Healer's Awakening

HEALER'S AWAKENING

-Avalon Awakening I-

David Hochhalter
and Tom Crepeau

This is a work of fiction, not a work of history. All characters portrayed in this book are products of the authors' imagination. Even when a character is modeled and named for a person who really existed, what emerges on the page is a portrayal of a fictional character who did what they did on these pages to create a good story. It is not presented either to praise nor to diminish the actual people. Instead, our characters are used by the authors to present a good story, nothing more, and (hopefully) nothing less.

Cover Art by Anjali Banerji
Editing and formatting by Anessa Books
Proofreading by The Editing Hall

Published by Anessa Books
Virginia, USA
http://anessabooks.com

Chapter 1

The seven realms which make up the Lands of Gawain and Texas share several similarities. Both lands are extremely large and situated on the southern edge of their respective countries. However, while the southern tip of Texas meets the ocean, Gawain meets a vast misty forest. We highly recommend not entering; No one will come looking for you. The eastern boundary of Gawain is worse. That's the dragon's forest.

—Guide to Avalon, 3rd printing

Three little pixie children shook in fear as they tried to hide under my braided hair. The rest tried to climb under my shirt. I giggled at the tickling sensation and held onto the tree branch tighter so I wouldn't fall off. They were afraid, and I didn't want to laugh at them; that might make them feel bad. I felt like a pixie mommy this morning. Mothers don't laugh at the silly things babies do.

Normally I would wave to the pixies as they woke up while my feet dangled over the lowest branch of the big tree. I liked watching all the animals as the sun rose. But on this morning, a dense rolling fog was pushing out from the forest. As it approached, all the pixies flew in different directions, desperately looking for places to hide. They seemed terrified of being caught in the mist. Standing on the branch next to me was a pixie warrior, ten inches tall with a twig for a spear.

"I will protect you, milady," he squeaked out.

It made me feel good the pixies trusted me. "My name is Petra," I said. "Together, we will be strong."

He pushed out his little chest, then threw his twig like a spear at the approaching mist. It disappeared.

"What is your name?" I asked.

He looked up at me in confusion.

I guess pixies don't give each other names. As I watched the fog push past the tree I was in, I felt happy I could help the pixie children, but another part of me felt like I should be afraid too. My parents always told me the mist was dangerous, but up in the tree I was certain the mist couldn't get me. Leaning over to look down, I couldn't see the ground anymore. I tried not to shiver; if I did, it might frighten the pixie children. I had to be strong for them.

I looked back up to see a gigantic elk stride out of the forest mist, taller than any elk I had ever seen before. A green sylph was standing on the elk's head, holding onto the massive antlers while leaning forward. When the elk turned his head, green sparkles trailed off the sylph's feathers.

I had never seen a sylph before, only heard about them in stories. They were powerful, magical female spirits. Suddenly the giant elk raised its head and bugled, the sound echoing over the lands. I gripped the branch I was sitting on very hard. Part of me wanted to run through the fog to meet this elk; another part of me didn't want to move. If I did, the pixie children might become more afraid and cry.

It bugled again, even louder as an even bigger elk stepped out of the forest a little farther away, pawing the ground while facing the first elk. This bigger elk looked very old; most of his hair was white. Instead of a sylph, there was a large blue spinnel with dragon wings riding this larger elk. Like the elk, the spinnel looked old, but it held itself upright even as the elk he was riding bugled a challenge back.

Both elks pawed the ground and bugled again. Suddenly, they began charging toward each another. The green sylph screamed out a challenge and the blue spinnel raised one clawed wing in the air. I held my breath. It felt like the world was waiting for the outcome. At the crash, all the fog burst away from them. The larger, older elk stumbled but kept his footing. The slightly smaller elk crashed to the ground and the green sylph rolled to the side. Quickly jumping up, she flew to her elk, even as it was shaking its giant head.

The older white elk huffed and looked down at the younger elk. <*"My time is not yet over."*> Its voice sounded in my mind, deeper than any voice I'd heard before. But it also seemed very old and tired.

The smaller elk stood up while shaking its head again. The green sylph clung to the antlers. <*"My time is soon, old man. She is awakening."*> This voice was female and just as strong as the other voice, but it sounded young.

<*"True,"*> said the larger elk. <*"But will she be ready?"*>

<*"For power, yes."*> replied the smaller elk dipping his head. <*"But her judgement is still that of a child. To grow without falling into darkness, she will need a guide. Someone slightly older who has the balance to stand next to her without becoming lost. Without that, the future becomes even more uncertain."*>

The white elk pawed the ground. <*"There is wisdom in your words. I agree, a guide must be chosen. But we are not permitted to choose directly. However, if we both agree on a Voice, they could choose a guide."*>

<*"Agreed,"*> replied the younger elk, and it swung its head to look at me. <*"But to request this burden of someone there must be a gift."*>

<*"Agreed,"*> said the larger elk, and it too turned to look at me.

A gift? I got gifts on my birthday and Yuletide. Since today was Spirit's Day, was I going to get something sweet? I really liked honey bread. Instead, I felt a tingling in my head and the words our lady's scholar had me write out started making sense in my mind.

Both elks turned to walk back into the forest. Just before they disappeared into the mist, I heard from the younger one, <*"It is a gift, Petra Abara. Freely given. Use it as you wish to nurture whom you choose. When she emerges, there will be a light brighter than any day. We only ask you to make a choice of who her guide will be, but it is your choice to make.">*

As both elks disappeared, the mist retreated. I ran back home faster than I believed possible.

Since that day, I enjoyed sneaking into our lady's library so I could read her books. I wanted to name all the pixies. The one who had stood next to me the day the mists came became Sir. Lancelot. The prettiest pixie girl became Queen Guinevere. Each morning, I would greet them and imagine we were having breakfast together.

The books I read were full of stories about other places and magical people. I wanted magic to find me. If it did, I could help others besides just the pixies. I told myself if I just imagined it enough, magic would come. But my parents did not have any, nor did my older brother or my older sister. Well, that wasn't exactly true. Hattie was prettier than I was; she had a magic that attracted boys.

Where my hair was a dirty blond, hers was a shining yellow-blonde. I overheard people describe me as *cute as a button*, while the same women congratulated my mother when talking about my sister. Hattie would make *a fine catch* for a merchant once she was of age—boys liked watching her.

While I preferred being outside except for my time spent with the scholar, my sister disliked learning from the old man and would find any excuse to stay indoors. The only exception to this was when she snuck out to deliver or bring back letters for the two noble daughters.

I discovered my sister sneaking out one day, and like me, she was very good at sneaking. She told me Marrit, the eldest of our lady's two daughters, could cast simple spells and had enchanted a tree stump. When a boy sat upon it, she could see the boy's image in her hand mirror. If Marrit liked the boy or he brought her a gift, she would send my sister to deliver a letter to him and bring back the gift. Sometimes I think the boys wanted to see my sister more than they wanted to send a letter to the little sorceress.

One day, when my sister came back with her hair down and unbraided, she got yelled at by Mother. For weeks afterwards, my sister was laden with more chores. But what really stopped her from going out again was Father. He was disgraced by my sister going outside with her hair down before her thirteenth birthday and demanded she stand in front of our lady and apologize. After that, every morning, Mother made sure Hattie's hair was braided and pinned up properly before she could leave for breakfast.

Other than reading, my own favorite activity at the time was watching the animals near the edge of the misty forest. Some of the trees towered over the others. My parents forbade me from going into the forest. They said many magical creatures hunted within the swirling mist which came from the forest on some days. I believed them. One day I even saw a griffon. It had chased a mistwolf out of the forest, then took to the air, circling around and looking for it. I hugged my tree and stayed very quiet. When I couldn't see the griffin anymore, I ran home. It was three days before I had the courage to go back.

I was so engrossed in reading I didn't hear the footsteps. When our lady saw me with the book, she seemed surprised. Then I got afraid; these were not my books. My parents didn't own any. I didn't want to steal them, like some people tried doing with her silver, I just wanted to read her books.

Our lady found my mother, and the two of them sat down next to me. Instead of taking the book away, our lady asked if I would read her a story. I was so relieved she hadn't yelled at me. She just wanted to hear a story! With pride, I found the page about Lady Guinevere and began reading to our lady and my mother about how she met King Arthur.

Some of the words I had to read slowly. I didn't know what all of them meant. When I stumbled on a long word, our lady put a finger under it and pronounced it slowly for me. Before the story was over, she had to help me with eight other words. Once finished, I looked up in delight. However, our lady and my mother were looking at each other. Was I in trouble?

I liked our lady. She was very kind to us. She made sure we had spare clothes and food. It was my mother's job to oversee her house.

Her lands where so large, I would have to ride a pony for three hours before entering another noble's lands. In the evenings, after our chores were done, we could play with her children.

"How long have you been reading, Petra?" asked our lady as she carefully took the book and put it back on her shelf.

"Oh, my lady, since after the great battle."

She cocked her head, then looked at my mother again. "And what battle would that be, young miss?"

"Do you remember the day the morning mists swept down all the way to your house, milady?"

"I do," she replied. "That was five months ago, the night we celebrated the fallen spirits. People say they saw strange things in the mist. Did you see something too?"

I bit my lip. Uh, oh. To help hide my nervousness, I put my hands under my legs and clicked my feet together while looking at the ground. My parents didn't know I liked going to the big tree in the morning.

"Petra," chided my mother softly. "What are you hiding?"

I wanted my sister here. She knew how to say things to hide where she had been. Mostly, she liked meeting boys or spending time with her friends. Like me, she would do her chores quickly, then find a way to slip off.

"Um ..." I clicked my feet together a few more times and tried to be smaller.

Our lady laughed and pointed at her few books. "If you tell us the truth, Petra, and your mother allows it, you may read my books again."

The books won. So, I told my mother and our lady the story about the day I saw the two elks. Once I finished my story, I said, "After that day, I decided to try reading. I wanted to name all the pixies."

Our lady stood up and asked my mother to join her around the corner. I couldn't hear what they were saying. Soon they came back. The lady looked down at me. "Petra, do you like spending time with the scholar?"

Avalon law dictates that a noble house provides education to their staff commiserate with position and standing. Since my family is of the Nabal class—educated indoor servants who were expected to understand proper etiquette—I was taught, along with my older sister and even my older brother, my letters and numbers. While the noble children were taught many times each week, the scholar would teach us twice a week, one hour each. I enjoyed the time with the scholar and always wanted more, but he would not teach me longer without someone paying him. Besides, I had chores to do, and I never had any money. Also, most of the time, my sister made excuses to be away. Unlike me, she hated sitting down with the old man and his books.

"Yes, my lady. But I don't have any money."

The lady cocked her head. "Why do you need money, Petra?"

I kept my eyes lowered. "He won't teach me more unless I pay him." I started banging my feet together again. "I don't have any money, my lady."

I felt my lady stiffen. Now I was going to get it. I whispered out, "I am sorry, my lady. I did not mean to make you angry. Do you want me to do more chores?"

Our lady excused herself. Soon after, I heard her shouting, then something shattering. Quickly followed by the sound of the front door of her manor slamming shut. I had never heard our lady angry before. I looked up now, tears trickling down my face. "Mother, I didn't mean to make her angry. Does this mean we have to go away?"

Mother hugged me.

I broke out crying and hugged her back. All I wanted to do was name the pixies and read.

When our lady came back, I wiped at my face and clung to my mother. I could not meet her gaze. I didn't want to see her angry.

She knelt down in front of me. Why wasn't she angry with me?

"Petra," she said quietly. "I have more chores for you to do. I will have a new scholar for my children soon."

"Yes, my lady," I said quietly. "What are my chores?"

"To spend more time with the scholar."

I looked up at her in astonishment and wiped at my face again.

"Also, it's about time you learn how to ride a horse." She winked at my mother. "Providing, of course, your parents allow it."

I liked the new scholar, and he didn't smell all musty like the other one. Besides reading better, he taught me how to count very high, along with multiplication and division. Instead of just two hours a week, I was allowed to spend three hours a day with him. He was kind and left books for me to read with a warning not to crease or smudge the pages. Books were very expensive, and our lady allowed me to read them only with my parent's permission. My father warned me, should a single page be damaged, the lady would no longer allow me in her library, for it was there she kept her few books.

My other chores expanded as well. Part of my additional duties was learning about different types of plants. Master Pucher was the local potions master. His apprentice had passed his journeyman tests and was away, learning with another master. I was to spend three hours a day looking for plants the master needed across our lady's lands. To help me with this, I was allowed to ride Star, a large pony owned by our lady. My father and the stable master instructed me how to ride him properly, put on his saddle, and how to care for him.

My sister was very proud of me and helped me groom him sometimes. But she refused to help me clean out his stall.

Star and I traveled across our lady's lands almost every day. I got very good at finding the types of plants, bulbs, and other ingredients our potion master needed. I even got to help him a little in his workshop, preparing the plants and learning more about them. For helping him, he let me read some of his books on plants.

The other chore, which I quickly became excited about, was working with the local healer. She was an older lady who traveled across the various noble lands as needed. Our lady had several maps showing where each lower-ranked noble lived that made up our greater lord's lands. Unlike the potions master, she had an apprentice, a young lady a little older than my sister. Our lady wrote to the healer and asked if I would be allowed to be instructed by her.

For weeks, nothing came back. But when a stableboy got sick from accidentally cutting his leg on a rusty nail, a day later, the healer and her apprentice arrived.

Master Healer Plaist was very stern with her apprentice and had her read from a book about how to treat the boy's injury and clean the wound properly. During this, the master pulled out some small knives, needles, plus a large mortar and pestle. When the apprentice stumbled, I put my finger underneath the word just like our lady had done for me and slowly pronounced it for her. The healer shot a glance at our lady, who was watching us at the doorway of her barn.

Our lady smiled at me.

"Petra," announced the healer in her old crackly voice. "Read the entire page to me."

The apprentice seemed relieved, so I began reading. The words were about blood poisoning and how to treat it. There were three words that I did not know, but by now I had learned how to pronounce them slowly, and how to work out what they meant. On the next page were magic symbols—runes! I was very excited and looked up at the healer. "Ma'am, what does each one mean?"

"Brilliania," demanded the healer, looking at her apprentice. "Explain each one *properly.*"

I understood testing by now. Our lady's scholar would test me sometimes, but he was always very kind. The healer's voice was direct and cutting. I could imagine if her apprentice got just one thing wrong, she would have more chores to do. I looked over at the hurt boy laying on the table and felt sorry for him. "I can come back another time," I said.

The healer reached over to touch the boy's leg. Her hands glowed for a second, and the boy gasped in relief. "Brilliania," said the healer. "Now!"

So she did. I had seen runes before. Mostly from the scholar who taught our lady's children about magic. The nobles had the gift and passed it down to their children. When I began asking Brilliania questions about the runes, the healer interrupted, "Let us begin."

I was also learning that once you enter a healer's room, there is one master—and the healer is it. Even our lady seemed to defer to her. I did not want to make any mistakes and be told to leave, so I patiently waited for instructions. Other than having me move out of the way, I got to stay in the room and watch. The apprentice was ordered to ground together into a pulp the ingredients on the page I had read. Then the healer added water and two drops of something else. After being pulped again, it looked like a thick blue liquid. Then the healer began casting, and I watched white runes glow in the air around the paste. I was trembling with excitement. Did this mean I could see magic?

Then the apprentice pulled out a long hollow needle and pulled the mixture into it. After putting a bit into the boy's mouth, they injected it into his leg. I held the boy's hand as tears trickled down his face. Then he slowly began to relax. Within moments, he was asleep.

"Even if you had the gift," the healer explained, "you are too young for it to emerge. I cast the magic in such a way so you could see it." She looked over at our lady, who was checking up on the boy. "From the letter I received, it implied your parents do not have any magic."

"No, ma'am," I said politely. "They don't."

She nodded. "Very well. I cannot be everywhere and having another assistant to help sometimes will be useful. Master Pucher thinks highly of you."

I jumped up and down. "He does?"

"A trade—your time helping me, for teaching. But I am very stern." Before I was able to answer, she quickly added, "You must have your lady's blessing as well as your parents. I am not taking you on as an apprentice. You don't have magic. Just as an assistant to help."

So, my chores increased even more. The healer was very stern, but I learned a great deal from her. Properly disinfecting without magic, stitching, setting broken bones, and other things. Also, I helped several times birthing large babies. Then, I wondered why Mother had wanted another child after my brother. It surprised me I was around. Why would a woman want to go through that more than once?

My days were now busy. Over the next three years, I grew another six inches. My body started to change, but so far only just a little. I had not begun bleeding yet. Mother commented she didn't think I would be as full as my sister. I wasn't certain if I wanted that to be true or not. Some boys looked at me differently now, but if I stood next to my sister, I was nearly invisible.

Between my chores, the extra learning with the scholar, occasionally helping the healer, plus riding Star and looking for plants, I thought it would be impossible for me to do more.

I was wrong.

Chapter 2

The four most power guilds within Avalon are the Wandmaker, Banker's, Healer's, and Potion's Guilds. Nobles generally go out of their way to ensure the safety of these guildmembers when on their lands. Occasionally there will be a person who belongs to more than one of the upper guilds. The nobles of the land where they are from often entrust them to be their Voice as well.

–Guide to Avalon, 3rd printing

Once a month, the cook and others traveled to the marketplace. Our lady asked if I would go as well with Bernard, her senior man-at-arms. When my sister heard about this, she demanded she had to come too. Just to get some peace, my parents relented. However, my sister was downcast when she learned our mother would be coming with us. I knew what my sister wanted to do. Already there were boys from other villages who stopped by to talk to my sister. She was not the age to wed yet, but soon.

My lady gave me a silver pin to wear and told me that Bernard would explain my duties. She pinned it above the Healer's and Potion's pin I was told to wear as well.

Other than Bernard, I was the only other person to ride. He and I rode side by side. He on his large horse, me on Star. My mother, sister, the cook, and a few others rode in the back of a cart pulled by a horse. We started out just after sunrise and left our lady's lands three hours later. As we passed other noble lands, additional travelers began following us. By noon, we had four more carts pulled by oxen and many others walking. There were two other men-at-arms as well, but they rode on top of laden carts pulled by the oxen. Almost all the people from other lands nodded their head at me as if I was a lady. I wanted to laugh. Me, a lady! True, I was on a pony with a man-at-arms beside me on a horse. But, a lady?

"You are our lady's Voice," came Bernard's deep voice next to me.

I looked up in surprise. He was large, muscled, and carried a sword and a bow. On his leather armor, he wore the symbol of our lady. It was similar to the pin I wore that had been given to me.

Even more amazing, Bernard had a magic ring, gifted to him by our lady. I had seen him use it once. When he said a special word, a flash of light would appear where he pointed. I watched him scare a wolf away.

Seeing my confusion at being "our lady's Voice," he added, "Your word is law. If someone insults you, it is an insult to our lady."

I scrunched up my nose.

"But I'm just Petra," I protested. "My sister is older than me."

He looked over at Hattie, riding in the back of the cart with my mother. I could tell he enjoyed watching her. Many did. "Your sister will make many fine babies."

Then he said formally, "You want to learn, you work hard, and you can read almost as good as our lady. You understand healing and bring valuable plants to the potions master. I overheard our lady say other masters have spoken your name." He leaned down to pat me on the shoulder. "When you are of age, I expect our lady will introduce you to a Castellon. Someday, one of my sons may work for you."

A Castellon was the second son of a noble who was sent away at thirteen to become the officer on another's lands; All men-at-arms reported to him. I wasn't sure what to say to that. I was just Petra. I liked to learn, explore, find things, and help people.

"Being a noble would be silly," I said.

He laughed, "And why is that, just-Petra?"

"Because then I couldn't explore. I want to see so much." I thought about all the wonderful places in the books I had read. Then I sighed. "But my parents have no magic." Aside from bards, masters, or men-at-arms, only people with magic were in the stories. While I was very excited to travel to the marketplace, I remembered the griffin flying, looking for that mistwolf. There was so much out there.

"Aye," Bernard laughed. "And neither do I." Grinning down at me, he said, "Let us move to the front. Your sister is taunting me. My wife will be annoyed."

As he said it, I looked toward the wagon. Mother picked up that Hattie was showing off and chided her. We edged our horses forward, so we rode in the front of the caravan. Once there, Bernard scanned the horizon; I did the same. If something ran from the forest to attack us, we would have little warning. Seeing nothing, Bernard asked me, "Tell me, just-Petra, what plants go into a healing potion?"

By now, I knew what plants the healer wanted and why. "The potion first requires a base. Something that the magic can bond to, such as sap or honey. You generally mix it with ..." Bernard let me finish. He nodded his head now and then as I talked.

"Just-Petra, of all the people following us, how many do you think can explain or understand what you just said?"

I hadn't really thought about that before. "I don't know."

"I can read some words," commented Bernard. "I believe your father can, as well." He looked behind for a second as another cart joined our caravan, this one with two cows trailing. "I doubt any of those behind us could read more than ten words. Why do you think our lady wanted you to come with us to the marketplace?"

I wasn't sure and said so.

"So, the cook and others are not cheated. You can count, read, and make sure the weighing of things is fair. Not all coins are the same. You know this?"

"Sort of," I replied. "Unless it is talon-stamped, the coin may have less silver or copper in it." I read about coins in one of the lady's books, and our lady showed me several types of coins and how to recognize their worth, along with how to use a scale properly. I thought about it for a second and asked, "But what happens if I find a coin that has the talon symbol stamped on it that is fake?" The books said a talon imprint meant the there was a minimum amount of gold, silver or copper in it.

Bernard looked down at me. "That is what my sword is for, and men with shovels."

Oh.

Soon after, our caravan stopped by a stream with an old stone statue of a lion near it. From the packed earth, animal droppings and other items about the place, I could tell this was used as a watering hole. The large statue was intact but covered in thick moss and the bottom of it was partially buried, probably from age.

We ate lunch while the various oxen and other animals drank their fill. By now, we had people with goats and even more cows traveling with us. From listening as I ate, these shepherds hoped to trade or sell them at the marketplace. Bernard, plus the two other men-at-arms, had strung their bows and stood guard. We were still near the forest. However, much of the surrounding area had been cleared of underbrush, so we could see a distance into the trees.

After eating with my sister and mother, I brought a thick slice of honey bread and cheese over to Bernard. Leaning his bow against a tree, he began to eat. Once he finished, I asked, "How much longer to the trading grounds?"

He looked at all the animals with us. "It is better if we all stay together, so perhaps three hours. I imagine we will spend the night and head back tomorrow. I recommend refilling our waterskins here. Don't drink water at the marketplace unless you have mixed in wine. Even then, it might be bad."

I opened my mouth in surprise. "Really?"

He nodded at me. "Really. I suspect the grounds may have an apprentice or two about who can cast a purifying spell on the water if you want. For a price, of course."

That got me excited. "So, people will be there who can cast magic?"

"Simple magic, yes. Probably." Seeing my excitement, he smiled. "Petra, if we traveled to town, you might find twenty people who can read, plus a few true journeymen. Out here, apprentices only. Masters only come when they are needed."

I pointed to the statue where several children played. "Who carved it?"

Bernard shrugged. "My father said he remembered seeing it there when he was a child. Perhaps it is a guardian from long ago. I have never seen it move or heard of a story where it did."

I wished so much I had the gift of magic. I hadn't started bleeding yet, and the stories suggested your magic came in when you stopped being a child. So, maybe? But in the back of my mind, I knew that it wasn't going to happen. Neither of my parents had the gift. But I was curious about something.

"You don't need your own magic to use the ring?" I asked.

"No. But it must have sun touch it for several hours before it can be used even once."

I asked hopefully, "Do you think there will be any books at the marketplace about how magic things work?"

Bernard broke out laughing. "Petra, I can guarantee there won't be. Aside from you and perhaps an apprentice, who would read them?"

Before we left, my sister and I headed upstream along with others to refill our waterskins. Something caught my attention. I was used to being out on my own as I rode Star across our lady's lands looking for plants, so little sounds were very important to me. Tapping my sister on her shoulder I put my finger to my lips and pointed up the stream.

"Go get Bernard," I whispered to her.

She followed my gaze. "What is it?"

I rolled my eyes. "I thought I heard something. Go get Bernard."

My sister reluctantly left me and went back to the caravan. I put down my waterskin and crept upstream. The faint breeze was blowing toward us, so whatever it was couldn't smell me. I didn't want to upset the others around me; they would probably start shouting or crying. It was odd, I was the youngest here and somehow, I felt as if I were the oldest.

Slowly sneaking forward, I paid careful attention not to step on any twigs while trying to use the trees to hide my approach. Around the fourth tree I saw it only because the creature moved its tail. A griffin was perched on a large branch, high enough that it probably could see some of the animals. From the sounds they were making, I bet it could hear them too. This griffin was a smaller than the one I had seen years ago. Even so, I bet it could fly away with a goat or a child.

Slowly turning to the side, I watched Bernard following my footsteps. Making sure the griffin could not see me, I signaled for him to be very quiet and pointed up into the forest. He understood and crept forward. When he saw the griffin, he hissed in surprise, before creeping back to me.

Without letting my sister or mother know what the actual problem was, I asked them to quickly and quietly get our lady's cart ready to go. I love my mother very much, but she is not very brave around monsters. The other travelers just followed, and pretty soon the caravan was back on the road. They were to wait for us around the corner.

It was odd; these three master-of-arms were treating me as if I was the one in charge. Well, two of them were, the youngest wanted to be a hero. Against a griffin, he would quickly become a dead idiot. A *heroic* dead idiot, but he could get us all killed.

"We should attack it," said the youngest man-at-arms again. "I can shoot it out of the sky."

I rolled my eyes. "Have you ever *seen* a griffin attack before? They are lighting fast. Besides you have a standard bow. I doubt your arrows would pierce its hide unless you hit it in the neck."

"Child, are you calling me a coward?" he said and spat on the ground near me.

Bernard wrapped his hand around the pommel of his sword. "Watch your tongue!"

"Her name is Ms. Abara," replied the deep voice of the oldest man-at-arms. This was the first time he spoke. Up until now, he had only listened. "My lord knows her name, and she is right." He looked at Bernard then tilted his head toward the other man. "Kill him if you must, then we can dump his body near the griffin. By the time he is consumed, we will have left."

Bernard nodded and began to slide his blade out. My eyes opened wide. The older man-at-arms wasn't kidding. The younger one began drawing his sword as well.

Bernard was going to kill the younger man-at-arms as if he was a rat to be discarded. I had seen hogs, chickens, and other animals killed before. It was done quickly, and they didn't know it was going to happen. I had even seen wolves and foxes killed from a distance. But they seemed more aware of what could become.

"What is your name?" I shouted at the younger man-at-arms as he raised his sword while stepping back from Bernard who had begun advancing.

The older man-at-arms put a hand on my shoulder. "Lady Abara, Kayden is a fool. The lands will be better off with him as food."

There it was again, Lady Abara. Even Bernard called me the lady's Voice. *Clang.* Kayden's first blow was easily parried. Bernard snorted in contempt, even I could tell Kayden was going to lose.

I am Petra Abara.

Clang. Bernard's blow seemed too high, Kayden pushed forward, and Bernard kicked him in the knee. It had been a ruse and the younger man stumbled backwards. The noise of the battle was drawing attention. My sister and others had come at the sounds and were staring at us open mouthed.

I am Petra Abara. I have said the assistant's Oath to the Healer's and Potion's guilds and wore the pins identifying me a member of both.

"If Bernard hurts him, I will heal Kayden," I said to the older man-at-arms. It was a stupid thing to say. Bernard would probably shove his sword through Kayden's chest. No one could survive that even if I had the gift of healing magic and poured an entire healing draft down his throat.

Clang. Kayden was retreating now. The older man-at-arms patted me on the shoulder as if he was comforting me. "This is about our safety. The death of one man is worth it."

There had to be another way. I was a healer. Healers must sometimes hurt too, but that is what numbing agents were for.

Clang. Bernard's sword was streaked with red. Kayden was trailing blood from a cut in his side. It wasn't a killing blow. I could heal that. *That's what numbing agents where for* I thought to myself again. A plan began forming in my mind. It was a stupid plan, but if it worked, it meant no one had to die. I just needed to get the three men-at-arms to follow me. From a distance everyone was watching the battle now. Bernard's sword rose, Kayden was about to die, and he knew it. I could see desperation on his face, his bravado being replaced with the horrid understanding his life was about to end.

Who was I? Out of desperation, my voice rang out, "My name is Lady Petra Abara, and I am the Voice." I put everything I had into what I said next. "And I command you to stop."

Bernard lowered his sword and turned to look at me. Kayden stumbled, dropped his sword, and gripped his side while sucking in breath at the pain. I bet his adrenalin was beginning to wear off. The older man-at-arms tilted his head to look down at me. "As you say, Lady Abara. What is your plan, then?"

A moment later I heard a sleepy <*"Yes ..."*> within my head, like the speaker hadn't fully woken up yet. The voice was powerful, but growly. At first, I thought it was one of the elks, but this voice was different. No one else was reacting, they must not have heard it.

Swiveling my head to track the sound, I noticed something different. Near the stream, a small amount of mist had formed around the base of the lion statue. Already it was breaking up and dispersing. The statue's eyes were now open, but I watched in wonder as they closed again as if the stone was going back to sleep. Within a heartbeat you would not have known anything had changed with the statue. No one seemed to see the movement but me. How could they? Everyone had been watching the battle and now they stared at me.

My mother and sister looked at me open mouthed as many of the women traveling with us curtsied to me.

My idea required a goat, which Bernard liberated from one of the shepherds for six copper pennies. After money changed hands, the shepherd asked what we were going to do with the animal—a little late now to ask that question. I shrugged. "Well, it was his goat, he can watch if he wants." As I explained my plan, the shepherd wanted to be as far away from this as possible. Too bad. I couldn't afford him running back to the caravan and causing a panic.

"I can kill the creature," whined the younger man-at-arms.

"Hush," I demanded. "You can't fight with stitches in you."

Bernard cuffed him on the ear, but not very hard, his glare suggesting next time it would be with his sword. The older man-at-arms had his sword halfway out. The whiner wasn't making many friends today.

Ignoring them, I whispered, "Come on. Take the bait."

The five of us were hiding behind some trees down the road. The caravan was even farther away. For a creature that flew, the distance was nothing. Could we kill the griffin, maybe? Would we lose people in the process? Probably. What I wanted was for the griffin to decide it didn't like goats, or hunting here, without any of us getting hurt. I was willing to sacrifice one goat for the cause.

Said goat was staked to the ground in the middle of the road. For good measure I poured a bit of blood on him. Petra Abara, maker of griffin snacks. The poor beast didn't have long to live in any case. We watched from a distance as it bleated and pulled at its rope. Suddenly the griffin was there. In a blink it had launched itself out of a tall tree and flapped its wings backwards, landing next to the goat.

The shepherd next to me fell to his knees. "Little Wimby," he whispered. The goat for its part, strained harder and bleated in panic.

Now I was going to feel bad; the goat had a name.

With razor sharp talons, the griffin tore into the goat and began ripping out chunks of meat.

"Now," pleaded the younger man-at-arms. He was almost crying. "We should attack it now."

The older man-at-arms' fist smashed into his face.

The griffin paused at the sound, cocked its head, and then finished eating the goat. It hadn't taken ten seconds for the animal to eat an entire goat. After preening itself for a bit, it spread its wings wide and launched into the air, then promptly crashed to the ground. The griffin righted itself, stumbled, stood up, shook his head, and flew again. It hit a tree some thirty feet up and fell to the ground, snapping off some branches on its way down. Then it began vomiting, violently, before collapsing.

I am Petra Abara. I am Petra Abara, I repeated to myself as I walked toward the griffin with my knife out. Bernard and the older man-at-arms had arrows knocked in case this went wrong. By now the griffin was panting hard and barely moving. I had put a lot of dried angel's trumpet into the goat. Healers use just a bit of it to relax their patients. The amount I used would have killed three people.

The griffin eyed me as I approached and tried to move. At best, it flopped slightly. I knelt down close to one of its eagle eyes. "I am Petra Abara," I said softly and touched the tip of my knife to the side of its neck hard enough that it drew a pin prick of blood. "I want you to leave us alone. We don't taste good."

Slowly backing up, I put my other bundle near its mouth, then walked away. There was a limit to my bravery. Opening a griffin's mouth, not going to happen. I never turned away from the beast. By the time I was back with Bernard, the griffin started licking at my package. Then it ate it.

Good boy. Now get up and fly away.

It hopped up and turned toward me. Uh oh. I could hear Bernard and the other man-at-arms' bows creak.

The creature squawked at me, turned around and flew off.

I fell to my knees in relief.

"Petra!" shouted my mother. She had walked back to find out what the delay was. "Are you sick?"

Bernard started laughing.

The older man-at-arms offered me his hand and hauled me to my feet.

Just before I mounted Star, my sister hugged me. Mother appeared to not know what to do. She was looking at me like I had gone crazy. As I walked toward the front of the caravan to take my place, everyone began nodding at me like I was a noble.

Once the caravan pushed forward, I overheard my mother talking to Bernard.

"But Petra is not yet ten."

I could imagine Bernard shrugging. A moment later, I heard his reply. "She is the lady's Voice. Her word is law. While we are off our lady's lands, Petra outranks you."

I wasn't sure what to make of that. Head-of-house and age where very important in a family. If you disobeyed your head of house, legally you could be arrested and whipped.

CHAPTER 3

The art of bartering is a way of life in Avalon. People will barter with anything from a wand costing a king's ransom to spices. Progressive nobles who provide open marketplaces with flat taxes and good security like Navartis, Lohort, Gawain, Vimmer ... we recommend visiting. However, a word of warning; the simple merchant selling fabric probably knows more about bartering than you. While fun to play the game, you will likely leave with empty pockets. Previous travelers have implied the average Avalonian merchant can sniff a copper penny a mile away.

–Guide to Avalon, 3rd printing

The marketplace was huge, consisting of twelve large, covered barns without walls, set in a great circle. Within the central open area was a Maypole with colorful long ribbons tied to posts. Farther behind the barns were stalls and pens for the animals. Very quickly I learned nothing was free. To rent a table within a barn costs a copper penny a day. A smaller stall that might hold ten goats, another penny. All the money went to the lord of our area. Our lady and everyone else traveling here owed him allegiance. Furthermore, any sale required paying a small tax. There were men standing about in the lord's colors making sure the taxes were collected. I didn't like them. They seemed very shrewd and disdainful toward the people milling about.

Before we began to explore, Bernard asked me to speak to those who came with us. Since this included my mother and sister, I felt a bit awkward.

"Bernard is carrying all the money," I said. "Before you purchase anything, you must come and get me. Our lady wants to make sure the scales are correct."

The cook seemed almost relieved.

Bernard stood on my left as I walked through each barn looking at the things for sale. Food, honey and spices, homemade clothes and blankets. I saw some simple machines such as pulleys and hand cranked meat grinders, plus so many other things—but no books. When I came across a merchant with the healer's insignia on some of his clay jars, I looked closer.

"How much for the dried angel's trumpet?" He had a small clay jar full of it.

The stooped, dirty man eyed me, glanced at Bernard, then smiled. Most of his teeth were missing. "Half a silver talon."

My mouth hung open. That was outrageous. "One copper talon."

"You are killing Weil," he said dramatically. "I could not sell it for fewer than ten copper talons."

I stared at his dramatics, then narrowed my eyes. A challenge. This was our lady's money I was spending, and I wasn't going to waste it. "A copper talon plus a copper penny."

"The noble is destroying Weil," he moaned. "I will be homeless," he cried while raising both hands to the sky as if asking the gods for help. "Eight copper talons and I might be able to feed my four starving children."

I knew where angel's trumpet vines grew back at home. However, drying the plant and grinding it properly took some doing. If you breathed in any of it, it could cause you to fall asleep, or worse.

I was not even a healer's apprentice and everything I learned from the healer was memorized. I didn't have her books to fall back on.

"One copper talon and two copper pennies," I countered. "And that's only because you are giving me a good show."

You would think with his dramatics we would be drawing a crowd. Nope. His patter was almost reserved, compared to some of the other merchants around me.

"Four copper talons and eight copper pennies."

I began walking away.

"Two copper talons."

His voice was becoming urgent. Almost pleading. I kept walking.

Suddenly his tone changed, and he banged his fist to the table. "Fine. One copper talon and two pennies."

I turned back and nodded at Bernard. He counted out the three coins, and the merchant handed over the small clay pot.

Now that the deal had been done, the merchant was much calmer. "Is your mother a healer?"

I felt for the healer's pin in my pocket, the one Master Healer Plaist demanded that I wear whenever I helped her. I pulled it out. "I am Master Plaist's assistant."

"You are her apprentice?" asked the merchant uncertainly.

I shook my head. "I have not started to bleed. I am her assistant." It was unlikely I would ever become her apprentice. A small part of me hoped, if I imagined it enough times, maybe magic would come to me.

The merchant bowed to me. Once he rose, I could see something was different. Most of his teeth were there, now. They were crooked, just like everyone else's, but they were there. In his hand he had a thin, dirty curved section of wood. "What is your name, young lady?" His speech had gotten better too.

"Um, Petra. Petra Abara." Was everything here not what it seems? "Do you really have four children?"

"I have two." He winked at me. After putting his fake teeth back in and shifting his shoulders, he looked just as before, a poor merchant hoping to save his starving family.

"My four children are going to starve," he cried. "Petra has won, and now I will go home hungry."

I just shook my head and smiled, walking away with my purchase.

Making the purchase for the cook was very different. He knew some of the merchants, and they had apparently already settled on a price for the various spices and knives he intended to purchase. What was I supposed to do, except agree to it?

Just to be sure, I inspected the three knives. Potion makers need good sharp knives to cut up things, but for healers, a good knife can separate life from death. Granted, these were to be used in the kitchens, but still, this was for our lady.

I turned to the cook. "Isn't there supposed to be a maker's mark on them?"

Just about anything made for sale was supposed to have a maker's mark: a symbol that identified which master or person made it.

The merchant's eyes narrowed. "Young lady, we have agreed on the deal. By my mother's name, I guarantee these are good knives."

Considering what I just went through with the other merchant, I bet he didn't know who his mother was. "There is no maker's mark on them," I repeated.

Now the cook was frowning too.

Bernard shifted his shoulders.

"We have agreed on the deal," said the merchant, now annoyed. He signaled for one of the lord's men standing nearby to come over.

The merchant, cook, Bernard and I were escorted away from the barn. With us were two of the lord's men. The older of them looked at the merchant. "What is the problem?"

"We agreed on the price. Now this guttersnipe won't honor it."

The lord's man looked at my silver pin signaling I was our lady's Voice. He glanced up at Bernard, who was now looking very annoyed. His hand was on the pommel of his sword.

"What is your name?" the man asked me.

"Petra Abara," I replied. "I am our lady's Voice."

The lord's man addressed cook. "Did you let the merchant know the Voice of the lady must bless the deal?"

He swallowed and nodded.

The merchant shouted, "He has purchased many things from me before. The child probably doesn't even bleed yet. I bet she can't read five words. How could she ..."

"Merchant," came a quiet but deep voice from behind us, "are you suggesting my vassal does not have the right to select her own Voice? Or that her choice should not be respected?"

Approaching us was a tall man in green robes laced with gold. It took me a second to recognize him, Prince Lindon Gawain. Our lady had a painting of him and his father, Lord Gawain in the main hall. She was one of Prince Gawain's many vassals. Three men-at-arms flanked him. However, they each wore chain mail armor, versus Bernard's leather. Also, one of them looked like he had some kind of pistol. I had never seen one before but had read about them. What was more, the tall man in robes had a wand in a sheath.

Bernard hissed and immediately went down on one knee. So did the cook and the others. Understanding he was a lord, I curtsied.

"You may rise," said our prince. "Actually, I was looking for you, Ms. Abara. My healer has been detained and will be here early tomorrow. Would you be willing to stand in his place for the night, or perhaps longer?"

I looked up at Bernard's stunned face. "Ah, yes my lord. But I am just a healer's assistant."

"As I have been told. However, there is a large difference between nothing and an assistant."

The lord turned to the scared merchant. "Now, merchant. I believe you have something to say to my vassal's Voice." Then his voice edged down a notch. "And I believe you need to explain to my men why you are selling knives without a maker's mark."

As we were led away, I whispered to Bernard, "What is to become of the merchant? They aren't going to ..." I let my voice trail off.

"If this is the first time, probably not. Most likely a fine. And he will not be allowed to rent a table near the front of the barns for a season or two."

As we walked away from the barns toward a tree line, other men-at-arms joined the lord, men with crossbows. They were loaded.

"My lord?" I asked nervously.

"I heard an interesting story about your adventure with a griffin, Ms. Petra." He looked toward the tree line. "Is the story true?"

I gulped. "If you mean that I drugged a griffin, and then asked him to leave us alone, yes."

The lord nodded and waited. A few seconds later, a tall man I hadn't seen at first wearing leather armor strode toward us from the tree line. He held an impressive compound bow. As he approached, I noticed he had an amulet held in place by a silver chain.

"It's still there," said the man. "Hasn't moved."

"Ms. Abara," said the lord. "This is Acrum. He is a ranger from the Archer Clan. He works for me from time to time. Tell Ms. Abara what you spotted."

The ranger looked at me intently. "A griffin flew in low about an hour ago. Currently it's about a quarter mile into the forest. Just waiting."

"Oh. Um. Does it have a blue crest on each wing?"

He smiled. "It does. May I assume then this is the same griffin you talked to?"

I didn't know much about griffins except for the one I saw before and few stories. But none of the stories were consistent. The only ones that held any truth for me were in recipes from the healer's and the potion master's books. If I had killed the griffin and sold it, the money would probably allow our lady to build two new barns. Killing such a magnificent creature felt wrong. At least, not if I could make it go away instead.

"Maybe. But why is it here?"

"Griffins are interesting animals, Ms. Abara. You had the opportunity to kill it and you didn't. You spoke to it and let it go." He eyed me intently. "In other words, you bested it. Now I suspect, the beast sees you as its master. Very much like a dog."

My eyes went wide as I sucked in my breath. "I just wanted it to leave us alone."

"A commendable attitude. However, the real question is, what do we do next?"

All eyes turned to the lord.

"If it gets closer, you may kill it. If it leaves, let it go." He considered me for a moment. "Do you wish to try talking to the beast again, in hopes of getting it to leave?"

I intentionally did not look at Bernard. He would be shaking his head no. Addressing the ranger I asked, "If it attacks, can you kill it with one arrow?" He had a compound bow, and it was a stout one. His bodkin-pointed arrows could probably punch through chain mail. Our hunting broadheads weren't any good against an armored creature.

He grinned at me. "I always like a good challenge."

Bernard's deep voice growled out, "That wasn't a yes."

Chapter 4

Griffons are magical creatures. How they came to be is a subject of debate in Avalon. A popular story has a powerful but mad sorcerer from millennia ago building them. He wanted guards for his lands that could also fly. The other story is that God has a sense of humor, how do you get a giant eagle and a lion to mate. Very carefully.

–Magical Creatures of Avalon, 9th printing

\#

I resisted the urge to call to it. The griffin was about thirty feet up on a large branch looking down at me. The ranger was at the base of a tree about seventy feet away. I had to take it on faith he was still there, it was as if he had melted into the background. I couldn't see him anymore.

Bernard, standing a few feet behind me whispered, "This is a bad idea. If you die here, I get to listen to your mother all the way back."

"Ha-ha," I said dryly.

The griffin cocked its head at me and squawked.

"It's okay," I said. "You can come down."

It landed gracefully near me and squawked louder while extending its eagle head toward Bernard. Got it. Don't like you, go away now. It probably had some understanding that swords were dangerous to him. I gave Bernard a pleading look, and he backed up ten feet. What in the world would my parents be saying to me right now? I took a deep breath and held out my hand. The griffin edged forward and began sniffing it. I slowly stroked its head. The griffin closed its eyes and rubbed its head against my arm.

How do you tell a griffin to go find a nice forest to claim, away from humans? Short of a dragon, or humans with powerful bows, griffins were the alpha of the forest. Death from above. True to the ranger's comment, "Very much like a dog." The griffin enjoyed being stroked. Now it leaned in close and rubbed up against me. I had to brace myself or I would be squished. A memory surfaced from several years ago. *"She is awakening and will need a guide."* With just about every minute of my day so busy these last years, I almost forgot about the two elks. Was this what they meant? I rubbed the griffin's fur while kneeling down. Yep, the griffin was a girl.

<*"Griffins understand territory, Ms. Abara."*>

I jumped at the mental male voice. I had heard it before, but now it sounded even more tired, and as if from a great distance. Looking up, I saw the white elk some distance away, mist swirling around the creature seeming to pull at it.

I thought back, <*"Is this what the battle was about? The griffin?"*>

By now Bernard had spotted the elk and hissed out.

<*"You and I shall speak one more time, Ms. Abara. Know this. A darkness is coming, and many things will be lost. You cannot stop it. But remember, your soul is your own. As are your choices."*>

<*"But what should I do? And, what choices? Who are you?"*>

I felt the mental touch of the elk begin to retreat. He almost seemed to be falling into the mist.

<*"I was the herald of M—"*> and it was gone.

I grabbed onto the griffin's side and buried my face in its fur. Giant wings unfurled and covered me. I cried as I held onto her. Nothing made sense. I didn't want the griffin to die. I wasn't certain what to do at first, but a thought grew bigger in my mind, *"Your soul is your own, as are your choices."* I got a choice, and I was going to use it.

The griffin pulled her wings back and mock-pecked at my head. Laughing, I stroked her head again and looked up into her eyes. "You need to guard our lady's forest," I said. "It is what I want you to do."

We stared at each other, then she rubbed against my head, almost knocking me over. Then backing up, she launched herself into the air and within moments was above the trees, flying south. When I turned around, tears trickled down my face. I felt like I had lost and gained something at the same time. But if asked, I wouldn't be able to explain either.

"Did you see the white elk?" said Bernard excitedly. "Good fortune."

"I've seen him before." The memory was like mist in my mind. "Several years ago, I think."

He patted me on the shoulder as we caught up with the ranger. "You are truly our lady's Voice."

Our liege lord had been watching from farther away, surrounded by his men-at-arms. I ran up and hugged him.

Laughing, he asked me, "What was that for?"

I sniffled. "For giving me a chance and not killing her. Thank you."

I was almost ten, no child, but he picked me up and carried me on his shoulder for a bit, anyway. "So, tell me about yourself, Petra Abara, Voice of your lady."

So, I did.

He put me down before we left the trees. "Have you decided what you are going to do next?"

I kicked a small rock and looked away. "Mother thinks I will begin bleeding soon. Neither of my parents have magic. Perhaps if I work with the potions maker when my bleeding starts, magic might find me."

Our lord didn't laugh. That made me like him.

"I wish you luck in your plans, Ms. Abara. If it works, let me know through your lady. My second son is one year older than you."

I looked up in surprise but didn't respond. What could I say? Magic would either find me or it wouldn't. "My lord, where should I be to treat any wounded?"

The ranger laughed. "Men drink, Ms. Abara. There will be fights. You *will* have patients soon enough."

Our lord sighed. "Aye. Acrum, please show Ms. Abara to the healer's tent and stay with her. If anyone treats her with disrespect, you are welcome to have whatever is left after Sir Bernard is done with them."

I collapsed backwards four hours later after treating two concussions, a broken nose, multiple broken teeth, four broken bones—one of them bad—and a knife wound. So far, no one had died under my care. I had used up one of my precious healing potions, splitting it between four people to at least push the healing process forward. I only had three potions.

Closing my eyes to rest them, I said to Bernard, "This is idiotic."

"Aye," he replied, raising his flagon. "But the hard drinking hasn't started yet."

I opened my eyes to stare at him in surprise.

Acrum laughed at my frustrated expression. "Ms. Abara, this is normal."

"They are throwing their lives away!"

He snorted and looked at one of the bonfires for a moment. "Most people don't see the future. They live for today." He shrugged. "If I didn't join the Archer Clan when I was fourteen, one of them might have been me."

"I have read a little about the clans," I said. "But each story is different. What are they?"

Acrum contemplated me for a minute. "I have to keep reminding myself that you are not yet ten. I have met old priests who are less well-read than you." After shifting in his seat, he added, "When you join, it is an oath for life. But they taught me what needed to be taught. More often than not, with bumps along the way." He touched his amulet. "There is magic inside of this. I can use it to see farther and hide, but that is all. There are a few who can tap more of the magics, but I cannot." Then he grinned. "That is not all truth. My commander can talk to me through it, as well. Most of the time I want him to shut up."

"Really? Bernard has a ring that lets him cast light. Is your amulet like that, but with more spells?"

Acrum shook his head. "I cannot say. But as I said there are a few who can use more spells than me. I have heard different clan amulets have different spells."

This was fascinating. "Why don't more people get an amulet, then? I would think they would want to be able to do magic."

Bernard broke out laughing, and Acrum grinned.

"Ms. Petra, look around you," Bernard said, still chucking. "Most just want to drink and eat. They don't want to be oath-bound for life. Besides," he gave Acrum a sideways glance, "Many look down on the lower clans."

Acrum raised his glass in salute. "Yet the lord still pays for my services."

Before I could respond, another drunken man stumbled into my tent. He wrist had been broken in a fight. This was going to be a long night.

Some injuries were severe enough that the healing books said I needed to check up on my patients every half hour. I thought all of them would live, but the damage! The healer arrived just after sunrise. He seemed surprised I was there, but he listened as I explained how I had diagnosed and treated each patient. After inspecting my various stitches, bandages, and braces he seemed pleased with my work and grudgingly said so. Then he began casting healing runes on a few of the more badly injured, something I could not do. Even though magic still fascinated me, at some point I fell asleep.

Bernard shook me awake while handing me a mug of warm tea. "The healer would like to talk to you outside."

I took a wobbly step and looked down at myself. Never had I been so dirty. Mud, gore, and bits of stuff clung to my clothes. None of the books about the heroes from long ago mentioned this. Draining the mug, I looked around for something else to wear, but my other clothes were still in our cart. Stepping outside the tent flap I blinked my eyes. The morning sun was very bright. Maybe I had gotten three hours of sleep.

Instead of just one healer, three others were with him, plus an apprentice. "Master," I said, addressing the healer I met earlier. "You wanted to talk to me?"

"I did. Please explain why you injected a little of each healing potion ten inches away from the wound."

The other three healers watched me intently. They were much older men. Why were they here?

I was a little nervous. What I had done was not something mentioned in any of the healing books. "Um, I only had three healing potions with me. From the drawings of the blood vessels in my master's books, the deeper vessels flow toward the area while the ones closer to the surface flow away. After numbing the area, I used my brass needle to inject a little of the healing potion in hopes it would flow toward the damaged area."

It occurred to me as I talked this was not something I had ever read about before. If one of the patients died, would I be in trouble?

The healer cautiously asked, "Was this procedure taught to you by Master Plaist?"

I curtsied. "No master. I couldn't think of anything else to do. I don't have any magic myself, and I thought some of them might die without magical healing."

"Would you excuse us for a few minutes, Ms. Petra?" said the oldest healer.

I nodded and walked back to the tent. "Do you think I am in trouble?" I asked Bernard, nervously. The four men seemed very intent as they talked amongst themselves.

He snorted. "The lord asked for you personally and no one died."

Acrum was awake as well by now. While stretching, he said, "If they attempt to hurt you, the lord instructed me to keep you safe."

The healer's apprentice ran off at the behest of his master. The discussion among the other healers continued. A short while later, our lord and some of his men-at-arms strode over to them, the healer's apprentice following. They talked some more, one of the healers pointing at me. I stepped backwards and took Bernard's hand when the discussion took angrier tones.

One of the larger men-at-arms wearing our lord's colors pointedly put his hand on his sword hilt. The healers' angry words began trailing off. Our lord looked over and nodded at me. "Ms. Abara, I have a few questions for you."

I gulped and went over to the group. The healers did not look happy. The lord's men-at-arms where very pointedly looking at the healers. I curtsied again. "Yes, my lord."

"Your parents are oath-bound to your lady. As she is my vassal, they are hers."

"Yes, my lord," I said, confused. Why was this important?

"And you have never studied under another master, other than Master Plaist and Master Pucher?"

"Um, no, my lord. I, er, don't know if the teacher for the lady's children is a master. But I learn from him too."

Our lord smiled. "And would you be willing to take an oath to that effect?"

I felt very unsure of myself, but everything I said was the truth. "Yes, my lord." Then I blurted out, "My lord, am I in trouble? I tried as hard as I could to heal the men and keep them alive." Tears started trickling down my face as I remembered their injuries and feeling so powerless trying to heal them. I looked down at the ground and whispered, "I don't have any magic."

The rest of the lord's men-at-arms put their hands to their sword hilts and pointedly stared at the four healers. Now everyone was paying attention to us, the area had gone very quiet. At last, our lord spoke again. His voice was flat and hard. "You failed in your duties,

Master Niewash. I paid for you to be here yesterday. For your failure, I instructed Ms. Abara to take your place. Her father is the eldest of her family who is oath-bound to a vassal of mine. The healer and potion makers Ms. Abara learned from are oath-bound to me, and I pay their full salaries to help my vassals. You have no claim to her discovery. I recognize the importance of Ms. Abara's technique and the benefit it has. Does the Healer's Guild wish to dispute my claim as her lord? I will gladly stand in front of the Wizard's Council. Do you wish to do the same?"

I grabbed onto Bernard's hand again. What was happening?

CHAPTER 5

The traditional format which new ideas are named in Avalon is to use the initial of the Noble's lands where the idea originated and the last name of the inventor. The G.Abara healing method was purportedly developed by a nine-year-old healer's assistant.

—Guide to Avalon, 4th printing

My mother and sister helped me wash my clothes in the stream while I shivered in the cold water trying to get clean. Eventually I was forced to dive in and soak my hair. Once back on shore, my teeth chattered as they each rubbed me down with a cloth. I only owned one spare change of clothes. Even though I wore an apron last night, I didn't think the bloodstains would ever come out. Maybe I could purchase another set of clothes here. I sighed, more of our lady's money I was spending.

My sister pulled my shirt out of the water. It still looked dirty. "So, no one ever thought of injecting a little bit of the healing potion before?"

While combing out my hair, I shrugged. "It just made sense to me."

Mother pounded my dirty pants between two wet rocks, then rubbed her forehead. "I bet our lady will give you a gift."

"Maybe she will give me a pony too," said my sister excitedly.

I rolled my eyes.

"It was Petra's idea. I don't think you're going to get a pony."

"But boys would like watching me if I rode a pony," replied my sister. She posed while stretching.

Mother snorted. "You are of age in two months. Do not bring dishonor on your father."

My sister pushed out her chest. "Two months is a long time, Mother. Even the priest looks at me when others are not watching. I bet he would marry me off now if you asked him."

Argh. Different day, same argument. I finished combing my hair and got dressed. "I just want more books to read." Then looking away, I added quietly, "I met a clan member who wears an amulet that lets him do magic. He said you needed to be fourteen before joining a clan."

My sister said excitedly, "I heard they make you take a blood oath during the full moon without any clothes on!"

"Hattie!" declared my mother. "Hold your tongue. I bet Petra will marry a nice hostler. She likes being outside."

My sister held up my stain-soaked shirt. "Dirt does seem to follow her around."

I stuck my tongue out at her. Then scrunched up my nose. "Who do you think our father will find for you?"

She grinned at me. "I met a very nice baker apprentice with his master. They were purchasing flour and spices. His master has a shop in town."

"What's it like? The town, I mean." I had never been to the town. My sister had been twice, with my mother, to purchase bolts of cloth for our lady.

"It's very large. Almost forty shops, and many houses around it. People come from all over to work in the sawmill. But he's the only baker."

Mother nodded approvingly. "The apprentice was very polite. His master even gave me a cinnamon roll."

By now, I was dressed. The clothes that I had worn were ruined. "I want to see if we can purchase cloth for a new shirt before we leave."

My sister bounded to her feet and helped Mother up. "Maybe we will see the baker and his apprentice again."

Some of the merchants had already started putting their wares away. But I found one that still had various rolls of cloth on display. He gave me a very good price, and I went home with three yards of different colors. I had healed his brother.

The baker was just about to leave as well but stopped when he saw my mother and sister approach their laden cart. Considering the size of the cart and the two men-at-arms he had hired to guard it, the baker must be doing very well. My sister and the baker's apprentice talked for a short while and she even gave him a polite kiss on the cheek before turning away. She seemed almost reserved with the young man. The baker gave Mother three more bread rolls.

It took a bit longer to get back home as our cart was full of items the cook and others had purchased. He got a better set of knives, these with maker's marks, for half the price. My sister was happy, my mother was happy, cook was smiling, and even Bernard was happy. He sang various songs as he followed the cart on his horse. But I was not. My body had started changing even more. From what I remembered of my sister, she started bleeding when she was about this age. When it was my time, would magic find me then? Three days later it happened, but not the magic.

Father let me stay with the potions master at his shop in town. He knew what I wanted, for magic to find me. If I hadn't just started bleeding and wanted to be around his magic as much as possible, I would have enjoyed looking at the other shops. There was one that even had books.

The potion master had a backlog of requests. I helped him prepare every potion and pleaded with him to purchase more ingredients just so he would cast more magic. I held onto his arms when he did, watching the potions transform in front of me, hoping to feel the magic flow to me as well. While he slept, I read every book he had. Perhaps there was a special potion that would help a person find magic. Nothing.

During this time, Father came to town twice, both to check up on me, but also to meet the baker. They came to terms; I learned my sister was to be wed in twelve weeks. I was very happy for her, but my lack of sleep was making it hard for me to think properly. Father hugged me and bade me to get some sleep, but I shook my head. Something, maybe a passage in another book, would fix this.

For three weeks, I worked with the potions master, and at some point, I just collapsed. When I woke a day later, I was still Petra Abara, just another person with no magic. I looked up at the ceiling and despaired. When I was of age, my father would probably marry me off to a hostler or baker and my dreams would be gone. Worse, the new apprentice to the potions maker arrived, and I was sleeping in his room.

Father brought me back home. I hid under the blankets and cried for two days. My sister held me and eventually got me to come out and eat. I looked and felt horrible. Mother and Father were worried about me. I felt ashamed; this was supposed to be a happy time for my sister. Instead of preparing for her wedding, she spent her time helping me. My sister was beautiful, sometimes silly, occasionally a pain in the behind, but she loved me. More than anything, that made me stand up and be Petra again.

She and I walked our lady's lands every day. We took turns riding Star and laughing together. Soon my sister would be gone, married. I bet within a year she would have a child of her own.

I did spot the griffin three times. She had flown to the forest south of our lady's lands as I had asked her to. She never approached me again, but I could sense her watching as my sister and I talked. Next to her was a larger griffin, the one I had seen years ago. Had they found happiness together? I hoped so. It made me feel good that the griffin had found a home. My sister had found one too. Where was I going to go?

The healer did ask for my help, and I was glad to offer it. She was still stern, but she was also happy with me. Our lord had given her extra coins for my idea, of which she gave me two silver talons. It made me feel good that others valued me so. As head of our house, I gave both to my father. He used them to help pay for my sister's coming-out party held on our lady's lands.

Disaster struck in the ninth week after I first bled. While making a delivery, the baker's apprentice was struck by a fast-moving carriage. The wheels ran right over him. He was brought to the local healer, but it was already too late. My sister wore black for a month. It got so bad I thought she might take her own life to be with her love in the afterlife. To help, I told her stories from the books I read. She had loved me when I could not find any light. I tried to help her find some again, as well. Over three weeks, my sister slowly started eating and laughing again, if only a little.

A few weeks later, our lady received a letter from our liege lord. An old carver who knew the lord's father needed help. He wanted to know would I be willing to be his apprentice and look after him. My father decided that I should go. The carver didn't live in town, but near it, so father escorted me there. I didn't want to go, but he was the family elder.

I was allowed to take Star with me, but the carver did not have a stable on his small lands. Our lord paid for a boy to watch over her in a stable nearby. Also, once a week, our lord paid for a man-at-arms to escort me home and back so I could attend church with my family.

CHAPTER 6

The beginning of wisdom is to call things by their proper names.

– Confucius

Learning how to find your own name takes wisdom only a true master can teach you. Once you step into the light and cross the line, the journey never ends.

–Ambrose

The carver was old and going blind; now he only made small wooden toys. I reluctantly helped the old, stooped man with white hair.

His name was Master Reindil. At first, he had me sweep up the floor, then, by the end of the week, help the occasional customer at his small counter. Small wooden soldiers, dolls, and, of all things, trains were his best sellers. His entire house had just four areas; the front room, his shop where he carved, his bedroom upstairs and a storeroom which became my bedroom. While the potions master's house was larger, it also had an intense smell from the acids and other boiled-down ingredients. The carver's shop smelled wonderful, like being in a forest. The negative was while the potions maker had good ventilation, the carver's little house got hot quickly. Master Reindil didn't seem to notice it.

After I waved the latest customer goodbye, a woman who had purchased a wooden doll for her daughter, I heard from behind, "What is forty-seven minus eight, Petra?"

The old carving master was standing at the doorway leading into his work area. He squinted his eyes to see me better, making his white bushy eyebrows bunch up. After I answered his question, he didn't look angry, rather amused at something. He looked at me and began to chuckle.

"Master?" Why was he laughing?

Instead of answering me, he turned away and beckoned for me to follow him. "Come, young lady. I want to show you something."

I followed him into his little shop. He sat down on his raised wooden chair. In front of him, each of his carving tools were carefully laid out. He liked to hum to himself as he carved. I must have heard fifty different songs over the week. Some I knew, many I did not. If a tool was nudged out of place, his song darkened until everything was just so again. While watching him carve, I realized with his poor sight, his hands knew where the tools were, not his eyes. Master Reindil could see close up. But even a few feet away, almost everything was blurry for him. He couldn't see the far end of the room. He did have a pair of thick glasses, which he used when he needed to go to the outhouse. Other than that, he hated wearing them.

After pulling a small block of wood from his pile on the left of his bench he handed it to me and asked, "What do you think is inside, Petra? What wants to get out?"

I studied it carefully. It was a rectangular piece of wood, from the smell probably pine. Like all pine, it had knots. I looked up. "It's wood, Master. It will be whatever you want it to be."

"Ah. Now that's where you're wrong, young lady." He picked up one of his carving tools and touched a particularly large knot. "I see the end of a soldier's spear raised upwards. What do you see?"

As I twisted the wood to visualize it better, my mind began racing. Images popped into my head of all the things it might become. We were playing a mind game, and suddenly I felt excited. A part of my brain which had started to fall asleep began to waken back up. There was a small part of me which wondered if my parents wanted me to stop dreaming now that they knew I had no magic. Within my mind, the outer layer of wood fell away. The soldier was there, I could see it, but something else too, a building with a flag on top. When I told my master what I saw, he nodded and took the piece of wood back, then turned it just like I did.

"So, let us see what kind of building it will become," he said and began carving. It turned out to be a three-story bank, eleven inches high, with a pinnacle at the top so detailed I could make out ripples in the flag like there was a breeze. I carefully carried his creation to the front room so it could be sold. When I came back, he had a laid out a small wooden box opposite him; on top of it was a small silver piece.

"Master?" I asked confused.

He was carving again. Without looking up, he said, "Take the money. Tomorrow morning, go to town and purchase a book you like or a newspaper. Then you may read it to me for an hour."

I stared at him. He wanted me to purchase a book? I could hardly believe it.

"But what book should I purchase, master?"

Now he looked up at me and squinted his eyes as if he was studying a block of wood. "Whatever you like young lady. I like stories, or, even better, songs."

"And the box?"

"When you are done reading to me, let us see what your mind can carve."

I spent eight wonderful months with Master Reindil. Each week he would have me purchase a newspaper or a book and let me keep them. I would read to him for an hour a day, and sometimes we would talk about what I read. Then he would question me on the path that I took through San Piedra; the street names, what various lords or ladies were wearing, and the names of the shops. It occurred to me as I spoke, I was his eyes for the things he could no longer see. But his mind, oh, his mind was still very sharp.

His life slowly unfolded before me. This old, stooped man had been a soldier, a sailor, a father, and so much more. He had been to another planet, fought a kraken, and was adrift for six days with two others before another sailing ship rescued them. He had been married twice. His first wife died in childbirth; now, he had outlived his second wife by ten years. His son was grown and had children of his own, although they lived far away. He could speak many different languages. He knew everything.

He never told me how to carve, just some safety instructions so I would not cut my hand open. After that, all he cared about was what I saw inside the wood. Often, I would watch his hands as he carved before making my own cuts. In my fifth month, I sold my first piece, a little flower. I made six copper pieces! I was so happy. I brought the money to my father on church day. Mother kissed me, and my sister danced with me into the night. We pretended to be finely dressed ladies at a gala, each of us would take turns pretending to be a lord, asking the other to dance. I wasn't trying to save peoples' lives. I wasn't desperately trying to find my own magic anymore. But laughing and being with my family made me happy just to be Petra again.

However, the most memorable event was the spirit. A winter chill was still in the air, and a surprisingly dense fog had enveloped the area. Just after I heard the city of San Piedra's high noon bell ringing, which could only be heard when things were very quiet, I heard our small bell dinging, signaling someone had entered our shop. Fog rolled into the front room. I was about to greet whoever had entered when my master looked up suddenly. "Do not allow it to touch you, Petra," he warned. "It is here for me."

"Who? 'It,' master?" But then I saw it. Facing us was a ghostly image of a sailor, his tattered clothes moving with a breeze I did not feel. I could see right through him. Goosebumps ran up my arms. It felt like the air was trying to pull me under. "Master!" I whispered in alarm, "What does it want?"

"Me, Petra. I am the last surviving member of the *Alana*, the ship the kraken destroyed. Fifty-three years ago, this day."

"What should we do?" I asked in terror. Was I about to lose my master?

Instead of answering me, my master pulled out an old bottle and poured a bit of brown ale into a wooden mug. "For you, my friend," he said and pushed it toward the floating image.

It moved toward the mug and seemed to drink from it. Then it began to sing, but no words came forth which I could hear, but apparently my master could. All I could hear were the mournful notes.

"You always sang well. Rest, my friend. My time is coming, and then I will be able to rest as well."

The spirit looked at my master, bowed to me and faded away. Within moments, the fog inside and out had disappeared. I began to breathe again. "Master!" I cried out.

"It is the spirit of the ship, Petra. Every year, it visits the survivors. I am the last. Only when I am gone can it fully rest."

"It felt like a wave of water crashing toward me," I gasped out. Then I remembered my master's words, *my time is coming.* But my master seemed to know what I was thinking.

"It was not an evil spirit, Petra. And it does not mean I will die this day. But my time is coming. I can feel it."

I ran around the desk and hugged him. "Don't go."

He hugged me back. "Everyone goes, child, in their own time. But not today."

Later, I was finally able to sort through my thoughts. "Master," I asked. "Have you seen other spirits?"

He looked up and squinted to see me. "I have."

My mind was racing in excitement. "Where do you think they come from, master?"

He didn't answer me immediately but went back to carving. Knowing him now, I could tell the block of wood in his hands would probably become a train engine. Perhaps five minutes later, without looking up, he said, "I believe they come from us. When enough people name a thing and care about it, a little bit of themselves go with it, and it slowly becomes. Like growing a tree, it takes many raindrops, not just one."

"So, all spirits are good?" I asked, barely able to contain my brewing energy.

He broke out laughing. "Oh, Petra. Even at ten, you must have seen some people that have no goodness in them."

"Of course, master." My parents would steer me clear of them, but I saw them nonetheless. Also, when I acted as a healer's assistant, I wondered sometimes about the people we were healing. A few of them scared me. There were two healers in town, and I helped them on occasion when they called for me. My master always let me go and never asked about who I had to help heal.

"Aye. They can care about some things too. Maybe that's where evil spirits come from, from evil people."

Now it was my turn to be silent for a bit. My little flower was almost done. "Master," I asked. "Can you call a spirit?"

His head shot up. "Petra, calling a spirit is a tricky thing. You must provide something to them that has value to you. I don't mean gold or gems, but something you hold dear."

Now I was bouncing in my chair. "Did you ever call a spirit, master?"

His face turned impish making him look years younger. "There was an old dead dryad's tree I found, one time. After I called her spirit—" He coughed. "Then we, um, well, enjoyed our time together."

I blushed but understood what he did not say. While I thought the idea of liking a boy that way was silly, my older sister had told me, "Just you wait. In three years, you will, Petra." But I had my doubts. It still amazed me women had more than one baby after giving birth the first time.

We were silent again, but my master's cuts slowly began to take on angrier movements eventually becoming savage, his tools biting into the wood. He stopped just before he destroyed what it would become and turned his head away from me so I could not see his face. My master whispered out, "But I paid a horrible price. When I woke the next morning, three years had passed." After a moment he began caressing the little engine, feeling his recent marks. Now he turned back to me and looked me in the eye. "Should you ever need to call a spirit, Petra, negotiate up front. Never forget that."

The spring rains seemed to go on forever. No one had stopped by the shop in three days. After reading to Master Reindil about a Lord who had gotten caught in an inappropriate embrace with another man's wife, he laughed out loud. Then he began telling me a colorful story about his brother which made me blush. I made a go of a bawdy song, and before long we were singing together.

Laughing, then wiping his eyes, my master said, "Life is not just one piece of wood to be carved, Petra, it is many."

There was something in his last words. "Master?"

But he just shook his head and smiled. "So, tell me about your sister," he asked, changing the topic.

"Oh, she has found joy again, master. A knife maker's apprentice has asked for her hand. The heads of household are planning to sit together next church day to decide if they should be married."

"Very good." He nodded. "I will make a piece for their wedding."

He did make a piece; it was the last thing he ever carved. Three days after my sister was engaged again, I woke and found my master in his chair, eyes open. A block of oak was in front of him, the bottom half uncarved, but the top was breathtaking; two intertwined rings on a rock in the middle of a bubbling brook. I cried for ten minutes before I noticed something was on my seat. The box with the small carving set he let me use, and on it lay a folded piece of paper.

Sniffling and unfolding the letter, I read, *Petra, a darkness is coming to Avalon, my bones feel it. Wherever your path takes you, don't forget to add some of your own cuts to it. You have given me some of your light, and for that I am eternally grateful. Keep on learning, girl. Never stop.*

The next morning, I received a letter from our lord asking if I would put together what items of Master Reindil's should be sent to his son. Within the same letter, he asked if I would speak at his funeral, which was to be in two days. While I cleaned and carefully packed all his carving tools, I thought about what I wanted to say. Master Reindil gave me a safe place to be with no expectation that I would be anything but Petra. He encouraged me to read every day. It was very important to him that I imagined what something could be. Whenever I had to briefly leave him (to help the healers, or, occasionally, the potions master) he never demanded to know what I had been doing. Thinking back, he trusted me. And, trusted that I would make good choices.

I put off entering his bedroom until midday. There wasn't much. His clothes I put aside to be donated, and his glasses to be sent to his son. Then I opened the two wooden chests. The smaller one contained old letters wrapped in twine. Some were to his first wife, but most of them were to his second. A few of the later ones were from his son; the handwriting was terrible. The last letter he received was six years ago.

This good old man had been alone, not contacted by any family members, for the last six years!

Opening the larger chest revealed a military uniform in our lord's colors. He had been a captain! From his stories I knew he had been a soldier, but not an officer. Carefully placing the uniform on his bed, I pulled out other things. A few letters, mostly from Lord Gawain asking for his services. Farther down were his sword and matching dagger. The sword was many-times-folded steel and engraved! Toward the bottom I pulled out six wooden mugs which were engraved on the bottom of them with "the Alana." From the inscriptions, probably by six different people. Was this all that was left of the ship? Had he been its captain? Then a few smaller items of little monetary value, but which Master Reindil had obviously held dear. All these items I would send to his son. All that was left was a small wooden box at the bottom of the chest. After pulling it out and opening it, my eyes went wide.

Chapter 7

Embedded in the trail you take is your will to never give up, to never stop believing, and to find something bigger than yourself to fight for. But more than that; you have given the fallen a path, a path to remember, for until the last of us falls, they will be with us forever.

–Lieutenant Calvit

I looked down at the open pit and still didn't know what I wanted to say. His burial was scheduled to be in half an hour. Besides the priest, I wasn't sure if anyone else was coming. Master Reindil had been more my master than the healer or the potions maker, even though I never took apprentice vows. I certainly learned more factual knowledge at the hands of the other masters, but I learned more about life—and about myself—with Master Reindil. I was ten, going on eleven, and I already knew I wasn't going to stay with my parents for much longer. I didn't have any magic, but neither did my master. He never let that stop him from exploring.

The first of the attendees to arrive where a few older ladies from town, then six old men in uniform. Four of them couldn't stand on their own and had to be helped down and into wheelchairs. The youngest one introduced himself to me. They were the last of his unit.

My parents came soon after, along with my sister, shortly followed by my lady and her children. Others came as well. Most I didn't know or had only ever seen from a distance, an old healer, some younger officers. The last to arrive was our lord, helping his father, the prince, walk the short distance from the carriage to the grave. People parted before them. These two great men stood just opposite me. When they bowed their heads, we all did as well. After the priest said a few words, all eyes turned to me.

I took a deep breath and slowly let it out.

"Master Reindil was the wisest person I ever met. He didn't teach me the art of healing, or of potions, how to read, or do math. Instead, he taught me to see the hidden clues around me and recognize the beauty waiting to get out."

I looked across the grave toward our Lord Gawain and his son Prince Landon, meeting their eyes. Tears began trickling down my face. "When our lord asked for my help to care for this old man, I thought I was being punished. Instead, it was the greatest gift I have ever been given. I learned wisdom from a man who has been to another world, fought in battles, been a captain of a ship, lost love, and found it again. Every day he asked me to read to him. We sang songs, told stories and laughed together. No matter where I go and what I do, this old man will be with me forever."

I wiped at my face and looked at our lord again. "Thank you."

After others said a few kind words, our Prince stood up with the help from our lord. His voice was crackly but understandable. "Joseph Reindil was my friend, my confident, and my Voice. He always found a way to get the job done. Without him, myself and others would not be here. May God and all the gods take his spirit and bring him to safety. Amen."

After each person took a turn shoveling dirt, our lord invited me to meet Prince Gawain. My lady stood on my left, my father on my right. After curtseying, I handed over the small wooden box I found in the bottom of Master Reindil's wooden chest.

He opened it up and smiled. "I still remember the first time I requested that Joseph be my Voice here in the south of our nation. His exact words were, 'I'd rather suffer through the plague.'" After pulling out the gold lion pin, he looked at me and winked at his son. "Hopefully you're less stubborn than your old master was."

I think my mouth was hanging open. "My lord?"

Before I could respond, he pinned the little gold lion onto my blouse just above my heart. The two small green gems for its eyes sparkled in the sun. Then he winked at me, "This is the part where you go down on one knee."

After slowly going down on a knee, we exchanged vows of fealty: me to be a good vassal, him to be a just and kind lord to me. He tapped me on my shoulder. "Rise Ms. Abara, Voice of our Noble Nation, Gawain. Seven lands in all. I name you, my Voice." He smiled down at me, kissed me on my forehead and spoke, "You may rise."

Instead of a celebration, the talk turned to war. There were over thirty men-at-arms including Bernard, several full knights in plate mail, plus two sorcerers. I had no idea things were already so bad. From their expressions, several of them hadn't heard the news we were suffering an invasion and were at war, any more than I had.

The sorcerer bowed. "Three days ago, I lost all contact with the Master Ception to the East. He was supporting the gathering of men-arms."

Sir Awalt grunted out, "I lost three men yesterday. They are like no creatures I have ever seen before. I believe they are only the scouts."

"Can you cast an illusion of these creatures?" asked our lord. "Perhaps someone knows of them."

An image of a large spider-like figure emerged. Taller than I was. Short black fur, many eyes and pincers for the front two legs. Several people hissed out.

"Anyone?" asked our lord.

I had no idea and shook my head. Others did the same.

Our prince slowly stood up and addressed his sorcerers. "Send out the call. I want all knights and men-at-arms on the road tomorrow. We will meet these creatures in battle. Our nation has stood for over six hundred years, it will stand longer."

He was wrong.

Chapter 8

Nothing we do will stop the darkness from coming. How we find hope is stepping into the unknown, bringing nothing but our internal light and the might of our swords. If we stand together, we may have another day. Tomorrow we do the same and after enough days, we discover hope.

—Arthur Pendragon

Within a week, people started fleeing.

I met the prince one last time in his castle. Everyone who could swing a sword or shoot a bow was gathering there, then marching in groups. This included my father, brother and our lady's husband. After sharing a cup of wine with three nobles, Prince Gawain beckoned me to come talk to him. His mood seemed light and jovial.

But the moment his back was turned toward them, I was looking at a different man. Death was in his eyes. All his easy energy was gone. Now his wrinkled face showed the pain of his age.

"Petra, my Voice," he said formally. "Save as many as you can." My lord was old. He couldn't stand on his own for long without help. There was no way he could fight.

I curtsied. "Sir, you are going into battle?"

I was trying to understand. From the way he talked a moment ago victory was assured. Now looking at me, it was anything but. What was going on? There was a sense of finality about him. Being an assistant to a healer, I had seen death come before. This man before me knew the reaper had a hand on his shoulder.

He gave me a sad smile. "My Voice, I will stand with my knights. My sorcerer tells me by nightfall the first wave of monsters could come. We don't have enough firearms. Head North toward Avalon city. Run like the wind. Don't let the screams of the dying stop you. We will hold until the last.

I was horrified. Outside, some of the younger knights were singing and laughing. They believed they were going to fight, spill blood, and go home to their families as heroes. From what my lord described, they all might be dead by morning!

"My Lord," I pleaded, "what if we all retreated?"

"Many of the monsters can move faster than a horse. We are going to try to buy you, and others, time to escape. Take as many as you can. Run like a mist wolf is hunting you. Don't stop until you get to Avalon City."

I swallowed. "Yes, sir. How many other Voices are there?" I honestly wasn't certain.

He leaned over and kissed me on the forehead. "There are six others, seven in total. A Voice for each of my realms. I am asking a great burden of you. Like the others head north to Avalon City. I have paid two from the Archer Clan to be your scouts. Heed their advice." He smiled down at me. "Joseph believed in you, and I owe him everything."

I grabbed his hand. "Sir. The teleportation circles," I pleaded. I had never teleported before, but knew they existed and had talked to people who had used them. If the stories were true, we could be in Avalon city within the hour.

The prince touched my hair. "My advisors tell me this horde is not from our world. They have magic different from ours which can take over teleportation beacons. Whenever a teleportation circle farther south was opened, monsters erupted through. They are too close. The only option is to run north. Word has reached me the gate circle in Avalon City still works—Earth and the other planets may be our only salvation." My Prince slowly lowered himself to one knee. I could see the pain on his face as he bent down. "Find a way to live again, my Voice," he whispered to me. "Bring some light into this world. Through you, others will remember it can be done." He winked. "Said another way, make some cuts of your own, girl."

I helped him to his feet and ignored the popping noise from his back and knees. Before I could reply, he turned away.

His posture changed. Gone was the old man. He laughed, clasped arms with the knights around him and bade them welcome. Now, his page held his polished mail shirt to put on over his padded gambeson.

This kind, old man would be dead before morning. I was a healer and there was nothing I could do to help him.

As I passed the word we would be leaving before nightfall, people dithered, children cried, and most wanted to stay in the city. Stone walls had kept them safe from wolves all their lives, surely these larger walls would do the same. I was relieved to discover one of my two scouts was Acrun, from the Archer Clan. The other was Vero. Like Acrun, he was tall and strong, but stoic. I also asked Marrit if she would be my advisor just for the simple fact that I trusted her. I desperately wanted to ask for Father, just so I could save him. He, along with my brother, had already marched south. If you could hold a sword, you were drafted to fight. A part of my brain was numb knowing they would likely be dead soon.

Once it was just the four of us, I leaned over the stone walls and screamed into the air. I screamed at the prince for demanding this of me, for the absolute stupid idea of standing your ground and not retreating. The three just waited until I finished. When I turned around to face Acrun, tears where streaming down my face. I wanted to be back in my master's shop, singing with him, listening to his stories, and smelling the fresh wood from his carvings again. Not standing on our prince's walls knowing all this finery would be destroyed within a day and there was nothing I could do about it.

Acrun moved to stand beside me at the wall. "That's not why the prince is staying. If he doesn't, you and the rest of his Voices won't be able to escape. He is sacrificing his kingdom so it might have a future."

"That makes no sense," I said, looking down at the lower walls. They stood thirty feet high; we were another forty up. From this position the castle looked impregnable.

He followed my gaze. "The creatures will just climb the walls." He snorted. "We could be five times higher, and it wouldn't matter."

"But the cannons," I protested. There was a small part of me that wanted to believe we could stay. Cannons had been placed on parapets around the castle walls and in the higher parts of the city. Teams of people fed them gunpowder from the front, then slammed an iron ball home. The explosion, when they fired, was tremendous. I had seen a cannon ball splinter a tree.

"Will mean nothing," replied Acrun. "If we are not on the road before sunset, we will be dead. Would you like some advice, Lady Abara?"

Sunset was six hours away. I cringed at the Lady Abara. A part of me wanted to throw the emerald eyed gold lion pin over the wall, to tell everyone to go to hell. Then I remembered my old master's dying note to me, *A darkness is coming. My bones can feel it.*

"Yes."

"Leave the cripples. Take only those that are willing to come at your command, the younger the better, including the children. Beg, borrow, and steal as many horses, wagons, and supplies as you can. Speed is all you should care about. Do not be polite. Don't ask, but command. Death is coming and nothing will save those who choose to stay. If they attack like before, two hours past nightfall the first wave of creatures will hit the walls. They will be the scouts. I expect between those with magic, the cannons, and others who can fight, the walls will hold. If the creatures attack like before, then the real wave will appear just before midnight." Acrun put a hand on my shoulder. "What happens when a wolf pack brings down prey?"

"They eat it," I said apprehensively and turned my face away from him.

"True," he replied, "but that also takes time. The prince is giving us that time. If he retreated, his forces would be overrun anyway and we with them. This way, we will have a head start, but only that. If we slow down at all we die."

It was a good five seconds before I really comprehended what he just said. I took a ragged breath and looked at Vero. "Do you agree?"

He nodded. "As you know, our commander can talk to us through the amulets. A noble bribed a sorcerer in Mertual to open the teleportation circle there three hours ago. Everyone died. The town was sixty miles to the west, I expect the monsters will hit these walls from two sides." He shrugged. "I would bring a few cripples just so you have something to feed to the monsters as they get near us."

I couldn't believe he just said that, but the man was looking at me like it was the most reasonable suggestion in the world. Treating people like goats to be eaten. If I could cast magic, Vero would be dead right now.

Acrun put a hand on my shoulder. "Lady Abara needs guidance, Vero, not your dark wisdom."

He shrugged. "Just because it is ugly, doesn't make it not true."

I couldn't have him in front of me right now. "Vero," I commanded. "Please begin passing the word we will be leaving in four hours. Put teams together to gather supplies, everything you think we will need."

He bowed. "As the lady says." He disappeared around the corner.

Acrun grunted. "He is thinking short term, which is valuable. But a leader must not abandon her people. Any who follow, become your people." He fingered his amulet. "There is another clan member who owes me a favor. If he comes, we might have a chance. Do I have your leave to help get ready?"

I didn't want Acrun to go, but it was important he gathered supplies. My mother would be packing, my sister would whine but follow. Who knew how many people would come from our lands? "Go," I said. "I will meet you soon."

It was just Marrit and me. "I could give you the lion pin," I said, partially hoping she would say yes. "You were born a noble."

She had never said a word through the whole discussion. She'd just kept calm and listened. A far cry from the young noble who would send my sister out to meet the endless supply of young men who hoped to catch her favor. Marrit had been preparing to take her journeyman sorceress test when the war broke out. Like my father and brother, her father and two brothers had been drafted to fight. While her younger sister had magic, her entire goal had been to marry into another noble family and have babies to pass along her magic. That was unlikely to happen now. She would be more hindrance than help now. The girl could whine. She acted like the war was just getting in the way of finding her knight in shining armor. At least my sister could see the desperation of the people around us.

Marrit gave me a sad smile. "Petra, I could never be the leader that you are."

"You're sixteen," I protested. "Already a noble and have pushed yourself to learn and have useful magic. Everyone likes you too."

"But that doesn't make a leader. People respect you. While they like me, they listen to you." Before I could respond, she added, "Besides, I don't want the job. I am very happy being Marrit, counselor to the Voice, a low noble and sorceress in training."

I partially turned away. "Do you agree with Acrun about what will happen tonight?"

"Yes," she said simply. "My master was killed eight days ago. Before dying, he transmitted images from his wand to mine. They are coming. If not tonight, then tomorrow. But Petra, what I am really scared of is what comes next."

"Sorry," I said and turned around. "What do you mean?"

"Who controls the monsters," she said in a whisper. "What lies in the darkness waiting to pounce."

"I don't know," I said. "But I don't want to meet them either. Let's get going."

Six hundred and forty-four people followed me, not including my mother and sister. We made it fifteen miles before darkness forced us to stop. A runner found us before daybreak. The castle had been overrun. One of the other seven Voices had waited too long; there was six of us now. I pushed everyone north at first light.

At first, we followed the same road north. Barrels, boxes, and other random large items littered the side of the road as the travelers before us had lightened their load to move faster. I gave orders to do the same. If it wasn't food, medicine, weapons, clothes, family heirlooms, or spending money, I wanted it gone. When one of the merchants started arguing with me, Acrun slammed the merchant against his cart. "Hear that, fool? They are coming. Do what she says, or I will break your leg. Then, their scouts will eat you."

I wanted to cry. Instead, I asked, "How far back are they?"

Acrun looked up. Vero was in a tree looking in the direction of the castle. He held up four fingers. "Four scouts, less than a mile away," replied Acrun.

The merchant started blubbering but did as we asked. Half of his belongings fell to the side of the road.

"Vero and I will take care of the four," announced Acrun. "But we must be seven miles north as fast as possible. The one who owes me a favor is there. His spell has to be cast before nightfall."

I had the children ride with others, doubling or tripling up on a horse. Some of the more pregnant women went in the carts. When donkeys became stubborn Marrit shot a cracking ball of energy from her wand into their rump to get them moving again. I pleaded, shouted, and demanded people start moving faster. Two hours later only Acrun returned. Vero was wrong, there had been nine scouts and one very large spider.

The trees and bushes here looked just like the others we had passed. Acrun whistled, then whistled again. Suddenly, a section of the forest shimmered, and a path emerged. It was big enough for two horses to walk side by side down it. An old, weathered man holding a staff stepped out onto the road. Where Acrun wore an amulet of a bow on a silver chain, this man had a gold amulet in the shape of a tree, with two rubies in its branches.

Marrit murmured, "That was a really good illusion."

I had never met anyone from the Great Forest Clan before. What little remained of his hair was white and his face was a sun-browned mass of wrinkles. Acrun made the introductions. "Lady Petra Abara, let me introduce you to Testin. He's an asshole, but in a good way."

Testin's mouth twitched, then he bowed to me. "Acrun tells me you're not an idiot. The boy couldn't find his ass in the forest with both his hands, but I trust his judgement in people."

Considering Acrun could disappear into the forest when he was right in front of me, that was saying something. I had never seen anyone better at hiding. How good was Testin? He had an odd accent I hadn't heard before. English or at least our version of English wasn't his first language. "Acrun says you know a spell that might help us?" I asked.

"We don't have much time," he said, turning to walk down the path "It's two miles up. We need to move fast. The trees tell me there are creatures advancing through the forest."

I was a little reluctant to leave the main road. If we got stuck in mud or lost in the woods, the horde would probably overrun us before nightfall. I looked to Marrit for guidance.

She nervously rolled her wand between her palms. "We have to trust somebody," she replied.

I nodded and began issuing orders to head down the path.

"What kind of spells are in your amulet," I asked Testin, as he and I led the way down the path at a fast clip. I honestly didn't know.

"Mostly spells about plants, maps, tracking, and healing," he said and looked at me. "Why, thinking of joining the clan?"

"I'm a healer without any magic," I replied.

He looked behind him for a second. "Looks like you have some magic of your own, they're following you."

We walked in silence for a bit. The old man didn't seem to have a need to talk. "Do you like your clan?" I asked.

He shrugged. "Most of them are a bunch of worthless rags."

That was an odd thing to say. The illusion he had cast was amazing. "What do the two rubies mean?" I asked after we had walked in silence for a bit more.

"That I'm old and did idiotic things I had no business doing."

He certainly wasn't like my old master. I was about to ask him what kind of spell he was planning on casting when I stopped and stared. The path opened into a large clearing next to a shallow river. A single massive tree grew next to a curve in the land, like the river had grown around it over time.

"It's a weeping willow," he said. "Not very common around here. But there's another one about its size some two hundred miles north and west of us."

Okay. Beautiful tree, but why was this important. Marrit asked in awe, "You can tree teleport?"

He grunted. "Going to be hard keeping it open long enough to get everyone through. Leave the animals."

"What about the remaining Voices?" I asked. They were ahead of us. Each one had more people following them than I had.

Testin snorted. "I'm going to start, need about thirty minutes to get the focus right. When the door opens, start running. Anyone who doesn't go through gets left behind. I can't do it again with so many people."

I pulled Acrun to the side. "What about the other Voices?" I demanded. "What is going to happen to them?" There was only six of us now and four of them were only hours ahead of us. There were thousands of lives at stake, many of them children.

"Lady Abara." Acrun bowed. "The prince demanded I get you and yours to Avalon City. I am fulfilling my oath. This is not a war but an extermination."

Tears began trickling down my face. "Acrun," I pleaded, "they can't run fast enough."

"No," he said flatly, "they can't. They're going to die."

I hit him in the chest and yelled out, "Why didn't you tell them to stop here? Maybe some of them could be saved."

Testin turned to face me. He was leaning both of his hands on one side of the tree, concentrating hard. "Dammit girl, I don't know if I can get all your people through. With all the teleport circles out, it was lucky I got here."

Marrit nervously tapped her wand on her hip. "This is teleporting too. Won't the magicians who control the monsters detect this as well?"

Testin rolled his eyes and grunted. "Questions. Always at the worst times. This spell was designed using a base eight structure instead of a base ten, so they're probably not looking for it."

"Probably," Marrit said nervously.

"Well, if I'm wrong," hissed out Testin, "then it won't matter, will it? If the tree wasn't next to the river, I doubt I could get half of you through. Now, be quiet!"

It took me a few minutes to calm down enough to begin explaining what was about to happen to the people following me. No one was happy. This meant leaving behind everything but what they could carry on their backs. Two of the merchants started discussing if they should turn back to find another group farther ahead. I didn't have the energy to argue with them. Instead, I began issuing orders. Women and children first. When you see the lights form, run. Don't dawdle. If you get left behind, you die. Some of the children began crying, but I didn't know what to do to calm them down.

Three of the merchants did begin to leave. About thirty others decided to follow them; these were mostly the ones in better clothes or had horses pulling carts.

"Let them go," said Acrun, edging to the side of the clearing. "They won't make it to the main road." He jumped upon a high rock and held an arrow nocked but pointed at the ground.

I turned at Marrit's exclamation. Extending up from the base of the tree was an archway of light. "Almost there," Testin shouted out. "Get ready." With a great burst of energy, the tree lit up. Testin's eyes were closed, and he fell to his knees but continued his contact with the tree. Water from the shallow river near the tree was suddenly sucked into the ground. Water flowed in to take its place, bubbling over the rocks, and it too was sucked into the ground. Testin gasped out, "Run. Move your ass girl." His arms were trembling as he kneeled before the tree.

From the direction of the path which brought us here I heard screams. Acrun's raised his bow, and his first arrow struck a creature emerging from the forest. He hit it in the head, and the spider like creature crashed to the ground.

"Run!" I shouted to everyone. "Get through the tree." I stood just to side of the archway of light and beckoned people forward. Shouting both orders and accusation as some men tried to run in front of the women and children. The moment a person touched the glowing doorway of light they disappeared. If a person hesitated, they were shoved forward by the storm of people behind them.

More creatures stormed out of the forest and ran toward us. Some of those following me had bows, one even had one crossbow, but none of these people had the training of Acrun, his steel tipped arrows, or his composite bow. People pushed toward the tree even as those on the outer edge toward the oncoming creatures fired or held up swords.

Acrun's arrows took down creature after creature with a single shot. But there were too many. Marrit began shooting balls of fire into the encroaching horde formed when several had grouped together like a pack of dogs running toward us. I had no magic, there was nothing I could do but scream at everyone to run. Half were through the tunnel of light when a large spider like creature pulled a man down and tore into him. Marrit burned it alive, consuming the man as well.

"Acrun," I shouted pointing down the river. Creatures were running toward us following the riverbank. We were about to be hit in two directions. Acrun shifted and felled two then shifted back. He was running out of arrows. Marrit screamed as she let loose another fireball of energy, and I watched her stumble. She had used more magic than I thought possible. The creatures kept coming. Fifty of my people to go, I stood by the large tree and shouted at the remaining to run faster.

"Testin," I yelled. "Get up!" He was still on his knees, eyes closed; his hands were on two of the tree's massive roots repeating some spell. Sweat dripped from his face. I don't think he heard me; he was concentrating so hard. Ten people left. "Acrun," I screamed at him, "Run!" He used his last arrow to kill a creature as Marrit and I stumbled forward toward the light. Acrun pulled his sword and ran, cutting down two as they closed the distance. I tried to pull Testin up; instead, he pulled hard on his amulet, snapping the chain around his neck and handing it to me. His other hand was still on a root. "Go," he whispered. "Live your life."

I tried reaching for him, but my hand slipped off his sweaty arm. Marrit pulled me into the light just as a spider monster attacked Testin. The last thing I saw was Acrun running toward me. He didn't get to us in time.

Mother held me as I rocked back and forth. Wherever here was, it was a little cooler and raining. After coming through the light bridge, Marrit fell over unconscious. We were in a clearing around another giant weeping willow. All we had with us was what we carried, no one had the time to sort through their belongings before the creatures attacked. I could hear children whimpering, some crying, and others just sat in the mud, too stunned to move. Everything we all knew was gone. I couldn't tell you which were tears and which were raindrops streaking down my face. My sister leaned against Mother, and the three of us just sat there looking at nothing. In my hand, I held Testin's tree amulet. Acrun probably hadn't survived; there were too many monsters around him. Was Testin alive? I doubted it. My brain couldn't comprehend all the deaths over the last day; it was too much.

"We are alive," said my mother, kissing the top of my head. "Without you we would all be dead."

"Miltan might still be alive as well," whispered my sister. The knifemaker's apprentice. Her second intended.

He was dead, so was everyone else who had marched south. Instead, I said, "Maybe." There were over six hundred who had followed me; now there were about fifty fewer. Considering how fast the scouts had been moving, I couldn't see how some of the other caravans could survive. I might be the only Voice left within a day.

The rain began coming down harder, and a young boy approached me. "Ma'am," he said quietly. "My mum says her stomach hurts. She's growing my brother."

I nodded and pushed off the ground to stand up. In my backpack I had some basic healing tools. Half an hour later, I helped to birth Hayden Till. The first person in our new world. We had one more to add to our number. It was raining; we were muddy, tired, and scared. Soon night would come and with it the cold. But just knowing life happened gave me just a little hope.

If Testin was right, we were about two hundred miles farther north. We needed to find shelter even if it was only under trees. Once night came, the temperature would drop. If we didn't get warm and somewhat dry, we wouldn't have to worry about the monsters finding us, we would be dead. Marrit helped to start several fires, and I began asking everyone to pull out their belongings to determine our resources. We had food to last us a few days if we ate sparingly, some minor healing potions, and other remedies, half of which I deemed unusable. It's amazing what some families will brew up believing their grandmother's recipe has secret healing properties. Fortunately, those carrying bows still had them along with an assortment of swords and most had simple knives. Unfortunately, the number of arrows we had was limited.

I had never been this far north and wasn't exactly sure where we were. If there was a road near us, no one knew about it. Between Marrit and a few others who had some knowledge of tracking, they determined the southern most parts of Avalon city were about another hundred and fifty miles away. If we had horses and wagons, we could get there in four days, maybe three if we pushed ourselves. But with thirty some children, a newborn, and some not much older, plus some very pregnant women, we might be able to cover fifteen miles in a day. Some wanted to break up into groups, but I demanded we stay together. The arguments got so bad I had to step in and use the dreaded words, "Because I am Lady Abara and I said so." If Marrit wasn't backing me up, I wasn't sure what would have happened.

It rained for the next three days. We began foraging to survive. Fortunately, we passed by two small, abandoned hamlets. Chickens and some other small game animals roamed the streets, and we even found several goats still in their pen. Inside one of the small houses I discovered a sewing kit. At the rate we were going, these would be all I had for stitches soon. Each night I had to remind myself success was measured by the number of people still with us at the end of the day.

Was there no safe place? Even having been teleported two hundred miles away, some four days later some of the smaller creatures found us. They moved fast and made odd cackling sounds when they spotted us, drawing more creatures our way. I organized watches and made sure any with some experience with a sword stood their turn, guarding. Even so some of the smaller monsters still found us. By the seventh day of our journey, I had lost another forty of my people to them. But by now we were encountering smaller groups marching in the same direction we were. During the last three days of our journey, we had found a road, then a larger road. The farther we got, the more that joined my party. By the time we crossed the huge stone bridge over the Cloudburn river, over a thousand people had joined us. We got to Hurries Bridge, the extreme edge that made up Avalon City. I thought we were saved. People from Earth had come to help. I felt like I had aged ten years in that month.

CHAPTER 9

I'll knight any who follow me into darkness, but those who are able to weep at the loss then find the courage within themselves to stand up again, they sit at my table.

—Arthur Pendragon

A sea of tents had been set up some distance north of Hurries bridge where refugees could get food, healing, and a place to sleep. I tried to keep us all together, but it was impossible. Between others streaming in from the south and soldiers mustering to march south, every hour was chaotic mayhem. Within a day, I lost track of who was where.

Soldiers from Earth's Continental Republic had come, and they brought their machines. Men in grey uniforms with rifles would gather behind large, tracked vehicles and head south into battle. Accompanying them were sorcerers and sorceresses from Avalon along with other nobles who also brought their knights wearing chain or plate mail riding horses bearing swords and lances.

On the second morning after our arrival, I introduced myself to a tired looking master healer and showed him my assistants healing pin with an offer to help. He glanced at my lion pin while sewing up a wound.

Why wasn't he using magic? He was a master healer.

"Lady Petra," he said, "I will take anyone who has common sense and can follow instructions. How long have you been an assistant?" Then he cocked his head and looked at me again. "Lady Petra Abara?"

"Yes, master," I said a little apprehensively. "But I'm just a Voice. I have no lands. You have heard of me?"

"There is a new procedure being taught in the Healer's Guild called the G.Abara method. It has been attributed to Petra Abara of Gawain."

I think I blushed slightly. "Yes, master. I, um, came up with the idea almost a year ago." Then I blurted out, "Master, have you heard of any other Voices of Gawain who survived or grandchildren of Prince Gawain?" I was terrified of being the only Voice. If no children or grandchildren of Gawain survived, a Voice could declare him or herself the new ruler. Other than acting as the nobles' trusted advisor and Voice, they could assume the responsibility of the kingdom if the line died out. I was terrified it might only be me.

Once the master healer finished his stitching, we moved outside into the open air. After taking a long drink from his mug, he said, "I heard someone say another Voice had arrived, but he was in another base." He smiled down at me. "If it is true, I cannot say."

I was relieved but also surprised and looked around at all the tents; they seemed to go on forever. "There are more places like this?"

"Two. You and I are in the smallest one. For whatever reason, the Earth officers are calling this one Sparrow. The other two are Eagle and Hawk." He shrugged. "Probably because they're bigger. So, about your offer, if you are really willing to help, I have a job for you."

"Yes, Master," I replied. "I was able to get all the people who followed me into tents." Then I blurted out, "Master, why weren't you using magic to heal that man?"

"Before the war, I might treat fifteen people a day. My magic can only go so far, so I reserve it for the severely injured, usually burns. Which is where you come in, you heal without magic, and I don't understand the doctors from Earth. They don't heal with magic either. I want you to work with them and then teach me their words and how they heal."

"Oh. Do you think they will let me read their books as well?" I felt like a part of me was missing when I didn't have books to read.

"Lady Petra, let us find out."

As we walked toward another group of white tents with large red crosses on them, I said, "I'm not really a lady."

He shrugged. "Generally, within Avalon city when you wear a pin such as yours, people will refer to you as lady or lord even if you're not." Before I could reply, I was introduced to several doctors and a deal was struck; they would take me on as if I was a premedical student and even pay me a little. I wasn't entirely certain what premedical meant, but it apparently allowed me the opportunity to read their books while I worked with them. One of the Earth doctors grinned at me. "What it really means is you get no sleep while you learn."

Soon after, I went to go find my mother and Marrit. "Can you send as many as of our people over to the healing tents where I will be working?" I asked them. "At least, I can do a little more to help."

Marrit sniffed. "Petra, we're alive. Most of them know that, without you, they wouldn't be."

For almost five months, I worked alongside the healers from Earth helping where I could. Surprisingly, I knew more practical healing than most of their nurses, but the ones they called doctors, Earth's healing masters, began teaching me things I never knew existed about surgery, medicines, and diagnosing problems. They even let me read some of their books. If I got four hours of sleep a night, it was a wonder.

During this time, every Sunday I wore my lion pin and prayed with any who followed me. Sometimes others came who had lived in one of the other realms of our prince, but I didn't care. If only for a moment, we could sit, be together, and share stories. Early on, we learned Father was dead and the group my brother was with just disappeared. The same letters brought word that Hattie's intended had died in the same battle with our father. As she prayed, tears trickled down her face. Twice her union candle could not be lit. I was the Voice, the person people expected to stand strong. So, as my sister, Mother, and others wept, I held our prayer candle and refused to let my own tears fall.

As time went on, I still held out hope that one of my prince's sons or grandchildren had survived, but it all came to nothing. I heard the same rumor that another Voice of Gawain had survived, but things were so chaotic I wasn't sure what to believe.

Every day was the same. Wake up after too little sleep. A sponge bath, eat, and begin healing. Then, after dinner, read the doctor's books to keep my sadness away. I felt as if I started crying, I wasn't sure I could stop. But something began changing after the sixth week—we had fewer patients. That meant I could sleep longer, but with that came the nightmares.

It was the morning after a Sunday gathering when I woke and started to cry. I sat on my bed feeling empty and just couldn't stop my tears. Someone must have called for my mother. When she wrapped her arms around me, I gulped and cried harder. Mother just held me while rocking me back and forth. At some point, after I had no more tears to shed, she tucked me back into bed and kissed me on the forehead like I was a little girl. "I am very proud of you, Petra. Today, just rest."

When I woke up again, it was dark. I went to the area where we prayed and knelt in front of the bonfire while holding my lion pin. A part of me wanted to throw it into the fire and walk away from the responsibility of it, to be just Petra Abara again. Tears trickled down my face as I considered what to do. I just sat for a while listening to the crackle of the logs and watching the flames dance. What made me keep the pin was the memory of Master Reindil. Every day for him was pain; just standing up hurt the man. But he never let that stop him from sharing his joy and wisdom with me.

"I had no idea making my own cuts could hurt this much," I whispered into the night. Then I stood up and turned away still holding my pin. I looked back and said, "Thank you for teaching me how to stand up again." It might have been my imagination, but I thought I saw my old master's smiling face in the fire for just a second. When I woke the next morning, the pain was still there, but so was joy in helping to heal those in need. I was able to share in the stories with those around me again; to laugh and cry without fearing my emotions would consume me.

A few weeks later, Hattie became involved with a soldier. At first, Mother didn't approve and went to Marrit for her thoughts, who then came to me. It wasn't just my sister, though. Those who followed me, and others from the Southern realms, wanted decisions made and, apparently, I was the one they came to. Several times a week a person or small group would ask for my wisdom or blessing. I would listen to their story while performing my duties as a healer. I discovered that the more blood in front of me, the shorter their stories became. When Marrit came to me about my sister, I listened to her thoughts on the man as I finished treating my patient.

While washing my hands, I said, "So you like him? Her second intended died less than three months ago." Traditional Avalon custom had you wait at least six months before becoming involved with another, but I didn't think people cared anymore.

Marrit smiled. "It feels like two years ago, but I do. Once the war is over, he wants to bring your sister home with him to Earth."

"Well," I chuckled. "I remember a saying from somewhere that the third time's the charm. Let go say hi."

Marrit led me onto a different part of the Republic's base. I had no problem getting past their guards; they recognized me and had long since given me an Earth healer's pin to go along with my Avalon pin. Like Avalon, those from the Continental Republic treated healers with respect. Also, some of their officers knew what a Voice signified and occasionally asked my opinion on matters. I always found it very strange, standing with these tall men discussing matters when I was a third their age.

My first thought when I saw Steve Mulligan was how could my sister possibly birth any of his babies. The man towered over me and looked like he could lift three men with one arm. However, he was very kind, and introduced me to his officer, who assured me Sergeant Mulligan was a respected and honest man. What was I supposed to

Once above ground, I looked south. Few buildings still stood, and farther away, most were rubble or just burned-out shells. Even where we were, many of the buildings had suffered damage. A week afterward, something miraculous happened. The bugs began retreating, then running. Sorcerer Petotum's name was chanted in the streets. Apparently, he and some elite soldiers from Earth had located the main gate beacon the monsters used to get to Avalon. With that destroyed, they had no reinforcements. Two weeks after its destruction, the remaining monsters started fleeing toward the mountains. We won, but half of the city was gone, and no one knew if anything remained of our home.

I was able to get Mother in front of a master healer who was able to repair some of the damage, but her cracked bone had already started healing improperly. Short of breaking her leg again, she would always walk with a noticeable limp, but her pain was not as great.

I kept my promise to Hattie and traveled south with her, back to Hurries Bridge. Mother demanded to come, so I purchased a small pony and a cart for Mother to sit in; even healed, it would be hard for to walk that far again. With what little money I had left, I purchased food and water as well. Resources were scarce and everything was expensive. Before the war, the pony I purchased might have cost a silver talon, now it was eight, and I was lucky to find one. After the cart and food, I had very little money left.

Others who had followed me traveled with us. Like my sister, they hoped that the life they left behind was still there. Every day of our journey was depressing. There was nothing but ruins, but my sister kept her eyes forward resolutely believing Steve Mulligan survived. Some days later we found the burnt-out remains of the building where he'd lived. Hattie insisted on helping to search. After three days of recovering bodies, Lieutenant Calvit brought Steve Mulligan's 'dog tags' to my sister. The man had died, along with others from his unit, defending our world.

The winter winds had come early, and snowflakes danced in the air. We had no home and only a little food was left. For warmth, we huddled in an abandoned church that was partially standing. My sister just looked at the ground and shook; her tears were used up. There was nothing left in her to grieve.

CHAPTER 11

A noble's Voice has two broad general duties. First and foremost, act as his or her voice in the courts and other daily matters. While the Voice's decision can be challenged, it requires a three-judge panel to overturn the decision. The other is to assume the noble's title if the line dies out.

—Guide to Avalon, 3rd printing

The other Voice who survived was Sir Alden Little, a huge older man who had probably been a warrior in his prime. Where I brought some five hundred to Avalon city, he brought over four thousand. It wasn't until the war was over that we learned about each other. The two of us met at the remains of the bridge which had spanned the Cloudburn river. The first of many bridges which connected Avalon city with what used to be the seven kingdoms of Gawain. Nothing was left but the foundation rocks some two hundred feet below. Sorcerers had destroyed the bridge in the hope it would stop the attacking horde. It didn't.

Teleportation circles were being rebuilt, but slowly. So many people died, finding anyone with magical talent and experience was tough. Much of Avalon City was still in ruins. If anyone was still alive south of us, it would be a miracle.

When we met for the first time, Sir Alden hugged me. "I thought I was the last," he said and stepped back to look at me with a smile on his weathered face. His belly was probably muscle when he younger, now it was turning to fat. I felt like I had been squished into a giant pillow.

I couldn't help but laugh at his enjoyment at finding me. "Don't you dare die on me," I declared while patting his stomach. "I'm a healer and you need to eat better. Those are orders."

He laughed again, making his body shake. I grinned, and we just stood there for a moment looking at each other. Then his smile faltered, and he sat down on a rock and beckoned for me to sit next to him. While looking into the misty chasm, he said, "I knew the other five Voices, four of them were my friends. Sir Jeralod was an idiot. If he was still alive, I would want to kill him."

That one statement told me a lot. He didn't suffer fools no matter how jovial he appeared at this moment. Also, he outranked me; in other words, he was the eldest among the Voices. I had a job to do, and he expected me to do my best.

Noticing my pins, he said, "So you're an assistant healer and a potions assistant. What else are you, Lady Petra Abara, youngest Voice of Gawain."

So, I told him my story. He listened without interrupting. When I mentioned the elks, he grunted. He laughed at the story about drugging the griffon. When I got to the part of life with my old master, he grinned briefly. There wasn't much after that, but I gave him the detail of my journey here including the tree teleport and the awfulness that came after. If felt surprisingly good to be able to talk to someone who didn't shrink away from the stories, someone who walked a similar path to me. It felt good knowing I wasn't alone even if some of the stories were awful.

"Aye," he began, "I lost over a hundred. Some good people, a few children too. I think I know why our prince made you his Voice, do you?"

I didn't know and said so. It seemed so ridiculous at the time. I was ten.

"You're a healer, Petra. Not just of skin and bones, but you help others find a way to believe in themselves again. Not many have that. I think our prince saw that in you. When you found a new way to heal better, did you ask for anything in return?"

I shook my head. "Why would I?"

He gripped my shoulder as my father used to do. "You thought of the people first."

The two of us sat together some more. If felt good sitting with this man who understood what I had been through. "What should we do?" I finally asked.

His answer was immediate, as if he was waiting for me to ask the question. "We meet once a month at a church and pass the word among all our people for any who want to attend. So, those who followed you can meet me, and those who followed me can meet you. I have a little silver; we make sure no one goes home hungry the days we gather. We stand with our people if they must appear before the courts and offer encouragement where we are able. But it is their job to find a new life, as it is mine and yours as well. Do you know what you want to do?"

I showed him Testin's Great Forest amulet. "I am told there are healing spells in the Great Forest amulets. But I cannot say the oath until I am fourteen. So, for now, find jobs where I can and help my mother and sister."

"You are a healer in a city of ruin. You will never be without work. Regarding the clan, I have heard bad things, and I have heard good things. But it is your choice, I will not gainsay your decision."

It made me feel good he wasn't going to deny me the opportunity to make my own decision on the Great Forest Clan. "Sir, what will you do?"

He watched the rolling mist from the river below for a few seconds before answering me. "My wife has passed, none of my children survived. My prince is dead, and my country is no more.

What I have left is here. Help our people find work and build a new life."

I was curious. "Will you declare yourself?" I asked. In essence, he could formally declare himself the new ruler of Gawain. That was the purpose of the Voice, a person absolutely trusted by the ruler to be an advisor, but more importantly to assume the throne if the line died out suddenly so there was a clear transfer of authority.

He reached over and pulled me close. "No, Lady Abara, I will announce myself to the courts so I may stand with our people when needed. But I will not declare myself. That I will leave for you."

I pushed against him and stood up to face him. "I am twelve years old!" I said in indignation. "I don't even know who I am yet. I was forced to lead, and it terrified me. No matter what I did, someone died. If it wasn't for people sacrificing themselves, me and my people would be dead too." *The people who sacrificed themselves* I thought to myself again. Then I said in a trembling voice full of fear, "I am not ready to take that step. I don't know if I will ever be."

"What do you think your old master would say to you right now," he asked me. He didn't laugh at my indignation, or chide my reluctance, instead, he seemed to take my words seriously. A little part of me felt like I had a new father.

"That I need to make some cuts of my own."

"Wise words, Lady Abara. I wish my first master had been that wise. Perhaps one day you may be ready or perhaps not. That is your decision. But I agree, find a life for yourself first. I assure you, if the time becomes right to declare yourself, you will know it. If that comes to pass, I hope I am still alive to see it, but fear I may not be."

Once back at the room I shared with my sister, I put my lady's pin and Testin's amulet in a small wooden box and sealed it with wax. My emerald-eyed lion pin in another box. I had my orders and was glad of them. Once a month, I wore the lion pin when we met at church, and I became Lady Petra to our people. After church was over and food was shared, I put the pin away and became Petra Abara again and was glad of it too.

CHAPTER 12

Core potions transform the body, but they cannot add to one's life force. Even minor ones which adjust the eyes or make hair regrow are difficult to brew. For this reason, only a second-degree potion's master is allowed to brew even the basic ones and they must have the proper equipment. Furthermore, the Potion's Guild requires that they must be inspected by another master before the potion can be legally sold. If a core potion has impurities, this can affect the body in unexpected ways. Also, if not infused properly, the potion may attempt to use the drinker's own life force to power the changes.

—Potion's Guild Handbook, Introduction to Core Potions

Mother tried to find work suitable to our previous life, but no one needed a crippled handmaiden. Sir Alden was right; I was a healer in a ruined city. Every day I healed where and whom I could, however most couldn't pay me but a copper if anything at all. Occasionally, I got a little food. When I ran in to a minor potions master who was investigating his shop, I pleaded with him to stay and help those around us. He at least listened to my story, then I offered to be his assistant in payment for brewing healing potions. He laughed and spread his arms wide indicating his burned-out shop; only a single wall still stood.

"Ms. Petra, I have no ingredients and no one else has any either. If you can find even a base, you would be a miracle worker."

The healer meant honey, and it had to be still warm from the hive. He stayed for two days collecting his tools before leaving. During that time, I attempted to find anyone who had healing ingredients. Most laughed at me or just shook their head.

My sister was able to get help from the other Republic soldiers who knew her; they gave Mother some medicine that helped with the pain and allowed her to move faster, but it wasn't magic, and it always wore off. I knew about it already, but they warned me about one of their medicines, cocaine. They said if used too many times it could become addictive and make you believe things which weren't true and do anything to have more of it. Besides the medicine, they gave us a large chest full of food in containers we had to rip open to eat. We ate sparingly and hid the rest, for starvation was all around. The winter was hard, harder than any I can remember. Some of the food I brought to those who followed us. It was only a little, but it was all I could do. I felt like I was doing nothing but staving off the inevitable.

During a winter, Mother caught a bad cold. It spread to her lungs, and she could barely breathe. In desperation, I boiled my few remaining healing tools to sterilize them, then gave her a little of Earth's cocaine as a numbing agent then punctured her left lung at its base. Yellow putrid puss spilled out, then I sewed her up. She started to get better, but six days later the sickness came back even stronger than before, and she passed within a day. My sister and I buried her behind the church.

Now it was just my sister and me. At one point, she found work as a handmaiden, and I thought our life would be better. But several weeks later the handmaiden from these nobles turned up, and we were given leave. They paid us five copper pennies for our troubles.

We went back to the church, but others were there and had discovered our hidden food. They did not wish to share, and they were bigger than us. That night, in the cold, a Great Forest Clan member found us. He brought us to a big building I learned was their lodge and gave us warm soup and a place to sleep for the night. I wanted to stay longer, but my sister refused. To stay required an oath, and she was afraid of it. When I asked her why, she said she was cursed. Three times, men made an oath to her and all of them were dead. My sister would refuse any oath, she said, for there was nothing but death in it for her.

At some point finding work was hard, but there was something I had which many others did not; I could read, write, had a great deal of knowledge, and belonged to two guilds if only as an assistant. These skills, plus my willingness to do any work, no matter how dirty or hard, enabled me to get a series of jobs. Then I found a more promising position helping an apprentice to a potions master. He paid me a little to find ingredients so he could brew his concoctions. Getting anything was tough. Poverty was all around, but having grown up in a country district working alongside another potions master, I knew many types of plants. So, between healing where I could, my days were spent running from place to place looking for the plants he needed. It was like I was seven again. But instead of rolling hills, I spent my days searching throughout Avalon City.

I didn't have any magic, so I could not help him imbue his mixtures, but as always it was interesting to watch the potion's transformation while I measured out ingredients for him. Most often I was paid in food along with a few coppers. Not much, but it helped. As a reward one day for finding a rare plant, the potions master gave me a drink that helped to straighten my teeth out. He hadn't warned me about the pain beforehand though. Soon after I drank it, I felt like my face was on fire. The apprentice held me down as I screamed into the night, but by the next morning, I had straight teeth.

The potions apprentice did not need me all the time, so I took "odd" jobs, as the Republic called them, where I could find them. It surprised me to learn most people on the street didn't know how to read and couldn't count past simple numbers. So, I used it to my advantage to find work wherever I could. By the time I was thirteen I knew more than twenty apprentices of various sorts who were glad to have me help them. But each of them had something I didn't—magic. Their world was different. They lived in a real house with a master who was part of a guild. I don't mean their life was easy. They were apprentices, and they did all the hard, lowly work. They might be covered in sweat and dirt by the end of the day, but in a few years, most of them would get their journeyman's badge, and soon after, become their own master. What was going to be my future? Aside from working with the potion maker and offering my healing services, my favorite job was working with a blacksmith's apprentice. He spent his free time trying to build a small model of a steam engine. Anyone with a brain could see that was the future. His master had several books from Earth about how they worked, and I read them by mage light while he made parts by hand.

During all this, my sister took a different path. She would spend her time with one man, then another. There was one who did propose to her, but she became nervous and left him. As my sister could not write well, she begged me to write on her behalf, citing her curse. She did love him, I wrote out, but she didn't want to see him die (from her curse). As I finished, I tried to tell her this was silly. I knew many apprentices at this point, several of whom could easily confirm if she was cursed or not. But she shook her head, took my letter, and left it on his doorstep. She was convinced this man would die if he spoke any oath words to her.

We shared a small, unheated single room together in the basement of an old building. After leaving this man who loved her, my sister became associated with a Hallick. When a prosperous man wanted a woman to spend an evening with, my sister was sometimes called. The Lady of the Hallick would dress my sister in finery suitable to the caller. After my sister returned to our simple room, she would be despondent for days until called upon again. But between the money we both earned, we never went hungry. Anytime we had a little extra, she wanted to spend it immediately while I demanded we save it. However, I was not the head of the house, my sister was. Our finances (or lack thereof) spawned the first true argument we had in some time. When I mentioned I was our lord's Voice and therefore outranked her, she laughed in my face.

"You mean those gatherings in the church," she said to me derisively. "Every month you put out word to those who followed you to Avalon City to come and pray together. I go because you are my sister, but pray for what, Petra? Everyone is dead!" she screamed. Then my sister reached out with her hands and turned to point around our meager room. There were a few books I had been able to find, barter, or purchase. The two boxes containing the pins. A chest of clothes, most which had been stitched several times over, and a single bed we slept in together. "What are you hoping for? That magic will come find you, or that a lord will marry me?"

I was about to tell her she turned down an offer of marriage to a very nice tanner when she sneered at me. "Life has cursed us, Petra! I know you hope, but at least I get to spend a few moments in someone's arms. What do you do, but run around working in the dirt hoping for a few coppers? Go back to hoping but let me live the life I want."

There was nothing I could say to that. I had never seen such anger from her before. It was as if she mourned the living. So, each month I watched our small savings disappear.

Four months later, I started to notice the changes: my sister's hair was lighter, her skin almost glowed, and she was shapelier. How? When I asked her, she just shook her head and smiled at me like this was a great secret. With the right ingredients, a skilled potions master could make a potion that could enhance a person, but they were tremendously expensive. Also, if not brewed correctly, they could do horrible things to a person. There was no way my sister could afford even the simplest of these potions, even had she had been secretly hoarding all our savings.

My sister still refused to tell me. But soon a pattern emerged; occasionally, she would leave for an evening to return the next morning, but there was one constant. Every six days she would begin to tremble slightly. When she did so, she would immediately leave and be gone for hours, usually the night, but once she returned, she was giddy and happy again. Every six days, the same pattern. Now that I was paying closer attention, I could track the changes in her body. After some time, it was difficult to tell we were sisters.

On a day I knew when she would leave, I intentionally followed her at a distance. Instead of going to the Hallick, she walked past it toward an old warehouse. She greeted a large, fit man, obviously standing guard. He let her through, and I lost sight of her once she walked through a door. Taking a chance, I crept around and stayed in shadows. Eventually I found a way to the roof. Looking through an old window, I gaped at the scene. It was a party! Lords and some ladies were laughing and drinking while sitting on plush chairs. Some greeted my sister like they knew her. An older well-dressed man, who was obviously expecting her, handed her a large glass mug. Whatever was in it was bubbling. Some of the people in the room began chanting, "Drink, drink, drink." My sister posed for them, jutting out her hips and began drinking it down. What was happening?

Later that evening I confronted my sister. The story spilled out of her. She was introduced to Mr. Ruperton months ago. He offered her the potions, providing she worked for him at the "club," as he called it. He assured her she would stay pretty until the day she died. The obvious question came to my lips, how long would that be?

At my insistence, she introduced me to her new *friends*. It was like a constant party in an old warehouse. Outside it looked rundown and abandoned, but inside it was warm and plush. There were pretend cages where women and some men danced. A few of them had magic and called upon it to enhance their shows. At small tables here and there, a few Lords or, sometimes, Ladies, would sit watching those who danced while talking quietly amongst themselves. Also, there were back rooms, and sometimes a couple or more wandered off to them. At thirteen I was no child anymore. I knew what was happening.

There were others there like my sister, women from other hallicks who this older man brought into his fold. Like my sister, each one was the head of their own house, the oldest. Legally, they had the right to do whatever they wanted. These women all willingly drank his potions. Whatever he brewed, worked—each was exceptionally beautiful. I was made several offers to join, but I refused every one of them. To make my point, I cut my hair short, so it just touched my back. I begged my sister to get out, but she insisted on staying. Her life had been cursed, she said, why shouldn't she make others happy now. For that I had no answer but repeated my protestations that she should leave.

I brought my concern to the potions master I knew. But he just shook his head and whispered to me, fear was in his eyes.

"This man you speak of, Ruperton. He is not of the guild and does not sell his potions. But he pays a great deal of money to the guild for them to be silent. There is nothing I can do."

As I turned to leave, he said in a stronger voice, "Petra, whatever you do, do NOT drink anything this man offers you."

I spun around. "But master," I pleaded, "What will happen to my sister? Can't you help her?"

Now he looked very afraid. "There is nothing I can do," he said, backing away half a step. "Your sister has walked a path that cannot be undone."

It was months later when I noticed her trembling started every five days. Soon, every three days. Within a month, the man kicked her out. Her trembling got worse every day, then she started to age very fast. When I buried my sister, she looked older than our mother had been. Now I was the head of our house; it was just me.

CHAPTER 13

The power of the clans lay in the psychic spell which is bound via an oath. This complex spell links to the mind and allows those who cannot cast magic the opportunity to call magic. Unlike a sorcerer who can cast any spell they learn, the clan member only has spells available to them encoded for a particular clan. While this is a path some might reach for, one must remember it's for life. Once in place, there is no easy way to remove the psychic connection and you're now bound to the clan leadership. The final consideration is capability. Just as someone who has magic must learn to control it, calling magic requires a great deal of practice.

—Wand Guild, Avalon. Opening notes on Clan magic

I stood in front of the two small headstones. The grass over my sister's grave hadn't fully grown over yet. My mother was buried right beside her. It was my fourteenth birthday. If I wanted to, I could walk into the Great Forest Lodge. I could have done what I was about to do next, the day after my sister died, but I hadn't been ready.

"I wish you were here to help me with this, Mother," I said to her gravestone. My hair was still rather short, but I pulled out all my braids and let it hang down my back. It barely went past my shoulders. I spent a few minutes combing it out, then attached Mother's hair clip. I turned around as if my mother was here with me. "Well, what do you think?" I asked the empty air. I was declaring to the world I was head of my house. The one who made the ultimate decisions for all the house members.

Petra Abara, head of a house of one.

Petra Abara, junior Voice of a nation that didn't exist anymore.

Petra Abara, a healer without magic

What cuts did I want to make? I reached into my pocket and pulled out the gold Great Forest amulet. Testin said there was healing magic in the amulets. I didn't know how much. I was never going to be an Archer. The Fox Clan was out too. No one I had talked to there mentioned anything about healing magic, and the few people I met from the Mole Clan were just strange. There were rumors of other clans, but I didn't know any of them.

But this was for life. I wouldn't give up being Lady Petra Abara once a month or any other obligation I had. It was just that the clan I chose would become my home. A home I couldn't divorce myself from. In a sense, I would be getting married,

"What do you think I should do, Mother? I want to find a way to push forward but more than that, I want to be Petra Abara. To find a home for myself where there aren't any titles. Go through the day knowing there is a bed I can sleep in after having done a good day's work and maybe help some people along the way. I wish you could have met Lord Alden. I wish ..." My voice trailed off. Tears trickled down my face. "Mother, I am happy you found some peace. I hope I can as well."

Two hours later, I walked into the main doors of the Great Forest Clan's southern lodge. I chose this one as it was the largest and, I thought, the best maintained around Avalon City. The entry room was obviously a staging area for groups of people either preparing to leave or just returning. A man a few years older than me glanced up from studying what looked like a map.

"Need help?" he asked.

"Petra Abara," I replied, "I would like to join your clan."

He tilted his head. "You're from the south, I recognize the dialect. Sorry about your lands."

"Me too," I replied. "Are you the person who I talk to about joining?"

He stood up. The man towered over me. Maker, he was a huge slab of muscle.

"Hebin Siboot, and no. Follow me, I'll bring you to Royce. I don't belong to a team yet, so I'm stuck doing basic things."

Like picking up boulders, I thought to myself as I followed him past an open-air staging area and then to a solid looking oak door with the clan's tree symbol engraved on it. After he knocked, I asked him, "How come you don't belong to a team?"

He shrugged. "I joined three weeks ago. I'm waiting for Royce to select more group leaders."

I was about to ask Hebin where he came from when I heard, "Come in."

Royce was a very fit woman a good six inches taller than I was. After I told her I wanted to join the clan she pointed at a chair in front of her desk and sat down across from me. She studied me for a few seconds. "I've seen you before. You were helping a journeyman healer. Are you an apprentice?"

"No, ma'am," I said and pulled out my healer's assistant pin. "But I'm part of the Healer's Guild. I have been for seven years."

"I assume that means you can't cast magic, or you would be an apprentice."

I had come to terms with the fact magic hadn't found me. "Yes, ma'am."

She leaned back in her chair still studying me. "You realize this is for life. You don't give up your name, titles, or any other obligations. I'm telling you this as some think if they join, they can escape their past. But you don't look like you're running from anything."

"No, ma'am," I said. "I just want to make a difference where I can. So many people died following me."

"Explain that," she said, and I watched her eyes shift upwards for a second. "Who followed you and why?"

"Oh, sorry." I pulled out my golden lion pin. "I'm the junior Voice for Gawain." When Royce didn't say anything for a few seconds I added, "There's two of us."

"Very well," she said and wrote something down. "Do you have any other obligations to declare? By law you need to."

"Oh. Well, I'm an assistant potions maker as well," I said and pulled out my third pin.

"Let me guess," said Royce deadpan. "For the last seven years."

I wasn't sure what to say. I couldn't tell if Royce was happy or angry with me. "I'm sorry," I asked. "Are you angry with me?"

She pointed just above me. Turning around I notice a large pink crystal wrapped in silver wire just above her door frame.

"Everything you just told me was the absolute truth or you have the best truth blocking charms I have ever seen. When someone lies it begins to glow."

"Really?" I asked fascinated. "Does it use Meppule's truth spell? I've read about it but never saw one."

Royce snorted. "Petra, half the time I wonder if the people who sit across from me know what the word truth means. You're a ray of sunshine."

I couldn't tell if she was laughing at me or not. To change the topic I asked, "I understand there is healing magic in the Great Forest amulets." I had read some books in the library about them, but I wanted to make sure. Being allowed to check out books cost a silver talon—for me, a lot of money.

"If you learn how to call the spells, yes. Most can't. The other spells encoded in the amulet are survival-based spells, a great deal of plant knowledge, and tracking."

Oh. I tried not to let my excitement rise to the surface. I spent so many years hoping magic would find me, I didn't want to spend years pining away again. That almost led to my destruction the first time. Without my sister and parents helping me, it probably would have.

"I almost forgot," I said and reached into my pocket and pulled out Testin's Gold Tree amulet and put it on her desk. "I don't think he lived on Avalon," I said. "His accent was very strange."

Royce gingerly touched it. "How did he die?"

I looked down. "It was early during the war. He opened some kind of tree teleport spell between two weeping willows so my people could get to safety. He didn't make it. I'm sorry."

Royce stood up and walked over to her door then locked it. Sitting back down, she said while looking at me, "That isn't everything is it."

"This is going to sound crazy," I said.

"It's still morning, I've got all day."

I wasn't sure what she meant by that. But I went ahead and told her about the two elks and my responsibility to choose a Voice. Technically, it was an obligation even if I hadn't agreed to it at the time.

Royce just listened, never said a word but continued to shift her eyes from me to the crystal above her door frame. Once I was done, she pondered me for a few seconds. I was starting to get a little nervous at her penetrating stare, did she think I was crazy? Finally, she stood up, unlocked her door, and came back with an old book. I recognized it immediately; it was the first book I ever read. *The Lords and Ladies of Camelot*. However, her book seemed much older than the one my lady had.

"This is the first edition of the book," she said while slipping on white gloves then carefully opening it to the last page. "Please do not touch it, tell me what you see?"

I recognized the etching of the lady of the lake immediately. As in my lady's book, she was standing in water handing Excalibur to King Arthur. Just looking at this book brought back memories of being a child where I was safe, and I got to name pixies. Thinking back, my lady had a third version of the book, but it was still very valuable.

"Look at the right corner," Royce suggested.

My eyes moved to where she indicated. I knew who was there, Merlin. He was still in the same place, then my eyes noticed a small difference.

"Where did those trees come from?" I asked in astonishment. My memory was very good, I must have looked at this etching a hundred times before in my lady's book. I had even seen it few times from other books as well, but never a first edition. There was a small grove of trees beyond Merlin. I leaned in closer almost needing a magnifying glass to see what my eyes passed over at first—standing among them was a giant elk. The detail was amazing. The magnificent creature seemed to be swallowed by the trees, almost as if the artist was intentionally hiding him.

"The trees were not in the etching of my lady's book. Sometimes I thought I was crazy," I said to Royce, still looking at the etching trying to see if there were any other differences. After sitting back up I asked apprehensively, "What does this mean?"

"It means there are two versions of the etching. It was *only* when you told me the story of the elks, did I remember seeing the elk in this etching." Royce eyed me critically. "I imagine your memory is very good. So is mine."

I scrunched up my nose. "That makes no sense. There are people who live and breathe Arthurian legends, they must have seen the difference before."

"Maybe," said Royce, carefully closing the old book. "I only remembered it was there when you brought it up. If I were you, I would be careful who you told your story to."

"You believe me, then." Some days I wasn't sure what to believe. "What do you think the other elk represents?"

"I believe that you believe it," said Royce, without answering my second question. She glanced above her again. "Do you want some advice?"

"Please!" I said relieved. She wasn't looking at me like I was crazy or a problem that needed to be cracked open.

"Live your life, Petra Abara. Surely you have seen people who think they are owed something or believe they hold the keys to Merlin's tomb."

I grinned and almost laughed. "Yes, ma'am." Little things like truth and reality were unimportant to them, only maintaining a vision of their own importance. There were even a few Sir Alden and I had to deal with occasionally, mostly when they ended up in the courts.

Royce pulled a silver tree amulet from a drawer and placed it in front of me. "You're going to start as a basic recruit like everyone else."

That confused me. "Why wouldn't I, ma'am? That's how you learn the big stuff by learning the little stuff first."

"You really believe that don't you?" Royce said with some amusement.

"Sorry?"

"Petra Abara, junior Voice to the people of Gawain, assistant healer, assistant potions maker, and a young lady burdened with the responsibility of choosing a Voice, I accept you into the Great Forest Clan. Since you can read, here is the oath." She pushed a paper across to me. "Once I give it to you, it's for life. Do you wish to proceed?"

What else was there to say? I had already made up my mind, and it felt good that Royce didn't think I was crazy. Following the instructions, I picked up the silver tree amulet and held it in my right hand while I raised my left hand. As she began speaking her part of the oath and me mine, I could feel a swirling sensation of power reaching out from the amulet in my hand and encircling me. At my final "yes," I felt a tingling sensation all over, and I began sensing the amulet in my mind.

<*"Welcome to the Great Forest Clan,"*> I heard in my head from Royce, and my eyes went wide.

It occurred to me as Royce showed me around, my sister would have been disappointed. There was no blood lost in taking the oath, and all my clothes stayed on. As a basic recruit, I discovered, I didn't get my own room, which didn't bother me too much. Up until recently I shared a bed with my sister. Instead, I got my own bed and a locker where I could store my meager belongings. Each locker was spell-linked to an amulet, so only my amulet could open my locker. While all this was going on, I experimented with the amulet icon in my mind. It was fascinating sensing it floating there.

Royce eventually handed me off to Bea, a stern muscled woman whose job it was to train the basic recruits. While Royce turned away, I mentally pushed at my amulet and said to her, <*"Thank you."*>

Royce stopped and turned. I couldn't read her expression. She mentally said back, <*"I assume you are used to falling down and getting up again. Stubbornness seems to define you."*>

I almost giggled out loud. <*"Falling down happens every day. Figuring how to stand up again is my secret magic power. Occasionally it works."*>

Royce turned away again and was almost around the corner when I heard, <*"I expect you will get more practice at both in the Great Forest Clan."*>

I had a new home.

There were about fifteen others who joined in the same year I did. Some were worse off than me. Others faced life that was not as harsh. Surprisingly, I was the only one among them who could read and write. Dora was even from another world (but not Earth). No one knew where she came from, and she spoke very little, but I thought she sounded very educated. She was terrified of being near graveyards, and I heard others whisper behind her back they had seen spirits follow her. But as odd as she was, we all shared one thing; none of us had a home we could call our own.

We were paired up with older clan members, and for two days we were given simple orders. I recognized them as both teaching and learning tasks. They gave us orders and watched how we did them. Also, we were instructed on how to use the magic in the amulets. Five of the others about my age had magic of their own, and one of them could even cast a light spell, barely. Even so, aside from Dora, I had more education and experience than any of them, even though most were older than I was. Regardless, none of them or the rest of new recruits could use their amulets yet when I joined. Some of them had been trying for six months. Since I never had magic, I did not expect the amulet to work easily. All my previous efforts to have magic find me never worked. But I worked hard at what they asked me to do. Things can be get done without magic; I have done them all my life. It was nice, though, having a purpose beyond just surviving.

On the third day I was moved to a different group, with an even older leader. Royce gave him the job of exploring the tunnels beneath the eastern part of town. Two of the tunnels had collapsed, and the city asked our clan to check for survivors, dig them out if necessary and help the city with rebuilding. It was dirty, smelly work. I tried to call light several times from my amulet. One time, I thought I felt something, but then I laughed at myself. I was Petra Abara, daughter to a handmaiden, not Petra Abara, daughter to a sorceress; it couldn't be that easy. So, I moved closer to one of the clan members who could create light from his amulet to see better.

On our second day of searching, I shouted for everyone to be quiet, then I put my ear to the wall. Having spent many uncomfortable days in the darkness during the war I got used to hearing the shadows of sound. You had to recognize human footsteps from monster's footsteps, or your life would end very quickly. It was there, faint—someone crying. I began pointing at people and telling them where to dig. In my excitement, I forgot that these people were of higher rank than me, but they followed my orders, anyway. We found three children, alive. I helped carry one of them to the surface. By now we had a crowd. I was dirty and filthy. Despite that, I was hugged by the mother and the father. I never felt so good. The city paid our lodge a grand sum of money for our work. I imagined Master Reindil would have been proud of me.

CHAPTER 14

Avalon, as a world, takes gymnastics seriously and most cities will have at least one team if not more. There are several beginner and intermediate leagues which compete against each other, but the highest caliber teams are silver and gold. Of the twelve gold teams across Avalon, the Avalon city team has won the world cup for last two years.

—Guide to Avalon, 4th printing

Five days later my happiness evaporated; I was sent to Royce's office. Swallowing, I nervously knocked on her open door. She looked up from her desk. "You are to report to Lady Elizabeth Navartis so she can teach you amulet magic. You are excused from all other work until she tells you otherwise."

I just stood there dumbfounded. Finally, I got out, "Ma'am, I can't speak to her. She is a great lady." I had seen her before in our lodge. She was rich, beautiful, and smart. Not just smart, I heard she designed spells. She was a high-level lady, who could command both our amulet's magic, and sorcery without an amulet, sorcery driven by her presence. The only clan member that wasn't in awe of her was Royce. The lady my family used to serve would never have dared to approach Lady Elizabeth, unless formally invited to do so. It was ludicrous for me to even address her. The old prince of the nation I was from, if he were still alive, would probably bow to Lady Elizabeth and her father. Even if I wore the lion pin, I was at the bottom of the bottom of any measurement in this. The masters for whose apprentices I occasionally worked would be hesitant to approach her. The only reason I didn't refuse was my memory of Master Reindil and his last words to me. *"Make some cuts of your own."*

Royce finished writing her letter, ignoring my fear. Then she looked up. "She will be here in thirty minutes. Do not waste her time."

I wasted her time. Lots of it. Concentrating, breathing exercises to help focus, nothing worked. She tried not to show it, but I could sense frustration from her. When she realized that I could read, she tried math. That was hopeless. While I could easily multiply and divide numbers in my mind, her knowledge of math was so much more advanced than mine, I felt lost and couldn't keep up. To hide my embarrassment, I just looked at the ground. This was the first time I felt truly lost. Why would someone this smart, who could think that fast, work with me?

She did not spend all her time with me. As a great lady, she had other things to do. When not here, she gave me mental exercises to try. I never stopped, but I also realized this was never going to work. There had to be some great feat I had to master to call the amulet's magic. Also, the other recruits were grumbling behind my back; they were working hard outside while I was sitting in a comfortable room. The only hard work I was doing, in their opinion, was getting up from the floor. I had enjoyed being part of a group with a purpose again and didn't want to lose that.

The next day, I was back with my team. We were contracted to help rebuild a church. Surprisingly, it was the same church where my mother and sister were buried. We spent most of the day building a crane to lift the very heavy rocks. I found it fascinating watching how the wood, ropes, and pulleys connected to build this contraption capable of lifting such heavy things. At the end of the day, I was called into Royce's office again. A sorcerer in black robes with thin gold trim around his collar was sitting across from her. "Come in Petra. Close the door and take a seat," announced Royce.

Trying not to tremble, I did as she asked. Was I in trouble? I had not stolen anything.

He was a sorcerer of the realm. Although his gold trim was very thin, he still could arrest me. After taking my seat, I politely nodded at him and said to my commander, "You wanted to see me, ma'am?"

"You are not in trouble," announced Royce. "I want you to tell me and this gentleman what happened to your sister."

I had just come from the church where she was buried. With that to remind me, all the memories were fresh in my mind. Everything just started coming out. Royce and this sorcerer just listened. At some point I realized I was crying and wiped my eyes with the back of my hands.

The sorcerer asked me, "Did the man force this potion on her or demand she prostitute herself?"

I shook my head while pulling back my hair. "No, sir. When she met him, she was already working as a prostitute." I gulped and added, "She took the potion willingly, at least at first. Toward the end, they killed her."

The sorcerer sighed, glanced at Royce, and placed some notes on her desk and silently left the room.

"Ma'am, he's leaving to arrest him?"

Royce reached over and handed me the papers the sorcerer left. "Do you see your sister's name here?"

Looking through the notes, her name appeared three times on two separate papers. "Ma'am?"

"Petra, as you know, prostitution is not illegal. Nor is taking potions to enhance oneself. But with some of the poorer-grade potions, the energy comes from the life force of the drinker, not from the potion."

I held the papers in my shaking hands. I was too angry to say anything at first. "She didn't know the price she would pay," I spat out. "The potions killed her. He murdered my sister."

Looking me in the eye, Royce said slowly, "Can you prove it in a court of law that he forced them upon her or in any way took away her free will? The man your sister worked for does not belong to the Potion's Guild and never sold what he brewed, so their laws do not apply."

"What about the Hallick's Guild?" I demanded. "Surely their laws apply."

Royce tilted her head and sighed. "The various hallicks have never petitioned the courts to form a guild. Other than taking the prescribed potions to cleanse the body of diseases, there are no such guild laws."

The papers fell from my hands and fluttered to the floor. "No," I whispered. "Why is my sister's name on the papers?"

"Ruperton registered your sister as a prostitute, paid taxes against her earnings, and made sure she took the proper cleansing potions." She said flatly, "In other words, this man works the law in his favor and knows who to bribe."

I slid to the floor and began to cry. I got out, "So he goes free, and my sister is dead, along with the others he poisoned."

"Petra, I never said he would go free, only that the law is limited here."

I raised my head and blurted out, "What should I do?" My sister felt cursed, like the world was against her. I knew a few of the other women this man gave potions to. They were all like my sister, alone in the world, or by default head of their own households. For a time, they were very happy, then they died. I felt powerless.

Royce stood up and leaned over her desk to stare down at me. "I want you to learn how to call the magic in the amulet, Petra." I cringed at that. Royce sighed at my frustrated expression. "Petra! You must learn to command the magic in your amulet, else your voice in the clan will have little weight. Will you try again?"

My eyes found my sisters name among all the other words on the papers. "Yes."

Lady Elizabeth Navartis came again the next day. But instead of the lodge, we went to a large building she called a gymnasium and had me change into odd clingy clothes. I felt very exposed standing on this giant beam of wood where others could see the outline of my body. At first, I was afraid to walk forward, even though she paced me and had her hands on mine. How she could walk backwards so easily without looking at her feet was impossible, but she did it. But when music played from her little mechanical machine, my feet began to move with the beat, pacing hers. Some of the music I liked very much, my favorite was a song called *Rock Around the Clock*.

At some point my toes began tapping to the music as I balanced on the beam. I still fell off unexpectedly, but it was fun. Others in the gymnasium didn't laugh at me when I fell. Sometimes they fell off their beam too, but they were much better than me. Some of them were jumping or twisting on the beam, things I could not imagine doing. Then I realized many of them were watching Lady Elizabeth, hoping for something, but I did not know what they were seeking.

Over the course of the week, she never spoke of the amulet. She introduced me to other things in the gymnasium. I initially refused the springboard. To run, jump, and trust yourself as you spun through the air seemed horrifying, but Lady Elizabeth made it look easy. Whenever she did a jump or a small routine of her own to show me what I should do, the others in the gym stopped to watch. They usually seemed to be disappointed when she was done. To me they were amazingly complex, but to her it was like walking.

Other ladies in the gymnasium introduced themselves to me—ladies of stature. Like Lady Elizabeth, one other was a high lady, but regardless of their status, they treated me well. A few asked respectful questions about the Great Forest Clan. It was like I was also a lady somehow, just different. It made me feel good to be included in their discussions. There was one who was nasty to me. I later learned from others that her family competed with the Navartis family in contracts for trade and in influence. In an odd way, that made me feel happy that a mean person did not like me because I was friends with a good person. I had friends. I wished my sister could see me and meet my new friends. That night I cried once again, remembering my sister.

It was the sixth day that I learned what everyone was waiting for. I was practicing on the balance beam, trying to tumble correctly without falling off. Lady Julia, one of my new friends, was helping me. After finishing my first tumble, I felt it: a whisper from my amulet, but somehow coming from Lady Elizabeth. Lady Julia noticed my attention was drawn away, and when she turned to look where I did, she put her hands to her mouth in delight. Then she waved her arms in the air to signal for everyone else to stop. The nasty lady several beams over made a snide comment and looked away. All but one of us were watching Lady Elizabeth now. Her eyes were closed, and she bounced slowly on one end of her beam. I could feel this energy building about her, ready to explode. Suddenly she somersaulted in place and many little balls of lights just appeared and followed her. Her movements just got faster, and more complex. Her balls of light grew, shrank, blinked, and seemed to interweave themselves around her as she danced on the beam. After perhaps ten seconds, or maybe twenty, I am not sure, she did a final move and spun three times in the air, then landed on her feet beside the edge of the beam with her arms raised. People around the gymnasium were clapping, whistling, but I went air born. I launched myself off my beam and grabbed her.

"Teach me how to do that," I pleaded, and she did.

Three days later I called my first magic from the amulet, a small ball of light. My world changed. I spent the night huddled in one of the lodge's spell chambers wrapped in a blanket. I called the light spell within my amulet again and again, then watched in fascination as the little ball of light hovering in front of me faded out. Other times I tried mentally pushing it around the room. It didn't always go the way I wanted to at first. It was like my mind was learning to walk all over again. Part of me knew I was going to suffer the next day, but I didn't care. I could call magic! It was well after midnight by the time I had some control over where the light went. By the third bell, I was writing out large words in the air around me.

Each time I called the spell it pulled a tiny amount of energy from me. I had seen various versions of the light spell in rune format before. It was pretty much step one for an apprentice sorcerer or sorceress. The difference was they needed to charge the entire rune format, but they could alter any part of the structure. With the amulet, most of the structure was there in fixed runes; I couldn't alter them. But the last part I had to add, sort of like adding the last note of a song. Through experimentation, I determined I could make what I added as simple or as complex as I wanted, thereby changing the spell somewhat. After the fourth bell, I tried out an idea which pretty much doubled the size of the spell. I stood and shouted in excitement when it worked. Two small balls of light hovered in front of me. I lost track of the number of times I called the spell over the course of the night. I was exhausted, I'd had no sleep, but at my success I raised my arms in triumph. The world blurred, and I promptly fell unconscious.

"One hundred and eighteen times," I heard from a distance.

What time was it? My eyes were still closed but at the thought of the time, I sensed my amulet and suddenly I was aware it was six eighteen in the morning. Maker, my head hurt!

"Sorry," I mumbled. "One hundred what?"

Who was speaking? Where was I? I blinked and closed my eyes at the light. Who turned on the sun? I vaguely recognized I was in Royce's office. Someone was propping me up and trying to hand me a cup. It smelled like coffee. I blinked again and noticed the long black hair. "Dora?" I asked.

She helped me sit up, and I gratefully took the cup from her. It *was* coffee. "You're hired," I said.

Now it was her turn to blink. "I am?" she asked. "Hired for what?" Wow, her accent was strange. I think those five words were more than I heard her say before.

After I took another sip of coffee, I noticed Royce was looking at me across her desk. Was I in trouble?

"You called the light spell one hundred and eighteen times," Royce repeated, then leaned back in her chair. "So, you picked your first member, who are the other three?"

"Huh?" I asked. "What are you talking about?"

"I need another team lead, you're it. A junior team lead has four support people. You just picked Dora as number one, who are the other three?"

I wasn't sure how long I stared at her. "Ma'am," I finally said. "I really just want to be Petra Abara for a bit. Every time I lead anyone, I feel like the world kicks me in the face."

"Well, too bad. Dora can show you to your new room. You have two days to pick the other three."

Before I could protest, she added, "Since you're an assistant healer as well, I'm sending you and Dora to Cayton Street this morning to help out. You'll be supporting Journeyman Healer Appleton. I have reserved a spell chamber for you to use every night for four hours and here is your training schedule beyond that." She finished by handing me over a thick stack of papers.

I blinked a few more times. "Ma'am, I only had half an hour of sleep. I'm not sure—"

Royce cut me off. "Healer Appleton is expecting you in the next hour. That should be just long enough for you to take a bath and eat some food while you walk there." She eyed her door. "Get moving!"

"Yes, ma'am." I sighed, and Dora supported me as I stumbled toward the bathing area.

I smelled horrible.

How Dora had come into the bathing room and put another cup of coffee down for me I have no idea. I swear I never saw her enter. I would bet money the door never opened.

It was a long day, and Dora stood by my side through it all. Once I got back to the lodge I wanted to collapse in my bed, but Dora pushed me into the spell chamber. Four hours! I didn't think I could stand for four minutes. She just sat quietly outside the circle and watched me as I first called light. I looked at Royce's notes and grimaced. Without asking, Dora handed over a candle. Okay, going from calling light to calling fire. How hard can it be when you're exhausted?

Two hours later I got the candle wick to smolder, then promptly collapsed to the ground in exhaustion. Dora pulled me upright. Then I used my secret weapon, pure stubbornness. I think it was my twelfth attempt later when Dora laid down next to me, I was staring up at the ceiling too tired to move.

"The candle lit this time," she said simply.

"Uh huh," I said. "The floor feels really good. Do I need to move?"

"You have the spell chamber for eighteen more minutes."

"Okay, rest time." I closed my eyes. I was almost asleep when I asked, "Why does everyone else avoid you? I think you're really nice."

Dora pulled me to my feet. "I will show you."

Without saying another word, she led me to the room where she slept and touched a candle, which promptly lit, making shadows dance around her room

"Wait," I said. "You can call magic?"

She shook her head making her long, fine black hair shift. "I use a different kind of magic. Sometimes it's hard for me to control it, I'm not that old."

I wasn't sure what she meant by that. She looked just a few years older than me. I looked about the room. There were three other beds, all unoccupied. She wasn't a team lead, but I heard rumors no one would sleep in the same room with her. I never really thought about why until this moment. Dora chanted for a second and suddenly the shadows in her room began to move on their own and take shape. What was more surprising was the black, misty gargoyle. There were other things in here as well, spirits maybe? But they were very diffuse compared to the misty gargoyle. Dora pulled out a chess set and put it on her bed.

"He likes playing, but I'm not very good at it. I call him Autin." She held both palms closed in front of her. I tapped the left, and she held out a white piece to me. "I don't know how Autin does it, but he always gets the black piece."

I lost at chess and bowed to the misty gargoyle. My only comment before I left was, "Who you are is the choices you make and what you believe in. Nothing else matters. I'll see you tomorrow at breakfast." I hugged her and went back to my room, then curled up in a fetal position under my covers. I had a shadow caster on my team, who I was pretty sure I was going to make my second in command. My life just got stranger. But I know two things: first, the difference between good and evil has a lot of grey in it; and second, I sort of got the feeling Dora looked to me to help figure what was good and bad. But I know good when I see it, and Dora wanted to be good.

The following morning over breakfast Dora had six people sit down next to me to be interviewed. By the time I finished eating I had selected; Hebin, Franklin, and Gail. I was a leader again.

CHAPTER 15

The Healer's Guild is responsible for the training and certification of all healers across Avalon without exception.
—The Wizard's Council

The knock came after a long day and longer night. I was still getting used to automatically sensing time from my amulet. I woke up enough to mentally pick up that it was about an hour before daybreak. That meant I'd had less than four hours of sleep. I groaned while hoping the knock was for the person across the hall.

My own room! I had been the leader of a team of four for five months now, which meant I got my own room. So far, my entire furnishings consisted of a bed plus two old trunks. The first held a few personal possessions including my carving tools and the lion pin. The second was filled with books, mostly about healing, but stories and songs as well. My latest books were open and at the foot of my bed. Royce had enrolled me in two college classes: Pre-Algebra and Composition-Literature. My first class for each had been the day before. I'd thought my previous education meant I would be the shining star. See Petra Abara leap to the front of the class. However, fifteen minutes into the Pre-Algebra class and watch as Petra Abara crashes to the ground. Who comes up with this stuff—what is a square root and how is X and Y related to this? Then I had to run to the gym for my gymnastics training; fortunately, it was on campus.

A shower, then a quick dinner with Lady Elizabeth and Lady Julia, who were still helping me with my gymnastics routine. I wasn't sure if I was ever going to be able to use the springboard without pin-wheeling through the air. See Petra Abara as she crashes to the ground, again. Over dinner Lady Elizabeth tried explaining to me what a square root was. I just shook my head. "I need to mentally stop," I pleaded, which was true, my brain felt overloaded.

What I didn't say, she was so much smarter than me, I felt ashamed for taking up her time like that. The woman designs and sells her own spells, and here she is trying to explain page one of a pre-algebra book to me. Secretly, I liked being part of her inner group of friends. They were all nobles, but treated me like I was a human being and a friend too. None of them knew about my part-time job as 'the Voice,' as I thought of it. It wasn't that I was ashamed of what I did; rather it was that they were friends with me because of me, and that was worth more than any title.

After dinner, I was back to the lodge, where it was my turn to patrol with my team. We had to stop a ridiculous bar fight. Who cares if Sir Lancelot was left-handed or right-handed? Some idiot brought out a knife. By the time the constables got there, I had stitched up a nasty but not life-threatening wound. It was the first time I used the diagnostic spell in my amulet on an actual patient. I did all this while the rest of my team finished subduing the attacker. Hebin (my tank) held the man down while Gail (my general all-around support) put cuffs on the man. Franklin went outside to see if any others wanted to play (he's my sharpshooter). While Dora, my second-in-command, disappeared into the shadows, and watched my back as I healed the wounded. A few minutes later the constables arrived, took Mr. Knife into custody, then locked him into a caged wagon while a journeyman healer inspected my work.

The last bell of the day was a memory when I crashed onto my bunk. But instead of going to sleep, I read the first chapter of my Pre-Algebra book. Then I picked up my Literature notes; First question, why does Shakespeare's metrical pattern shift in Macbeth? Oh Maker, I'm doomed. When I finally put both books down, it was two in the morning.

Knock, knock, knock. There was one more knock this time, and it was my door.

"Go away!" I shouted. That ought to do it.

"Ma'am?" came a young female voice. "Royce wants to see you. Now."

Oh god. She's going to kick me out of college, and it's only been a day.

"Ma'am?" came the voice again. "She said it was urgent."

My eyes flew open as I flung the sheets off me. "Two minutes," I yelled back and reached for my clothes.

Please, please have coffee, I said to myself as I knocked on Royce's door. Was there a God of coffee? There should be. I could pray every morning. I was so tired from last night that I didn't bother to bathe, just fell onto my bed. My clothes were rumpled, my hair uncombed, and I stood there ready to be yelled at. I felt like I must be the worst clan member in history. Royce opened her door, invited me in and walked behind her large desk. She picked up a coffee mug while sitting down. She didn't have another mug in her office; that's just torture.

"Sit down, Petra," she said, indicating the chair opposite her. "I want to talk to you about your patrol."

"Ma'am?" That wasn't the question I was expecting. "What part?"

She had a book open in front of her, there was a Great Forest watermark on each page. She twisted it around to show me the spell. "This was the diagnostics spell you used last night?"

"Yes Ma'am. There was a knife fight, and I wanted to make sure no organs had been hit before I cleaned the wound and stitched him up." Then a horrid thought struck me. <*"Did anyone die?"*> I asked calling through my amulet, too afraid to say it out loud.

"I am told everyone is back at home and resting after having their wounds checked by Journeyman Healer Darvish." She leaned back in her chair and took another sip of her coffee while looking at me. "You're still in the Healer's Guild as well, correct?"

Royce knew this. "Yes, ma'am," I said slowly. "I keep up with the dues. They aren't very expensive." My patient was fine. Why was I here?

"And has the guild certified you in using healing magic?" Royce asked while torturing me by drinking more coffee while continuing to look at me.

I felt blood drain from my face. "No ma'am," I said in a small voice. "Until I got the amulet and learned ..." My voice trailed off. "How much trouble am I in?"

Royce leaned forward and handed me a folded slip of paper with the healer's logo on it. "You are to report to Healer Hochim this morning at the main Healer's Guild hall." Royce looked up at the clock on the wall above me. "In twenty minutes. I recommend not being late."

I grabbed the note and ran out of the room. I didn't bother changing, combing my hair, or bathing. If I used the local teleportation circle and ran the rest of the way, I might only be ten minutes late.

I was twenty minutes late, exhausted and felt like my lungs were going to explode when I finally got to the correct room. Her office was in the high master's suites.

Oh Maker. A high master. I'm doomed. Several people looked at me oddly as I ran down the halls. They were probably thinking how the madwoman escaped the asylum.

My first thought after I sat down across from her was that she looked like a nice grandmother. Maybe over tea and cookies she would share some wisdom, give me a warning, and send me on my way with a smile. I was beginning to think I might survive this.

She had a folder open on her desk. I could see my name on it. With a flick of her wrist, the door closed behind her. She asked, "Petra Abara of the Great Forest Clan?"

Her voice didn't have that nice grandmotherly ring to it. More like an annoyed officer.

"Yes, ma'am?" I said nervously. "It was a really deep wound and ..." I gulped when she closed the folder. *What did that mean?*

"How do you determine if the fibula has been cracked versus broken? Without magic," she clarified.

The question threw me off balance. The fibula was the smaller bone in the lower leg. "Um, well you would have to ..." I was able to explain the procedures used to examine the bone. I was looking for a reaction from her; satisfaction, annoyance, anything. Instead, she asked, "When a wound has become infected with Trimin, what is the proper way to clean it? Again, without magic."

Question after question. Each one assuming no magic was involved during the examination or healing process, Diagnosing wounds, diseases, drugs, and pathogens. She went at it for forty-five minutes with me. Never a pause or a hint of what she thought. At some point, my mind started shifting into automatic healing mode, and I began relaxing.

Click. I blinked at the noise. Healer Hochim had pulled out an old stopwatch. I could hear ticking sounds as the gears moved. "Now," she said, "what is the correct method to examine the back of the eye? Without magic."

She was timing me. Now I was even more nervous. I swallowed and began to answer her question. When I was about halfway done, I heard another click. *What did that mean? Should I stop talking, was I too slow?* Speaking faster, I finished describing the procedure. She just looked at me. Say something, I mentally pleaded. *If you're unhappy at least tell me.* Instead, she asked me another question, and her stopwatch started again. I was so doomed.

I think another ten minutes had passed, and who knows how many questions or clicks when I realized she hadn't asked another question in the last ten seconds. *Did I pass? Was she or wasn't she going to kick me out of the guild?*

Healer Hochim abruptly put the folder away and stood up.

"Come with me," she said. It wasn't a request.

I followed her down several staircases into the basement. It was very cold; they must have a charged spell crystal in place to keep it this cool. Opening a warded door, she had me step into a rectangular stone room with ten large spell circles carved into the floor. Seven of them were being used by apprentice healers practicing their magic; six young women and one young man. Magic runes glowed in the air around them as they cast through their wands. A master healer was slowly walking around watching the apprentices while drinking his coffee. Where he had one red cross on his collar, Healer Hochim had three.

I heard from the master. "Jeremy, you're not shaping the runes correctly. With what you have there, it will only tell your temperature not the patient's." The master took a sip of coffee and said in frustration, "Start over and try again!" His voice was direct and commanding but resigned at the same time, as if he wanted to be anywhere but here. I could see what was distracting Jeremy, the young ladies in the spell circles around him. He was having a hard time not looking at one of them. She was petite, cute, and very focused on building her spell properly while ignoring being stared at. I was fourteen and taller than she was, but she seemed older than me.

Healer Hochim cleared her throat. "Master Peopin," she called out. "May I use a spell circle and take some of Sebine's time?"

"Of course, Healer Hochim," he replied and bowed. "Lady Sebine, please ground out your spell circle and follow Master Hochim."

Lady Sebine waved her wand and all the energy of the runes fell to the ground at her feet, making the rocks twinkle for just a second. The circle glowed briefly, and she stepped out of it. Healer Hochim led the two of us to the farthest spell circle. "Petra Abara, meet Lady Sebine Lister," she said, introducing the two of us. I did a polite curtsey to the lady. Now that I was next to her, I could confirm she was a bit older than me. Also, while my hair was a dirty blond and still uncombed from this morning, hers was almost a white blond and done up in a braid to represent she wasn't the eldest. But what really struck me was her amazingly large jade-green eyes. So much so, I wondered if there was a hint of elf in her, or a past relative who had taken a core potion to change them.

"Sorry." I curtsied again. "I didn't mean to stare."

Lady Sebine cocked her head. "I've seen you in the gymnasium before."

I nodded. "Yes, ma'am."

She laughed and held out her hand. "Sebine, please, were both in the Healer's Guild." She tapped the side of her face near her left eye. "Grandmother took a core potion. I've been told her eyes almost glowed green."

I was curious. "You, um, still see the same colors as we do?"

She grinned. "That and more, I can see pretty well in dim light, but not total darkness."

Healer Hochim clicked her stopwatch to get our attention. "Sebine, Petra is from the Great Forest Clan, and she is an assistant healer. Since she calls versus casts magic, we are trying to determine the best way to place her for appropriate instruction."

Additional instruction? I was living on four hours of sleep a night. "Um, ma'am," I said hesitantly. "I don't know how much time ..." I stopped at her direct stare.

"You will make the time," she commanded.

Oh, boy. Who needs sleep, anyway?

Sebine grinned at my frustrated expression, but asked, "Calling magic?"

"Petra does not have any natural magical ability. However, her clan amulet contains a great many spells, some of them healing oriented. Few clan members learn how to tap those spells. Since Petra was already an assistant healer and understands the basics, she seems to be able to call them, or at least some of them. So, let us experiment."

She nodded at me and clicked her stopwatch again. "Petra. Please call the diagnostics spell you used last night, but I want to Sebine to be its focus."

So, I did. When I focus in on the amulet, I can sense the spells in there, layers of them. Through experimentation I was beginning to understand that I can make the bit I add as simple or as complex as I wanted it to be, thereby changing the spell somewhat. Unfortunately, the more complexity I add, the more likely things will go sideways. Maintaining the focus takes all my concentration. Also, if it's not a healing spell, I must go through a ritual before I can call the spell at all. Some of them I simply can't do yet.

Slowly letting out my breath, I found the spell in my mind. I focused it on Sebine while putting a little of my own energy into it. Suddenly images popped up around me; her skeletal structure and a faint outline of her body plus charts of information, temperature, blood pressure and pulse. Sebine stared at the transparent illusions. Healer Hochim asked, "Last night. How did you know the knife wound hadn't cut into an organ?"

I twitched my mouth; this part was hard. I mentally shifted the spell in my mind and focused in on Sebine's abdomen. This involved moving my hands like I was directing my illusion. As I commanded it, the illusion changed and expanded to her mid-section, now showing her organs in that area. "Um, if she had a wound, it should show up here. I can rotate the information, but I can only hold it in place for about a minute. Then I need to rest."

Healer Hochim clicked her stopwatch three times in quick succession. "Please drop the spell," she said, then turned to look at all the faces now watching us. "Why aren't you practicing? Back to your circles, or I will assign more homework personally. Sebine, Petra, please follow me."

As the two of us followed Healer Hochim, Sebine asked, "Did I see you with Lady Julia and Lady Elizabeth at the gymnasium?"

"They're helping me practice on the springboard."

"Any chance I could pass you tickets for them to come to my family's upcoming performance?"

"Sorry?" My face must have looked blank.

Sebine laughed. "My grandmother would be turning in her grave." Then she winked at me. "We're about as low as you can get and still be nobility. My family is Hovinar. We put on plays and other things."

"Sebine is a rather accomplished apprentice," commented Healer Hochim without turning around. "Who will soon take her journeyman tests."

"Could you help me with my literature class," I whispered to Sebine as we walked into Healer Hochim's office.

She winked at me again. I took that as a yes. Maybe this day wasn't going to be so bad after all. Famous last words.

Healer Hochim pulled out three old handwritten journals and handed them to me. "I searched through our guild records and found these. Ms. Aguilar was a Great Forest Clan member who was also a healer of note in our guild. She died over eighty years ago. You may copy her journals. Now, tell me your schedule."

There was another Great Forest Clan healer in the guild? I had no idea. I wonder if Royce knew. Healer Hochim clicked her stopwatch. "Your schedule."

"I, um, patrol three times each week, usually in the evening since I'm the youngest team lead. There are training courses I take as well. They take up another ten hours or so. Then there's my two classes, studying, and the time I spend in the gym. Oh, and I need to appear in court about once a month."

Healer Hochim cocked her head at my last statement. "Are you in some kind of trouble?"

"What? No. I am one of Prince Gawain's Voices. Now there's just the two of us. I'm the youngest." I shrugged. "Anyway, we take turns standing beside the people who followed us from the southern lands when they have to appear to court."

Sebine looked intrigued. "You're not nobility?" she asked.

I laughed. "I was born Petra Abara. But Prince Gawain made me his youngest Voice right before the war. I was ten."

Sebine murmured, "I can imagine a play being written about you." Then with a twinkle in her eye she laughed out, "Who knows, maybe you will end up being High Lady Petra Abara. Head of House Gawain."

I shuddered. "No, thank you." There wasn't enough time in the day as it was.

Healer Hochim wrote out notes in seven vertical grids, each representing a day of the week. Then she began writing in the events I mentioned organized by time. "So, you have free time Monday, Friday, then Sunday after church for healing classes. Plus, the class on Tuesday evening you're going to teach with Sebine so both of you can account for your training hours." She spun the schedule around, and I almost cried. There wasn't a free hour in the entire week except for church. She accounted for my time in the gym as well, but little else. "But studying?" I whined. "And what class?

"You will study as you eat breakfast, lunch, and dinner. The class will be for first-year students—healing without magic."

I felt a drowning sensation engulf me. Healer Hochim was completely serious. I could only imagine what Royce was going to say.

When I got back, I handed her the schedule Healer Hochim had written up for me. Her answer, "Dora will bring you food while you're in the spell-chamber practicing."

"Yes, ma'am," I sighed.

The next day I handed the theatre tickets over to my friends. Lady Elizabeth didn't come to the play, but Lady Julia dragged her parents along and that alone made a splash in the newspaper. Macbeth played for an additional two nights to a packed house.

CHAPTER 16

There are three known self-aware trees in Avalon. However, having conversations with them is an interesting experience, concepts we take for granted are foreign to them. There are ongoing attempts to force self-awareness—our goal is to determine the exact spark needed to initiate consciousness. This has so far proven beyond our reach, however there are a few things we have learned to date. It is far easier to accidentally make a new form of magical termite than to make a tree self-aware. Also, giant termites make it harder to get further funding.

–Professor Genark of Notir University

At the end of the school semester, I got an A in Pre-Algebra. I also learned something important about myself—when it comes to math, I am very competitive in class. I would rather lose sleep studying then get an answer wrong. Composition-Literature was another matter. I got an A-, but without Sebin's help I wasn't sure I would have passed. Reading Shakespeare made no sense to me, but hearing it played out by experts was awe inspiring. To help me, Sebine used something she called negative feedback. If I didn't read Shakespeare correctly, I got hit with an acorn. She, I, and others from our class would practice acting out plays under a giant oak tree nicknamed FaStill near the theatre-arts building. So much magic had been cast around it over the years (mostly by students creating illusions to set the scene for a play) that the tree had grown an odd sense of identity. FaStill couldn't talk to you in the traditional sense, but you knew when it had an opinion about something. Also, it had a habit of dropping acorns on people who couldn't perform to its expectations (usually Shakespeare); the tree's accuracy was good, hence the negative feedback. Additionally, there was a family of silk foxes that inhabited its branches. Sometimes you would see one of them peering down at you from above. For whatever reason, they loved *The Twelfth Night*. When it was reenacted, the entire fox family would peer out to watch it. When Sebine was helping me practice my lines under FaStill (for Hamlet), I heard an odd high pitched ow-ow-ow from above. Looking up, a small silk fox was wrapped around a branch. Its large brown eyes peered down at me. Considering its size, it was probably a child.

"Is it laughing at me?" I asked Sebine, as the two of us stared up at the creature. Getting Shakespeare right was hard. For Sebine, the words rolled off her tongue.

Sebine laughed. "I think that's Berrit. She's about nine months old."

I knew the theater department named every litter. When a young silk fox was about a year old, they either found their own tree to live in or occasionally attached themselves to a young sorceress as a bonded animal.

"Everyone's a critic," I mused. "Well, Miss Fuzzy," I said to the creature. "You can—"

Plonk.

"Ow."

I had been hit by an acorn.

Sebine fell backwards against FaStill's trunk, laughing even harder now.

"I'm with the Great Forest Clan, you know," I said to the tree.

It wasn't words per se, but I got a definite not-impressed vibe come from the tree. The little fox laughed some more. I heard more laughing from farther up in the branches. Joy, now I had an entire family of silk foxes laughing at me.

Sebine got her laughing under control. "I think FaStill believes you would do better playing in *A Midsummer Night's Dream*."

"How can you tell?" I asked, looking up to see if another acorn was about to hit me.

Sebine quoted, "You minimus of hindering knot-grass made; you bead, you acorn." When she spoke, it was like music.

I swear I could feel the tree purr.

Stupid tree.

Plonk. "Ow."

But at least I got an A- minus in my literature class. Playing out snippets from other plays was fun. I got to be someone else besides Petra Abara Great Forest Clan member, healer apprentice (I got upgraded), potions assistant, or Voice of a dead nation.

When I showed Reece the A- in Composition-Literature she just looked at me. "The lodge spends all this money for you to go to school and you come back with an A-," she drawled out. "How many languages do you know?" she demanded.

"English, of course, and I can sort of understand Basque, plus a great deal of Latin." You couldn't really be a well-read healer and not be exposed to Latin. But where was Royce going with this? I wanted an A as well, but there just simply wasn't the hours in the day for studying both.

"I have signed you up for Algebra, Geometry, and Etymology. Your classes start in two weeks."

"Wait," I said in alarm. "I don't get the summer off? And Healer Hochim has me taking the journeyman healer test in four months." I whined. Also, the gymnastics tryouts for the silver team were in six months. Lady Julia was pushing me to try, even though the springboard was still my nemesis. But on the balance beam I felt in my element. I stopped whining long enough to ask, "What's Etymology?"

"The study of the origin of words. Considering Avalon is a hub to other worlds you need to understand the basics on word origin forms. But I want you to focus on Earth versus the other worlds."

"Okay. Why?" I asked but I sort of already knew the answer. Earth's ideas, especially from the Continental Republic were cropping up in the streets of Avalon. They were the ones which made up the bulk of the armies which had come to Avalon's defense during the war.

Her answer still surprised me. "As you learn more of the inner spells within the amulet, having a foundation of word structure will become very important." Then she changed the topic. "How is Dora progressing?"

"Well," I said slowly, "with the amulet, she's ready to take the first step." Essentially, initiate a broadcast from the amulet. I discovered very quickly many of the people in the Great Forest Clan wouldn't even try. They were content doing only what was needed to get through the day, happy they had someone tell them what to do. Part of my job as a team lead was to train my followers on how to use the amulet themselves. So far Dora was almost ready, the others, not even close. I have been, so far, the quickest to learn how to tap into the amulet's capabilities of our year of inductees and am the only team lead from the bunch.

Royce eyed me. "What's the hesitation."

"You know she can cast magic. I've seen her do it before, and she doesn't need a wand, but Dora seems very apprehensive she might lose control."

Royce snorted. "Someone who is actually concerned about control. Will wonders never cease. Let me know when she can broadcast."

Somehow, I found a way to manage it all; I got an A in Algebra, an A geometry, and a B+ in Etymology. I also passed my journeyman healer test four weeks ago. The day I passed, took the oath, and got my pin, my friends took me out to dinner to a really nice restaurant.

Afterwards, I held the pin in my hand as I went to sleep. I did it. I was certified to heal with magic.

By now, pockets of Avalon City were slowly coming back alive. You could pass one street that had a house, or a shop being rebuilt among the rubble, then farther down the next street there was nothing but craters. Some of the explosives the Republic had used to destroy entire mobs of monsters had been huge. It made the equivalent amount of damage from one of our gunpowder cannons seem like a pixie's slap in comparison.

For the time being, markets were groups of tables at street intersections. When we put out the word the healing tents were up, we generally had customers within minutes. Since I was a journeyman healer now, I was expected to assume greater responsibility of the apprentices-in-training. At least once a week, me and my team had a handful of healing apprentices in tow. I would have the apprentices set up the white healers' tents while my team knocked on doors to announce we were here. Then, for the next three to five hours, we offered free healing to anyone who came by. The apprentices worked for free; it was part of their training, but our clan got paid a stipend from the government for my work by way of the Healer's Guild.

I discovered my abilities to call magic didn't translate into imbuing potions. Said another way, I ignored the warnings in Ms. Aguilar journal notes. She had written DO NOT DO THIS in all capital letters, underlined and circled it. Maybe she missed something. I mean there's a near infinite number of ways you can add additional rune structures to what the amulet provides.

Who knew such a large slime creature could bubble out of such a small cauldron! After I threw my half-melted club away—yes, it melted wood—I wrote in my own journals with all capital letters, underlined and circled the same warning. For good measure, I added the words, "and I really mean it" under my warning.

CHAPTER 17

Shadow casters are the stuff of legend. The problem is no one ever cast a good shadow caster in a story before. They work with darkness so they must be bad, right? Let's talk about that. By the way if you hurt my friend, I will find you.

—Petra Abara

There were other notable events during the summer. Probably the time we helped to search for the hunting party who had come over from Earth was the most dramatic. Dora came out, but not in the way you would think that means.

The hunting party wanted to 'bag an Avalonian bear,' as they called it and bring the trophy home with them. This happened right after Dora passed her first amulet test. This meant she could initiate a broadcast, which became very helpful during searching through the dense forest up north.

When Royce gave me my orders that day, I rolled my eyes at her. "Jingo bears need to eat too. Why is this our problem?" Jingo bears lived well north of Avalon City up in the hills, where it was even colder. From pictures I had seen, they made the American grizzly bear seem small. They were also smarter, very territorial, could move surprisingly fast, and liked meat along with a diet of berries and fish. To make it worse, if they ran fast, they could teleport short distances. You better bring a big gun and keep on shooting. If someone asks, "How big a gun?" You didn't bring one big enough. Anyway, Reece's response back to me was one of the people in the hunting party was the aid to some senator from the Canadian Union, and we were being paid well to find them. She pointedly didn't say alive or dead.

Since money was on the table, I asked for four from the Archer Clan to come with us. We outranked their clan so I could have ordered them to, but I never like forcing someone that way. Two stayed with me and Hebin while Dora took the other two plus Gail and Franklin. Three hours into our search we found what was left of one of the adventurers.

Hebin made a joke. "Well, his arm is over there, and his foot is back there so maybe he was trying to tell us the time he died."

I rolled my eyes. "Keep moving." I recalled the blood tracking spell from my amulet, but I didn't really need it to follow the tracks— mama had two cubs with her. Unfortunately, the wind changed direction a few times, and she probably knew we were coming. Six miles later we found the other three adventurers, plus the two Jingo bear cubs. The large fuzzballs were happily eating. We weren't bringing anyone back alive. But where was mama bear?

I signaled for the two from the Archer Clan with me to climb a tree. They nodded seeming almost relieved. Hebin was my tank, but next to a full-grown Jingo he was a chew toy. The two cubs were as big as him.

Hebin had two pistols, and the two from the Archer Clan had rifles. Even so, we were in her territory, and she could teleport. "We're going up," I said to Hebin. "We're dead if we stay on the ground." Like the rangers, he seemed relieved. There was a limit to his bravery.

Soon after we found a perch, I heard from Dora, <"*We're all up in a tree. Mama's near us.*">

I could pinpoint Dora's location from her broadcast. After I found her, I handed the binoculars over to Hebin and pointed. One of rangers with me whispered, "I see the mother." He had his back against the trunk of the tree; his rifle was resting on a branch.

I really hated to do this. She was a mother with two cubs, and this was her territory. The idiots from the Canadian Union had tried to hunt her, and she killed them. While I don't like seeing loss of life, this was nature—you try to kill me, I will try to kill you. It gets played out thousands of times each day from an ant up to man.

<*"Dora,"*> I called, reaching out to her. <*"One of the archers with me has a shot, do yours?"*> One shot wouldn't kill her. I wasn't sure if three would. If we had to, I wanted it to be a clean kill where the bear wouldn't know it happened.

I got back <*"Yes, but do I have your permission to try something else? I want to scare her away."*>

Since I made sure everyone was included in both broadcasts, the archers could hear us talk to each other via the amulets. I wasn't sure if any of them were good enough to initiate a broadcast through theirs. The archer next to me, who had dropped to a lower branch to find a better position looked up. "Scare her? That's a Jingo bear with cubs. You would need a platoon of tanks to actually scare her."

Ignoring him, I bit my lip. If Dora did this and she survived, it couldn't be undone.

Hebin whispered to me, "What is she talking about? Dora is half my size."

He didn't know.

I banged my head against the back of the tree. "Maker," I pleaded. Like always, I didn't get an answer. *Makes some cuts of my own*, I said softly. Well, damn it. Dora wants to help; she has every right to do so.

I closed my eyes and put a hand to my chest and replied back, <*"If it doesn't work, I can't guarantee we can kill her before she gets to you."*>

<*"I understand,"*> she replied in her soft voice, then she dropped to the ground and immediately disappeared.

"Holy crap," replied the archer who was tracking the bear. "Your friend just disappeared. That's no hiding spell. But ma'am, the bear's going to smell her, anyway. This is stupid."

"Garren, I have done stupid before. This is just one more to add to the list." Then my voice darkened, and I couldn't believe the words that came out of my mouth. "If you shoot my friend," I said in all seriousness, "I will hunt you and yours down. That's a promise."

Hebin turned to look at me in surprise. His mouth was open. I'm a healer, and I just threatened an entire clan of people. The other archer put a hand on Garren's gun barrel pushing it down. "I heard a rumor," he said quietly, looking in his friend's eyes. "You and I didn't see anything, and if you open your stupid mouth, I will say you're the biggest liar since Merlin's apprentice."

There were degrees of liars in Avalon. Merlin never had an apprentice that anyone knew of. Since Merlin was the big guy in our history, saying *biggest liar since Merlin's apprentice* was pretty much at the top.

The other ranger looked up at his friend and mouthed, *"What?"* Like Hebin or anyone else here, he didn't know.

I opened a broadcast to all of us, excluding Dora. She needed to concentrate now. Also, I didn't want anyone from her team to do anything stupid. I could feel Gail's spiking apprehension. <*"Don't do anything stupid,"*> I said to all of them. All the stupid was apparently reserved for me. <*"When it starts to happen, don't move,"*> I ordered.

I heard from Franklin. <*"I have a shot."*> Like the archers, he had a rifle pointed at the adult bear. Out here in the wilderness, having guns was fine. The Avalon courts disapproved of rifles being carried openly within the city limits. Pistols were fine, but rifles had one purpose—killing at a distance. Besides, if you were stupid enough to carry an unawarded pistol around, you got what was coming. An apprentice sorcerer could kill you with his wand; magic and gunpowder are an explosive combination. I don't know who Darwin was, but he came from Earth. His phrase pretty much sums it up; *The idiot was almost walking Darwin*, meaning you were too stupid to live.

<*"Give Dora a chance,"*> I said. <*"Don't interrupt her."*>

<*"Interrupt her?"*> shot back Franklin, confused. <*"I can't even spot her. It was like her body just flowed into the shadows."*>

<*"Franklin,"*> I pleaded. <*"Don't shoot Dora."*>

<*"Why would I ..."*> and as his words trailed off, I could feel his spiking astonishment.

From a distance I heard the soft chanting. It had an odd cadence to it that always made the hair on my arms stand up. Mama bear swung her body around trying to locate the source. Her two cubs stopped eating and stood up on their hind legs looking around as well.

Through our link I could hear Gail's frightened *eep*. All the shadows as far as I could see began shifting then flowed toward the noise. The trees were big; so were these shadows. What was coming together was huge, larger than mama bear by several factors.

I recognized the animal from a book, a tyrannosaurus rex from Earth, but this one was made of shimmering black shadow. Its entire jaw was larger than the Jingo bear. Mama took a nervous step toward her cubs, then another. The shimmering tyrannosaurus shifted its body to look down at her then it roared. The noise was deafening.

I remembered the frightening feeling when I was six at hearing the griffon's loud piercing squawk. This roar vibrated my bones. Birds flew out of trees. I could imagine every animal within miles running for safety. The tyrannosaurus was king, and the Jingo bear was food. Mother bear hit speed in two seconds and teleported next to her cubs. Taking the smaller one by the scruff of the neck, she never slowed down. The larger cub went tearing after her. The tyrannosaurus began charging after them, roaring again. I could feel the earth shake at each step, then suddenly the shaking stopped. At the edge of our vision the shadows broke apart and within seconds everything was as it had been before. Dora stepped out of a shadow and waved up at us.

I reiterated through my amulet. <*"Don't shoot her!"*>

Shadow casters were the nightmares of the magical word. Right up there with a Malumbrus. Everyone knew they were evil because the stories said so and, well, they called shadows. What else did you need to know? Grab the pitchforks, torches, and guns.

Garren's friend lowered his gun. "I wasn't here." He gave me a salute and climbed out of the tree not saying another word. Garren looked at me. "We go after her. You go after us. Understood?" Then he dropped to the ground. The other two met Garren, and the four disappeared into the forest, none of them saying a word or looking back at us.

It was just me and my team now. But did my team include Dora?

None of them looked at Dora as we picked up what was left of the hunters to be carried back. Please say something, anyone. Dora was always so quiet, afraid to be out in large groups. Why she glommed onto me I have no idea.

Chapter 18

Some think to know a person's true name gives you a great deal of power of them. That's ridiculous; first, because very few know who they really are, and the second, if they have any brains and ambition, they out there gathering new names even if they don't want to.

—Merlin

The competition for the gymnastics silver team was in a week. My next set of classes would start the week after, advanced algebra, pre-physics, and argumentative speech. When I read the syllabus for speech I cringed, I would have to write speeches which defended my point of view and debate with others.

My friends helped as I pushed myself in gymnastics. I secretly called us the eight nobles plus one. A little voice in my head wanted me to wear the lion pin around them, but Lady Elizabeth and the others didn't seem to care I wasn't a noble. They were my friends just because I was Petra Abara and that meant more to me than anything else. I was never going to compete in gymnastics at the same level as Lady Elizabeth, but maybe, just maybe I might be able to get on the silver team.

Also, I was happy for Marrit. I had met her intended at church three days earlier. She was getting married to a low noble from north of Avalon City who owned a plantation and a small mining operation. When I asked if she knew how Sir Alden Little was doing, she bit her lip. She told me he had been helping someone rebuild his house when he slipped off the roof and broke his hip. The healers helped him, but he was tired all the time now. She looked down and said in a soft voice, "He didn't want me to tell you."

I made a comment about stubborn old fools and made sure I would meet him the following day. I was a healer, and he hadn't called me!

As I made my way toward Sir Alden's house, I was working up my indignation so I could yell at the man. Four years ago, I would have been terrified of talking back, now I wanted to throttle him. Climbing a roof at his age, then falling off and breaking his hip? He was lucky he hadn't broken his neck! Worse, he didn't send word back to me! I'm a journeyman healer now! He had to have known I was going to hear about it. Even if I couldn't help him, I knew people who could. My rising anger was really masking my fear. If he died, all the people who followed us to Avalon city would look to me for guidance.

Originally, I'd wanted Sir Alden to be the only announced Voice in Avalon City from the lands of Gawain, the person the courts would call upon when decisions needed to be made about one of our people. But he wouldn't have it. Along with him, I had to raise my right hand and announce myself to the courts, as well. This translated to having legal authority as the elder of the house—the house being anyone who previously lived in one of the seven southern realms of Gawain. Here I was, fourteen years old, telling our people—some of them three times my age—that what they just did was stupid and please don't do it again. The ridiculous, idiotic things some people do! Fighting, stealing, dueling without posting the duel, even welching on a bet. In Avalon, welching on a bet is serious.

Depending upon the severity of the charge, the courts generally let the head of the house determine the punishment. Our judgement had to be approved by the judge, but the eldest (or in this case, the

Voice) was granted a great deal of leeway. The general idea is, it's your house, get it in order! For repeat offenders and cases involving capital crimes, the head of house's Voice is more likely to be overruled by the judge.

Once a month, the courts picked a day, Sir Alden and I sat through case after case. By the third month, I was pretty sure what kind of punishment Sir Alden would administer. On the fifth month, he demanded I take over, which terrified me. He just sat back and provided guidance if I asked. Fortunately, people came to court for good things too—taking guild oaths, couples posting marriage contracts, or purchasing property. Slowly, our people were finding a home. Without the good, I wasn't sure if I could have stomached the bad.

Some of the older people who followed us came to court just to watch how I administered judgement. I felt like every word and gesture of mine was being dissected. Of all the cases only two were truly awful. Capital crimes. In both, Sir Alden stepped forward to administer judgment. His voice was direct, cutting, and blunt. The judge rang his bell meaning he wasn't going to intervene. Both men were hauled out in chains to be hung the following day.

My anger evaporated when I saw Sir Alden. He must have lost thirty pounds in the span of a month, and he needed a cane to walk the distance to open his door. "Come in, Petra," he said, stepping backward while adjusting his cane. I could tell he couldn't swivel his hip.

After a maid brought in tea and left, I blurted out, "Why didn't you call me?"

He snorted. "And have you shout at me for days on end about what I fool I was? There isn't enough whiskey in my house for that."

"Alden," I protested, "I could have ..."

"Well, it's about time," he said, cutting me off. "Took you long enough."

"What?" I asked, confused. "Time for what?"

My mind was still pondering what it would take to fix him. If I broke his hip in just the right way, and a healer used the srinder method, then ... He cut into my running thoughts.

"Words have power. You called me by my first name," he said and pointedly added, "Lady Petra Abara."

"Sir Alden," I said slowly. "I might be able ..."

"It's Alden and you're not just Petra Abara anymore, no matter what you're telling everyone else." He snorted and banged his cane on the ground. "Whatever healing trick you're thinking about, you can keep it where it's at. You can't cure old."

No! My mind refused to accept this. "You have years in front of you," I pleaded. "Please," I said, "I'm not ready to declare myself."

"And maybe you never will be. But the people who followed us see Lady Petra now, and Sir Alden is a foolish old man who fell off a roof." He sipped his tea and continued to look at me. "I'm not dying today. You can stop by any time you want to discuss things. I'll give you whatever advice this old man can. Would you like some now?"

I refused to cry. My mouth trembled. I took a sip of tea to calm myself and tried not to spill any as my hands shook. "Yes."

"Petra Abara has done a good job of making some cuts of her own. Why don't you ask Lady Petra if she wants to make a few cuts too?"

"Alden," I said, putting down my teacup, so I didn't spill any of it. "Lady Petra is, well ... I don't know who she is."

He leaned back in his chair. "From what I know, Petra Abara is friends with some very powerful ladies. Do you think they know who they are any more than you do?"

I rolled my eyes at his statement. "They were born ladies, of course they know who they are."

Alden took a sip of tea. "So why haven't you told them you're Lady Petra Abara, junior Voice of Gawain?"

Suddenly, I felt very uncomfortable. "Well ...?"

To divert my feelings I blurted out, "Alden, why are you making this so complicated? This is about you being a stubborn old fool."

He raised an eyebrow. "I already know who I am. Never tried to hide from it. Why are you hiding?"

When I didn't say anything, he put his teacup down as well and asked me, "So do these ladies you spend time with go around saying lady this or lady that when they talk to each other?"

I shook my head. "No, of course not. Elizabeth, Julia, Joanne and …" I stopped, realizing what I just did. I called them by their first names, my friends. "Lady"—I swallowed—"Elizabeth is so much smarter than I am and prettier too. She teaches me how to compete in gymnastics. I learn so much from her. She and the rest of my friends are some of some of the nicest people I know."

"Do you trust her?" Alden asked and finished his tea.

"Without hesitation." I didn't even need to think about it. It just was.

Alden reached for his cane, leaned forward and with a grunt pushed himself to his feet. "Gawain was my friend. He trusted me, and I trusted him. Once you found out your old master had been one of the most respected Voices in his time, did you start thinking of him as a lord?"

I stood up as well, shook my head and tried to stop myself from crying. I was so confused at all emotions inside me. "I cherish every memory I have of him," I said. "He was so happy when he was sharing things with me, even simple things like singing together." I stopped, fearing I might cry and got out, "He trusted I would hear his wisdom."

Alden hobbled over to his door. "I have seen my fair share of nobility who pretend that their title makes them above fear or friendship." He opened his door and pointed toward the street beyond. "Friendship and trust go both ways, and it has nothing to do with putting a title in front of your name. Maybe it's time for Petra Abara to try practicing what your old master taught you." He gave me a little push. "Off with you, girl. I'll be here tomorrow."

Once I was outside, he closed his door. I wasn't sure what to do. I came to yell at the man and now felt like I didn't know who I was.

CHAPTER 19

I feel like a prized hog at a festival.
–Lady Julia Lohort

I heard Julia's voice from the other the side of the door. The hum of the power crystals around me drowned out her words. I was hoping for darkness, but the crystals gave off a faint greenish glow. Above me I could hear cheering and then people stomping their feet. Someone else made it onto the team; I bet it was Helena. She was good and already on the silver gymnastics team. I wasn't even sure why the coach was having her try out. Helena was beautiful, personable, an amazing gymnast, and I really liked her. If I got on, that meant someone else didn't.

The Avalon City silver gymnastics team was considered one of the top three teams of its class on Avalon. The only class higher was gold and, well, Elizabeth won that last two years. To compete against Elizabeth? Good luck and don't hold your breath. She has had offers from Earth, but she's been firm. Either the entire team she's on gets to compete in Earth's Olympics or no deal. So far, it's been a standoff.

Elizabeth, Julia, and Joanne talked me into signing up for the silver trials. If you ignored the springboard, I would charitably call myself not bad on a good day. I'd signed up four weeks ago. Three weeks ago, I wanted to back out, and Elizabeth had to stop me from hyperventilating. A week ago, I was certain this was a horrible idea— between classes, studying, my responsibilities with the Healer's Guild, my responsibilities with the Great Forest Clan, and having to spend a day in court as Lady Petra Abara meant I didn't have as much sleep as I needed.

Three days before the competition, Dora said she could handle things at the lodge without me for a bit. My teachers pushed my due dates back, and Healer Hochim wrote out a prescription for me. It read, and I quote, "You have my permission to tell the rest of the world to take a hike." So, I was able to get some sleep.

However, right now, I wanted to throw up. Every seat was taken in the stands. It brought back memories of running during the war. If I won, someone else had to lose. To escape, someone else had to sacrifice themselves. There was no way of winning then, there was no way of winning now. Before my fears dragged me under, I ran to hide in the basement.

I heard Julia's voice again, this time louder. "Petra. Can I come in?"

How did she know I was here? I'm the one good at tracking. Another cheer from above. I hesitated and answered back, "The door's unlocked."

The door opened and light erupted into the crystal power room. Julia held her glowing wand just above her head. The sudden light interacted with the power crystals, casting odd greenish rainbows around the room. I was educated enough to know what has happening, it was a refraction effect—the same way rainbows are made. Fortunately, this was just light. When magic is refracted, odd things could happen. My physics teacher reinforced that odd usually meant bad in that case. No one really understood if it could be mathematically explained. I wished I was back in class right now, so I could escape my memories and my impending humiliation.

I was sitting on the ground against the far wall. Julia came over and sat down beside me.

"How did you know I was here," I asked. I'm not great at hiding, but I know how to move silently when I need to. My turn wasn't for another twenty minutes, and I couldn't stand being there any longer without turning green. Throwing up was a real possibility. When everyone's back was turned, I slipped away and headed to the basement.

"Elizabeth told me," she said. Julia shrugged. "She's got an amulet too. What's wrong, Petra?"

I pulled my legs tighter to my chest. "Half the school is in the bleachers. Plus, I'm not that good."

"Compared to who?" she asked and lowered the light from her wand.

"Well, you for starters, and Helena is amazing. So is everyone else."

Julia looked straight ahead. "And I have been practicing for six years. Helena even longer. You started learning from the best in the world three years ago."

Did I detect a hint of jealousy? Someone jealous of me? "Julia," I said slowly. "You learn from Elizabeth too," I repeated. "I'm not that good."

Her next statement surprised me. "Who is Elizabeth going to marry? Who am I going to marry?"

I twisted my head to look at her. "What are you talking about?" We went from talking about gymnastics to marriage. My brain couldn't connect the dots.

Julia dropped her light spell. The room went back to its almost near darkness. "We're both high nobles, Elizabeth even more so than me. The only reason we aren't married is because we compete and win. The moment we stop, we're on the market. I have already had several offers—one king and three princes, all from different countries." Like me, Julia hugged her legs tight. "One of them is even from the planet Brittia. He's the second son."

Julia and Elizabeth never talked about this before with me. "Um, do you like him?" I really didn't understand why the subject came up.

"He's twenty-four and a bore. I personally think he's waiting to get married to a high enough noble, so he can assassinate his father and older brother. He takes the throne, and my job would be to look pretty, wave adoringly at his subjects, while having lots of children." She banged her head against the wall. "It's worse for Elizabeth. She's related to Arthur."

That sounded horrible. "So, you don't want me to compete?" I cautiously asked.

Julia laughed. "Just the opposite. Petra, you're a healer. You belong to a clan and you're working on getting a math degree at college. Elizabeth mentioned you're a Voice for some people from wherever you came from, but she didn't mention who." She shrugged. "Since you don't talk about it, we figured it had something to do with the war. If you wanted us to know, you would have said something."

"Um, the noble lady where I grew up made me her Voice. I announced myself to the courts so I'm sort of their de facto elder. It's weird." Was I omitting that I was the junior Voice of Gawain? Yes, I was.

"See?" Julia said as she took my hand. "You're Petra Abara. That means something in Avalon City. Outside of gymnastics, Avalon sees my value as a trade negotiation. I'm a princess to be married off. I take classes, help others, but Avalon will never allow me to be like you. A person with my own voice."

"I am really confused." I wasn't kidding. "You want me to compete, but if I got on the team, it could mean you're off, even if that's really unlikely. Then your family would ship you off to be married to some prince who sounds like a murderer in the making. What am I missing?"

"I want to be on the team. I like gymnastics and it's fun. But so many people think winning means having more subjects or having more land." She leaned into me and whispered, "You're Petra Abara, a woman with your own voice and no one had to lose. I want that too."

The memories of the ugliness of the war hit me. I cried out, "Yes, they did!" Tears started trickling down my face as I remembered Acrun, Testin, and others. I sucked in my breath. "So many good people died just so I and others could survive." A realization hit me. "It's not free, Julia. To have a voice means you must be willing to fight, to make some cuts of your own. Maybe the old Avalon was like you said, and maybe some want the new Avalon to be like that as well. But you know what? It's not!" I said with conviction.

Julia was staring at me open mouthed. "What do you mean?"

"Look at the guilds," I said fiercely. "For every man in a junior position, there's probably three women now. And by guild law, they get a vote. Avalon's different even if no one has seen it yet." I laughed. "Hell, in the Healer's Guild it's more like five to one."

"So how do I fight?" asked Julia. "I'm a Lohort, a high noble. Everyone wants me to be a princess. How do I, um, make some cuts of my own?"

Just hearing my old masters' words reflected at me made me relax a little. "I don't know. But the wisest person in the world never told me how. Just to never stop trying."

"Well, Petra Abara," said Julia, rising to her feet while grabbing my hands to pull me up. "Let's see you fly through the air and afterwards we can talk about making a few cuts."

I laughed. "More like pinwheeling through the air." Everyone on the team really was better than I was.

While climbing the stairs, Julia asked, "So, you're a Voice and you stand in at court?"

"Once a month. The idiot things some people do," I said.

"Are you ever going to declare yourself? You could become Lady Petra Abara. Head of the land you won't talk about."

Before I had a chance to respond, we entered the gymnasium and the cheering hit us. Julia took her turn and like always was amazing.

My turn came a few minutes later. I was still nervous, but once I stood up on the balance beam, I felt like my old master was watching me, and that made all the difference in the world. The crowds faded away. At the end of my routine, I spun twice in the air and nailed the landing. As expected, the springboard was my nemesis. I made my landing without falling, but no one would have called me graceful.

After I took a shower, the coach asked if I would like to be an alternate. I won, and no one had to lose. Elizabeth joined us, and we went out to celebrate. Over lunch, Julia and some of my other friends took turns guessing which land I was the Voice of. All their guesses were from small kingdoms. It made me feel good that they didn't need me to be a high noble to be their friend. Whatever Petra Abara turned out to be was good enough for them. The only person who didn't make a guess was Elizabeth.

Chapter 20

The job comes with endless worry, nerve wracking decision making and staying up at night wondering if you made the right decision.

–Lord Gawain

Janson Planter's parents had died in the war. He and his grandmother were one of the many who followed Alden to Avalon City. Several years earlier, Janson's grandmother had asked for Sir Alden's and my blessing if the boy could take a job on a farm helping a blacksmith repair equipment; Janson was eight at the time. When I demanded he learn how to read and write too, his grandmother found someone who would work with him after dinner while he sweated during the day.

Alden always seemed baffled whenever I requested children of House Gawain learn to read and write. "He's a good stout boy. I bet he'll make a fine blacksmith. Why does he need to read?"

Learning to read was very important to me. It was the only time I ever pushed back. Sir Alden wasn't angry at my demand; rather, he was baffled. Since he wanted me to assume more responsibly as the junior Voice, he never overrode me. He just thought this was an unnecessary burden I was placing on the children who came before us. If a parent wanted our blessing so their child could legally work, mine came with, "Your child needed to learn to read too."

Being able to read and write brought a tremendous advantage. I wanted my people to have it as well—at least the ones who were willing to push themselves.

Three years later, when Janson started to notice girls were spruce (his words), his magic came in, which surprised his grandmother. As far as she knew, there wasn't a drop of magic on her side, and if her daughter-in-law had any, she never knew about it.

We paid for Janson to take the magic entrance exams to help place him based on the strength of his magic, affinity, and his intelligence. When the instructor found out Janson could read and write, he was moved to a smaller group of children, most of whom were dressed much better than the other group.

I smirked at Alden, who pretended not to notice. The man was still in his carriage; it was painful for him get down from it. He rarely left his house, but for special occasions he would. It's a big deal for a house when a new magic line emerges.

After his testing, Janson was interviewed by several street-level master sorcerers who needed an apprentice. By the end of the day, he'd received three offers. Two weeks later, Alden and I read through the offers. He snorted at me. "If I had a pin strong enough, I would pop that head of yours. But I don't think anyone makes one stout enough."

I patted him on the knee affectionately. "No one ever credited you with brains. But someone's got to think for the two of us."

He grimaced while leaning forward, then kissed me on my forehead. "It's an honor to know you, Lady Petra Abara."

"What's that about?" I asked, perplexed. The only other time someone kissed me on the head like that had been Prince Gawain.

"It's exactly what I said!" he growled out like it was nothing. "Now, which offer do you want to pick?"

Four days later, I announced Janson's apprenticeship at church. A nervous Janson and his equally nervous grandmother stood with me as I asked for donations toward a beginner's wand. I started it off by putting two silver talons into the donation basket. Alden put in eight, then we passed it around. A very (with the emphasis on *very*) basic wand crafted for a street-level beginner apprentice from a respected wand maker would cost ten gold talons. It would be guaranteed not to overload, providing you didn't store more than three basic spells in it.

Because Janson tested so high, the Sorcerer's Guild would pay half. It was up to our house to pay for the other half. To pay for this, we would need donations from our people, and they would need to be generous. We wouldn't be walking into a shop that sold Retorian or Darci wands. I think they would turn up their nose at the idea of providing any wand for ten gold talons. I heard a beginner's wand from them started at over a hundred gold talons.

Janson's new master (Sorcerer Nanton) was a firm believer in Pomodo wands. So, we would be meeting him at the Pomodo wand shop later in the day. Alden wasn't feeling up to traveling that far, so he declined to come with us. That left me signing all the paperwork as head of house, which I didn't mind at this point. The courts knew Alden had me sign for most things now and just checked up on him from time to time. Also, Janson would have to take two oaths: one to the Sorcerer's Guild by way of his new master, and one to our house administered by me. He would be bound to both.

I followed Janson and his grandmother as they nervously walked between the glass double doors held open for us by the well-dressed porters. Above the marble entranceway, large silver letters spelled out *Pomodo and Sons*. Then, underneath, *Wandmakers. Est 1585*. I was pretty sure the letters were made of pure silver.

I am not a wand aficionado, mostly because I can't use a wand, but I knew Pomodo was a respected wand maker. Sorcerer Nanton, Janson, his grandmother, and I were brought to a small, warded room where Cooper Pomodo brought out beginner wands for Janson to try. Cooper was about my age. At some point I started feeling a little embarrassed watching the three of them as they handled and then discussed each wand. When I asked Janson's grandmother if she would like to take a turn walking around the main floor with me, she seemed relieved and immediately agreed.

Off-duty realm sorcerers who were being paid as guards were present, but in the background, as we walked past glass etched counters with wands inside, I recognized the etchings as runes, but these were very intricate. Also, each wand was balanced on a thin silver plate. I bet the slightest change in weight would set off alarms. As we moved about the room, I noticed that not all the wands were made by the Pomodo family. When I asked a saleslady about this, she seemed happy to help. "Lady Petra." She curtsied. "We have agreements with other wandmakers. This allows their wands to be sold commercially without maintaining the expense of a store."

"How did you know who I am?" What I meant was, how did she know I was Lady Petra to these people?

"Grandfather believes it is important to know the names of all the Voices." After another curtsy she added softly, "But we do not sell or give away any of our information."

I gave her a forced smile. To change the topic, I was about to ask about the wand in the triple glass enclosure, when I noticed one of the realm sorcerers standing guard shift and pointedly look at me. I heard, "Yes sir. She's here." Who was he talking too? There wasn't anyone around him.

The Realm Sorcerer strode forward and introduced himself. "Lady Petra, I am Realm Sorcerer Birgultan. The Chief Justice has requested your presence." Before I could respond, he took my arm and guided me to the front of the store. Two more realm officers met us outside. One of them was holding open the door of a sleek carriage pulled by six large horses; this could move fast.

"But why do I need to see the Chief Justice?" I asked the Realm Sorcerer as he pushed me inside. Then a horrid thought struck me. Did one of my people do something truly horrid? Did a child die? Before I could ask another question, Sorcerer Birgultan climbed in and sat opposite me. The door slammed shut, the driver cracked his whip, and the carriage lurched forward, slamming me against the back cushions. I recognized the crest on the seat pillows: *Pomodo and Sons.*

Two realm sorcerers all but carried me to the Chief Justice's chambers, with Sorcerer Birgultan in the lead.

Please don't be a dead child. I felt close to despair.

There were almost thirty people gathered here. More were coming in even as I arrived. I recognized every one of them, these were the family elders of Gawain households. The Chief Justice was in his robes and strode forward to shake my hand. "Lady Petra, thank you for coming." An aid stepped forward and opened a box, a golden lion pin almost identical to mine was inside. Lord Alden's pin. His had blue sapphires as eyes versus my pin which had green emeralds.

"Alden," I whispered while putting a hand to my mouth. "Please, no."

"Lady Petra," said the Chief Justice formally. "By all indications, he passed peacefully. Avalon law requires at least eight heads of houses to be present for the transition of power."

Before I could say anything, he turned to the gathering people. There were more than forty now and still more were coming. "Lady Petra is the Junior Voice of your house. Sir Alden has passed. Do you believe Lady Petra is fit to perform her duties as Eldest Voice of your house?"

I was still staring down at the pin. *Alden, how could you?* I reached out to touch the pin and felt a surge of power. With it came an odd growly, sleepy, voice in the back of my head. I remembered hearing it, years ago, the lion statue near the watering hole. This time it spoke two words instead of the one I heard when I was almost ten. <*"My queen ..."*> In surprise, I pulled my hand back.

In the background I heard a chorus of sound. Every one was a yes.

Alden, how could you die on me?

The Chief Justice nodded solemnly. "Lady Petra, the family elders of your house have acclaimed you to assume the role as Voice of the House of Gawain. However, you were the Junior Voice. Avalon law allows you the opportunity to abdicate when the Elder Voice passes. If you choose to do this, the eldest of each family will gather to select a new Voice. Do you wish to remain and announce yourself as the Senior Voice for the house of Gawain or do you wish to abdicate?"

He said it like it was just a formality. He hadn't waited for the arrival of any other heads of households who we could see were approaching. He'd assumed unanimity. *Why was that?*

More elders arrived, mostly men, but enough women were there you could tell they held a presence too. I knew every one of them. They were good people. Like me, they struggled to find a way, to find hope. Sometimes that meant there was food on the table at the end of the day. They all looked back at me, waiting. Not one of them challenged me. I remembered Alden's words from six months ago. *"Why don't you ask Lady Abara if she wants to make some cuts of her own?*

I could feel this presence which had spoken to me just a few moments ago, waiting.

My fear was palpable at standing alone, but these were my people. I repeated it again in my mind slower this time. *These were my people; I was their Voice.* I looked at all the eyes waiting for my answer and said it out loud, "I am your Voice, my place is at your side. I will stand with you"

The Chief Justice smiled at my words, and I heard a powerful <*"Yes!"*> within my mind, followed by a roar like a lion's. Then, like before, it was gone.

My people cheered, and then the Chief Justice raised his hand. "Lady Petra, please raise your right hand and place your left on the Bible (it was old and had a raised etching of Excalibur on it). Do you swear to uphold the House of Gawain? Do you swear to administer justice to both the high and low in your house? Do you swear to respect the integrity of the house elders?"

After my final "Yes," I lowered my hand and began to shake. I was it. I was the Voice of House Gawain.

The Chief justice flipped a page in his book. "Lady Petra Abara, Voice of Gawain, do you wish to declare yourself this day? All applicable conditions have been met."

I shook my head. "I'm not ready yet. I don't know if I will ever be."

He nodded and gently picked up Alden's golden lion pin. He pinned it right next mine. I wore two of them now. Another cheer broke out, and I heard in the voice one last time, a sleepy, <*"My queen."*>

My first official action as the Eldest Voice of House Gawain was giving Janson Planter his house oath as Gawain's second sorcerer since the war. He was only a beginner's apprentice, but I thought the young man's chest would explode with pride. His grandmother was crying.

Chapter 21

Unlike a commoner who may visit court without any fanfare, a noble must have their right of entry be challenged by a peer of sufficient rank. Should they be deemed unworthy, the noble must stand before the Wizard's Council and be judged.

–Arthur Pendragon

Healer Hochim finished going over the medical records I was required to update—my grades and comments about me from other masters who I've worked with. She had been my guide in the Healer's Guild for over three years now, and during that time I had gotten used to her stopwatch. How hard she clicked the buttons and the duration between clicks told me a lot about how this woman felt at any given moment. Her last click was over thirty seconds ago, and it was gentle. She was happy—well, as happy as the woman ever seemed to get. I still didn't know much about her as a person outside of the Healer's Guild.

After closing my second notebook, she gently clicked her stopwatch again, the ticking stopped. "I'm proud of you, Petra. You have my permission to take the senior healer's journeyman test."

"Ma'am?" I said, trying to speak past the lump forming in my throat. "Thank you." Without Healer Hochim constantly pushing me, I might never have gotten here.

Click. This one more forceful. "You can thank me by not only passing but getting one of the highest scores." She sat back and gave me a direct stare. "You are aware there is a small but vocal conservative faction within the Healer's Guild which dislikes the changes happening around them. You're a woman, you assume a leadership role, and you call versus cast magic. Don't give them an opening."

I knew the three masters Healer Hochim was referring to. One of them was Master Neiwash from the lands where I grew up. I first met him when I was almost ten. He seemed unable to believe the idea I had come up with shouldn't belong to him. But he didn't think up injecting a little of a healing potion close to a wound. I was a woman, he was a man, and therefore he was right. The courts disagreed with him. The other two masters were almost as bad. Except for those three, the other male masters I learned from ranged from friendly to it's a job. None of them were hostile toward me.

Whenever I had to work with Master Neiwash, I had to remind myself that he outranked me and force myself to ignore his snide comments. Afterwards, back at the lodge, my team would watch in fascination as I called fire spell after fire spell in a spell circle to work through my anger.

"Ma'am?" I asked Healer Hochim curiously. "Why does Master Medicus tolerate their kind of bigotry? Good healing ideas can come from anywhere—me, you, even doctors from Earth."

She snorted. "Did someone come along and decree everyone needed to be nice to each other?" After giving her stopwatch a firm click, she added, "Has Master Niewash physically attacked you or forced you into servitude beyond that of reasonable Master Journeyman work expectation?"

I shook my head. "No, ma'am. He just, well, hates me."

"Welcome to the guild. I trust you have a way of venting your anger that doesn't involve drugs, heavy drinking, or extreme gambling."

I grinned. "Three hours in a spell circle, ma'am."

"Good."

Just before Healer Hochim put away my folder, she asked, "Is there any other work experience we missed? It will go toward your ranking as a senior journeyman. The closer you are to the top, the more likely it is that you can choose the masters you want to work with."

I leaned forward, and she turned my folder around so I could see the notes. There was a summary of my experience on the first page. Everything was there except for one thing.

But you never know. "During the war, I was hired as a premedical student by some of Earth's doctors. They even paid me for my time."

CLICK. That was a direct sound. I looked up in surprise to see Healer Hochim's direct stare.

"I thought you knew, ma'am," I said, a bit confused.

"Petra, did these doctors ever give you any tests to take?"

"Yes, ma'am, every week. I worked with them for four months." I gulped as she continued to stare at me. "Every day I worked alongside teams of doctors." I shrugged. "When we first met, you asked me lots of question on how to heal without magic, so I thought you knew."

"Young lady, I am not a mind reader." She made a note in my folder. "I will reach out to the Republic healers I know to see if you are in any official records. Also, we need a journeyman or two to work with a group of healers at a symposium. Since some of them are doctors from Earth, I am going to recommend you. Considering what you just told me, I think you'll do well."

Uh-oh. Did I detect a hint of a smile from Healer Hochim?

"Ma'am, I don't have much free time."

I knew it was the wrong thing to say even as the words came out of my mouth. The woman seemed to consider sleep a necessary evil which you could push aside on occasion. "Can I have Sebine as a partner with me for whatever this is?" I added quickly.

Healer Hochim clicked her stopwatch. "Agreed. The job will be rather bloody."

"There aren't enough hours in the day," I whined to Sebine, who pretended to ignore me. Classes during the day, gymnastics practice, study at the Healer's Guild, and then the night before I had to patrol from eight to the final bell. Royce wouldn't give me any slack even though Dora insisted she would cover for me.

Normally, I would sleep in a bit on days I had to patrol, but for the last five weeks, Sebine and I had worked the morning shift of this year's healer symposium. It was a six-week conference held every year where healers from all over, including doctors from Earth, would gather to try out the new stuff being developed. Better tools, spells, drugs, microscopes, even enchanted items. Having the least seniority of the journeymen assigned to the symposium, Sebine and I got the early shift, which meant being there at five in the morning to clean up from the previous night. This was grunt work but assisting with the experiments I found fascinating. Ideas were bleeding not just from Earth to Avalon, but also the other way around too. Forward-looking guilds were pushing hard, hoping to find a new market on Earth. Other than lack of sleep, the other part I found a bit distressing was the animals. Since everything was experimental, the patients by and large were farm animals, usually pigs.

Sebine was laying down on a gurney taking a short nap. She opened an eye to glare at me. "This is all your fault. I could be sleeping right now."

I gently banged my head against the wall but couldn't argue that one. After slowly standing up, I looked around at the mess from the previous night. Maker, I was tired.

I whined again, "Why can't we have apprentices do this?" Cleaning tools and mopping floors was what apprentices were for.

Sebine snorted without opening her eyes. "Some of the magic items are experimental. Apprentices would probably blow themselves up."

She extended an arm and pointed at an odd contraption in the corner with several extendable appendages ending in scalpels, powered by crystals. "The edges of the spells making up that thing are beginning to fray. I'm not touching it."

I attempted to call a spell so I could see the magical signatures around me better. It was technically used to disarm traps. Like anything else, it's all about what I add to the last part of the spell. I felt the energy begin to form, then break apart. Drat. It wasn't a healing spell. Without a focus, which for me was a candle, the spell was hard to call. "I'll take your word on it," I responded and threw a smock at Sebine. It landed on her head. "I volunteered you. We're a team, suck it up and help me clean up the operating room. Besides, tell me you aren't having fun with some of the experiments."

Sebine pulled the smock off her head. "Yes, ma'am, senior journeyman healer," she said mockingly and sat up. While she stretched, I noticed her grin.

"What?" I asked.

"Are you tired because of Mr. Tall and Handsome?" she smirked. "That doctor from Earth who asked you out?" She winked at me while putting on her smock. "Did Petra have fun last night?"

It was my turn to snort while I handed Sebine a mop. "I had to patrol. I wasn't going to go out with him, anyway. Not interested in married men."

"He lives on Earth, have some fun. What happens on Avalon stays in Avalon," she sang out while smiling at me.

I raised an eyebrow while taking my own mop. "What about Doctor Grabbyhands from Earth? By the way, loved how your eyes went wide when he patted your behind."

Sebine thrusted her mop forward like a rapier. "I do have standards. Too bad the Healer's Guild won't let me put a hex on him."

We were silent as we began mopping the floor. Between the two of us and some applied magic, it didn't take long to clean the floor and sterilize the tools. By agreement, we left the thing in the corner alone. After we were done cleaning, I opened my thermos and pulled out two coffee mugs. It was the unwritten rule in the Healer's Guild, the senior person on the job was responsible for making sure their team was properly caffeinated. Sebine clinked her mug against mine and asked, "Healer Hochim actually picked Master Neiwash as one of your three instructors for the senior journeyman test?"

I rolled my cup between my hands remembering the test I took just a week ago. "It was horrid. The barrage of esoteric questions never seemed to end. Eventually the other two instructors had to restrain him. Toward the end, he was almost shouting in my face." I raised my mug in salute. "But I answered every one of his questions correctly, then passed both the practical and knowledge healing tests." I was immensely proud of becoming one of the youngest senior journeyman healers ever. Master Healer Petra here I come. Little things like men could wait.

I was curious. "What's Master Niewash like when you have to work with him?"

She shrugged. "I'm a woman, therefore he thinks I won't be any help. But he doesn't go out of his way to make me miserable." She stretched again and added, "When I have to work with him, I imagine I'm in a play, it helps."

I never considered that. "That's a good idea. Thank you. I always go back to my lodge and shoot fireballs in a spell circle."

Sebine drained her mug and extended it toward me hopefully. I poured her more coffee. I considered her idea from another point of view. This coming Friday was my day in court as Lady Petra. "You're nobility," I said. "When you have to be Lady Sebine, do you put on a mask like it's a show or is it part of you?"

Sebine seemed to get where I was going with my question. "I've seen you transform into Lady Petra before. That's no mask. But for me, it's a game. My family is about as low as you can go and still be nobility, so I just have fun with it. Personally, I think Arthur got soused while one of my great-great relatives was putting on a show for him. Afterward, he suddenly found himself ennobled. I bet no one knew if it was a joke or not, so everyone treated it like it was real." Sebine posed dramatically. "So here I am, Lady Sebine, traveling noble of storytellers and healer, in awe of the great High Lady Petra Abara."

I rolled my eyes at her. "What does nobility get you?" I asked. For me it seemed to be endless worry and work.

She shrugged. "We own land, of course. Not that we have much, but the important part is we can't be prosecuted for putting on our plays. Some of the more conservative nobles would like to rewrite history." Sebine suddenly grinned, making her large green eyes almost sparkle. "My aunt wants to write your story. She asked me to pass along an invitation for tea." She raised her hands as if in celebration. "I would, of course, be Samwise, the true hero of the story."

I stuck out my tongue at her. Ugh. Someone trying to write about me? To the change the topic, I said, "Elizabeth might be coming to watch me in the courtroom."

Sebine lowered her hands. "Nervous?"

I looked away for a second. "A little. What if it becomes weird between us? I don't think she knows I'm the Voice of Gawain." Sebine was about my only friend that did, and she didn't seem to care. If Sebine's aunt wrote the truth about me, just about every chapter would end in: *See Petra step in something new and stinky.*

Sebine put down her coffee mug. "Look, Petra, technically I'm a noblewoman of Avalon, and I'm not worthy to step in Elizabeth's shadow. No one is knocking down my parents' door with offers of marriage in return for trade rights or land acquisition. Think of the pressure on Elizabeth to get married. She is related to Arthur, beautiful, smart, the best gymnast in the world and, from what I hear, one of the top three sorceresses of our time."

I rolled my eyes. "Thank you for reminding me of everything I'm not."

Sebine bumped her hip to mine. "Seriously, no one is. She's like Arthur reborn as a lady, but you're missing the point. She's *the* most desirable princess of Avalon. Kings from other worlds are probably competing to land her as the wife for their son. But you come along, become the Voice of Gawain, lead people to safety during the war, become the Senior Voice of Gawain, turn down declaring yourself and become a senior journeyman healer in record time, all while you answer to a busy clan."

I stared at Sebine. "So? And for half that stuff you just mentioned I was terrified the entire time, and for the rest, it was pure stubbornness just to survive."

Sebine ignored my dramatics. "You are showing other women, even princesses, that they can have a choice. That they can forge their own path. Maybe Lady Elizabeth, Princess of Avalon, is in awe of you."

I was about tell her she was obviously drunk when the double doors to the operating room swung open. Two master healers and a doctor from Earth came in; trailing were four apprentices pulling two pigs on leashes. "There you are, Petra." Doctor Grabbyhands smiled. "Master Healer Harmon is going to demonstrate the experimental organ transplant procedure being developed in Avalon. Why don't you be my assistant today?"

Sebine nudged me toward him while whispering gleefully, "I want to see your eyes go wide too."

I shot her a dark look, then put a smile on face. "Yes, sir."

Learning about organ transplants, that was going to be fun. Spending alone time with this doctor, not going to happen.

Before court began, I went through my notes again trying not to show how nervous I was. Behind me were all the people who came to court for my judgment. There were some good things, a few stupid, and, thankfully, nothing truly horrific. Early on, Sir Alden had coached me to be very consistent with my negative judgements. "Let people know your rules," he reinforced, "and stick by them." I wish he was by my side now.

Looking down at me from the back of the courtroom, set in a half circle, was the common audience. They were non-nobles who came in to watch, generally they were house elders or families of those in the main courtroom. Any visiting nobles got to sit in comfortable chairs off to my right. Currently, it was empty. Honestly, it usually was. Since my day in court was considered 'house judgements,' it was never printed in the front the newspapers or pasted on the boards. Backpage boring stuff.

I could tell the judge was getting ready to sit down and ring his bell signaling the start of the cases, so I sent a ping through my amulet to Elizabeth. <*"Are you coming today? The judge is almost ready to start."*>

I got back an immediate, <*"We're almost there, can you ask him to wait for a minute?"*>

Now my nervousness increased. <*"What do you mean we? How many others are coming?"*>

<*"Just Julia, her father, and my father. Who are you a Voice of? I can tell my father knows and thinks I'll be surprised when I find out."*>

Instead of answering her first question I pinged her back. <*"Let me talk to the judge. Hang on."*> It was ridiculous not telling her. She was going to find out in a few minutes, anyway. But once she was here, she was, well, here. I wanted Elizabeth to be with me when she found out. That made little sense, even to me, since I could talk to her through our amulets, but it's how I felt.

After my request for a short delay, the judge looked up at the clock, then pulled out a law book. "Two minutes, Lady Petra. Which noble is coming to watch?"

"Lord Navartis and Lord Lohort," I said. "Along with Lady Elizabeth and Lady Julia."

The judge froze for a second and signaled for the courts majordomo to come over. "Lady Petra, by tradition, before another noble is admitted, a noble of sufficient rank must challenge the arriving noble before they can enter the courtroom. It can be done by the court's majordomo, but Henry here isn't of sufficient rank for Lord Navartis or Lord Lohort."

I blinked at him. "Huh? Sir, you don't challenge me. Where is that tradition from?"

"You are the Voice, Lady Petra, should you declare yourself and assume the title, then that tradition would also apply to you. Regarding where it come from, Arthur. I hazard a guess he wanted to remind the nobles they did not have free rein in court." He smiled.

"Of course, back then it was just the court of wizards, but the tradition holds."

"Wait a minute, is that why nobles generally don't visit when I'm in court?" I could count on one hand the number of nobles who happened to stop by and watch me over the course of three years.

"I believe so. Now regarding a high enough ranked noble ..." He let his words trail off while looking at me.

"You're kidding," I said. "You just said the rules only apply to me after I declare myself."

The judge grinned. "True, but once you step into the courtroom, you're High Lady Petra, Voice of Gawain. So, go stand on the court's front steps and challenge those four as to their right of entry. While Lord Navartis outranks you, legally you're both high nobles, which is all the rules stipulate."

I stared at him while feeling an overwhelming sensation of drowning engulf me. I would be challenging my two best friends and their fathers to their right of entry to watch me? Could my life ever get any weirder?

I blurted out, "There's got to be some ritual words to go with all this."

The judge turned around the law book he had opened. "Yes, there is, Lady Petra. It's right here." I couldn't tell for sure, but I thought the judge might be trying not to laugh at me. The majordomo looked like he was ready to start chuckling. I turned to him after reading the short protocol notes. "The rules say I can call you to stand by my side as well. So, I'm calling you—and no laughing."

With what I thought was effort to not laugh, he bowed and said, "Of course, Lady Petra."

I made sure my two lion pins were in their proper place, grabbed the judge's book to make sure I didn't mess anything up and walked outside. The court's majordomo paced me. My timing was perfect. Within ten seconds of walking outside, the grand Navartis carriage pulled up. Their majordomo hopped down and opened the door. Lord Navartis grinned when he saw me.

Suddenly, I got it. The man had to know the rules, knew I would have to be standing out here, unless he contacted the courts ahead of time to have senior enough person there to challenge him. He planned this. Oh, that sneaky man. Any apprehension I had faded away.

Well Mr. Lord Navartis, highest noble of the land, you're about to be challenged by Lady Petra Abara. Ha!

When Elizabeth stepped out of the carriage, her eyes went wide.

Afterwards Lord Navartis bought lunch for us at a local restaurant. Julia was reenacting being challenged by me, and Elizabeth was smiling. It wasn't weird, they were still my friends. After we clinked glass, Julia said, "You know, while you're Lady Petra, you technically outrank my father." She batted her eyelashes at him. "So, Father, if you ever get into trouble, I can put in a good word for you. I know people."

Elizabeth burst out laughing. I definitely had friends.

CHAPTER 22

So, you think boys are smarter than girls, do you? See my hand hit your face?

—Petra Abara

Welcome to trigonometry. It was very strange sitting in a class comprised of mostly young men older than I was. There were a few young ladies as well, but not very many. I was the youngest of the students, and the other ladies tended to cluster around me, this shield of femininity in a room full of men. It was very odd being the "tough one." I wanted to laugh.

Surprisingly, and to my delight, some of the apprentices I had befriended were in my class. It is also where I met Lord James. Whenever he walked across the campus, he had a horde of young noble women following him. So why was I the lucky one? Mr. Tall and of the Beautiful Blue Eyes decided I would be his focus. When he sat down next to me in class, my girlfriends and I moved a row backwards. Between classes, my responsibility with the clan, and gymnastics training, I didn't have any free time even if I wanted to date (which I didn't). My sister became a plaything of a very evil man, and I didn't need a fresh reminder of her fate, even if Lord James smelled really good.

Lord James, if anything was stubborn. It became a game of cat and mouse. He would wait until I sat down, my girlfriends would surround me and he would sit next to us and strike up a conversation with one of them. As one, we would stand up and move several rows over. Halfway through the semester, I heard a rumor there was a betting pool going on of who would give in first.

Our not-relationship came to a head right after the final. I missed the last two extra-point questions. The professor said the exam was going to be hard, and it was. My palms began sweating as I looked at the dreaded clock on the wall and realized time was running out. Without more time I could not answer them. I finished the test, but I wanted to get all five extra point questions at the end. The professor immediately graded the papers, then handed them back. Lord James, god's gift to women, answered the same three extra point questions I did and part of the next one. I got an A+ and he got an A++ while everyone else got a B or less.

Worse still, he asked me out on a date. Smiling down at me with his beautiful hair and amazing eyes, he said it was tradition that, "The person who got the highest grade gets to ask any girl he wants to out on a date."

I shot back, "So this tradition assumes boys are smarter than girls?"

His smile got wider. "I am only," he said, putting his hand to his chest and looking very noble, "reflecting what is in front of us. I got the A++." His smile widened, showing perfectly white teeth. "And you did not."

I slapped him. My girlfriends surrounded me as I stormed out.

Apparently, the news of the offered date made its way to the Lodge before I got there. Someone made up a mock wedding advertisement—I was to be married in three days and become Lady Petra Vimmer. I ground my teeth at their laughter. Worse, I had been almost beginning to like him, right up until he demanded I go out on a date with him. The toad.

Royce came out of her office and pointed at me. "Petra, you're with me, NOW!" Her stern expression brokered no refusal. She had a carriage ready for us. We rode in silence toward Lord's Street. I was still filled with riotous anger toward Lord James. But a small voice in my head wondered how much trouble was I in?

"You slapped a lord in public, Petra," Royce said through gritted teeth, as our carriage pulled up to a large constable station. "You're going to stand in front of a Sorcerer of the Realm."

A junior constable opened our carriage door, and we filed out. The place was huge with constables all over the place. A few of them recognized Royce and waved in greeting. An older man with six stripes on his sleeve came over to us. His nameplate read Captain Griston. After reaching out to shake Royce's hand, he asked in a teasing voice, "Have a potential recruit?"

After giving me a quick look, he added with a smile, "She's kind of small."

"Ms. Abara is here to see the realm sorcerer on watch."

Captain Griston's teasing tone disappeared. "She stepped in it, then?"

"Neck deep," replied Royce. "I might need help burying the body."

"Hey," I said with indignation. "Doesn't anyone want to hear my side of the story?"

Royce ignored me as the captain led us around the corner to a large office and opened the door. "I'll be outside if you need any help," he offered to Royce and promptly closed the door. I swear I heard a lock click shut.

I felt trapped. Royce still wasn't saying anything to me. Was I about to be kicked out of the clan? There was shouting coming from behind the other door in the room. From the tone, I was betting it was Lord Vimmer. Oh crap. A lord could get someone like me hanged. Over time, Lord James had transformed into my opponent, and I sort of forgot he was a lord. The last remnants of my indignation from earlier vanished. How deep in it was I?

Just when I was beginning to think no one would come in, the far door opened, and a tall, handsome, well shaven man in uniform wearing a gold-laced blue robe said, "Come in, Ms. Abara. I would like to hear your side of it."

Lord James, my nemesis, stood against the far wall. He looked annoyed and frustrated. "Father, it was my fault ..." But he was cut off by the older man, obviously his father. They shared the same build and hair, except he didn't have that same casual energy Lord James had.

"No!" shouted his father. "This guttersnipe slapped you, in public. If she is not punished, our house will be dishonored. Others will think ..."

I felt a pressure wave of energy in the room cutting off the lord. "Actually, it is my job to decide what punishment, if any, should be merited," said the Realm Sorcerer. "As a lord, you have had your say first, Lord Vimmer. Now it is Ms. Abara's turn. As she must address you as my lord, you *must* address her as Ms. Abara, as she is the head of her house."

Wow, he had some power to him.

He turned to Royce. "Do you wish to stand by Ms. Abara of the Great Forest Clan during this trial?"

At Royce's, "I do," I felt a little better. Even if I was found guilty, she would be by my side. That meant a lot to me.

Turning back to me, the Realm Sorcerer asked, "Ms. Abara, you are being charged with striking a lord. How do you wish to plead?"

Lord James jumped in, "She barely touched me. I don't even have a lasting bruise. Besides, I probably deserved it."

The Sorcerer turned and eyed him. "I am sorry, young Lord. Did I ask you a question?"

Even I could feel the temperature plummeting in the room. My nemesis gulped—and he could do magic directly. Since I felt something as well, I bet this Realm Sorcerer wasn't kidding around.

"Ms. Abara, how do you wish to plead?" repeated the Sorcerer.

I was beginning to like Lord James. He was trying to get me out of this. I bet he didn't want to be here anymore than I did. But lying in front of someone with this kind of power seemed absurdly stupid. "Yes, sir, I did. I slapped young Lord James."

It looked like the Realm Sorcerer relaxed slightly. Was I imagining that?

"Very good, Ms. Abara, thank you for that. Now, a follow-on question. Did you in any way profit from the bet, or have agents who profited from the betting pool?"

"Huh?" I said. Oh, the betting. I had known there was betting. I blinked, stalling trying to think. Why was the fact there was some kind of bet important? "What?" It was the only lucid think I could manage.

"He means the bet at school on whether you would go out on a date with me or not by the end of the semester," added Lord James, helpfully.

"I heard about it," I said, turning to him. "I thought it was a joke. Surely no one was betting money on it?"

He grinned. "Yep. Last I heard it was up to eighty ounces."

My eyes went wide. "Of silver?"

"Gold," he said. "The clans don't get along very well with the nobility. Also, a lot of apprentices apparently know you. For some reason, the story spread all over Avalon City."

I think my heart stopped. Eighty ounces of gold was a huge amount. People killed for just a fraction of that. "That's ... that's just ridiculous. How could it get so large?"

He shrugged. "As I heard the story, the original bet made its way up to the Dean of Mathematics. Naturally, our teacher recused himself from assisting either of us in it, and took no part in the pool. After that, it sort of took on a life of its own, including teachers, and once the College of Sorcery began betting ..."

Lord Vimmer broke into our conversation looking a bit confused. "Bet what? She slapped my son. Eighty ounces of gold? Why aren't you punishing her?"

The Realm Sorcerer ignored Lord Vimmer and focused in on his son. "Same question, young man. Did you in any way profit, or have agents that profited from the bet?"

"No, sir. If I did, that would be cheating, wouldn't it?"

"Yes, exactly. Very well, then." Turning to Lord Vimmer, the Realm Sorcerer said, "You brought this to my attention as you should have done. Your son, by his actions, and when an accredited institution codified it, together created a legal bet. Essentially, he enacted a duel. Indeed, many people consider dating just that, jousting for position. Legal precedence for similar actions has been adjudicated, even before the Wizard's Council. There are precedents going all the way back to King Arthur's Round Table."

What? At what point had I begun dating him? I think my face had gone white.

I stepped toward my nemesis and looked up at him. "Excuse me. I am NOT dating you. I would rather date a turnip. You are a fathead who thinks men are better than women."

"That's not what I said," he replied with frustration and stepped toward me. We were nose to nose now, except he was taller, and I had to look up into his frustratingly beautiful eyes.

"Oh yeah?" I replied, leaning upward. "I distinctly remember ..."

Bam. I think ice crystals began forming on the wall.

"Before I was interrupted," replied the Sorcerer of the Realm, "jousting for position while dating is often bet upon and has legal precedence. However, I cannot ignore the fact a lord has been struck in public."

"Ha," shouted Lord Vimmer.

Ignoring the outburst, the Sorcerer continued with, "Ms. Abara, you are hereby ordered to stand guard from dusk to dawn, patrolling the university for two nights." Then he turned to my nemesis and added with that same flat voice, "A lord is expected to go into battle and defend the realm. You obviously need to work on your dodging skills. Therefore, you are ordered to stand guard from dusk to dawn for one night also, patrolling the university."

"Wait!" I said to the Realm Sorcerer. "I need to stand guard *with* him for an entire night?"

"Yes. That's exactly what I said, young lady."

I turned back to Mr. Beautiful Eyes. "I hate you."

It might have been my imagination, but the Sorcerer of the Realm might have been trying not to laugh. Royce and I rode back to the lodge in silence. After we got back, it sounded like I could hear laughing from her office as she explained what had happened.

I hate men.

CHAPTER 23

Wingman (noun): A man who helps a friend with potential romantic relationships. What's a woman's best friend called when examining a man?

–Petra Abara

I don't need your help," I said to James while running down the purse snatcher. Who attempts to steal a purse in a university full of mages? That's just idiotic. Lord James and I were doing our court appointed rounds at the Notir University. The Realm Sorcerer set the date, a month after my court appearance. The University constables were waiting for us and gave us temporary cloaks and badges to wear. After signing some paperwork and showing us our rounds, they left us alone. I distinctly heard one of the constables mention something about another bet; it was probably about us. Maybe it might be who killed who first. There's a lot of space in Avalon, they'd never find his body, honest. Sorry, Mr. Realm Sorcerer, sir, young Lord James must have fallen down a well.

Since this was a rest day, it meant every student would be out partying. After we heard the scream, we ran around the corner and almost got knocked over by the purse snatcher flying past us. His victim was in the process of pulling out her wand when I shouted back that we would handle this and gave chase. James sprinted ahead of me. *Oh no you don't, you are so not going to get to him first*, I thought and called a spell from my amulet. A white ball of energy flew from my hands just missing James and heading toward our perpetrator's left leg. Technically, it's a spell to trip-up prey in the forest, but hey, you use what's available, right? A small part of my brain really wanted to just edge my spell ball a bit more to the left and "accidentally" hit my partner. *This is a one-night thing. We are so not dating*, I thought to myself. Got that?

Except Mr. Thief seemed to sense my energy ball, tumbled to the right and jumped, pulling himself ten feet up onto a ledge. He made it look effortless. Okay, maybe he wasn't the idiot I thought him to be at first. James cursed and pulled out his wand and got a shot off at our thief, but his spell went wide. Whatever he cast had a blueish tint to it, probably a stunning spell. Hitting a target when both of you are moving is really hard. Magical dueling is very competitive in Avalon, but I don't belong to any of the clubs. Not that I don't think practicing magic is important, it's just that I think dueling is stupid. In real life, your opponent is not going to follow the guidelines or "stay in their lane." They're going to use whatever works, be it a wand, a gun, or a simple quarterstaff. Just as James was getting off another spell, our thief threw something behind him and James's spell suddenly veered toward it. When the small black ball and James's spell collided, the area exploded into darkness.

"Gremlin dust!" I shouted. "Don't cast any magic until it wears off." James and I were only in the cloud briefly, but if either of us attempted to cast or call any magic for the next three minutes, really odd things would happen. With magic, that translates into bad. Who was this thief? Gremlin dust was very expensive and had to be packaged correctly. Only someone with excellent herbology knowledge would even try it.

"Maker's nostril!" shouted James at the criminal. "Stop."

"Seriously?" I sneered while running as fast as I could to keep up. "Like that's going to work." Being slightly shorter meant I was falling behind.

James shouted, "If he goes around the corner ..."

But I cut him off, "Stop and bend over."

He glanced back at me while we ran. "What?"

"Just do it," I screamed at him. This partnership thing wasn't going very well. Our very first chase, and this lug of man wouldn't listen to me.

James cursed, stopped and stooped down like he was ready to hike the ball in a rugby game. I ran as fast as I could and used his back as a springboard to propel myself upwards and forward while somersaulting into the air. Elizabeth would have been proud of me; I'm trying out to be a permanent member on Avalon's silver gymnastics team instead of a backup. I crashed into the thief, and my momentum was such that he and I careened off the narrow brick wall. Splat, we hit the edge of a trough, upturning it, then slid to a stop deep in mud. Moments later random bits of food and other things landed on top of me. The large boar seemed surprised two strangers suddenly appeared in his sty, but he sniffed me once and began eating an old banana peel which had landed on my head. There wasn't an inch of me that wasn't covered in muck.

The thief attempted to get away but slipped. I grabbed his ankle and pulled hard. He tried kicking me in the face, but I was expecting something like that and twisted his foot.

"Lucifer's ass, girl!" he screamed out. "Let me go, I don't want to hurt you."

In his right hand was a throwing knife.

I growled back. "I bet that gremlin dust is still on me. Let's see what happens if I call a really nasty spell with you right here with me and both of us covered in shit."

We turned at the noise. James and several other constables had rounded the corner and stood at the edge of the sty, looking at us incredulously. James called out, "I would do what she says. Ms. Abara doesn't like losing."

There was not so much as a splatter of mud on my partner, and here I was looking like a pig's rear end. I wanted to kill someone.

The thief's eyes widened. "You'd do it, blow both of us to hell and back?"

I looked over at James again, he was perfect, not a strand of hair out of place even after our chase. A gentle breeze made his blue cape fan out slightly. His image could be on the cover of one of those romance novels from Earth. I turned back to the thief, and something in my expression made him gulp.

"Just try me."

After we turned the thief over to the university constables, I headed toward the gymnasium. To put it correctly, I walked toward the gymnasium and James followed me. We got a few stares. I bet more than a few people thought James was "bringing me in." I was still covered in mud and worse.

"Where are we going?" James asked. "The main constable headquarters is the other way."

I gave him an incredulous stare. "James, I want to get clean. The gymnasium has a shower." This time of night the water was probably cold, but I would take it. I bet the constables' idea of getting clean was filling a tub of water from the pond in the back of their station. They would probably give me some privacy, but it would take all night to get this stuff out of my hair if I was forced to stand in a tub.

Please be dark, I hoped. Nope, I could see the mage lights flicker inside the gymnasium as we neared it. I swung toward James. "Is there anything I could say to make you go away?"

James almost growled at me. "Look, we're supposed to be partners for the night. Why is this so hard for you?"

"What in the world are you talking about?" I demanded. "We're not dating. You're smart, good looking, smell really nice. For a Lord you seem okay, so go find a nice Lady and walk around the campus with her."

"So, you like me," he said with a sudden smile, making me regret everything I said. It was hard to concentrate when he looked at me like that.

Argh. I stomped toward him. Before, I was trying to keep my distance, so I wouldn't get any mud on him, now I didn't care anymore. "At what point did I say I liked you?" I asked, poking him in the chest leaving a dirty fingerprint. That made me feel better. Share the pain Mr. Perfect. I pointed in the direction we came from. "While I get cleaned up, you can walk around the campus a few more times, then head home."

He folded his arms, refused to move and continue to stare at me. "No. Look, Petra, if you don't want to see me again, say it. I honestly like you. You're beautiful, smart, interesting and stubborn as hell," he said, growling out the last part. "But say it," he demanded. "Tell me to go away, and I will."

Oh, for the love of ... "James, you're a Lord," I shouted. "Why can't you get it through your thick head that being with you ..." But my retort was cut off by a voice I knew well. Oh no!

"They're really cute together," came the elegant, educated voice. "Should we invite poor Mr. Vimmer in, or leave him out in the cold?" The voice continued, "I would agree, he is good looking. However, the rest ... requires a closer inspection." The last part was almost said as a command.

Please Maker, no. But she was there, along with the rest of my friends. All ladies, all high rank, and all them wearing gym clothes outlining their bodies while I was covered in mud.

I sighed, defeated. "Lord James, let me introduce you to Lady Elizabeth Navartis and her friends."

For the first time since I knew the man, Lord James looked stunned. Eight beautiful women stood in front of him, and none of them looked self-conscious. Three of my friends probably equaled his rank. Three others were definitely higher; Julia, much higher.

And then there was Elizabeth. And all of them looked at him like a thing to be examined. I couldn't help myself. "Okay, pretty boy," I teased. "This is the place where you bow and show you're not just a country bumpkin."

To his credit, James got himself under control. "Lady Elizabeth," he said while executing a perfect bow, "I don't believe we have been introduced."

She turned to me and smiled. "Well, he recovers quickly too. Let's get you cleaned up and while you do, I want to hear the story." At that, Elizabeth took my hand, ignoring the fact I was covered in dirt and pulled me toward the gymnasium. She said, almost in a whisper, "And don't leave out any details." Then she looked back over her shoulder. "Ladies, he's yours. I think a closer inspection is in order. Don't you?"

Ha! By the time Julia and the others get done with him, he'll be squished flat.

Oh God, the warm shower felt wonderful. Elizabeth must have had the gym sorcerer charge the heating crystals earlier. I was in heaven. Water cascaded off me. Eventually, somewhere underneath, I would find clean skin. I had to shampoo my hair twice to get all the dirt out.

"So, nothing's broken?" she asked, seeing the bruises beginning to show on my shoulder.

"I called a basic diagnostic spell," I said while squeezing water out of my hair. "Just royally bruised." Come the next day my shoulder was probably going to be purple.

Elizabeth gave me a nebulous look like she didn't believe me.

"Look," I said, "if anything was broken, I would have headed toward a healer. Not a fan of being my own personal guinea pig with healing spells."

She snorted. Even that sounded elegant. Through the soap in my face, I saw a smile form on her lips. "So, you used Lord James as a spring board and catapulted yourself into the air to catch the thief?" Now she laughed outright. "How many rotations?"

"Two. I got extra impetus when he stood up in shock as I jumped, but then I hit the thief at a bad angle and well, it all went to shit."

Elizabeth slammed her palm into the door frame while laughing uncontrollably at my pun. "Only you, Petra," she finally gasped out. "Only you."

As I was getting my gym clothes on (my cloak and other clothes smelled to high heaven), Elizabeth said, "So, a professional thief. That's unusual on this campus. Who was his target?"

I thought about it for a second. "Um, Lady Manchester. I don't know her."

"Hmm," replied Elizabeth. "Her family manages some of the contract inspections with things coming from other planets." At my questioning glance, she shrugged. "They make sure nothing ... *inauspicious* is going to Earth or coming through here *from* Earth. That type of stuff."

I stood up and stretched, feeling the tightness in my right arm, I had to work it out or I would be stiff for days. "So, you think this is a target of something bigger?"

"That would be my guess. However, whoever 'they' are has probably been set back. But I expect they will probably try something else. Somebody threw real money to get this thief."

"Speaking of money," I asked. "Who won the bet? It was over a month ago, and I haven't been able to figure out who the winner is. It's like it's this big secret."

"Well, now," she said, buffing her fingers on her clothes. "If you just happened to know that Lord James had a private math tutor, and someone told said math tutor that the teacher liked the problems in a certain book for extra credit on his tests. And," she drawled, "if such a very sneaky person suggested to the math tutor studying said book might be a good idea before the test ..."

I stared at her open-mouthed. "You're the one." Then my indignation kicked in. "You cheated! And besides, you don't even need the money."

"I did not cheat, I planned," she retorted, not looking the least bit uncomfortable. "They don't know about your sister's history, and I believe her story would be news to young Lord James and others." She shrugged. "Besides, I split the money, and donated all of it to four churches." She grinned. "Under your name, of course. They should be getting it soon."

Oh god. I groaned. As I was thinking of a retort, Elizabeth said, "Blue."

"Huh, what?"

"Blue," she stated. "Sky blue. You need to wear a sky-blue dress."

"Whatever are you talking about?" I said, almost ready to scream now.

"For your first date with Lord James, of course," she replied, eyes sparkling. "Not right away, of course. It's still too soon after winning the bet for NOT dating him. But you do know he's going to persist. I think you may find you change your mind once he gets over himself and tries to understand what went wrong."

"You are so going to die."

"Promises, promises."

Working on the balance beam helped to stretch out my sore muscles. Elizabeth took the beam next to me. I was still grumbling on the inside, *Go out on a date with James, ha!* Inspiration struck, and I asked sweetly, "So how is Lord Vestule?" Said Lord was older, arrogant and boring. I had the displeasure of meeting him twice at the Navartis estate. He was the current man Mrs. Navartis was parading in front of her daughter. She wanted my friend Elizabeth married to a man she could control socially; for this she needed an older man. The reason was obvious—head of house. In Avalon, women by themselves have very little power except for four conditions; one, as head of house; two, you're a sorceress; three, you're aligned with a guild; or four, you're aligned with a clan (which I am). Outside of clan affiliations and being my own head of house, my individual power stopped there. Avalon is very backwards. At least, slavery is illegal. I hear on some planets it is a way of life.

Lady Navartis wanted her daughter's future husband to be older, so Mother could rule the roost (which I thought was unlikely). Elizabeth was a sorceress—and a good one. She was sort-of aligned with the Great Forest Clan, and had other affiliations as well. I couldn't imagine any Lord holding her back. I knew she liked men, but I honestly couldn't imagine a man worthy of her.

Elizabeth stuck her tongue out at me. "Sky blue," she said, "and your dress needs to show just a hint of decolletage."

"I would rather kiss a pig," I hissed back at her. "Why are you doing this?"

She rolled her eyes at me. "Petra, I had him checked out. He's a good man." She sighed at my frustrated expression. "I'm not asking that you marry him, just give it a shot."

I looked away. "I wouldn't even know how to get his attention that way," I declared softly. Which was true. Men were a mystery to me. My sister could wiggle her finger and men would come flocking to her. Whatever skill she had obviously missed the mark with me.

Elizabeth smiled mischievously. "Is that all? Let me show you." She suddenly stood up and waved at James, who waved back from the bleachers. Elizabeth slowly bent her body backwards until her hands were almost touching the beam. Then she adjusted her stance so her feet slowly rose in the air whereupon she split her legs. James looked embarrassed and didn't seem to know what to do with his hands. He settled for sitting on them. She winked at me still upside down and said, "See? Men are very visual."

"I hate you," I replied. There was a part of me, deep down, that was annoyed Elizabeth was capturing his attention that way. She was normally rather proper about such things but seemed to delight in embarrassing me and teasing James.

"That's what friends are for, Petra," she said, rolling, then sitting up. "Seriously though, talk to the man. After tonight, if you don't want to see him again, say so." Her face took on an impish expression. "Or you could get Bethiah to make him go away."

I rolled my eyes and glanced at James. "I don't want him maimed." Bethiah's (i.e., Lady Gloster's) opinion of men was better off dead. She was one of my friends, but her stance on some things was pretty extreme.

"So, a date then," replied Elizabeth firmly.

"I'll think about it," I growled back and continued to stretch out my muscles.

CHAPTER 24

Calling spirits is a tricky thing. You must offer them something they hold valuable.

—Captain Joseph Reinhold, Voice of Gawain (deceased), Petra's Master

Anyone who says gymnastics isn't real work should try holding a handstand for thirty heartbeats. Once I had some feeling back in my shoulder, I worked on other aspects of my routine I was planning to use when I tried out as a full member of the silver gymnastics team. Most of my friends were much more advanced than me, some amazingly so. Then there was Elizabeth. When she was "in the zone," as she called it, the air around Elizabeth became charged; you could sense something spectacular was about to happen. I hoped she would be able to go to Earth to compete in their Olympics.

A part of me wanted to go home after I worked out the kinks. The Sorcerer of the Realm who set my punishment probably wouldn't say anything to me since I caught the thief, but he said from dusk till dawn, and it was still before the tenth bell. Just before James and I left the gymnasium, Elizabeth assaulted him with her famous dimples, leaving him gasping while my other friends either giggled or outright laughed at him. To save him from doing something stupid, I dragged pretty boy toward the constable's headquarters so I could get another cape and badge.

We were patrolling again. The midnight bell was about twenty minutes away. Most of the students had left, but there were still a few pockets here and there.

"Your friends mentioned your sister," James said suddenly. "But didn't tell me much of the story. Sorry for your loss. I lost my older brother and an uncle in the War." Still walking, James looked at me. "And my father's never really been the same."

"Thank you," I replied. Then I asked, "Did you fight in the war?"

He would have been young, but it wasn't impossible. Many, who were the age he would have been, had fought.

"I was a runner," he replied. Now looking straight ahead, seeing things only he could. "I carried messages and did anything else the officers needed. On any given day, I was lucky to get four hours of sleep." He waved at some people he knew and turned to me. "You?"

"I didn't fight in the war if that's what you mean. But I helped a lot of families keep moving. Some of them just wanted to stop." I paused and edged toward a painful topic. "I lost both my father and my brother in the war. I was the youngest in my family."

"Do you still miss them?" James asked, quietly.

"Every day," I replied and edged a bit closer to him. "What was your father like before the war started?"

James kicked a small stone. "Excited, energetic. He wanted to start a brewery with his brother. After the war, he just stopped talking about new things."

We were both rescued from the painful topic of the war by the cursing. Two young men were circling each other, each ready to draw a wand. "Hey," James shouted. "If you want to duel, then you need our approval, and it better follow the rules," he said intently.

I tapped him on the shoulder and pointed to the two beer mugs next to a fountain.

"And dueling while drunk is illegal on school grounds," he said, his voice getting dark. "I either throw you two into the fountain, or you can come back tomorrow and properly post the duel."

The larger of the two looked like he might draw on James but thought better of it. They went away, grumbling. I smiled inwardly. It's always someone else's fault. When I patrolled the streets of Avalon with my team, some of the more unsavory drunks wouldn't hesitate to start a brawl.

After the two were out of sight, I turned back to James. "Does everyone do what you tell them to do?" I asked.

"Not everyone," he said, smiling at me.

Damn his smile; it made my brain go sideways. To protect myself from him, I started walking again. Within a few steps, James caught up with me. We walked in silence for a bit. Just to say something, I blurted out, "Do you know Lord Seltin?"

"What kind of question is that?" he asked, bewildered.

"Sorry, but do you?"

I had to know, was this man really a monster in disguise? A part of me wanted him to say yes, they were best friends since childhood, so I could convict him on the spot.

James looked at me, a bit confused. Probably wondering why this was so important to me. I was looking him in the eye, waiting for his answer. He tilted his head. "I have been introduced to him and his family, but don't know him well. His father redefines unscrupulous. I don't like his kind of parties; everything seems to be for sale. I get the feeling his children think the world should be handed to them on a silver platter." He shrugged. "Other than that, I actually find the Seltins pretty boring. Why?"

I broke eye contact and looked away. "Why can't you be evil?" I asked under my breath. "It would make things so much easier!"

Now James looked truly confused. "Did I say something wrong?"

"I need to sit down," I said. Memories and emotions were boiling up in me, and I didn't trust myself to stand. After sitting down on a park bench facing the fountain, I grabbed some pebbles and began throwing them into the water. Throwing things helped. I wished I could hit something. James sat down beside me and waited. After another round of pebble throwing, I stopped. The university frowns on people throwing rocks into their fountains; someone has to clean them out.

I said slowly, so my emotions wouldn't break free, "The eldest child of Lord Seltin, Lars, often called upon my sister. He encouraged my sister to drink more of the man's potions, even gave her trinkets of ..." Then words just started spilling out of me, mixed with emotion, and at some point, I noticed tears hitting the ground. My tears. I felt like a ship floating in a sea of anger. Everything bottled up was breaking free in a torrent. James said nothing, just listened. At his touch, I leaned into him and started crying harder. At one point, I started hitting him and cried out, "Why, why, why?" I must have hit him pretty hard; he huffed a few times.

Once I was down to just sniffling, James said softly, "Your sister sounds like she was a wonderful person."

I pulled back my hair and wiped my eyes. A fog had crept into the night, making all the mage lights twinkle. "She was beautiful, headstrong, and full of life. She was also one of the stupidest people I know." I laughed harshly. "She was just so afraid to love again."

"Is this club still there?" James asked while rotating his arm. I guess I did hit him hard.

I shrugged. "As far as I know. I try not go back." I watched him wince as he stretched his arm. "Are you okay?"

"I'll just tell my younger sister I was assaulted by a beautiful woman."

I hit him again, this time in the chest.

"What was that for?" exclaimed James.

"Because you're a man," I blurted out. "And you probably deserve it."

James laughed. The fog was getting thicker. The mage lights across the pond were barely there. "So, about this club, why doesn't—" But I cut him off.

"The man who runs it isn't part of guild, doesn't sell his potions, and knows who to bribe."

James looked around. "I've never seen it this foggy before ..." Then his eyes widened at the sensation. I felt it to, like being pulled under. What was going on? Just moments ago, I felt like a ship at sea ... Oh God. An old memory surfaced ... *You must offer something of yourself, something you truly value.*

I had cried, spilling water on the ground. My emotions, sharing them with James. But how did the spirit hear me? I thought it was at rest now.

"James," I shouted. "Where those two men were fighting, bring their mugs here, now. I need alcohol."

"What?" he replied, looking around and trying to see through the fog. That feeling of being pulled out with the tide was stronger now.

"James, please," I said, taking and squeezing his hand before letting it go. "This is very important."

He did leave, confused as ever, but following me in this without question. *Argh, don't like him, don't like him.* But a part of me did. James held me as I cried, didn't push me away, didn't try to get closer, he just let me be me. I lost sight of him after ten feet. A part of me didn't want him to go.

Dong. The first bell signaling midnight came. It sounded very far away. *Dong.* This one sounded even farther away. "James, where are you?" I asked, hoping he could hear my voice and find me. At each dong, I called out "James," so he could hear me through the fog.

Dong ... On the seventh bell, I could see the edges of him carefully holding two mugs walking toward me.

Dong. The eighth bell; it was barely a whisper now. "Sit next to me," I said, taking both mugs and placing them on the far side of the bench.

Dong. The ninth bell. I sensed more than heard it. The feeling of being someplace else was stronger. I swear I could see fish swimming in the fog.

"Petra," James said frightened. "What is happening? Is this from you?"

Dong. Did I hear, or only imagine, the tenth peal of the bell?

"No. Yes, sort of," I replied, half hysterical. "Don't touch it when it comes."

"Touch what?" he asked, pulling me closer to him. But it was here.

Through the swirling fog, I could make out a ship broken in half laying at the bottom of the sea. From it, a sailor walking toward us. He looked just like before; weather worn, long beard, and tattered clothes moving to an unseen current, but this time I felt it.

"Petra!" James whispered in alarm. "What is it?"

"It's a spirit," I replied, gripping his hand. "Not an evil spirit," I clarified, "but I thought it was at rest."

The sailor took one of the mugs and drank from it, then began to sing. It was a happy song, full of life about a pretty girl on shore waiting for her lover's return. There was a beat to it, something they could keep time with like a striking hammer or pulling an oar. On the second stanza I joined in.

James looked at me, confused. I bet he couldn't hear it. At the end of the song, the sailor's form shifted, becoming older and stooped. I stood up in surprise. "Master?" I called out.

Like the sailor, he was incorporeal, but it was him. One hand still holding onto James, with the other I reached out to touch my old master's chest. It was like touching a thin sponge. But with the touch came smells: old pine, and other wood. It was like being ten again and in his old shop.

"Your tears called to me, girl," my old master said. "Did the darkness come?"

I sniffled. "Yes, master, it did."

He nodded. "My bones felt it. I'm glad you survived."

I cried out, "But my sister, my mother, everyone ... They all died. I am the last."

He just looked at me and smiled. "You remembered me, girl. Do you remember them?"

I nodded.

"Then their spirits still live on, through you. Only when all the memories fade can they be truly gone." He looked at me fondly and reached out to touch my hair. I leaned my head into his ghostly hand. "Did you make some cuts of your own?" he asked.

"I'm trying. Sometimes the wood is very hard."

He laughed. "Aye. There is a right many knots in the world. But don't you stop, girl."

I reached up to touch his hand. "Are you with the ship, the *Alana*?" Was my old master stuck forever under the waves?

He pondered me for a second. "A small part perhaps, an echo nurtured by the spirit. But the rest of me has moved on."

"Can," I quavered. "Can I call you again?" I would give anything to laugh with him again. To sing songs and read to him. He was so wise. The little girl in me remembered being so happy with him.

"Not without something much greater, Petra, and the price would be high." He smiled sadly at me. "It's time to let me rest. Go and start a new block of wood. Life is not just one of them."

As the ghostly visage of my master withdrew his hand, his form shifted until it was the sailor again. It bowed to James, turned, and walked toward his watery grave. Within moments, the fog cleared, and we were back. I could see the mage lights around the pond once again twinkling at us. It was like we never left.

Chapter 25

Reece's Raccoons are named after Sorcerer Glander Reece who died some fifteen years ago. During his lifetime he was intrigued by what he described as "Id intelligence." Essentially, in Reece's theory, the Id is what made humans self-aware. When Sorcerer Reece learned of an animal on Earth that had opposable thumbs unrelated to humans, he apparently became obsessed with studying them. He brought several dozen of the small fuzzy creatures over to his family estate whereupon he began to experiment on them magically. No one knows what he did, but everyone knows the results, talking raccoons. After his death, they escaped and formed groups around Avalon city.

The Reece's Raccoon is nocturnal, stealthy, and extremely intelligent. They can speak better than a pixie and can apparently sense magic, to a limited extent. They use this to avoid both traps and people (even magicians) trying to catch them. They're intelligent enough not to invade an occupied house, so for the most part you only see them when they want to be seen. Like a pixie, they will steal things they consider valuable. They occasionally steal imbued items often with hysterically funny results. On occasion, one might become fascinated with a particular human or family and play with them. No one knows why. They also love ginger, and, as *an exception to the not-invading-occupied-houses, will invade kitchens during the dark of night to get more of the spice. It is illegal to bring them to Earth.*

—Guide to Avalon, 4th printing

W e continued our patrol walking side by side, occasionally getting closer to each other. If our fingers brushed, I sidestepped to move farther away. I wasn't certain but James seemed very nervous. Did he want me to hold his hand? When we came across deep shadow, he carefully edged around it. After the first, bell I decided to take pity on Mr. Perfect.

"It's not coming back tonight," I said with a hint of amusement. A part of me was enjoying watching him off balance.

James almost jumped. "How do you know?" he asked nervously. His feet were at the edge of an extended shadow. There was no way around it. It was either take the plunge or backtrack.

"The last time it came was seven years ago. I wasn't the one who called it then, either."

He marched up to me and demanded, "Petra, it said the price would be very high if you called it again. Don't do it!"

Huh? "I'm not planning on calling the shadow again," I said, getting annoyed. How dare he tell me what to do! The little girl in me did, but I wasn't going to tell him that. While she was still in there, the older me's voice was stronger now. I could call magic, had a team, and did good things for the city. I liked the life I had carved for myself. I still wasn't sure if I wanted Mr. Of-the-Beautiful-Eyes in it, though.

James leaned into me. "Petra, don't do it." His words were commanding.

Okay, now I got it. It made him feel better if he "took care of me."

"While I'm not planning to, Mr. Perfect. You're not my husband to order me around." Now I leaned forward as well. We were nose to nose. I hit him in the chest, hard.

He *oofed*, but held his ground. Almost growling, he said, "You solve a lot of problems by hitting them, don't you?"

I pointed backwards where we came from. "That was my old master, the wisest man I ever knew. He taught me how to carve my own path, and sometimes I need to dig hard to make it stick." Yelling now, I pushed him backwards. "Unlike you, nothing comes easy for me. I need to study at night because I'm too busy during the day. Some days I'm lucky to get six hours of sleep." I pushed him again. "I lead a team, and I'm worried that I might make the wrong decision and get one of them killed." I tried pushing him again, but he grabbed my wrists. I growled at him. "Let me go," I said softly. Oh, I was pissed.

He did but refused to step backwards. "You said your sister was afraid to love again," he said. "Are you afraid to love at all?"

We stared at each other for a few heartbeats. I was so tired. "James," I said. "I'm not really a Lady. Even if we made a go of it, I don't want to stop pushing forward. That's just a part of who I am."

"Isn't that what nobility should be?" he said softly, then smiled. "If my mother was ever invited to Lady Elizabeth's house, she would probably think it was the biggest event of her life." He shook his head. "Can't you see how amazing you are?"

I patted his chest, then leaned into him. He slowly hugged me. I sighed contentedly. "I'm thinking about letting you have one date. If I do, you'll get one date to get me to change my mind about you. One date. Only one."

"Deal," he replied. I could feel him smile.

"I haven't agreed. I'm still thinking about it. But if you do get one date, and then say something stupid," I warned. "I get to hit you."

He laughed. "I wouldn't have it any other way."

I just enjoyed his warmth, the strength of his muscles. He was just the right height to ...

"Cookie?" came a soft voice near us. I froze, and I congratulated myself on freezing. It wasn't easy, but I didn't want to startle the speaker.

It was difficult not to jump at the intrusion, but I managed it. The voice was unhuman, soft, hesitant. Somehow, a bit deep, a bit resonant.

Meanwhile, James spun around and went into a crouch, his wand was out, ready to cast. Me, I crouched down, v-e-r-y slowly, and then turned. I was staring at two luminous eyes in the darkness. It stood about calf high. I was still looking down, but not as far down as James had to be. When James spun, it had jumped back. Now that I was down nearer his level, he took a hesitant step toward me.

"Cookie?" came the soft pleading voice again. I saw the edges of two small hands extending something toward us.

Could it be?

"James," I said in a whisper, "I think it's a Reece's Raccoon."

The fuzzy little guy in front of us stood up on his hind legs and held the stick in his hands as if in offering. "Cookie?" it asked again, in its little voice.

I knelt down and carefully kept my distance so as not to startle the creature. "James," I said softly, "I think it wants to trade the wand for a cookie."

"I don't have anything with me except for some jerky and water," he said and looked sideways at me. "Besides the wand is probably stolen. I doubt anyone gave it to him. Should we try to take it from him?"

That earned a soft snort from me. "I'm done chasing down criminals through mud tonight. I doubt we could catch him even if we tried." Looking at the raccoon, I pointed at me and said, "Petra. I am Petra." Then I pointed at him. "Do you have a name?"

It considered me for a moment. "Jumper of Haystacks. I am Jumper."

Well, that was a very descriptive name. He probably lived on a nearby farm. I tried remembering the few articles I read about them. Considering his smallish size, I think he was an older adolescent. He held the wand up higher. "Cookie?" he asked again, hopefully.

I knew what he wanted now. In my locker where I kept a change of clothes, I had a box of cookies. Eating a little after practicing helped me to keep my focus. Now I remembered placing a few in my backpack to eat later in the night. I bet there was some ginger baked into them. It was amazing the little guy could smell them. As I slowly pulled my backpack off my shoulder, he backed up a step, probably ready to bolt if I tried to grab him or pop the bag over him.

When I pulled out my three cookies, his face quivered in excitement.

I pushed a cookie toward him. He considered me and said, "Two. Two cookies."

James started laughing which made Jumper growl at him. My partner was interrupting a cookie negotiation; very serious!

"Hush, James," I said quite softly. James forced himself to quiet his laughter.

"I will give you all three if you give me the wand, and something else magical." I bet the little guy had other things squirreled away.

Now he looked sad. "Only have Wan with Jumper."

Interesting, he couldn't pronounce the "d" sound on the end of "wand" very well, wand was wan.

"You may have all three now and you will give me the wand but you owe Petra another item."

It was like lightning. He dropped the wand, ran forward, hugged my knee, grabbed the three cookies and vanished into the night. The thief we caught earlier was easy compared to what attempting to catch Jumper would have been. Any attempt to catch him would take planning, skills and some serious luck. The little guy was lightning-fast.

James and I examined the wand, there was no maker's symbol engraved into the length of the wood, which was very unusual. However, a circular silver piece was embedded into its bottom. Three symbols were clearly visible on the silver piece: C.S.L.

"Well, no idea," I said to James. "I don't think it's an apprentice's wand, this feels too well made. Who's C.S.L.?"

"I'm not a wand afficionado," he said, rubbing his jaw. "I know the names of the wandmaker houses which make up the guild today. But none of them have a last name starting with L that I know of."

"Well," I said with a hint of exasperation. "What's the use of having a Lord as a boyfriend if he doesn't know these things?"

"Aha," James said in glee. "So, I'm boyfriend material."

I hit him. "We'll see. After we finish our rounds, we can turn it in." I put the wand in my backpack.

The rest of the night passed without incident unless you count me hitting him three more times. Got to make sure Lord James never forgets I'm not a "Lady," even though the people who followed me from my childhood lands seem to see me as such.

Just before dawn, we arrived back at the constables' main entrance. The Captain of the night watch was being shouted at by a Sorceress of the Realm. Listening in, we gathered the thief had escaped before he could be questioned. One of the sergeants had both of us fill out a form so we could detail any events or occurrences of note. By agreement, we left out the part about the spirit arriving since we knew it wasn't connected to the thief.

I was exhausted and headed toward the Great Forest Lodge for some sleep. I had to do this tomorrow night too! Groan.

CHAPTER 26

Sorcerers and Sorceresses of the Realm are the glue that holds the nobles and guilds in check. They ultimately report to the Wizard's Council via way of the courts. Traditionally, the newest member on the Wizard's Council is responsible for acting as the head of the Realm Knights.

—Rules of Avalon

It's not fair. I was only able to get five hours of sleep before my body woke me up. Dragging myself out of bed, I ate a late breakfast in our Dining Hall before being accosted by my team. Gail and Hebin sat down across from me. Dora sat on my left and Franklin on my right. I was surrounded. After draining my coffee mug, I glared at them. "What's going on? You all have the day off. Don't you have anywhere better to be?"

"Ah, the dulcet tones of our commander," laughed Gail. She placed a silver talon on the table in front of me and pointedly looked at Hebin. "So," she drawled slowly. "Is Lord James getting a date?"

I gave her the stink-eye making her laugh again. There was not enough coffee in me for this conversation.

Hebin tapped his finger on the table eyeing the silver talon. "It doesn't count unless there's an actual date set. I bet they didn't cover that part."

I rolled my eyes. *More coffee,* I mentally pleaded, but apparently no one was reading my mind. As the four of them began a spirited discussion of what constitutes setting a "date," I got up to refill my mug. I knew coffee was not going to wake me up right now, but it was that or kill someone. I absently wondered how many people were still alive today because their potential killer had a full cup of coffee with them and didn't want to spill it.

Walking by them, I said, "I didn't kill him, and he's *possibly* getting a date. However, we haven't set the day yet." I knew I was talking myself into meeting Lord James again. Admittedly, I'd had a good time with him if you leave out landing in a pig sty.

"Ohhh," Dora smiled. She must have picked up on my threatening tones. She almost giggled out, "Was there bruising involved in determining if he was dating material?"

I gave a small smile as I drank from my mug. "When I left him, he was still massaging his right arm."

Hebin laughed and banged the table. "You always like leading with your left." Hebin liked anything physical, and being six-foot-four and made of muscle, if he decided to flatten James, I wasn't sure if there would be anything left.

This was getting annoying.

"Okay. Why is everybody interested in my love life?" I growled out, loud enough that others in the room turned to me.

Ignoring me, Hebin put his fingers together and bent them backwards in satisfaction while looking at Gail. "I win," he said.

"Oh yeah?" replied Gail. "They didn't set a date yet, so it doesn't count. The bet continues."

I left them arguing and headed back to my room, drinking my coffee as I went. Just before I got there one of our newer recruits found me. She looked terrified. Was I that scary? I was wearing my best smile too. "What can I do for you?" I asked while trying to remember her name.

"Sorry, ma'am," she said, backing up slightly. "But the commander wants to see you." She blanched and gulped. "There's a Sorceress of the Realm in her office as well."

"A few inches taller than me, with black hair turning a bit white?" I asked. My guess this was the same Sorceress of the Realm I saw yelling at the captain last night.

"Ma'am?" she said in terror. "I'm not sure."

I sighed. This kid seemed terrified I might bite her head off for not knowing. "That's okay, what's your name?"

"Belinda, ma'am," she said softly while looking down at the floor.

Okay, give her something to do to make her feel better. "Thank you, Belinda. Please let Royce know I'll be there shortly."

The kid popped up and ran around the corner. Jeez, they get younger every year. Had it only been four years ago that I joined? It felt like a lifetime ago. After changing into some clean clothes and running a brush through my hair, I headed over to Royce's office. The door was open, and I could see her sitting behind her desk. Yep, it was the Sorceress of the Realm from last night. The two of them were talking and apparently sharing some joke. I bet it was about me. Everyone seemed enthralled with my life. I knocked on the door frame and asked, "You wanted to see me, ma'am?"

"Come in, Petra," replied Royce. "Realm Sorceress Bardot would like a moment of your time."

After sitting down, I asked, "Is this about the thief or the wand?"

"Wand? What wand?" asked the Realm Officer.

I shrugged. "I met a Reece's Raccoon last night, and I traded a cookie for a wand. I figured the creature probably stole it. I turned it in before I left."

The Realm Sorceress suddenly laughed, making her look younger. "Which clan, Haystack or Pipe?"

I stared at her. "Ah, er ... Haystack, ma'am." I wasn't aware the Reece's Raccoons lived in clans, or that there was more than one clan of them living on the University's grounds. *The hidden world around us*, I snorted to myself. The things you don't know.

"Then you were lucky, Ms. Abara. Reece's Raccoons from the Pipe Clan are notorious pranksters." She grinned. "I'll have a look at the wand after I head back." She shrugged. "If no one claims it after a week, technically it's yours."

"Ah, okay?" What was I going to do with a wand? I can't cast magic, just call it. This conversation was so different from the one I had with the other Realm officer. She almost seemed nice.

Royce cleared her throat. "Realm Sorceress Bardot has a request of you, Petra."

"What do you know about spectacles, Ms. Abara?" the Realm Sorceress asked me.

"Um, that I don't need them?" I replied, looking confused. "Sorry, why is this important?"

"We belief the thief you caught last night was employed by the Glass Maker's Guild," she replied. "An offshoot of their guild makes the various glasses for people to wear who need them. They are very expensive and made by hand."

I started to get it. "And they don't want competition from Earth," I said, remembering Lady Navartis's comment about inspections. "They're trying to force the Manchester house from allowing glasses from Earth. I assume they're cheaper?"

Royce leaned back in her chair. "I told you she was smart."

The Realm Sorceress nodded. "Extremely. Apparently in the Republic, machines can make glasses in large quantities. Even accounting for transportation and import taxes, they would be much cheaper than glasses made in Avalon by hand."

"Got it," I replied. "But why am I involved? I stopped the thief and returned the purse."

"We think the Glass Maker's Guild is getting desperate and may attempt to kidnap Lady Manchester. The ransom, of course, being either that import taxes are elevated to the point selling glasses here makes no sense, or an outright refusal of them to be allowed through the gate."

I whistled. "No offence, isn't that what the Realm Sorceresses are for?" I shrugged and looked at Royce. "Why would I put myself between a Noble house and powerful guild? There's no win here. Either of them could squish me flat."

"You're absolutely correct on the first part, Ms. Abara," replied the Sorceress. "But without the thief, we have no proof. Late last night, a request was submitted to the Wizard's Council asking we be allowed to question certain individuals in the Glass Maker's Guild under Sorcerer's Oath."

Ouch. I heard stories "under oath" meant some very nasty things as it related to a Sorcerer or Sorceress of the Realm. "What happened?" I asked, intrigued.

"We received a Decision back. It was written by Mr. Petotum. A person's guild rights against physical and mental intrusion were sacrosanct unless there was proven evidence suggesting otherwise." She shrugged. "Essentially we can't bring them in for questioning unless we have evidence. None of us were surprised by the Decision." She looked at me directly. "We need that thief."

"Hey, I'm not the one who let him escape," I retorted. Something else crossed my mind. "Why aren't the Glass Maker's Guild trying to build their own machines to make glasses?" I looked over at Royce. "I'm assuming it could be done in Avalon?"

Realm Sorceress Bardot snorted. "I know. I want to kick the captain from here to Earth. That was a professional thief you caught. The captain should have known better than just to put him into a simple lockup, even though he's only patrolling the University." Now she seemed frustrated. "Regarding your very good point about investing in their own machines, no, although not because it couldn't be done. They aren't because the guild is backwards, paranoid, and just plain stubborn."

None of what she just said surprised me. There were a lot of people in Avalon who didn't like the changes happening around them. Earth ideas, especially ones from the Continental Republic, seemed to be bleeding into our streets and turning everything upside down. "I get it, ma'am. But what do I have to do with this? I have no power."

Royce got up and closed her door, then sat down again. "Yes, you do," she said simply.

I rolled my eyes. "No offence, ma'am, we're the Great Forest Clan. We look after our own, and we're respected at the street level, but we don't have a great deal of political power."

"I didn't say anything about our clan," replied Royce. "I said *you* do," she emphasized.

Huh? What was she talking about?

"I don't think you completely understand your position, Ms. Abara," jumped in Realm Sorceress Bardot. "You are part of the inner group of ladies which comprise some of the most powerful houses in Avalon."

What? I gave her a stare. They were my friends, sure but ... "I'm not a lady." I blurted out.

"Outside of the time you spend as the voice of Gawain, you're not," she replied immediately. "You're something different." She eyed me critically for a moment and looked at Royce. "What do you think the Navartis house, indeed any of the houses of Ms. Petra's circle of friends, would do to the Glass Maker's Guild if an agent of theirs harmed her?"

"They would vote to disband the guild," Royce said deadpan. "And with their combined power, they could."

I stood up. "No," I said. "I am not a lady. I'm unimportant." They were making me out as someone with power, who walked in dresses and commanded servants and ...

"Petra," said the Realm Sorceress softly. "Please, sit down." She must have picked up on my frustration. "You're something new in Avalon. You're not alone, but there are precious few like you—people who are intelligent, educating themselves, and unafraid to interact with people of all walks of life, including lords and ladies." She smiled briefly. "As well as Reece's Raccoons. Avalon is changing, and you're leading the charge."

I snorted at that. I took my seat again but crossed my arms. I am no lady! "Half the time I either end up in the mud, or I feel like life has kicked me in the face."

The Realm Sorceress's voice darkened slightly. "Petra, to a certain extent this is a war, but a cultural war. The first ones always get bloody, always." She reached beside her and pulled up a small canvas bag. "These are all the things the captain removed from the thief." She looked over at Royce. "We think the guild is getting desperate, the first shipment of glasses from Earth is scheduled to arrive in three days. A contact of ours picked up a rumor that a large sum of money has been paid to agents to kidnap Lady Manchester. If that happens, things will spin out of control, and Avalon might go up in flames." She looked at me evenly. "We need that thief so we have something we can use to force this out in the open." She put the bag on Royce's desk and pushed it toward me. "Find him, Petra. Others are looking of course, but the Great Forest Clan is known for its tracking, and you have friends and contacts across Avalon."

I don't like hidden agendas; they always explode in my face. Pointedly ignoring the bag, I said, "The other part to this, even if I fail but it 'appears' as if the thief intentionally harms me, is that you have a political wedge to force the guild's hand." Still staring at Sorceress of the Realm, I remarked, "You're a sneaky bitch, you know that?"

The Sorceress looked back at me, unconcerned. "You're more than a pawn, Petra, but that doesn't mean I won't sacrifice a piece to win the game."

I snorted. Nice to know where we stand. I tilted my head. "And what game are we playing, ma'am?"

"To keep Avalon for imploding. That's my job. And, at least for now, it's yours too."

CHAPTER 27

Goblin (noun). Short, intelligent, cavern-dwelling, humanoid creature.

—From the pages of Dangerous Magical Creatures

Sneaky backstabbing realm sorcerers," I grumbled to myself as I slipped on my leather gloves. I didn't want to touch any of the items directly yet. There wasn't much. Two silver talons very clean; nothing there. A well-made set of locking picking tools, but no maker's mark on them; probably hand made. Two more gremlin bombs, which surprised me; just one was expensive. But like the lock pick set, there was no maker's mark on them. Then I examined the four throwing knives and smiled. Gotcha. Like everything else, no maker's mark, but one of them had a smudge of blood on it.

While Master Onthur looked at the unexploded Gremlin ball through his eyepiece, I tried not to fall asleep. He liked to hum to himself under his breath. This was hour eighteen plus since I woke up this morning, and it was hard to keep my eyes open.

Right after the Realm Sorceress left, Royce called a Level Two. This meant anyone that was free was now on the case, even if they had the day off. Teams of Great Forest Clan members spread across Avalon, most heading into the seedier parts of the city, all looking for the thief. I was able to transmit a mental picture of him to their amulets. However, I knew they weren't going to find him in the lower-class bars or brothels. The guy I captured was high class all the way. Intelligent, well spoken, and honestly seemed to have a sense of morality, of all things, considering his profession. Not places the Great Forest Clan traditionally ventured.

I started with examining his knives first. They were perfectly balanced and exquisitely made. Like the few other items taken off the thief, there was no maker's mark, or anything else indicating where they might have come from. No hair, either. The thief planned this out. I bet it was a way of life for him. *Leave no mark.* When I found what looked to be a smudge of blood, I thought I might have won.

There's a spell in our amulet, that if done right, allows us to trace blood. It is much more complicated and involved than the spell to follow a blood scent. To call this one properly, I have to slow my heartbeat down and be in a quiet place. Once in the right mind set, I called the complex structure from my amulet along with a trace amount of energy. While holding the energy in place, I mentally started to add the final piece, the part which came from me. Hence the difference between calling versus casting magic. With casting, the entire structure comes from you, like Elizabeth, or any other person who uses a wand. To me, a wand is just an expensive stick. But calling magic, that I can do. It apparently has something to do with the clan oaths and how the amulets are made.

Royce tells me the higher clans have vastly more complex spells woven into their amulets. Fine with me, I'm still working my way through all the spells in the Great Forest amulet. I didn't need to experiment with something that would probably just explode in my face. That already happens often enough with the spells which *are* in my amulet.

When a first-year walked into the spell chamber I was using, without paying attention to my do-not-disturb sign, and therefore breaking my concentration, I screamed in rage. I was almost there! I could feel the called energy wafting away. Now I had to start from scratch.

"Can't you read?" I screamed at him. "This is a spell chamber, and that's a Do Not Disturb sign."

His face went white, then his eyes went wide. He dove backwards, thereby just missing the brass candle holder I threw at him. Now it was going to take another fifteen minutes to get myself in the right mental state. I later heard Dora found the young man cringing in a closet. He honestly believed I was going to come after him. How in the world did I get that kind of reputation?

I stomped out of the spell circle, yelled down the hall for everyone to leave me alone and picked up the candle holder. Once seated back in the middle of the circle, I lit the candle with my mind and amulet. I don't know why this is important, but after mentally lighting a candle, I begin to relax. It took some time to sort through the spells in my amulet and bring what was needed to the surface. Then I slowly began to pull the structure out. Holding the knife up in front of me with the blood stain, I added the final key to activate the spell. The blood was consumed. Moments later, a complex illusion began to take shape around me. Buildings, and streets grew from the ground: Avalon City. A section glowed slightly, farther North. Carefully stepping toward the pulse, I could make out a farm. I knew where to go. Got you!

Soon after, my team and I invaded the Mountberry horse farm. A large family owned the place, and they didn't look anything like the thief. These people were large, solid, and talked with a decidedly uneducated ascent. When I created an illusion of the thief, the elder suddenly smiled at me and said with excitement, "Aye. You want the letter!"

Huh? He hurriedly walked inside and soon came out with a folded piece of paper and handed it to me. He smiled the entire time and bowed to me, like he was delivering a precious item to a lady. What was going on? Opening the letter, I read, "Whoever you are, congratulations! You just trailed Boo-Boo. Well done!" Then the entire letter burst into flames. It was consumed in an instant.

"Who is Boo-Boo?" I asked, through gritted teeth.

The family elder escorted me to one of his stables, inside was an ancient plow horse. It stared back at me, unconcerned by this stranger peering at him.

"How long ago," I asked, very calmly, "was that letter delivered?"

The elder bowed to me. "Lady, three seasons ago." He beamed at me and added, "There is a prize for finding Boo-Boo. You are the first!" He opened the stable door and handed me a set of reins to put on Boo-Boo. "Congratulations, he is a very nice horse."

Boo-Boo's best years, if he ever had any, were years ago. Oh, I am so going to kill that thief.

Three false alarms and another dead end, and I was ready to fall over. This was it. There was nowhere else to go. While still looking through his eyepiece at the gremlin dust bomb, Master Onthur said, "It's not mine." He shifted it in his hands and added, "I always put my maker's mark on everything I build."

"But do you know who made it?" I asked. I already knew there was no maker's mark on it. I doubted Master Onthur made any "on the side," but it wouldn't be impossible. Without that mark, I had no idea if he could trace it. But his shop was full of interesting things realm sorcerers probably wished didn't exist. Years ago, I did some odd jobs for him, mostly when his toys needed calibration. More often than not, they needed a lot of calibration. But he paid well and appreciated my feedback.

"No," he said slowly, and I forced myself not to hit my hand on his glass countertop in frustration. This was my last lead.

He pondered me for a moment then handed the gremlin dust ball back. "I know someone who *might*," he stressed, "be able to tell where it was made, generally."

My spirits rose. I cautiously asked, "How much will this introduction cost?" Negotiating was a way of life in Avalon. He smiled at me. *Uh-oh. This was about to become expensive.* I was desperate, and he knew it.

"For the right price, I will make the introduction. However," he said, "the individual will probably request something difficult for them, and for you, to get."

Oh. Realm Sorceress Bardot and I never talked money. It was more do-this-and-I-won't-have-you-killed-and-make-it-look-like-the-thief-did-it. I couldn't get a solid sense of who she was. A part of her seemed almost respectful, as if I was a person with title and power. While in the next breath, I was a thing to be discarded or allowed to die to further her agenda of keeping Avalon from blowing itself up. After she left, I yelled at Royce ... who then looked me straight in the eye and said, "You just met one of the nice ones."

I looked at her incredulously. "That was nice? She threatened to kill me with a smile on her face!"

Royce snorted. "You think keeping the guilds and nobles in line takes niceness?"

Oh. Good point.

"Hang on a second," I said to the Master and called through my amulet to Royce. <"I may have found a lead. How much money do I have for this?">

While I was waiting for a response, I asked Master Onthur, "How much do you want to make the introduction?"

His answer made my jaw drop. What did he think, that we were made of money? Before I could tell him that was preposterous, Royce reached back. <"Whatever you need."> It was a statement.

I rolled my eyes and told her what he wanted. I was expecting Royce to blow up; instead, she immediately replied, <"As I said, whatever you need.">

I blinked. *Ah, okay?* I said to Master Onthur, "Royce says yes."

"Very well," he said. "Follow me." In a back room he had me help him roll up a rug. He disabled a magical trap, and then a door on the floor appeared.

Ah. An illusion, very ingenious.

Pulling the handle upwards, a waft of cold, dusty air hit me. After walking down the first few steps, he turned back to look at me. "Well, are you coming? Your answer lies in this direction."

The steps ended about sixty feet down in near-total darkness. There was a trickle of light from above. The air had turned cold, damp and moist. I could hear nothing whatsoever. Just breathing seemed loud. Why wasn't he casting light? I had been in dark places before, but nothing like this. Just as I was about to call light, he whispered at me, "No magic! Wait!"

Okay?

He made a guttural sound, then repeated it. Down here, it echoed. How deep did this cavern extend? I felt him about to call out again when I saw a faint blue light pulse out somewhere in the darkness, far away. My amulet registered something. Whatever spell was involved in making that blue light wasn't from traditional magic. The faint light bobbed slightly as if someone was slowly walking toward us. Without looking at me, Master Onthur whispered, "If you insult her, I can't protect you."

Okay, got it. Whoever was coming toward us was female and this was *HER* land. On a pure power scale, Master Onthur was about a three, but he knew how to store magic with the toys he made. Usually, he used gems, linking them to his devices to power them.

As the short creature shuffled toward us, the smell hit me. Okay! I have hit a new low. This rancid smell was a new one, even for me. She wasn't wearing traditional clothing, but leather rags stitched together. Around her neck were the bones of small animals. From the looks of them, a few still had some meat on them. Everyone carries snacks around; she just doesn't use pockets. Her thinning hair was black, as were her large eyes. I blinked; her skin was green. Was this a goblin? In her left hand, she held a large bone staff. Had it been carved from one of those giant southern lizards? They were the only creatures that I knew of which were large enough. Fastened on the top of it was a blue gem; that was what was giving off the faint glow. Now that she was standing in front of us, it was all I could do not to retch.

Master Onthur and the goblin grunted at each other a few times. The language was very guttural. Just about every word seemed to contain a "gul" or "shi" sound in it. How you expressed the sound apparently changed the meaning.

Suddenly she turned to me. "You have," she rasped out, "lost dirt, which must find home?"

There could be only one thing she meant. I pulled the gremlin dust bomb out and held it toward her. She sniffed it, then licked it. Ugh.

"Three mounds of dirt," she said, looking at me and banging her bone staff on the ground. "One from Richmond, Virginia. One from the lands of the Dragon. And one from a famous tomb I will not name in the Haunted Lands," she stated, then turned and began shuffling away.

Master Onthur translated for me. "She wants the dirt in return for telling us where the dirt from what is in your hand came from, more or less. As much as she can find out."

"But we didn't negotiate," I said, perplexed. "Why is she walking away?"

He shrugged. "That the way she is. If we follow her, we have accepted her terms."

"How am I going to get dirt from a tomb she won't name?" I asked him.

"Can't you think of a famous tomb of someone no sorcerer or sorceress will willingly say their name?"

"What?" I screamed, the noise making the sound echo throughout the caves.

The answer, of course, was Morgan Le Fay. *Wait a minute, Le Fay's tomb is in the Haunted Lands?* I hadn't known that.

"How long do I have to get her dirt?" I asked.

I couldn't believe I was considering this. Trying to get dirt from the dragon's lands would probably solve my problem of finding Le Fay's tomb. I would be dead.

I had the definite feeling that if I removed even a small mound of dirt from the dragon's lands, that he would notice. Yes, the Great Forest Clan is allowed on the dragon's lands, but we were expected to ask permission every time we entered them. I shuddered.

Master Onthur shrugged. "Goblins traditionally think in terms of seasons. Probably four months." He gestured for me to follow her. "If you take a step toward her, in her mind you have accepted the deal."

Grumbling under my breath, I followed the Goblin Priestess. She looked ancient. This being the first goblin I've ever met, she might be a spry teenager, but I doubted it. The ground was very slippery, and her gem only cast a faint blue glow.

"Why can't we cast own our light spell?" I asked.

"We're about to be teleported," said Master Onthur. "Goblin magic and human magic don't mix well together." He looked at my chest, "or amulet magic, either."

Oh, joy.

Sure enough, I could see little sparkles of blue light beginning to surround the two of us. Suddenly, the walls shifted. We were someplace else. My amulet felt it. Wow. It was not happy. This was the first time I ever got an emotion from it. I had no idea my amulet had feelings. Was it alive? A question for another day. First, I had to survive this.

The two of us were standing at the edge of the opening of a vast cavern. The light from her staff reflected off thousands of rocks from the high ceiling. What was more amazing were the little mounds of dirt, hundreds of them. There was no particular order, some were closer together and others just off to one side.

"I have only been down here a few times before," Master Onthur stated. Even so, he seemed just as awed as I felt. "Each pile of dirt is from a different part of Avalon."

"So, she listens to dirt?" I asked, confused.

He shrugged. "She's a goblin priestess. Goblins love dirt."

A thought crossed my mind. "How many goblins are down here?" I had no idea these caves even existed. For that matter, I had little enough idea where we were.

"You're welcome to ask her," he said. "I expect she would want even more rare dirt for the answer."

"Ah, no. I'll pass, thank you."

She took my gremlin ball and began chanting while moving around the room. As she passed a mound of dirt, it began to glow, then faded as she walked away. But I detected there was a timing to this; some of the glows lasted longer than others. Eventually her chanting got louder, and the echoes seemed to take on a life of their own. Soon she began walking in a circle, then a smaller circle. The mounds of dirt around her glowed continuously now, a few a bit brighter than others. Eventually she stopped, planted her bone staff, and said, "High dirt. Long deaths."

I had no reference point to where this was in Avalon. "What does high dirt and long death mean?" I asked.

Now the goblin priestess looked back at me like I was an idiot. "Dirt from Noble house, and many buried there over long time," she said to me.

I got it. A long-standing noble house, in their family graveyard. "Which house?" I asked excitedly. "And where is it?"

She eyed me critically, looked around her at the glowing mounds of dirt on the cavern floor as if studying a map. "It is at the setting sun. Before the river, but where the water turns."

"That's all?" I asked, ready to explode. I was exhausted. This was my last lead. Now I owed her dirt from places so dangerous that traveling there would likely get me killed, and all I had in return was a geography riddle.

Master Onthur put a hand on my shoulder to stop my explosion. He said formally, "The dirt is wise."

I got that this was the equivalent of saying "goodbye, and thank you very much," in Goblinish. The priestess led us back, and we teleported again. My amulet made a whining noise in my head, almost like an unhappy puppy. It didn't like being teleported with goblin magic any better the second time. Turning to look back, the short green creature was gone. I guess she didn't come with us.

Now Master Onthur created a ball of light. Considering the darkness, we had been in, it was like looking at the sun. "You have to think like a goblin," he said. "The first part is obvious. It is at the setting sun, means the gremlin bomb was made in the west part of Avalon."

My brain was beginning to re-engage. While climbing back up his stairs, I said, "So before the river, is probably just east of the Coyoun River?"

He looked back at me and nodded. "That would be my guess as well."

"So, what about *where the water turns*?" I asked perplexed. What in the world did *that* mean?

While closing his trap door, he shrugged. "I have no idea. As I said, general. Maybe that's something Royce can help you with."

He gave me a firm stare. "I wouldn't wait too long before delivering the three buckets of dirt. Goblins have long memories."

"What!" I said in frustration. "Before, you said four months."

He smiled down at me. "Ms. Abara, that is only my guess."

While I glared up at Master Onthur, he said deadpan, "I expect delivery of the promised emeralds within a week." He bowed to me. "It is always a pleasure doing business with the Great Forest Clan."

I blew some hair out of my face. Thanks a lot.

Then a wonderful, wicked thought crossed my mind. I was technically working for a Realm Sorceress on this job. *Let's see her get dirt from the haunted lands. Hah!*

CHAPTER 28

Avalon evolves through charters. By law, any group of people regardless of status, are allowed to post a decree for consideration. If enough guild members sign in favor of it, the courts will formalize the request and send it to chambers. There, the high nobles will decide if it should be brought to the floor for a full vote. If it passes, it becomes law in Avalon.

−Guide to Avalon, 4th printing

I vaguely heard Elizabeth say, "Where the water turns," for about the tenth time under her breath as she walked around our map room. Stopping near me, she kicked the side of my chair. "The goblin didn't say anything else?"

After shaking my head to clear it, I said, "No. Sorry."

It was going on hour twenty-six. Now back at the Great Forest Lodge, I took over the map room. We might have our faults, but maps we do well.

I had sent runners for Elizabeth and my other friends, asking if they would join me. All the clues suggested the thief was a noble or associated with one. My friends would have more knowledge than me of which nobles lived out west.

Joanne had been the first to arrive, Julia soon after, within an hour my other friends trickled in. I have good friends.

After saying my goodbyes to Master Onthur, a part of me wanted to head west with my team. But Royce had drilled into me again and again, think. Don't blindly react to the first piece of information you get, so I called my team through my amulet and headed back to the lodge.

Elizabeth had sniffed the air, and cautiously took a step back from me. The Great Forest Lodge doesn't have a shower, but we do have a stream running behind the lodge. So, I went out back. While I waited for one of the first years to fill a tub for me, I tore off my clothes and jumped into the cold water. The rancid smells from the goblin had permeated my clothes and seemed to stick to me. Even after I took a second bath inside with vaguely warm water, my hair still smelled.

Why me?

Joanne giggled as I gave Elizabeth the stink eye.

Let's see you walk behind a goblin priestess without retching, Lady.

Since the Coyoun River was large and went north to south, the area to search was huge. I stood up and stretched, then looked back over all the maps. Still nothing. Julie circled around the table to look at the various maps again. "There's an inlet," she said, pointing to Askook, a mid-sized town off the river. "The docks sort-of form half a circle."

"Maybe," I said dubiously. Calling those docks a half circle would be a stretch. "Who are the noble families in that area?"

Elizabeth shrugged. "I believe all House Pemble."

Joanne tapped the table. "So not our thief, then."

I looked up and tilted my head in question. She shrugged. "House Pemble's concept of education stops at addition. They give lip service to running the schools on their lands."

So, probably not the family where our thief came from. The man I caught honestly seemed to have morals and appeared very educated. It was about this time Dora knocked on the door frame. My team gets nervous around nobility. A lot of people do. She was keeping track of where the various teams were that had headed west on Royce's orders.

"What's up?" I asked her. "Did a team find something?" Since I would have heard it through my amulet as well, probably not. To be a team lead meant you could at least use your amulet to talk to each other through it, but most of them still couldn't focus in on a particular person. I don't understand; it's not that hard. But the idea of "practicing" a skill before we needed it in the field seemed to be a foreign concept, even with Royce pushing them.

Dora looked just as tired as I was, but there was a mischievous smile on her face. I was too tired to play games. "What is it?" I asked snappishly.

Instead of answering, she backed up and Lord James walked into the room. As always, he looked perfect. I exploded, all my anger and frustration coming out. "James," I snarled. "I'm busy."

The room had gone quiet. My friends waited while I glared daggers at the man.

My life was on the line, I had no sleep, my hair still smelled like rotting goblin, and Mr. Perfect was standing there looking like he had a good night's sleep.

Instead of retreating, he said, "I came to help." He glanced around the room at my friends watching us. "When you didn't show up last night at the university, I sent a message to Royce asking if you were okay."

Elizabeth looked at me and raised her eyebrow slightly. I remembered her words from two days ago. *He's a good man.* I never imagined my first date with him would be trying to re-catch the thief. How come every time we meet outside of class, I either smell to high heaven, or I get covered in muck? Maybe there is an Abara curse after all. I sighed. "Come on in, James. Here's the story ..."

As the story unfolded, James spluttered out, "A Sorceress of the Realm implied she would kill you if you didn't find the thief?"

"That isn't going to happen," retorted Elizabeth. "I contacted the Wizard's Council before I came here."

"What?" I screamed at her. "You didn't tell me? For the last hour, I thought my clock was running down."

Joanne banged the flat of her palm on the table to get my attention. "It is, Petra, but for all of us. Avalon City is ready to tear itself apart. If it wasn't for the Wandmaking, Potion's, and Healer's Guilds coming down hard on the other guilds, it would have exploded already. The rest of them are scared that their world is changing, and they want it to go back to the way it was."

I was taken aback. Joanne usually took her cues from Elizabeth and waited until she spoke first. It must be really bad. A part of me wanted to scream, but I unclenched my fist and asked, "How come you didn't tell me?" *Why were they keeping me in the dark about something this big? They are my friends; they should tell me.*

"Is it because I'm not really nobility?" I asked. It hurt to say it. But was I really just the tag-along?

Elizabeth cocked her head at my statement. Then she looked me in the eye. "No Petra, and yes. It's because we don't know what to do ourselves. This is the first time we have actually been involved at the street level. And we thought you already knew, even though I now realize you haven't been in any of our family conferences, where we learned it, sometimes from spying on our fathers and brothers."

She took a deep breath. "Also, it feels good trying to make a difference." Elizabeth looked around the room at her friends, my friends. "The old Avalon wants its ladies in their 'proper' place. Not everyone here has a father like mine, who includes me in these things." She opened her hand, making a large ball of light appear, then closed it, letting it wink out. "Old Avalon be damned. I want the new Avalon. But I don't want to burn it down in the process."

Wow. I had never heard such fierce intensity from her before outside of the gymnasium.

"Um, thanks." But I wasn't sure what I was thanking her for.

"So does the club have a name?" asked James.

We all turned at James's comment. "What are you talking about?" I asked him, perplexed.

He shrugged. "If you form a club and post the charter, then it becomes a legal entity. One of the articles of your charter could be a sort of ladies' investigative service." He looked at us all, staring at him. "Then it gives you legal right to do whatever is in the articles unless someone has the legal oomph to dispute your charter."

Bethiah said in amazement, "A man I don't want to kill. Who knew?"

I snorted. "Wait until he says something stupid. Then I can enjoy hitting him for you."

"Oh," she replied, suddenly happy. "I like that. Do I get to hit him too?"

"No knives," I said quickly.

Bethiah pouted, "Spoilsport. That takes most of the fun out of it."

Joanne said to the air in general, as we pulled out more maps, "The Noble Protectors."

Elizabeth rolled her eyes. "Too formal. Besides, Petra is part of the club."

That made me feel better. As we studied the maps and considered places to send our teams, we discussed names for the club. By the way they talked, I thought they were really considering doing it. During this, James edged his way to stand beside me to help examine the maps. The residual smell about me was fading, but it was still distinctly there. "So that's what Goblins smell like," James said uncertainly. He was probably thinking I might hit him again. After his idea, my friends didn't seem to know what to do with him. He was with me, that was fine, but he somehow became part of our group, and I don't think all of them were ready to accept him yet. Hell, I wasn't sure if I wanted to accept him yet. But I did allow him to take my hand.

I shook my head. "Worse, much worse. I wish I could just have continuously dunked—" I stopped.

"What?" James asked, turning his head to look at me.

"Could it be?" I asked.

Elizabeth tapped the table to get my attention. "Spill. What is it?"

I said slowly, "Where the water turns ... I was wishing I could have attached myself to a waterwheel after I met the goblin to try to rinse the smell away as I went under, again and again and again."

James squeezed my hand. Joanne said, "Damn!"

I yelled for Royce through my amulet.

Royce snorted. "You would need a master thief to get in there. I bet the place is magically trapped to high heaven."

We were looking at some very old maps of the Winton estate, sprawling lands over thousands of acres. They were rather prosperous, and well liked. Unlike House Pemble, House Winton spent money on education for their people. The result had brought prosperity. In addition, they commissioned a system of locks off the Coyoun River which feed a series of waterwheels. Blacksmiths, bakers ... everyone in the area used them. A good waterwheel was equivalent to having ten apprentices. The masters could make more for less money.

From the combined knowledge of my friends, Lander Winton, the youngest son, was about ten years older than me, had been educated on Earth at Duke University. He was a sorcerer and liked to experiment with things. He had an old stone mansion as his work area abutting the family graveyard.

Elizabeth snorted at Royce's comment. "The man's likeable, extremely intelligent, and incredibly devious. If he's our man, that's an understatement. I bet ..." Her voice trailed off.

"What?" I asked. "You've met him before?" Which I thought unlikely, mostly because when I brought up the image of him to my friends, none of them had recognized the man.

"Lord Winton, yes. Briefly. He tried to pull my father into some trading agreement a few years ago." She shrugged. "Father refused. There is a passing resemblance of your illusion to Lord Winton. But I was thinking, what if there's a bastard? Lord Winton plays the high road while bastard brother works in the shadows, both working toward some hidden agenda."

Julia reddened slightly, then shrugged. "Everyone knows that I have a bastard sister. Father is paying for her education." Looking toward Elizabeth, "Your theory would explain a lot. If you're right, the Winton family could disavow the man if he was caught. But they're playing a dangerous game going after another noble house. What's their end goal?"

Bethiah blew some hair out of her face. "Too bad we can't just kill him."

Before I could jump in, Elizabeth growled back. "Grow up! If I'm right, we need them alive or this could blow up Avalon City. While I don't approve of the Realm Sorcerer threatening Petra, she wasn't wrong about how bad this could become."

Bethiah grumbled but was otherwise silent. Joanne looked around the table. "Anyone know any master thieves we can call?" She shrugged. "You need a thief to catch a thief."

An insane idea popped into my head. "Does anyone have any cookies with ginger in them?"

"Starving, are you?" Bethiah shot back at me.

"Oh," James said.

"What?" Bethiah asked.

"Well, do you?" James asked, in a perfectly serious tone, back into the blank stares of Royce and my friends.

CHAPTER 29

The first date is very important. It sets the tone for the relationship going forward.
    –Cook's Guide to Dating

I was wondering if Jumper was going to come. James and I had been sitting on the same park bench for the last twenty minutes. Within my pack were ten Red Dawn cookies, the ones the little guy smelled before.

Two benches farther away were my friends, waiting. I could tell they were discussing James's idea of forming a club. That's how things get started in Avalon. A group of people get together, post articles around the city about whatever their club is about, pay the initiation dues to the courts and off it goes. If enough guild members or nobility sign it, then the articles go before the courts for deliberation. Conversely, if three high nobles and three senior guild members sign against it then it goes up to the Wizard's Council for deliberation. Most posted articles never get anywhere, the members generally can't get enough signatures, so it stays in limbo until the article permit runs out. The members can do whatever it is they wanted to do, but the courts generally won't allow them to renew their proposed charter without a much larger fee or extenuating circumstances. Without their proposed charter being approved, their club or guild is disbanded.

I could imagine the firestorm in Avalon if Elizabeth posted some of the articles I heard suggested. Women, insinuating they have rights like a man! Heads would explode. What many people didn't pay attention to, though, was that there were a lot of women in the lower echelon of the guilds now. So many young men died in the war that young women developing any kind of magical power were being picked up by the guilds out of desperation.

James broke into my thoughts. He leaned over slightly, and I could feel his breath on my neck, giving me little goosebumps. Damn, the man smelled nice. He whispered to me, "Maybe the little guy is afraid of the extra people."

After rolling my eyes, I leaned into him. I was so tired.

I could "feel" him grin at me. "Maybe we should try hugging," he said, chuckling. "Last time he came, you were in my arms."

And then he broke the mood.

"If I remember correctly," I said with a hint of exasperation, "right before Jumper arrived, I was hitting you." I hit him on his thigh for good measure, but not that hard. "Better watch out, maybe he likes strong women. You might have competition."

James went back to softly blowing on my neck. I leaned into him more. We sat there watching the sun set. The far clouds were still tinged with red. Soon it would be dark. While the stories had Reece's Raccoons as generally nocturnal, I didn't know when they woke up. Did they have rounds? Wake up at certain times? No one knew. Three nights ago, Jumper found us at the first bell, an hour past midnight. It was a good six hours until then.

Royce had three teams of people converging on the Winton estate to canvas the area. She was pulling visuals from their amulets and recreating it on our scrying table, then several clan members drafted quick maps before Royce shifted the viewpoints. Like I said, we do maps well. The table is completely different from a traditional scrying table. Our table uses actual materials to make the images, versus glass or water. The dirt, sand and other substances flow together to recreate whatever the clan member on the far end is seeing. Ten minutes ago, I got a report from Royce. <*"It's probably him. The closest team just hit a trap. I'm having them retreat slightly then try a different route."*>

Thinking back to her. <*"Urban's team?"*> Urban Mustor was all about being the "first." It was a thing with him. Little things like safety and looking out for traps; that was for the losers. I overheard Royce shouting at him on more than one occasion.

She snorted. <*"Of course! Jesten's out, but alive."*>

Good. We needed all the manpower we can get, even if Urban's team was full of idiots. They don't understand anything about complementary skill sets. Almost every member of his team is male and large. I swear they start more fights than they stop.

James shifted. I sense he wanted to say something when we heard a soft, "Cookie?"

Turning around, Jumper was right behind our bench. Also, there was another Reece's Raccoon with him, slightly bigger, but the body was leaner, more elegant. My first guess, this was Jumper's older sister.

"Petra frien," said Jumper. "Jumper olth-er sister, she has other glow."

Got it in one. The markings on their face were nearly identical.

Jumper's sister opened her hands and showed us a small green glowing crystal.

James's eyes opened wide. "Is that a healing crystal?" he whispered in awe.

I knelt down in front of Jumper's sister. "I am Petra," I said and tilted my head toward James who had knelt down as well, just to my left. "He is James."

She nervously looked at James, then said to me, "Burrow. I am Burrow."

Now that I was closer, I could tell Burrow wore a small cloth backpack. The stitching was really well done. I bet she made it herself.

Greetings done, I asked, "Is that, er, glow for me?" I said, indicating the magically glowing crystal in her hands.

She nodded and extended her hands. I gently took the crystal from her. "Thank you."

Her face quivered in excitement. "You have more cookies?" she said while standing up higher to get a better look at my backpack.

This was so surreal, I felt like we were at a swap meet. My bet? Burrow had other "acquired" items in her backpack she was willing to trade for ginger-infused cookies. A large part of me felt guilty. While I knew they probably stole the items, the exchange rate was insanely weird. A true healing crystal was very rare; even Elizabeth would have a hard time affording one, if one was ever offered for sale. I essentially just traded a single cookie for something that could sell for more than twice my own weight in gold. And that might well be underestimating it.

"Petra has more cookies," I said, trying not to use words with a "d." That is harder than it sounds. I didn't want Jumper or Burrow to think I was intentionally talking down to them.

Jumper's body quivered in excitement while Burrow gave him a sidelong glance, then backed up a step. "Burrow wants something for clan," she said in all seriousness.

Hmm. "Okay," I said and slowly pulled off my backpack. "I have ten cookies." My guess is Burrow wanted to share with the entire clan. Maybe I could get an entire clan of Reece's Raccoons helping me. At my "ten cookies," Jumper ran forward and hugged my leg. I gently touched his furry head and stroked his back. Did he just begin purring? I stroked him again, and he hugged me harder.

"I want something too," I said. "Petra needs help."

Burrow cocked her head. "Honor help, or home help?" she asked. I could tell Burrow had some understanding of negotiation.

I glanced at James, and he shrugged at me. "The little guy really seems to like you." After stroking him once, he added, "Probably honor help."

Burrow nodded at James then pointed at me. "Jumper must walk," she said in all seriousness. "He walk *to* Petra."

"Ah, what is, '*To* Petra?'" Did I just become a mommy?

My friends were slowly edging their way toward us. Burrow gave them a glance, then hissed at them. Okay far enough, she's got boundaries. "Jumper of age to walk," she said. "He is allowed to choose guide. Jumper walk *to* Petra."

Oh. Not a mommy then, sort-of a big sister. Jumper looked up at me. "Please?"

How in the world do I get myself into these things? James started laughing, so I hit him with my free hand. Burrow nodded respectfully at me, like hitting males was the thing to do, which just made James laugh harder.

"Jumper," I said. "Why me? My life is very dangerous."

He stood back and looked up at me. "Petra can jump, Petra calls spirits, and Petra calls magic." He thumped his chest. "Jumper to learn calling magic."

I put my hands to my face. He wants an amulet. What in the world am I going to tell Royce?

James started laughing harder. He asked, "What do you mean Petra jumps?"

Burrow pointed at my friends. "Petra jumps with friends. Petra is a jumper."

Elizabeth was close enough to hear Burrow. "They must watch us at night while we're in the gymnasium. I had no idea they were there."

I had to remind myself we were on the clock. I pulled out all ten cookies and gave one to Jumper, who began eating it immediately. "Petra has honor problem." I gave Burrow the simplified version of the story. She listened without interruption. As I finished, she nodded at me and said, "I will get Royal." Like that made all the sense in the world, then she was gone.

Jumper was both excited and reluctant to meet my friends. He started bouncing then doing flips ... It took me few seconds to see it; he was recreating some of our routines. When Jumper was introduced to Elizabeth his eyes went wide, then he looked at the ground.

"What's wrong, Jumper?" I asked. He was okay with meeting everyone else. Hell, half of my friends wanted Jumper to go home with them.

While still looking at the ground, he said, "She is Royal. Jumper must *to* walk."

There it was again, the emphasis on the to, like it was a journey. Elizabeth said slowly, "I think it's a rite of passage. Jumper is male. I bet he must go on a quest," she emphasized, "to earn an adult name. I bet Royal is their way of saying the group elder."

Jumper grabbed onto my leg. "Yes, *to* walk. Jumper is small name."

James asked, "How long does walking take, Jumper, and where do you need to go?"

Jumper suddenly jumped onto the back of the bench. "Flower is very pretty. If I call magic, Flower will see me." He tilted his head and added, "Petra sees you. I want Flower to see me."

James grinned at me. "See it's official. You're my girlfriend."

Bethiah snorted.

I hit James, and Jumper laughed. "I bet Flower hits hard," he said in all seriousness, like it was a mating ritual. My life is so weird.

The biggest Reece's Raccoon I had ever seen said to Elizabeth, "The Haystack Clan greets the Navartis Clan." At a guess, I'd say he weighed 45 pounds. When standing erect, he was taller than her knees, but not quite waist high. There were about thirty other Reece's Raccoons around us, ranging in size from almost Jumper's size to almost twice as large. Also, this one wore a cape and a hat.

She curtseyed. "The Navartis Clan will hear the Haystack Clan."

Elizabeth knows how to do pomp when she needs to. The two of them looked at each other, sort of weighing what to say next, now that the pleasantries had been done. Had this ever happened before?

"What will the Navartis Clan offer to the Haystack Clan to help Petra and her mate?" Royal said.

My mate!

Elizabeth only gave the briefest of smiles.

Hell. At the rate this was progressing, James and I would be married by morning.

Elizabeth suggested, "Twenty cookies?"

The large Reece's Raccoon snorted. "A child's offering."

Interesting; he could pronounce the "d" sound without a problem. I wondered if their palate changed as they grew.

Elizabeth tilted her head. This was a real negotiation. "Please explain *to Petra*," she asked, glancing at Jumper (who held onto my leg), then back up to the big Reece's Raccoon in front of her.

"If Petra agrees, she will have three challenges for him. She may also teach him to help succeed at each challenge if she wishes. Once Jumper has completed all three, then she will name him. Today he is *to* Petra. If he succeeds, he will be *from* Petra, with an adult name."

"Very well," replied Elizabeth, without missing a beat. "Petra will have your answer in three days."

Now it was the Reece's Raccoon's turn to tilt his head. He looked around at all his fuzzy friends. "The Haystack Clan wishes to have land. Our own land."

Okay, this just got serious.

Elizabeth's eyes went wide. "Ladies," she said, looking at all of us, "I think we need to adjust the Charter we were about to write. This is going to create quite a stir." Then, formally addressing the Royal, she replied, "The Navartis Clan will sponsor you, but Avalon must decide. Where do you want your land to be? Here, next to the University?"

There was silence for ten seconds.

"Yes, here. Agreed," Royal replied back, and then took off his hat and bowed to Elizabeth.

My god, Jumper could whine. "No, Jumper," I said for the third time. "You are not coming with us. You do not have an adult name." James and I demanded he stay behind. I almost felt like the two of us were arguing with our child over his bedtime, but in this case our child was a grumpy twenty-five pound talking raccoon.

Jumper was about to protest again, when Burrow hit him on the back of the neck. "You are *to* Petra," she said. "Petra has spoken."

Jumper looked up at James, hopefully. When James reiterated my "no," the little guy picked up a pebble and tossed it in the fountain.

We lost sight of him as he wandered off into the darkness. I hoped he was going home, wherever that was.

Now we could focus in on our fuzzy thieves. Not including Burrow, there were seven other adult Reece's Raccoons whom Royal had picked out to come with us. They arranged themselves into two groups, based on sex; five males and three females. The eldest of each group were the de facto leaders, Winter and Star. Winter was by the far the oldest, the largest and, I thought, the most intelligent. He was fascinated by my illusions of the images I pulled from our scrying table back at our lodge and asked some good questions about the traps our advance teams had encountered so far. It made me wonder if Reece's Raccoons got smarter as they got older.

Star's intelligence apparently leaned more toward making things. She and her friends wore handmade leather vests decked out with odd little tools and tiny glass bottles containing who-knows-what.

James was staring at the vests. I knew him well enough now that I could tell was looking at the magic. After I gave him a nudge, he looked at me in wonder. "There are all sorts of magical components in those vials. It's like a home-made magical chemistry set."

Star gave him a nasty smile. "We make the wards go boom. Fun."

"Uh, how big of a boom?" I asked in apprehension.

Star gave me a bigger smile "Depends on how tight the trap is."

I was about to ask what she meant by that, but I was interrupted by Royce. Instead of my hearing her through my amulet, she was walking toward us carrying a bundle under her arm. Behind her were ten others, all wearing clan amulets I didn't recognize right away in the darkness. As these newcomers approached, icons began appearing in my mind; little floating images of their faces with their clan symbol just underneath. With Royce were five from the Mole Clan, three from the Fox Clan, and two from the Archer Clan. Technically, the Great Forest Clan outranked them. These were about the only clans we did.

I gave Royce an inquiring look while telling Winter and Star, "Don't run. They're friends."

At my comment, the Reece's Raccoons stopped backing up, but still looked apprehensive. The ten Royce brought with her seemed just as apprehensive at approaching Elizabeth and her noble friends. Like I said before, a lot of people are afraid to be around nobles.

I looked behind Royce, at her new companions. They were staring between the Reece's Raccoons and my friends. "What this?"

"They're your additional help for the night." Royce shook out the bundle under her arm to reveal two thin silver-trimmed cloaks with a seal sewn into them.

"No," I said flatly. I was not going to be an agent of the Sorcerers of the Realm. Elizabeth was staring at me, open-mouthed.

"Yes, you are," said Royce. "Both of you are." She handed over two waxed sealed letters. "The first is from the Wizard's Council, granting both of you authority till the morning light. The second is to be given to Lord Winton if he decides to be stubborn."

I was about to explode at her when James touched my back. "What?" Now my anger was directed at him.

"Petra, she's right. If a group of nobles got together and stormed another local's land, then it would be open war in Avalon. Think about it. Ancient grudges would rise again to the surface, and nobles would begin raising armies to attack each other. That's what Realm Knights are for, to keep the various powers in check and bring them to the courts instead of men and women dying in the fields."

"Petra," said Elizabeth slowly. "He's right."

"Yeah? Well, why isn't Miss I'm-going-to-kill-you front and center, then? She was the Realm Sorceress involved in this from the start."

Royce sighed. "For the same reasons as before. They have no official proof. All we have are the ravings of a Goblin priestess, her cryptic message, and then our best guess of where the breadcrumbs lead. A second-rate lawyer would tear apart the prosecution's case in a minute and get it thrown out of court."

Elizabeth added, "I get it. You and James are the best witnesses. Both of you saw the man in action and caught him. If you get close enough and both agree Lord Winton or his bastard brother is the man, then the prosecution has something to work with." Turning to look at Royce, she asked, "Why the second letter?"

"It's a decree from the Wizard's Council stating that the Winton house attacked the Manchester house with no provocation. It grants the Calvit School the right to march on the Winton estates and hunt down the Winton family. The courts would then appoint another noble line as guardian of the lands. If you *and* James believe you found the right person, give the letter to the family elder. They either cooperate or the council officially posts the decree to the courts."

Royce indicated the ten she brought with her. "Along with your team, these others all report to you and James." She pointedly looked at the Reece's Raccoons and my friends. "And any other support you two bring along. Sunrise is ten hours away."

Chapter 30

Our parents use a tracking spell on our wands to keep tabs on where we are. Elizabeth designed a spell when she was twelve that interrupts the tracking spell to suggest we are at a friend's house when in fact we are someplace else. Watching Petra and Elizabeth stand together is amazing. I can only guess who will flinch first, those two or Avalon.

–Lady Julia Lohort

We were near the Winton estate. I thought I was quiet when I moved through the forested area to help spot any guards, but the two from the Fox Clan made my breathing sound loud. They could cover more territory than I thought possible between the fifteen-minute clock bells without making a sound. They weren't invisible, but something else. It was like they blended into the background. After scouting the castle, we met up at our pre-arranged spot about a mile away. In total, we had spotted five guards patrolling in two groups.

"Did you see any of them check in at the castle?" asked James and shifted the map he held so others could see it. He had pulled it from our map room before we left.

Trilt, the older of the two Fox Clan members pointed to a small building at the front of the castle. "That's a guard house. The first guard team checked in ten minutes past the first (quarter) bell, second team at the second bell."

James shifted the faint ball of light hovering above the map in his hands so it traced the route the guards walked. He looked up at Trilt. "Is that about right?"

She looked at him approvingly and put a hand on his arm. "Yes. Those guards check in every twenty minutes."

Through my amulet, broadcasted only to Trilt, I said angrily, <*"Back off. He's mine."*>

What was I doing? At what point did I lay a claim on the man?

Trilt grinned at me but pulled her hand down. <*"His scent is not on you, Petra Abara of the Great Forest Clan. Tonight, I report to you, but tomorrow I do not."*>

James tapped the map softly. He seemed oblivious to Trilt being interested in him. Good boy, stay that way. Suddenly I remembered all the women trailing him at the university. Was he really that clueless? Part of me hoped so. If it came down to some of the noble women versus me, I bet I wouldn't stand a chance.

What was I doing? I thought to myself. *Get my head in the game!* These thoughts had to be because I was exhausted. We were about to begin an assault, I hadn't had any real sleep, and I was wondering how many women I might need to fight off. I am not my sister I growled to myself; I don't know if I even want to be with the man. My unconscious however, seemed to have a different opinion on the matter. Trilt grinned at me like she could hear my thoughts.

<*"Shut up."*> I told her.

James looked at me. "I bet they check in like that throughout the night. Let's position ourselves so we can quietly take on each group at a place where anyone from the top of the castle can't see them."

I had never been on a midnight assault before and didn't think of that. I put a hand on his arm while pointedly looking at Trilt. "Good idea. Let's do it that way."

As we moved closer to the castle, I heard faint laughing whisper in my mind. *<"His scent must be on you, or it doesn't count.">*

<"Shut up.">

<"What did you shoot them with?"> I asked Rainer. He was one of the two from the Archer Clans who reported to me for tonight. I had never seen a blowgun before and was a bit dubious when I saw the little dart. Rainer and Selcor had some gooey substance in which they dipped the darts in just before loading them. A soft *swiff* and each of the five guards walking around the edges of the Winton estate fell to the ground, asleep. Well, would you look at that.

<"Elder rituse extract.">

Oh. Rituse vines were the apex hunters of the plant world. The scent from the flowers would make an animal sleepy. Then the vines would wrap around its victims, digesting them over a period of days. Small rituse vines where occasionally found growing in the remote areas of Avalon City. When cats, dogs and other small animals suddenly disappeared, often rituse vines were suspected. Once discovered, the vines were burned out; you don't want to let them grow big. I heard stories that in the wilds, massive versions of these vines could take over an entire forest.

Ask questions later; we had a job to do.

<"Any other guards?"> I asked Dora, my second in command.

<"Not outside. But we just found our first magical trap; I've never seen anything like it. I think the Fuzzballs are up.">

After Dora gave me her location, I looked at Winter and Star. "Star, your team is with Dora, she found a trap. Winter, follow the other team, and see if you can find another way into the castle."

Team two was led by Hebin; he had the five Mole Clan members with him. If you wanted to track someone through a cave or sewer system, then the Mole Clan was your best bet. I literally don't understand why they even exist as a clan. Why would anyone want to join them? However, for tonight they might prove useful.

This was an old castle, but well maintained. No one builds castles anymore. I had been to a crumbling one on Elizabeth's estates, where we were celebrating Julia's fifteenth birthday and she wanted to have it in a real castle. The Navartis family hadn't bothered with the upkeep because it cost too much. Modernizing a castle can cost more than building something better to live in to replace it.

The one in front of us was even older than the crumbling Navartis Castle but had been recently repaired. Also, the graveyard next to it was gigantic, with all the usual memorial stones and statues. Creeping around at night added immensely to the scary factor.

If we discovered a trap that woke the dead as zombies, I was so out of here.

Let the Wizard's Council deal with him if he turned out to be a necromancer. Dora almost broke down when she learned about the graveyard and that we were getting close to it at night. For her, as she described it, the darkness is full of monsters. Since she can do things with shadows which seem impossible to me, maybe the nightmares she's so afraid of are real. This just reinforced that wherever she came from was someplace I didn't ever want to go.

I put her on the frontal assault team versus the let's-circle-around-the-graveyard team. Team three acted as lookouts. I had spread them out around the area in case there were more guards wandering about that we had missed. According to James, we probably had a limited amount of time before someone in the castle expected one or more of the guards we had dropped to check in. James said that timed check-ins are a basic security measure.

This was the part I hated the most, the waiting. I wanted to be front and center, but this time I was one of the people in charge. The other reason was that James was beside me, and as much as I hated the idea, we were the "officers" for this operation.

He and I were now alone in the dark at the edge of the forest facing the castle. Elizabeth and my other friends politely retreated to support the lookout team.

Don't say anything stupid, I told myself. I wasn't sure if I was just telling myself that, or mentally pleading with him as well.

"My father says he's sorry."

Huh? What? "Sorry?" I asked. "Sorry for what?"

This wasn't the way I thought a conversation with him was going to start tonight.

James pulled off his pack and offered me a cookie. "For yelling at you during the trial."

I gave him a glare but took the cookie. They were good cookies, and I felt like I was eating sugar just to keep my muscles going.

In the darkness, I could sense James turn away slightly, and heard him rummage in his backpack.

Standing back up, now holding a thick tube, James looked directly at me. "He's trying, Petra. Would you be willing to meet him over a beer?" James unscrewed the top, and suddenly I smelled coffee. With a wave of his wand over the container, I felt a hint of heat.

"Hot coffee!" he announced.

"You're using my lack of sleep to your advantage," I said. But I didn't turn down the offered coffee. "You play dirty."

James sat down on a log and pointedly look at me. He did bring me cookies and coffee. After sitting down next to him, I took a sip and leaned into him. He put his arm around me. That felt nice.

"How is it," I asked between sips, "that you still smell good?" My mind was fantasizing about reaching under his shirt to run my hand across his chest. *Shut up mind, more coffee.* I took another sip.

"You never answered my question," James replied.

"Which question?" But I knew what he meant, about sitting down with his father. I countered, "What does your mother want?"

James laughed. "To marry off my two younger sisters without our house exploding. Kiera has two offers, and I understand a third is arriving. Our house is one big game of cat and mouse. Aspen's coming-out ball is in three weeks. Especially with Aspen, Mother is running out of patience. Between my father and me, we've received over ten requests to be the first to dance with her."

I sat there drinking coffee, listening to him describe his house of chaos and missed my family. Then the memories of my sister surfaced. James must have picked up on my sudden tension. "Your sister?"

I took another drink of coffee. This was really good coffee. "I wish my father or older brother had been around after the war. Someone who could have influenced my sister's decisions. She never listened to me."

James kissed the top of my head. "I find that hard to believe. People listen to you, Petra. I bet your sister did too. She just, well, got caught up in something she shouldn't have."

"I bet your mother is hoping for grandchildren soon." As soon as the words were out of my mouth, I wanted to take them back. I was talking about his sisters, but the implication in my words were about me too.

Me, a mommy! Not anytime soon. I wanted to take more classes. And, well, what did I want beyond that? After the war, it was all about surviving. Now that I had found a home in the Great Forest Clan, I wasn't ready to settle down yet. You could be married and part of the clan; that wasn't a problem. Some who started a family became reservists, buy many didn't. Part of it was the pay; a basic member didn't get much, but it was something. Reservists get only a little bit of that. As a team leader I got more, plus a part of any bonus the clan earned. For all of us, the housing, basic food, training, and education were paid for by the clan. So, unless you wanted to eat out or enjoy other activities, you didn't need to spend much. Surprisingly, many did. Like my sister, once a coin hit their hand, they had to spend it.

Did I want to be a mother? Someday, maybe. Since I was the youngest, I never really saw what my parents had to go through to raise my brother. My sister could shift from a model child to a pain in the behind in the span of five minutes. Also, any gymnastic aspirations I had would end once I was pregnant. While I don't think of myself as beholden to having children, the underlying expectation within Avalon society expected a woman to embrace that path at some point, preferably sooner. If I had any native magical talent and my husband was in a guild, they would be giving him bonuses for each baby we produced. While not law, the children of a particular guild have a tendency to grow up working in the same guild. Considering the amount of people we lost in the war, I sort of understood what was happening, but it made me feel like half of Avalon was brood mares for the other half.

"Copper for your thoughts," James asked.

Damn, the man was being polite about this. He had the opportunity to use my grandchildren remark, and he was letting me off the hook. I tentatively reached over and touched his chest; there was some muscle under his shirt. "After this is over, a beer with your father sounds nice."

I put down the coffee mug and looked up at him, my hand still on him. James twisted and pushed some stray hair out of my face. He smelled so good. Just as he started leaning down to kiss me, I heard from Hebin, <*"They found it. The Mole Clan says there's a tunnel in the graveyard that leads into the castle."*>

A deep thought bubbled up inside me. It wanted me to tell Hebin to wait so James could kiss me.

Shut up, brain.

Pushing against James, I said, "Wait. They found a tunnel."

Reaching out to Dora, I asked, <*"How are you doing with the magical traps?"*>

<*"Um. Petra,"*> she replied nervously. <*"They found three of them and have linked them together to set them all off at once. Star seems really happy, like this will be big."*>

Standing up, I grabbed James's hand. "It's about to begin. You're a noble, you take the front and introduce yourself after the traps are disarmed. I'm heading toward the graveyard. Once we set these off, I bet our thief is going to run out the back door. Without him, were back at square one. And I want some payback."

I met Hebin in the graveyard. Now that we knew what to look for, I could sort of make out the lever that opened the hidden door. It was built into a statue. Twist the marble hand, pull down on the arm and a well-hidden trap door opened slightly. I would have missed it completely, but I guess that's what Mole Clan is good at, finding things underground. It made me wonder if they had a spell in their amulet that helped them with these kinds of things, like my spell for tracking blood.

"Do we wait for him to come out, or head into the tunnels?" Hebin asked me, quietly.

"What's with the rope?" I asked. Several of the Mole Clan were pulling up on two ropes when Winter appeared. Oh, they had lowered him into the hole.

Once he pulled himself out completely, he shook his whole body. "Bad traps. Deadly. Need more time if we don't want to die."

Shera, the leader of the Mole Clan group with me, said, "There are three bodies down there. They didn't die well."

"Uh, how do you know?"

She shrugged. "My amulet can feel them. Their spirits are unhappy."

Okay, keeping Dora up front was a good idea.

Shera pulled me to the side and nervously whispered to me, "You do know your friend, Dora, is a shadowcaster?"

I understood her concern. Shadowcasters were instinctually shunned. Fear what you don't understand and all that. The other part was obvious. Most people feared the night to some degree or another. The sun brought light and life; the darkness, wolves and other creatures that stalked you.

I rolled my eyes. "She is not evil any more than you or I."

Shera looked at me sideways. Probably trying to determine if I had a hex on me. Then she walked back to stand with the other four Mole Clan members.

I knelt down and indicated Hebin and Winter do the same. After whispering out a plan I ended with, "Let's wait for him to come up." It was about this time I felt the hair on my arms being tugged at by an invisible force. Uh, oh. Looking at Winter, I noticed some of his fur seemed to be frizzing out. "How big is Star's explosion going to be?"

Before Winter could respond, a huge blue comet streaked up into the sky and exploded perhaps a hundred feet above the castle. As the energy expanded, it seemed to be taking on the form of a giant butterfly. Then it broke apart into falling sparkles.

Holy Crap. How in the world did she harness the energy of the traps to do that?

"Big," said Winter, in wonder. "Wow."

Everyone started looking between the falling blue lights and me. "Okay. People, hide. Let's wait for him to come up. Move on my signal."

I closed the trap door by moving the statue's arm up again.

We could hear shouting from the top of the castle, light spells going off everywhere up there. I heard James's voice from a distance telling them to open up, and that he was a realm sorcerer. Since we were in the rear of the castle, we didn't hear all the back and forth, but I got that there was at least one person who wanted to pick a fight. Suddenly I realized how real this was; someone could die. It might be James, or one of my friends. My stomach went into a tight ball when it dawned on me if Elizabeth or one of the other high nobles was injured or worse, this could get very ugly, very fast. It sucks being in charge and not knowing what was happening.

After another round of shouting, the trap door opened, and in the darkness, I could see the shadow of a man emerging. "Boo Boo says hi," I said, grinning at him while calling the strongest ball of light right in his face. As he started to twist away Hebin's massive fist slammed into the side of his head.

CHAPTER 31

The foundation of our state is the education of its youth.
–Diognese

Lord Winton poured brandy into snifters for us, and handed them to James, me, and Elizabeth. He leaned back in his chair with his and took a sip. After glancing over at his brother, who was still tied up, he asked, "How did you track us?"

Several responses came to mind, but I settled on, "I'm from the Great Forest Clan. That's what we do." Better not to give him any clues. Let him come to us.

"Very well," he said and bowed slightly to me. Then he addressed Elizabeth. "Lady, I respect your father. What part do you play in all this?"

"We don't want to see Avalon City, or perhaps all the former Pendragon Lands, burn to the ground." She looked around at all the other ladies with her, my friends and hers. "Petra and James asked for our help."

He swirled his brandy slightly. "Interesting. Neither do I, but sometimes it is necessary to allow the flames to spread to save the forest." His voice deepened and with a hint of an aggressive tone he asked, "Are all my guards still alive?"

"Yes, they are," James replied. "However, one of them on the roof refused to surrender immediately. He's being tended to." Looking at me, James added, "Petra, I believe the man you caught is our thief. What do you think?"

For an answer, I pulled out the second letter and placed it on the table next to Lord Winton. He made no move to pick it up but eyed me as if I was suddenly more interesting.

"This is in case you decide not to cooperate," I said.

Ignoring he letter, he addressed Elizabeth again. "What do you want Avalon to become, my lady? If I'm right, your mother is probably trying to marry you off to some boring older man so the whole absurd play can be reenacted all over again. I applaud you for trying something different." He twisted slightly to look at our thief. "You can untie my half-brother. Do you agree not to run away, Franklin?"

Our thief laughed. "Oh indeed. If possible, could I have a bit of that brandy?"

"There you go," said Lord Winton. "On my honor, I pledge he will hold true to his word." He eyed both James and me with amusement. "Lord and Lady of the Realm, the stage is yours."

As I began to cut him free, Elizabeth asked, "Did your half-brother take the contract for the Glass Blowers Guild independent of you, and are either of you involved in the planned kidnaping of Lady Manchester?"

Lord Winton said, "For the second, no. I understand a group with little scruples has been hired, but before you ask, I don't know who they are."

With a snap, the last piece of rope was cut away. "You're wasted in the Great Forest Clan," said our thief, as he massaged his wrists. "How is Boo Boo?"

"Doing well. He is working with first-year clan members who have never ridden a horse before."

"Thank you for being kind to him," he said, in what appeared to me to be sincerity, as he accepted the brandy snifter from Lord Winton.

"I don't get you," I said. "You're educated, polite, seem to have morals, yet at the same time, a thief?"

He put a hand to his chest as if I wounded him. "A thief! My dear, Lady Manchester would have found all her belongings returned within a day. What I want is what my brother wants—to stop this appalling disease called ignorance."

"Okay," James interjected. "You have bought yourself a few minutes. Explain."

Our thief looked at Lord Winton and held up his glass. "Should I take this, brother, or will you?"

"I think I should take this one." Lord Winton said while swirling his brandy glass once more. He bowed to Elizabeth again. "Avalon is at a crossroads, my Lady. We don't have Earth's grasp of technology." He laughed to himself and shook his head. "Just getting the waterwheels designed and installed was a huge effort. Not because I didn't have the manpower, but for the simple reason there was precious few who understood the math and had any practical knowledge of the forces involved." He shrugged. "Within a generation we will be overrun. Enough of us aren't adapting. Earth, especially the Republic, understands that in order to expand, they need to grasp the fundamentals of magic. Furthermore, they don't see the machine as a threat, just the opposite. We have the upper hand right now because technology is even less stable on the other worlds with which Avalon has direct connections. But Avalon is a place where some technology, if designed properly, can function, in addition to magic. If we don't harness this, soon we will become the puppets of Earth." He drained his glass. "To adapt, we need to educate the masses, unshackle them, and watch in wonder as they build."

Elizabeth tilted her head. "And the women? Or does your vision only include the men?"

Our thief laughed. "My lady, Avalon cannot have one without the other. Either we all become slaves to Earth, or we all adapt."

Lord Winton tapped the letter beside him. "I assume this a declaration from the Wizard's Council? If I don't play nice, they tighten the screws."

James took a sip of brandy. "They're calling in the Calvit School of Magic and Combat if you don't agree to our terms."

Lord Winton sniffed. "Just like the Council to have someone else do their dirty work. Very well, what are your terms?"

James and I looked at each other. James tilted his head. "Petra?"

"Your half-brother comes with us. He agrees to cooperate fully with the Realm Officers and to stay under house arrest until the Realm Officers close the case. Afterwards, he will serve a one-year sentence working on the Notir University campus as part of their security team." I glanced at our thief.

"Agreed," he said. "Very diplomatic."

Lord Winton smiled. "I take it there's more."

"Two things," I said. "First, your half-brother will assist me in fulfilling several obligations I was charged with in order to find him. And, the second is for you, Lord Winton. Elizabeth and the other noble ladies here are about to post two charters. You will publicly sign and support both and in the case of the second, offer up lands, which you may have to buy, in Avalon City."

"Interesting," he said. He seemed to be looking at me with renewed interest. He glanced at James and winked. "From the way you two interact I assume you are wooing her, and she is returning your affection?"

I cocked my head at him. What game was he playing here? Playing for time? He was cornered, I and he knew it.

"I suffer a few bruises along the way," James replied. "But I think we're getting there."

Lord Winston smiled, then turned to me. "If you decide he isn't the right man for you, look me up, young lady. While I am, I admit, a bit old for you, I still have some good years left in me." Before James or I could respond to that direct statement, he said with a chuckle, "To whom would I be offering lands?"

"Lord Winton," I said. "Have you ever met a Reece's Raccoon before? Let me introduce you to Winter." His eyes went wide as I fetched a nervous Winter and escorted him into the room.

"Hello, mate," said Winter. "She's a crafty one, isn't she?"

Our thief started the round of laughter.

CHAPTER 32

Sorcerer Petotum was a hero during the Avalon war. He is also the youngest sorcerer ever to be tapped for the Wizard's Council. Considering his responsibilities, the man is rarely seen without his coffee mug. Rumor has it when chambers suggested raising import taxes on coffee, a noble asked, "So who's going to tell Sorcerer Petotum about this?" The measure was dropped, and the subject never came up again.

—Avalon Press

L eave me *alone,*" I screamed, and reached out from under my covers to grab something. Without opening my eyes, I threw it at my door. Whatever I just threw made a satisfying thunk. The knocking stopped. Good!

I rolled over and tried to go back to sleep. After James and I handed over the thief to the Realm Sorceress, Royce debriefed me. Then I crashed in my bed. Ah sleep ...

Knock, Knock.

Someone is so going to die. "What!" I yelled, as I dragged myself out of bed and opened the door.

A young man, maybe thirteen, was there staring at me open mouthed.

"What?" I asked again, bleary-eyed.

Blinking to clear my vision I followed his startled gaze; he was looking at my chest. That's when I noticed I didn't have any clothes on. Not enough sleep. Don't care. "What. Do. You. Want?" I asked through gritted teeth. Apparently, my anger was focusing the magic in my amulet. I could feel something taking shape behind me. Didn't care.

The kid stumbled backwards and said in a whisper, "Royce wants to see you, ma'am."

Ignoring the ma'am, I glared at him. Part of me wanted to yell at the universe and tell everyone to jump in a lake. "Fine." I growled and slammed the door. I could feel the forming energy break apart. Problem for another day. Too tired now.

Grumble, grumble. I stumbled around the room. Shirt check ... no bra. Sigh. Take shirt off, put on bra. Put on shirt. Just simple things required an enormous focus. The part of my brain that kept time seemed to be stuck. How much sleep did I get? It didn't feel like very much.

I looked at myself in the mirror. I wasn't wearing my undergarments on the outside, my hair was somewhat combed, and I still looked like death warmed over. If James saw what I looked like in the morning before coffee, any romantic overtures he had would die a quick death.

Wait! Did I agree to meet his father?

Yes, I did. I distinctly remember saying yes right before he was about to kiss me. I briefly banged my head against the mirror. What am I doing?

As I stomped my way across the lodge, people gave me a stare and got out of my way. *Didn't want to talk to you, anyway.* From the angle of the sun through the windows, my guess was that it was somewhere around ten in the morning. That meant I got about five hours of sleep.

Approaching Royce's closed door, I noticed three Sorcerers of the Realm standing guard. Didn't care. Ignoring them, I walked forward to knock on her door. One of them made as if to stop me. I glared at him. "So help me, if this is something stupid, I will find you." Was I threatening a Sorcerer of the Realm? Yes, I was.

"Petra Abara?" asked the one with the widest gold trim on his collar.

"Yes."

He opened the door and stepped aside, so I could go in. *Okay, you get to live today.* My eyes saw it immediately. There was a steaming cup of coffee at the edge of Royce's large desk. I strode toward it, picked it up, drank deeply and sighed. That's when I noticed all the other people in the room were staring at me. Realm Sorceress Bardot was standing against the far wall. However, she didn't have that "I'm in charge" attitude about her this time. Instead, she had more of a "please, don't notice me," expression on her face. That's when my brain registered Royce was standing at attention as well. I blinked, turned and stared. It took my brain a second or two to register the two people next to me.

Sorcerer Petotum of the Wizard's Council was smiling at me. "That's okay. I didn't need any more coffee this morning, which you clearly did."

My foggy brain froze. I had just stolen that cup of coffee from the person with the single greatest authority in the city of Avalon. The man was a legend. During the war, he was instrumental in helping to lead the Republic's special forces across the Eastern Mountains. He was also believed to be the single youngest person, ever, on the Wizard's Council. In his spare time, he led expeditions into the Bookstore to recover people who were overdue returning to the outside world (in other words, people who had gotten lost inside it). Rumor put his success rate at almost ninety percent. I bet the man never sleeps as there simply aren't enough hours in the day to allow him any. And I just took his coffee. He probably lived on the stuff.

If someone took my coffee in the morning, I would be deciding which way they were going to die. Instead, he was still smiling at me.

"Hi," I said and put his coffee mug back on the desk. My brain was suddenly very awake. "Sorry about the coffee. As you are probably already aware, I'm Petra Abara."

Royce cleared her throat and pointedly looked at me. "Petra, Council Wizard Petotum and Realm Commander Othiel would like a word with you."

My gaze switched to the older man with a full head of white hair who was standing next to Council Wizard Petotum. Realm Commander Othiel. He had a deep scowl on his face, and I felt like he was deciding how he wanted to bury me. Either of these two could stomp our entire clan flat. Realm Commander Othiel looked like he wanted to. He glared at Realm Sorceress Bardot then swung his piercing gaze to me. He demanded, "Who else did you tell about the tomb in the Haunted Lands?"

I could feel gathering energy around him as he spoke. Eeep! Brain, start. Mouth, talk. "Uh, well Royce and James, I mean Lord James. Also Master Onthur knows as well, as he was translating what the Goblin Priestess said into something that almost made sense to me."

"We have already visited the Vimmer estate this morning," replied Sorcerer Petotum with an easy smile. "Young Lord James was very cooperative. That's where I had my first cup of coffee."

While pulling out a thick scroll and unwrapping it on Royce's desk, Sorcerer Petotum said, "We would like you, Royce, and Realm Sorceress Bardot to sign this Codicil."

"Um, you make it sound like I get a choice."

Sorcerer Petotum tilted his head at my comment. "Master Onthur had the same choice. He displayed a certain reluctance to sign it. At first."

Realm Commander Othiel cracked his knuckles, as if wishing I'd refuse to sign it too, so he could crush the life out of me. He looked like he wanted to suggest how much he'd enjoy my not signing right away.

"If you choose to sign it, then you may *only* discuss any information you know about the tomb with members of the Wizard's

Council." Sorcerer Petotum pulled out a long thin wooden box. Opening it revealed several quills and what looked like small bandages from Earth.

"Ah, but what about my obligation to the Goblin Priestess?"

"As far as you are concerned, that has been discharged. What you used to owe has been addressed by the Wizard's Council," replied Sorcerer Petotum with a sunny smile. "Which hand do you write with, Ms. Abara? I assume it is your left. Most people hold their coffee cups in the hand they write with."

I nodded, but said cautiously, "Uh, why do you want to know?"

He held up a quill. "For the blood, Ms. Abara. You will be signing this codicil in blood." He gave me another smile. "Or would you like to explain to the dragon why you are taking dirt from his lands?"

Between getting fried by the dragon or signing my name it was an easy decision. I shot both hands forward. "No time at all. Ready to go."

Sorcerer Petotum pulled out a quill and pricked my index finger on my right hand. Blood seeped up into the tip.

"Thank you, Ms. Abara," he said, holding out the quill for me to take. "Avalon City would hate to lose your services."

Chapter 33

Cogito, ergo sum.
−Rene Descartes

fterwards, Sorcerer Petotum asked me to come outside with him.
Uh-oh. I had signed his scroll in blood, my name was just below James's. Below my name were signature lines for Royce, then the two Realm Sorcerers. Part of me found it surreal that I signed before them. Usually in legal documents, I'm told, the highest person signs first. Maybe Codicils are different. The article on top, written in swirling gold-and-red lettering read:

"If the signed attempts to convey via *any means,* intentionally or otherwise, the location of the tomb of the Unspoken (you know who she is), except to a member of the Wizard's Council or a to another signatory of this Codicil, they will be instantly teleported together with any person or people they have told to Room 843B-5 in the Bookstore."

I asked uncertainly, "So James and I could, um, talk about it, and we would be okay?"

Sorcerer Petotum held the door open for me. "Perhaps. However, the spell is very powerful, if a third party was secretly listening in, it is designed to activate. Please bear that in mind."

He smiled down at my astonishment. "The wording does not require intent, Ms. Abara, only that the event is about to occur. I think this is one of those moments in life where experimentation can be regarded as a bad idea."

I was trying to think of something to say to that when I saw them—James and Elizabeth. Except Lord Navartis was here as well, along with a dozen household guards. I recognized the family crest they all wore.

As we approached, James gave me a tired smile. "I had less sleep than you did." He gave Sorcerer Petotum a nervous stare, then looked back at me. "I was visited over an hour ago. Mom's still running around in circles."

Sorcerer Petotum gave a small bow. "Your mother does stock wonderful coffee. I believe it's a French Roast from Earth."

Before James could respond, Sorcerer Petotum switched his gaze to Elizabeth. She was looking up at him in wonder, her face was almost glowing. Was she taken with him?

James offered his hand, and I took it. We both watched in fascination as Elizabeth gave Sorcerer Petotum an inquiring glance. What was going on?

"I know a very good oracle, Lady Elizabeth," smiled Sorcerer Petotum. "When I asked her to do a reading on you, she says her entire crystal ball turned green."

Lord Navartis cocked his head. "Sir, what does that mean?"

"That is a very good question, Lord Navartis, for which I lack an answer. However, I am going to politely decline the offer for tea. I think our paths will cross from time to time, but not intertwine." He gave my friend a direct stare, and she nodded back. Sorcerer Petotum suddenly smiled. "The oracle said my future was bathed in red."

"Fire," Elizabeth said, swallowing nervously.

"I think not. Or, perhaps, I hope not. She did not get a sense of doom with it, but something else. Regardless, it will be interesting to watch it all unfold." He tilted his chin down the street. "Gentlemen, Ladies, it's a beautiful day. If you would walk with me, please." It was *phrased* as a request, but it was anything but.

I don't know how it happened, but I was on one side of Sorcerer Petotum with James holding my hand, and Elizabeth with her father on the other. The collective household guards plus four Sorcerers of the Realm walked behind but flanking us. To say people got out of our way would be an understatement.

"Lord Navartis, Lady Elizabeth, Lord Vimmer," the Sorcerer said, addressing the three of them. "Thank you for coming."

So, he planned this. Why? As we walked down the street, none of us knew what to say to the Sorcerer, or why he still needed to talk to us. The fact James held my hand made me feel better. Part of me was oddly happy that he looked a bit disheveled. Mr. Perfect had his limits. I really just wanted to curl up next to him and sleep. But I doubted one of the most important people in Avalon just decides to go for a walk. Were we about to be smacked down?

Sorcerer Petotum remarked as we passed a hive of pixies playing in a garden. "If one makes the wrong turn in the Bookstore, you can meet some interesting individuals."

"Sir?" replied Elizabeth. I was with her. *What?*

James looked just as confused. Sorcerer Petotum was trying to imply something, but it went right over my head.

We rounded a corner, and Sorcerer Petotum chuckled. "Perhaps I was being too oblique. I was trying to imply it is possible to meet individuals who are, strictly speaking, not human. Yet like us, they are interested in reading and writing."

Okay, still not getting it. Apparently, something clicked with Elizabeth.

"Oh," she nodded slightly. "The Charter about the Reece's Raccoons."

"Indeed, Lady," replied Sorcerer Petotum. "While I look forward to reading your charter, I do not wish to see your House, or the Houses of your friends diminished."

Lord Navartis asked sharply, "How so, sir?"

We walked in silence and rounded another corner. "Your daughter, Lord Navartis," began Sorcerer Petotum. "Indeed, all her friends are very popular in Avalon, both due to the gymnastics events they have participated in, but also due in part because they make themselves available to the common man. They are approachable, and because of that society holds them close. I entirely believe, should they leverage their collective might to get the required signatures on the Reece's Raccoon Charter, as I have heard your daughter is going to call it, they could. But in doing so, their actions, while well-intentioned, would ultimately diminish your daughter, her house, and those of her friends."

"They fought alongside us," I said with heat. "They can talk, build things, and have their own culture." Then I realized who I was challenging. I added, "Sir," in a small voice.

"You surprise me, Ms. Abara. Please keep doing that. I thought—"

Elizabeth, who had been sputtering, indignantly interrupted, "They have a right to be heard!"

"Elizabeth," said her father beside her. "Perhaps in this, we might want to step back."

James squeezed my hand, then added his own thoughts. "Sir, I agree with Petra and Lady Elizabeth. When someone stands up and says they want to be heard, we become less if we don't give them the chance."

Yes. Yes, he is my boyfriend. Decision done. I wanted to kiss him right there.

Sorcerer Petotum broke out laughing. "Oh, I wish I could get the three of you in the room with the rest of the Wizard's Council." Then, looking at Elizabeth, he said, "I never said you should not post the charter, rather that you and your friends should, then step back and allow Avalon City to decide. For if you take their voice away, even with good intentions, then you become what they ultimately fear."

We turned another corner. Where were we going? Now Sorcerer Petotum looked at me. "Tell me, Ms. Abara. We can talk to a pixie, and they can talk back. The same for some other creatures, as well.

However, aside from the dryads and the dragon, the courts do not grant them any rights, and are unlikely to do so. Why?"

James squeezed my hand. I was beginning to get it. "So, the Reece's Raccoons need to demonstrate they can read and write, as well as talk?" I asked.

"Almost, Ms. Abara," replied Sorcerer Petotum. "They must be able to read, write, and interact with others while displaying a grasp of emotional concepts. For example, stand tall and openly discuss the merits or lack thereof, of a written law with a human. To purchase items at the market and exchange coin, so Avalon can see they understand the fluid concept of money." He smiled at me and James holding hands. "They must show the people they belong on their own merits."

Lord Navartis said nervously, "Sir, there will be some who will be angry at the thought their place in the world is being challenged."

Sorcerer Petotum tilted his head in apparent acknowledgment. "I agree. Some will. But if we give in to those fears, then nothing will ever change. The thought of change ultimately causes fear in many. You can't have change for free." Now Sorcerer Petotum stopped, and we all did as well, looking at him. "The question for you, Lord Navartis, is do you want to live in an Avalon that gives in to that fear, or an Avalon that wants to ask and discuss the hard questions?" He stepped back and bowed. I could tell he was about to leave.

It was about this time I noticed we had stopped in front of a brewery. The entire front window was full of people who had their faces plastered against it, looking at us. Sorcerer Petotum winked at me, then added, "This is where I must say my goodbyes. I hope you two enjoy the rest of the morning. Ms. Abara, I believe I see Lord Vimmer inside the brewery. Have a good day." Then he was off, the other Sorcerers of the Realm following him.

I swung to face Elizabeth. "Did you plan this?" I asked her accusingly. I probably still looked horrible, and here I was about to meet my boyfriend's father. Why can't life ever give me a break?

Elizabeth just shook her head. She looked just as surprised as I was. Turning to James, I said, "Let's go meet your father."

He stood up for the Reece's Raccoons against Sorcerer Petotum. I owed him for that.

Chapter 34

When meeting your boyfriend's mother for the first time, expect to be interrogated. Don't worry, Avalon law forbids turning guests into toads when they have granted safe passage. There is some debate on other spells, however.

—Cook's Guide to Dating

Royce gave me and my team two weeks off to recover. I heard our Lodge was awarded some money from the city for finding the thief and bringing him in. If so, as a team leader, I would probably get a bonus five days after the new moon. Bonuses were paid out every month. There were some new wood carving tools I had been saving up for; I just needed three more silver talons. Good carving tools are expensive. Even so, I shared a portion of every bonus I received with my team. Some of the other team leads were annoyed at me for this; the field people on their teams were grumbling. Dora mentioned there were several requests to Royce from other team members asking to transfer to my team. When I suggested to Dora she might consider being a team leader herself, she just looked at me like I had two heads.

"Wherever you go, that is where I will be," was her direct reply. From her stare, I think she meant every word of it.

Any extra money after that I divided in half. The first half went into my savings, the other I brought with me to my bi-monthly meetings with the people from Gawain, for any that needed it. Sometimes I might get a few people from my lands, occasionally the church was filled. Regardless they wanted me to keep up the tradition, so I did so. It meant something to me, as well. I would always light the first candle of remembrance for the fallen, then others would follow my example. Even if I only had a few silver talons to spare, I could guarantee on any given month someone needed it more than me. There were a few others who started following my example and had made something of themselves in a guild. The total never amounted to much, but it made sure someone who had fallen on hard times didn't go hungry. The next gathering was going to be in eight days. With the bonus, I might have a bit extra to bring.

I looked at myself in the mirror. I thought I looked okay in the blue dress. To my surprise, Elizabeth had it made for me. It hadn't needed to be adjusted at all. My hair was now washed, combed, dry, and cascaded down my back. My mother's hair clip held it all in place. Dora and Julia helped me get ready. At some point during the recent adventure, those two became friends. The Noble and the Night they called themselves. After they pushed me out on my date with James, they were planning on getting dinner together.

Jumper put down his coloring book to stand up at the edge of my bed. Leaning forward, he sniffed, then scrunched up his nose. "You smell funny."

"It's called being clean," I said. Then looking down at the open book, I saw that he didn't finish drawing out the five words. The coloring book was meant for a three-year-old. Something about a cat and a hat. It was from Earth. Rather expensive, but odd enough that I thought it might make a good starter for Jumper. "Rainy doesn't end with 'ie.'" I corrected. He tossed the blue crayon across the room. "Well, it soun-ds like that." He still couldn't pronounce the 'd' sound well, but he was getting better. Then crossing his arms, he demanded about the fifth time this afternoon, "Want to learn magic. Not writing."

"Well, tough. I won't teach you any magic until you learn how to read and write properly."

Jumper took the red crayon and began mashing it on the page. "Magic ... want to learn magic."

Julia rolled her eyes, and I had had enough. This was his second temper tantrum. Before I could tell Jumper to stop, Dora began chanting under her breath. Immediately I could feel a cold breeze blowing out from under my bed; wisps of darkness came with it, and Julia's eyes went wide. She grabbed onto my arm for reassurance; she hadn't seen shadows called before. Believe me, it's creepy. As the slivers of darkness began edging up the side of my bed, Jumper somersaulted to the middle of my bed and held the red crayon before him like a knife, ready to strike.

"Back ... back ..." he shouted, stabbing the gathering shadows next to him, his raccoon eyes going wider. Within moments, a shadowy Reece's Raccoon took form next to Jumper.

"What's it going to be, Jumper?" asked Dora in a menacing voice. "Are you going to be polite tonight or is my shadow going to eat *you*?" At her last words, the shadow form broke apart into tendrils that leapt toward Jumper but dissipated just before touching him.

"Ahhh-hhh-hhh ..." Jumper leapt upwards and attached himself to my ceiling. All four of his paws grabbing on for dear life. His shaking fur was frizzed out. "Jumper will be nice," he screamed. "Jumper nice!"

Julia gulped. "I heard stories, but never met a shadow-caller before." She swallowed and looked at me. "I thought you were joking."

"Nope," I laughed. "Makes you wonder what's really in the darkness at night, doesn't it?"

Now it was Dora's turn to shudder. "Sometimes if they're powerful enough, a spirit can use the darkness to take form. The really crazy ones are scary." She eyed Julia's nervous expression and looked at the ground. In a whisper, she said, "Are we ... still friends?"

Dora rarely called shadows around strangers. Most people would run for their lives and then reach for the guns and pitchforks. People were instinctively afraid of the shadows, and the few stories about shadow casters generally had them as the bad guy—or in this case, girl. I gave Julia a pleading look. Dora really needed friends, and I didn't want her to feel even more isolated. As my second-in-command, she did a good job. The others of my team liked and respected her, but she intentionally didn't go around calling shadows around them.

Julia took a deep breath. "You just startled me. We are."

Dora's eyes lit up.

"Where are you two going tonight?" I asked.

"The Green Garden," replied Julia. "It'll be fun."

I raised my eyebrow. "Isn't that the place where the waiters and waitresses are painted green and wear ... um, not much else?" It was also a famous gambling establishment. People from all over, even from other planets visiting Avalon, would stop by. Personally, I didn't see the thrill in gambling, having spent a great deal of my time during the war hoping I didn't get eaten by a monster on any given day.

Dora reached out a hand, and Julia took it. "It's okay, Petra. I will be fine. Thank you for working with me."

Julia gave her a curious look. Dora shrugged. "I'm afraid to be around large crowds. Petra's been working with me." She noticed Julia's worried expression. "I do really want to go. Just, stay with me, please?"

Julia squeezed her hand. "Of course." Then they both turned back to me. Julia pulled out a little box and handed it over to me.

Uh, oh. "What's this?"

"In case you decide to stay over for the night," Julia said with a straight face. Then her grin got wider. "Or invite him over here."

I opened the box to reveal a copper ring with a small red stone inserted into it.

"I am so not sleeping with him tonight," I said angrily. "Just having dinner with his family. What is wrong with you people?" If I wore this ... well, aside from a powerful potion, or, say, pollen from a dryad, it would be unlikely I could get pregnant. The stone was really magic-imbued glass. Once it became clear, the magic had worn off. They generally lasted a few weeks. You could buy them for about a silver talon. Some of the more conservative guilds refused to allow anyone in their guild, and that included family members, to wear one. I heard a rumor there were some women banding together about this that they planned on posting a charter suggesting it was their right to do so. If that charter got posted, the streets might turn ugly, quickly.

Flump. Jumper dropped from the ceiling to land on my bed. "Why not?" he asked. "I like him."

Dora started laughing. Julia grinned at me.

"I am not taking dating advice from a raccoon," I said. "Finish writing out the words on the first five pages. You can go home when you're done."

Jumper rolled his eyes and plopped down on my bed. He grabbed the coloring book and grumbled but tried to write out the words again. While very dexterous, writing apparently used muscles in a way that was new to Reece's Raccoons. We quickly discovered pencils were right out, and so were quills. Remembering seeing them before, we, or rather Elizabeth, purchased a set of crayons brought over from Earth. They were expensive. So far Jumper could, with effort, copy a short word if he held his energy in check. We hoped to post the charter by the beginning of next month, and we were taking turns working with some of the raccoons; teaching them to read, write, and understand the concept of money. One of the older female Reece's Raccoons could already read a bit and was trying to help us. She liked cooking and had learned to read to understand human recipes. So far, our combined efforts had mixed results. A great deal of patience was required. Part of it was the money. Why would you need it, when you could just steal what you wanted?

Dora picked up the ring, eyed it, and put it on my palm. "You need to set a good example, team leader." With eyes full of laughter, she said, "Safety first."

"Get out of here, both of you." They both laughed and left.

Jumper looked up. "Me too?"

I sighed. My life was so weird. "Bring the book home with you, Jumper. But I want you to copy all the words on the first five pages before tomorrow."

Ten minutes later, I was standing outside the lodge. Before walking out my door, I hemmed and hawed, then put the ring in my pocket. I am so not going to use it, but there was a little voice in the back of my mind suggesting other ideas. *But it will make Julia feel better if I took it*, I said to myself.

An elegant four-horse carriage pulled up and stopped. I recognized the Vimmer coat of arms on the side. A servant stepped down, placed a stool by the door, and opened it to reveal James. He offered a hand, and I took it. My God, he looked and smelled good. And in the carriage, I couldn't get away from it. My senses were being assaulted. I unconsciously patted the side of my dress to make sure the ring hadn't fallen out. James made a motion with his hands, and the two magical lights lowered a bit. It was just him and me in here. I wasn't sure if I trusted my hands, so I sat on them.

"Wow, you look fantastic," said James.

I bit my lip. "You too," I said uncertainly. "So just a date, then."

"Petra." He laughed. "You've already met my father. It's just dinner. Besides, I bet most of the conversation will be about Aspen's coming-out ball. It will be fine."

When I didn't say anything at first, he gently pulled on my arm. I let him take my hand. "It's our first date, Petra. You're not committing to anything." He laughed at my uncertain expression. "Just share some more war stories with my father."

Four days ago, when I'd sat down with James's father in the brewery, I hadn't known what to say at first. Everyone in the place was looking at James and me like we were visiting royalty. Both of us looked horrible (me more so than James, of course). But just about the entire place had stuck their collective faces to the window to watch Sorcerer Petotum, Lord Navartis and Elizabeth, two Sorcerers of the Realm, and a platoon of household guards stop in front of *Tate's Brew House*, with one unknown and one barely known individual (probably only James's father knew who he was), who looked like sleep had been last week's luxury.

After all the important people left, all those eyes turned to James and me. When we walked in, the place was silent. The owner jumped to his feet and bowed to us as if we couldn't possibly be gracing his establishment. I was so tired, and so out of my depth. James nodded at the man and asked if we could have the (empty) table in the corner, plus three stouts. After we sat down, Lord Vimmer walked over. He stood there looking confused, blinking at us a few times. He seemed not sure what to say. I certainly didn't. Before I could say anything, James began, "Petra grew up in South Avalon, Father. Her entire noble nation was destroyed during the war. In her own way, she fought, just like you and I did."

Then the owner brought over three tall beer mugs of dark beer. Lord Vimmer sat down across from me, took a long pull of beer and looked at me again. But instead of anger or indignation, he seemed sad. He raised his mug. "To the survivors." The three of us clinked mugs. Surprisingly, I was able to tell some of my stories without crying.

At some point during the carriage ride, I ended up sitting next to James. Then I kissed him. Or was he kissing me? I'm not sure, but I liked it. Outside of kissing my father when I was little, this was my first kiss.

I didn't remember exactly how it happened, but I began sitting in James's lap. Then kissing him again. His arms pulled me in close. When I found my hand sneaking toward his belt, the image of Julie handing me the ring popped into my head. My hand froze.

Did I want this? Oh yes! Did I want to meet his family disheveled? No. But more importantly, I wanted to be proud of myself. Sleeping together in the Vimmer family carriage on our first date made me feel uncomfortable. If James and I were really going to make a go of it, his father as head of the Vimmer house had to give his permission. I wanted Lord Vimmer to see me as the woman I had become, not as someone my sister often presented herself as, later in her life, whose affection could be purchased.

James had his hands around me and was kissing my neck. I pushed against his chest, kissed him quickly, then smiled. Sitting on his lap like this, I could look him directly in his eyes. "After your father gives permission," I said, smiling at him. "But I really want to."

James took a deep breath. I could feel all those muscles shift along with other things. There was a little voice inside me which really wanted him to continue. Reaching a hand into my pocket to slip on the ring would be very easy.

His left hand ran down my back making me shudder, and he kissed me one more time. Then James shifted to the left, and I was suddenly sitting next to him again. "I hate it when you're right," he said, looking forward. "I really want to as well."

"Thank you for stopping," I said and leaned into him just being happy.

James kissed the top of my head and wrapped his arm around me. I leaned in closer and sighed. I wasn't a noble, I reminded myself. There had to be titled women his mother would prefer he date. *Shut up brain*, I said to myself, *just enjoy the ride.*

James kissed the top of my head again and opened the curtains. It was fun watching the streets I normally walked down from inside a closed carriage. I couldn't quite put aside my apprehension about meeting his family. But even if his father said no, he and I could still be friends. That meant something to me.

A bit later the carriage made the turn onto his family's lands. The horses began cantering down a long pathway. If I wasn't used to the sprawling Navartis estates or those of my other friends, I would have felt very out of place as the carriage pulled up to the Vimmer's main house. We passed men and women maintaining plush gardens. I noticed two man-made beehives and at least one large garden full of pixies. If there was one thing the Great Forest Clan excelled at, it was plants. In our amulets were a mental encyclopedia of sorts on plants, thousands of pages. Instructions on how to identify a plant, which ones were edible and which ones could kill you. The book appeared in my mind when I called to it. However, like anything with the amulet, you had to practice to get it to work. By now I could mentally search it and cross reference a plant within moments. It had become second nature to me.

Some of the flowers in the gardens we passed where local to Avalon, but many you would only find in deep forest. From a certain point of view, there was a fortune in potion ingredients growing on their lands. James never mentioned being interested in plants before. When we passed three large stone otters, frozen like they were playing in a garden, I twisted around to see them better. Where they guardians? The main Navartis estate had about twenty guardians. Some of them were huge. There was even a larger-than-life cheetah that occasionally animated at night to protect the family lands.

From the rumors, to make even a small guardian was hard and required very complicated spells. I'd been told there were only six masters capable enough to make the larger ones. The prices they commanded were right up there with some of the better wands. The spells make a guardian hold together pretty much forever, providing the family bloodline stayed intact and the rocks didn't break. Most guardians were very old.

James must have picked up on my excitement. "After dinner we can walk around." He pointed at the three stone statues. "That's Taos, Belter, and Sunshine. Every once in a while, they begin playing. Mostly at night, though."

So, they were guardians!

James laughed and ran a finger down my back, making me shiver. "Their idea of guarding the lands is to jump all over an intruder. For them, everything is one big game." He laughed. "One time we found Belter frozen in place, but he had wrapped himself around a thief. Getting the thief out took some doing."

"How long have they been in the family?" I asked.

"I think they were created twelve generations of Vimmers ago, by my ... nine times great Grandfather."

I gaped at him. To think back that far! I don't remember my grandparents, and only heard vague stories about them. Suddenly, I felt how different our families were. My apprehension came back. James squeezed my hand for reassurance.

As the carriage neared the house, I felt him tense up slightly. In front of the house, standing outside, were his father, what had to be his mother, and probably Kiera, the eldest sister. Flanking them was a minor army of servants. *Just a date* I said under my breath ... But where was ... and James cursed under his breath.

"What's wrong?" I asked. "Is Aspen sick?" His youngest sister. Whenever James talked about her, I always picked up a hint of exasperation.

"No. Nothing like that." James squeezed my hand again. "Can you give Aspen some slack? She's very sensitive, right now."

Huh? "Oh, her coming-out ball." For my sister, her coming-of-age party was the biggest thing in her life. She talked about it for months. For a young woman in Avalon, it's the transition to adulthood. You're allowed to begin officially dating, providing the family elder gives permission. My sister's coming out party consisted of borrowing our lady's west garden for the day. Combined, there were about twenty guests. Friends and suitors attended. Total cost for the entire affair was two silver talons, which, for my father, was a lot of money. I bet Aspen Vimmer's ball will be "the event."

He grinned. "Yep. It's all she talks about." Then James tilted his head. "Did you ever get a coming-out ball?"

I shook my head. "When I turned thirteen, my sister and I were doing anything to earn money just to eat." I shrugged. "It was also about that time she really got into trouble." Now it was my turn to squeeze his hand. "I guess I never really thought about it. Once my sister passed, I was my own head of house." I was about to add more when the horses stopped. A moment later I felt the carriage jerk slightly and settle back down on its springs. Through the window, I watched the same servant drop down and place a stool in front of the door, then open it for us.

James's Mom, Lady Vimmer, was just a tad taller than me. A bit plump, she wore it well. She was very cheerful and didn't seem to care that I wasn't a noble. If she thought less of me because I didn't have a title, I couldn't sense it. She greeted me like a human being. After she introduced me to Kiera and Lord Vimmer, she declared she had the sunroom ready, which apparently meant following her inside—and leaving James outside with his father.

Kiera followed and mouthed, "Sorry," to me. I got that I was about to be grilled away from the prying ears of the men. From my initial impression, I liked Kiera. She was about my age, reasonably fit, and wore her dress for comfort versus showing off her curves. Sewn into the left sleeve of her dress were two emblems; the first indicating she was a journeyman sorceress and the second which mistress she was associated with. Attached to her thin belt was a small sheath holding her wand. A part of me wondered as we walked through the house, whether Kiera was my guard. Did they believe I was dangerous?

As we walked, I asked, "How is Aspen?"

Kiera rolled her eyes.

Did I catch the edge of a sigh from Lady Vimmer? She replied, "My youngest daughter believes she is a full adult before her ball."

Got it. Daughter and mother weren't getting along.

The sunroom was filled with plants, but they didn't take over the room. Six chairs dominated the center. Lady Vimmer took the second largest, her daughter just to her right. One of the butlers stood next to a smaller chair, facing them. The meaning was very clear: welcome to our house, and the interrogation is about to begin.

Chapter 35

It is not impossible to bypass house wards, but it requires an extremely complex and powerful spell. Assuming you survive the attempt, you then need to prepare for the energy backlash.

–Protective Spells, 2nd printing

James said you two met at college?" asked Lady Vimmer, eying me while I sipped my lemonade. A maid had brought over three glasses for us then retreated out of the room.

"We did. He, um, well ..." I trailed off, not sure how to say the next part. *Yes, Lady Vimmer, we did. And I slapped your son. What a nice room this is.*

Kiera saved me. "I heard the bet of who would give in first was over ten gold talons."

"Bet? What bet?" asked Lady Vimmer, looking between her daughter and me in confusion.

Okay, here it comes. Well, at least I got to meet her. So, I told the entire story from beginning to end. James's mother's eyes went wide, and then she started laughing. That's a good sign, I hoped.

"Petra, that's wonderful," replied Lady Vimmer after dabbing at her eyes. She must have sent some signal to the three servants standing in the background. They quietly walked out of the room and closed the doors behind them. It wasn't lost on me I was being cornered.

Kiera asked, "Do you plan to continue college?"

"Yes, Royce—she's my lodge leader—has signed me up for pre-calculus and introductory physics."

Lady Vimmer was studying me intently. "I have met one or two Great Forest Clan members before. They were very earthy. You're very different. Why is that, Ms. Abara?"

I was back to being Ms. Abara again.

How to say this without knocking my clan? I said slowly, "Most people I have met don't really want to push themselves. They are satisfied with doing the least amount of work."

Lady Vimmer's eyes wrinkled in laughter. "Young lady, that concept bleeds across rank and title." She took another sip of lemonade and studied me closely again. "You would not be surprised I asked around about you?"

I shook my head. "No, ma'am. After you report on me back to your husband, I might be dating your son." I was expecting it. What I didn't know was what she had learned. She gathered up several sheets of paper and brought out thin eyeglasses. She looked over at her daughter for a second. "Kiera doesn't want me getting my eyes fixed by a potions master. She says such potions could change the way one casts magic, as well." Lady Vimmer gave her daughter a long-suffering sigh. She began reading the papers on her lap.

Without thinking about it, I replied, "She's right. Especially if the ingredients aren't absolutely pure."

Lady Vimmer cocked her head at me and pulled off her glasses, holding them in her left hand. Then, leaning back in her chair, she said, "Explain. Assume I know something about plants and the art of making potions."

There was a hardness in her voice. I didn't think it was about me, but something else.

"I am an assistant potions maker," I said, watching Lady Vimmer's face. "Making sure there are no impurities in the ingredients is extremely important." When her left eye ticked slightly, I almost swallowed. "It's not too bad for minor healing potions and the like, but for core potions designed to change the body, even trace impurities can cause the magic to do odd things." As I finished, I could feel the unspoken anger in the room, not directed at me. "Sorry." I swallowed. "Am I boring you?" My glass of lemonade was empty.

Lady Vimmer looked away for a second. When she turned her head back her anger was gone. "Not in the least, young lady," replied Lady Vimmer. "Before I was married, I was a potions journeyman myself. It's been a few years since I advertised my services. I never tried to achieve full Master status. Running a household and raising children takes a great deal of my time. However, I still keep my hand in, now and then. I do the requisite work to keep my Potion's Guild license valid."

She took another sip and asked, "So that brings us to the topic of children. What is your opinion about having them?"

My face reddened a bit, remembering sitting on top of James's lap earlier. "Maybe," I said uncertainly. "James are I are helping to teach, well you could think of him as a three-year-old, but our patience is being tested ..." I trailed off seeing Lady Vimmer's expression shift. Her face was now a mask.

Had I said something wrong?

Lady Vimmer cleared her throat. There was a lot of command in that sound. She asked softly, "Is this young individual you are helping to rear going to be my grandson?"

I stared at her, then broke out laughing. "Jumper ..." But I was laughing too hard to add anything else.

Lady Vimmer looked at my illusion of Jumper in curiosity. With practice, my ability to call illusions had gotten pretty good. I'm technically using the spell in my amulet designed to recall geographic features and plants, but it works on other things too. You just need to be creative in how you add the last part of the spell, the part that comes from me. The image of Jumper in front of us was just like he looked in real life, a bit over two feet tall if he stood upright, along with the signature black and white fur.

"So, you and James are teaching him how to read and write?" Kiera asked me. "Why?" At my confused expression, she added, "I'm not suggesting reading and writing aren't valuable skills, but what does it get him?"

"He'd like to know that, as well. Jumper is fighting me every step of the way." My and Keira's laughter was a bit madhouse, despite its short duration.

"Um, James, and the rest of my friends," I said. "We're working off and on with about thirty Reece's Raccoons, at progressively different levels of skill. I'm stuck trying to help Jumper, who is pretty stubborn about not wanting to learn it. He wants me to teach him magic, instead." I shrugged. "There's about to be a charter posted that declares them sentient in order to have the right to purchase and hold property. Sorcerer Petotum indicated that would be one of the expectations. If they can't read and write, they aren't eligible to deal with the contractual laws of property."

Kiera's eyes widened. "How would you ..."

James's mother, Lady Vimmer cut off her daughter by clearing her throat again. While looking down at the papers in front of her she asked in a worried voice, "Petra, can you explain the 'Last Lion.' Are you involved in a gang?"

"Um, no. Not really. It's something the Last Survivors call me. The Last of the Survivors is what we call our ourselves." At Lady Vimmer's blank stare I added, "Twice a month, those from our original lands who survived the war get together at the Church of the Beloved Fallen for a day." I shrugged. "The church used to have another name, but it was abandoned. We asked, so the city let us take it over. The Church of the Beloved Fallen is what I call it. They always ask me to light the first candle to honor the fallen. I'm their Last Lion. We're meeting again in another eight days."

The room was silent for a few seconds. What can you really say to something like that? Everyone lost something in the war. "Which nation where you from originally?" inquired Kiera softly. "No one we talked to seemed to know, just that you are said to be from the south originally. It's as if it's a secret that they don't want strangers to know."

That didn't surprise me. Seven major nations got wiped out. Probably a third of Avalon City are refuges. "Um, the Cloudly Lands of Lord Gawain. My mother was a handmaiden to one of his vassals."

Kiera's eyes had gone wide again. "Did you ever meet the prince?"

Before I could answer Lady Vimmer tapped her chair. "Petra, can you explain what 'the nine' means? The term came up several times during my investigation."

Well, at least I was Petra again. I must have looked blank. "Sorry?"

Lady Vimmer moved her finger down the second page, stopped and read out loud, "Petra Abara is part of the nine." Looking up she asked again, "What does that mean?"

"Still lost," I said. "Who's saying that?" Maybe figuring out where the statement came from might clue me in. *The Nine?*

Lady Vimmer pursed her lips but seemed to decide something. "Realm Sorceress Bardot. She and I went to school together."

Something clicked. Elizabeth had a group picture taken at the gym and declared us "the nine." While they were my friends, it was really eight nobles plus one if you asked me, but I never said that out loud. None of them seemed to care I wasn't a noble and never made me feel like I shouldn't be one of them.

"Got it," I said with relief. "Now it makes sense, she means Lady Elizabeth Navartis, Lady Joanne ..." I listed out all my eight noblewomen friends. I shrugged. "And I'm number nine."

Lady Vimmer just looked at me. Kiera had her mouth open.

After a moment Lady Vimmer asked quietly, "Of these other ladies—does my son know any of them?"

I nodded. "He met them recently. You can't really spend any time with me and not meet my other friends. Is everything okay?" The two of them were looking at me like I had two heads.

Lady Vimmer carefully folded the papers on her lap and took off her eyeglasses. "Well, it's apparent my son has decided to keep many things from me," she said. "I'm not angry, Petra. More surprised. If you don't mind me asking, how do you know Lady Elizabeth?"

"I met her almost four years ago, ma'am. She taught me how to call magic from my Great Forest amulet. And, to balance, and also, to laugh, but more importantly, to believe in myself. Elizabeth offered friendship with no expectations in return. She helped me learn that falling down doesn't mean I have to stop. That education should be open to both men and women equally." I was surprised at the conviction in my words. Not that I didn't mean them, but how strongly I believed in them. I finished with, "If there is anyone in this world I would follow to the gates of hell, it would be her."

As I talked an idea was forming in the back of my mind. I really needed some guidance, and Kiera might have some suggestions. "Kiera, I mean Miss Vimmer?" I asked. "Would you be willing to help me try to teach Jumper magic? We don't know whether the Reece's Raccoons can work with any of the three variants which I know can be taught. We *do* know some of them can do potions, but that isn't any part of what I'm talking about."

Kiera blinked a few times. "Sorry, Petra. Can you repeat that? I haven't gotten past the 'Lady Elizabeth' part. Is she as impressive as the stories make her out to be? I have only seen her from a distance, when she won the Avalon Cup."

I nodded. "Wicked smart, she can both call and cast magic. She designs spells, is amazingly beautiful, has gymnastic talents I wish I had just half of. When she walks into a room, you just know she's the queen, and somehow it's okay." I shrugged. "She's my friend, and I'm in awe of her every day."

Kiera was about to add something when Lady Vimmer asked, "Does Lady Elizabeth have an opinion of you and James dating?"

I nodded. "She suggested I date him. She said she had him checked out, and that he's a good man. I was ... a bit reluctant at first but warmed up to him."

Lady Vimmer tapped the side of her chair again in apparent thought, then cocked her head at me. "Three variants? I am only aware of two and admittedly know little about calling magic."

Kiera looked at her mother. "Sorry, three variants? What do you mean?"

I jumped in. "There's casting magic, which is what you do." I shrugged. "For that, the entire structure of the spell comes from you. Then there's calling magic, which is what I do. All but the last part of the spell structure is held in my amulet, I can call it out, focus the framework of the spell and then add the last part, sort of like the last note in a song." Looking down at her wand, I said, "You can learn and cast just about any spell, but I can only call what's in my amulet, and only the bits I've practiced with. So, I need to be creative sometimes."

"Got it," Kiera said slowly. "Is there a way to add more spells to your amulet?" she asked inquisitively.

"No idea," I said. "But different clans have different spells. I heard rumors that some of the higher clans have some pretty powerful stuff in their amulets. Also, as I move higher in my clan, more spells seem to become available to me."

"So, what's this third variant?" she asked.

"Calling shadows." Then, looking at their uncertain expressions, I added softly, "And it's even creepier than it sounds."

Lady Vimmer said quietly, "You know of a shadow caster?"

"Not exactly. I personally know a shadow caster," I corrected her. "She's my second in command."

"Oh," was Lady Vimmer's comment. Kiera swallowed.

I had to know. "Ma'am, Lady Vimmer. Do you think I have a shot at dating James? I could understand if—" But she cleared her throat again, and I stopped talking.

"Petra, I look forward to the conversation with my husband. As the elder of the family, he has the ultimate say, but my vote would be yes. I'm thinking it might be quite complicated for him to decide."

Kiera said under her breath, "So, you follow Lady Elizabeth, and a shadow caller follows you?" Then she just shook her head.

I was about to say Dora was really nice, but I stopped and turned. We had heard an indignant scream. Female, annoyed, and from the rising pitch, ready to explode in anger.

Kiera closed her eyes and banged her head on the back of her chair while muttering, "Not again!"

Lady Vimmer made a gesture with her left hand. I felt the magic locking the double doors release, and they opened. She addressed the two servants standing at attention, who were now cringing at the sound of something else breaking.

"What is upsetting my daughter this time, Dickenson?"

The older butler turned and bowed. "Apparently Master Marion is still in the field and unavailable, my lady. His apprentice is here, delivering the flowers Miss Aspen picked out." He rolled his eyes slightly. "From her tone, I suspect she feels slighted." We heard another crash, this one followed by a secondary sound like glass falling. "I believe that was one of the lower windows, my lady," sighed the butler.

Kiera pulled out her wand and grimaced. "Can't we just push her out the door and let the first poor fool marry her?"

Another crash.

Lady Vimmer stood up. "I apologize, Petra, for airing out our family squabbles in front of you. But I need to deal with my youngest daughter now." She gave me a nod and left the room, flanked by the two butlers.

Kiera reluctantly put her wand away. "I want to bury that idiotic child." She eyed the doors, and with that same hand gesture her mother used, they closed. Eyeing me for a second, she sighed then said, "James dotes on her, he feels somewhat responsible for her condition."

"Sorry," I said. "From the way James describes her, she's very lively and, well, um ... attractive."

Kiera snorted. "I would rather you hear it from me, but please don't share it outside of our family." Then she said something under her breath, and I could feel energy wrapping around me. House wards demanding my oath.

At my nod, I could feel the energy binding to me. A blood bond to the house wards had made a decree. I accepted them and could not speak what she was about to tell me except to another holder of a blood bond to the wards, or with her approval.

Once Kiera was satisfied, she told me the story. "When Aspen was almost ten, I had just started my apprenticeship, so I was away. Mother and Father had business across Avalon and were gone for a week. James had finished up his sorcerer's apprenticeship in only eight months—my brother is rather brilliant. He was at home sleeping. During that time Aspen slipped out by bribing three of the servants to look the other way. She'd apparently planned this out. It wasn't until hours later when James woke up that he learned the twit had left."

Kiera tapped the side of her chair not really looking at me anymore. "She and two of her friends each paid a king's ransom to purchase core potions from a potions master." She shook her head and stuck out her tongue. "They wanted to be the loveliest ... Well, it worked, but at a cost. Aspen's magic is a bit random. Worse, she blames James for not stopping her."

I blew up. "That's ridiculous. James is one of the nicest people I know." I checked my anger and asked quietly, "He would have stopped her, wouldn't he?"

Kiera banged her fist on the side of the chair. "Of course! Getting James to understand it wasn't his fault has been an uphill battle." She sighed. "Mother and I tried different things to get him moving again." See shook her head in remembered frustration.

"As I said, my moronic brother is rather brilliant. Father sent him away for a year to work with another master to meet the requirements for full journeyman. When he finished and returned, I could see the light in his eyes again. My brother was back. But he still excuses most of Aspen's antics, more than she deserves." Kiera tapped her chair again. "Anyway, instead of working toward becoming a Master, he decided to go to college. Apparently, that's when he met you."

My mouth hung open. I had to know. "Did the potion's master infuse the potion correctly?" What I was really asking, did the potion draw upon a bit of Aspen's life force to take effect?

Kiera eyed me as if she understood my implied question. She said slowly, "I heard rumors someone was making such potions, but no." She sighed.

"Once we figured out what had happened, my parents called in a favor. They had another Master Potions-maker examine the remains of what my sister and her friends drank." She shook her head, "It was," she stressed, "infused correctly. But the idiot hadn't cleaned his equipment properly. There were trace amounts of strawberry pollen mixed in with the primary mixture. When he found out, he broke down." Kiera shook her head. "The man didn't know. He thought it was pure."

Remembering back from conversations I had with other Potion's Guild members I asked, "Wasn't he supposed to get another Master to examine his potion before selling them?"

Kiera spat out, "The man had racked up gambling losses and didn't want to pay the guild fees. He honestly thought his potion was correct." She calmed herself down. "So, my idiotic sister paid the price."

"I am so sorry," I said and meant it. "My sister died because of bad potions."

Kiera reached over to open the papers her mother had left behind. "We learned your sister became a registered prostitute and after some time died. But that's all. What really happened to her?"

I had told the story enough times that it I could tell it without crying, suddenly stopping, or shouting in anger. "My idiotic sister did become a prostitute, she honestly thought she was cursed. However, at some time she met a very bad man ..."

As my story unfolded, Kiera put her hands to her mouth. Once I was done, she asked, "Is this still going on? I can't believe the rumors were true."

"I don't know," I said honestly. "But I do good things for the city, and that makes me feel like I'm making a difference." Now it was my turn to look away. I whispered, "There are so many bad people out there, and sometimes it's hard to tell what requires intervention, and which evils to leave alone."

Kiera echoed me, "I know. Part of me wishes we had another Merlin."

I laughed. "Me too. But who would have the power and yet want the job?" The stories had Merlin as a half-dragon—personable, beyond powerful, and who only stepped in when Arthur got really pissed at something. There were lots of bars around Avalon which had plaques on their wall stating Merlin drank here. If even twenty percent of them were true, the man liked his beer. The stories became kind of vague on what happened to Merlin after he confronted his sister. The Wizard's Council is all that remains of his authority, the roots of our governmental structure. Legend had it that it was always difficult to find anyone for the Council since actually wanting the job typically disqualified a candidate.

I half wonder if the various guilds and nobles had drugged Sorcerer Petotum. When he woke up, they grinned at him and said, "We took a vote, you lose."

I tilted my head, remembering the stories ... "After Merlin confronted his sister." I tried to think of her name. It was there, I knew it, but it was like some compulsion was keeping it down.

Kiera looked at me quizzically. "Some very powerful magic just started swirling around you. I have never seen anything like it."

"It's um, a compulsion I had to sign, from the Wizard's Council. I'm not allowed to talk about it."

Kiera's eyes went wide. "I could see the energy surface when I mentioned Merlin. Is it about—" Suddenly, Kiera and I weren't there anymore.

Chapter 36

The average spirit in the graveyard is scary, but it can't harm you. At best they are random bits of memories held together by wafts of magical energy and strong emotions. The person they used to be in life has moved on; what's left has only one purpose, find enough energy to exist for another day, usually by taking some of your heat and trace energy.

A ghost on the other hand is really a spirt with enough of its memories intact, it has some awareness of who it used to be in life and a limited ability to interact with the real world. They traditionally exist within a confined space, usually a house, graveyard, and the like. Should you encounter a vengeful ghost, we recommend getting a good shaman.

Guardian spirits are full memory copies of an individual but lack true free will. They serve a defined purpose and are maintained by an extremely powerful magic item or artifact. Within their domain to protect this item, they have near absolute control limited only by their capabilities in life. If you encounter a guardian spirit, words are both your savior and your curse as they become bound forms. Treasure hunters beware, very few people survive meeting such a spirit. The only known ways to get rid of a guardian spirit is *to help it complete its goals or call in a very powerful shadow caster*.*

(*) see page 489 for shadow casters, under the nightmare section. Depending upon which story you believe, LeFay was purportedly a shadow caster, who transformed into a necromancer (**)

(**) see page 515 under KYAG section. Kiss Your Ass Goodbye.

—From the pages of Dangerous Magical Creatures.

—L eFay," finished Keira.

We were in darkness. What was more, all the background sounds suddenly disappeared. There is almost always some sound in the background. When it's gone the brain notices the gap, or at least mine does.

Kiera gasped out, "Where are we?" Her voice echoed slightly as if we were in a tunnel. I felt as much as heard her shift and suddenly I could see a bit. The tip of her wand was glowing.

I called light through my amulet and between the two of us, I could make out we stood in a large, old stone room. Correction, some kind of wide passageway, both sides extending into shadows. Around and near us, old books and random bits of paper were haphazardly stacked on the floor. A single book here, several books there, in no apparent order.

I whispered out, "This must be 843B-5."

Kiera turned to look at me in confusion. "What?" She swept her wand left and right to see into the shadows. "That almost sounds like coordinates."

"It is, sort of. 843B-5 is a room in the Bookstore." I didn't want it to end this way. "I am so sorry," I said. "I didn't want you dragged here too."

Kiera's eyes had gone wide. She looked scared. "Petra, what's going on?" she whispered, then jumped at the skeleton. It was sitting against the wall, with a book in its lap looking for all the world like it was still reading.

I spotted another one and pointed. "Farther down," I said while edging my ball of light down the hall. "There's another one." Like the first one, this one just sat there like it was reading a book.

"Petra," Kiera almost shouted. "Get us back."

"I can't," I exclaimed. I could feel tears beginning to form. I really liked Kiera and didn't want her to die. Well, I didn't want to die, either.

Kiera grabbed my shoulders and shook me. "Petra," she shouted. "How can we be in the Bookstore?"

I backed up until I bumped into a wall. "I signed a codicil with the Wizard's Council," I said, groaning. After kneeling down, I took a deep breath. "It was about not discussing her." Seeing Kiera's confused expression, I added, "Merlin's sister. I accidentally found out where she was buried."

Kiera backed up a step. "We started talking about Merlin ..." Her eyes went wide. "But I was only thinking about her. The spell was that sensitive?"

I banged my head against the back wall. "Sorcerer Petotum warned me," I said, rubbing my eyes. "He said if the spell *thought* the discussion might happen, it would activate."

Kiera looked down at the skeleton next to her, then at the one I found. I could hear her casting, and a large ball of light appeared next to her. With a hand gesture from her, it began rising until it hit the ceiling some thirty feet up within the corridor. There were at least three more skeletons farther down the passage. I could hear her take a gasping breath. "Why did I have to come?" she finally asked.

"Hey, I didn't write the Codicil," I said angrily. "I just signed the damn thing since the alternative was annoying the dragon."

Then, looking down at the ground, I said softly, "I am so sorry."

My life was so weird. I bet Dora would know what to do in a place like this. I didn't have a clue.

The two of us were silent for a minute or two. Kiera finally asked, "Do you think we're in the black section?"

"Maybe," I said. "If so, I didn't know there were rooms."

Kiera took another deep breath and seemed to gather herself. She walked over to me and offered a hand up. "I'm not ready to give up yet."

I took her hand, and she hauled me to my feet. "Thanks," I said and meant it. "This might sound bad, but I'm glad I have someone here with me." I looked around again. "Wherever here is."

I looked down both passages. They looked pretty much identical. Normally I could get a sense of direction from my amulet. If it had one, it wasn't sharing it with me. Do you want to know true north? Just ask a Great Forest Clan member. Right now, down here, I couldn't tell you if the sun was setting, much less any direction. I was about to grab some of the books to make a diagram with them, when Kiera grabbed my arm.

"The skeletons," she said. "Each person died reading a book. I bet the books are trapped."

"Good catch," I said. Then lowering my ball of light so it was just above the book in front of me, I carefully knelt down. After gently blowing off some dust, I read C.S.L. My eyes went wide, and I jumped to my feet, backing up against the wall. "Holy Shit," I murmured.

"What? What did you see?" remarked Kiera, looking afraid. "Did a curse get you?"

"No. C.S.L. That's what's on the lower part of the book. I bet this is an old library."

Kiera stooped down to get a closer look at the book without touching it. "Okay? Who's C.S.L. and why would a bunch of people literally die reading them?"

"Um, I don't know, and I don't know," I said.

Kiera slapped the ground with her hand. "Petra!"

"No, I'm serious. I found a really old wand about a week ago with silver embedded in the end. It had C.S.L. carved into it."

Kiera looked at me for a few seconds. "That can't be a coincidence. You find the wand, and now look where we are."

"Maybe." I shrugged. "Explore time?" I suggested.

"I'm game if you're game," replied Kiera.

I snorted. "Or we could pick up some trapped books and die reading them."

Kiera rolled her eyes at me while I scuffed the floor and made several arrows to indicate the direction we were about to take.

After the second turn and eight more skeletons, I said, "You're remarkably calm."

Kiera snorted softly. "It's either that or start screaming." She looked at me and tilted her head. "There's something about you, Petra, which makes me believe it will be okay."

"Please," I said. "I can't tell you the number of times I have been starving, covered in mud, running from monsters or just plain frustrated at the world."

Kiera grinned and carefully stepped around a pile of books, neither of us wanted to touch any of them. "That's the point. After you fall down, you get up and still have hope. I can see why James likes you."

That made me blush, but I didn't say anything. After rounding another corner, Kiera asked innocently, "Well?"

Huh? "Well, what?" I asked her.

She raised an eyebrow. "Have you slept with my brother yet?"

I blushed and whispered, "Almost. It's getting harder not to."

"Do you trust him?" she asked.

"I do. Elizabeth kept on telling me what a good man he was. It took me some time to believe it myself."

As we rounded another corner, I remembered sitting on James's lap in the carriage and wanting him. I *so* didn't want to die right now. Assuming we got out of here, even if his father said, "No, you can't date my son," I might jump James, anyway. I had a ring and everything. A night of just the two us alone sounded very nice right about now.

Kiera grinned at me. "Plotting a seduction?"

I gave her a sideways glance and edged around another skeleton.

Kiera giggled and sent her ball of light forward. Then her expression became serious. "If Father says no, don't become his mistress, Petra."

She smiled at my astonished expression. I asked slowly, "Do you?" I left the rest of question implied.

"I do. He's a rather gifted Journeyman blacksmith." She smoothed out the front of her dress. "He and I are very good for one another. But we both understand our position. He's actually courting a rather nice seamstress. I wish him the best, and if they come to terms, I will probably help pay for the wedding."

At my astonished expression, she gave me a rueful smile. "Petra, you're so much more than Mother and I expected. As much as I like my brother, don't take a back seat." Now, Kiera laughed at something. "I honestly thought James had lost his mind when he invited you over. What I was expecting was nothing like you."

"Um, what were you expecting?" I worked so hard to get where I was. Actually, I didn't really know *what* I was besides being Petra Abara. Except for my friends, I noticed most people wanted things—including people—in nice easy-to-understand boxes.

Kiera shrugged. "At a minimum, a higher-class version of your sister." She ruefully shook her head. "Just by watching you during the introductions, I knew I was wrong."

I pointedly looked at her wand. "Did you actually think I might be a threat?"

"Petra!" Kiera said in exasperation. "The information we gathered about you was just so strange. Mother honestly thought you might be a master thief."

Now it was my turn to laugh. Like Kiera's laughter, it echoed. Then, seeing the footprints in the dust, I groaned.

"Shit," Kiera said.

"Yeah," I echoed. Our scuff marks were right in front of us. We just made a circle. There were no doors or any other immediate way out we had seen.

"Daughter of a ..." I was about to yell out in frustration when something obvious came to me. I rolled my eyes at my own stupidity and grabbed my amulet. <*"Royce!"*> I mentally shouted. <*"Can you hear me?"*>

Nothing.

"You know," a female voice said from the shadows, "there's never been a clan follower down here. I wasn't sure what would happen."

She slowly walked forward as she talked. She was old with thick glasses. Very stooped. Kiera almost sobbed in relief at the sight of her. But I had felt this sensation before. Tilting my head slightly, I could see right through her.

"Hello," I said. "Has anyone ever gotten out before?"

"There have been a few," she said, looking at me. "Most don't."

Kiera stepped forward, probably to introduce herself when I grabbed her arm. "Don't," I whispered. "That's a spirit. I bet she wants to bargain, or she would have just let us die." Then I added, "Don't give her anything personal, such as your name."

The old women nodded. "Wise advice. But I know who you are Petra Abara, the Last Lion." Then tilting her head, she added, "And you, Lady Keira Vimmer. The question is, do *you* know who you are?"

"Are you C.S.L.?" asked Kiera.

"Kiera," I hissed. "If she answers you freely, you are bound to her."

The old lady raised a thick white eyebrow. "And what would you give to free your friend, Petra Abara?

Kiera was backing up. I could sense fear beginning to consume her. "What do you mean, 'bound to her?'" she blurted out. "Petra!"

"You asked her a personal question. If she answers, you have made a connection with her. If I'm right, she's a spirit linked to this place and her words become bound law."

The old lady bowed. "In a sense. I assume you learned this from your old master and from your friend, the one who follows you in shadow."

I nodded. "She introduced me to a few minor spirits and gave me the basics on the rules." I looked at the spirit, trying to see if I could figure anything out about her. "Also, as you implied, I have met two other spirits before, and not evil ones either."

The spirit snorted. "A ship. That is nothing compared to the power that holds me here."

"I don't doubt it. Compared to the *Alana*, I expect your power is like the ocean." I looked around me. "And we are in your domain."

She cocked her head, studying me. "And yet you are not scared now?"

"You are wrong, spirit," I said. "I am very afraid and because you were wrong, my friend is free." I cocked my head at her. "Don't the rules go both ways?" I really was afraid—white knuckle terror, but I found the courage to continue. "Isn't that how the game is played? If you are wrong, we can ask a boon of you. Mine is, my friend is to be free from you and from this place."

The spirit nodded. "Very well. I agree on both the letter"—here she gave a wicked grin—"and the spirt of our laws." A door appeared opposite Kiera. "You are free to go, Lady Vimmer. May you enjoy your life." She said it fondly. There was no threat in her words. So, she wasn't an *evil*, or vindictive spirit. But as I was learning, there was a lot of space between good and evil.

Kiera started reaching for the door and stopped. She seemed ready to ask the spirit something then turned to me instead. Good girl! Learning fast.

"What about you, Petra?" she asked quietly. Her hand was holding on to the doorknob.

I eyed the spirit. "You want something of me yet. Don't you?"

"Like all spirits, girl, I want to rest. My time is coming. But I'm not allowed to tell you, girl. You know that. You have to figure it out yourself."

I was still terrified, but something in me relaxed a notch. She followed rules. She might not be good, but she certainly wasn't evil. Without turning my head, I said to Kiera, "Whatever you do, don't let go of the doorknob, and don't ask her any more questions. Got it?"

I heard the doorknob partially turn and stop.

"Something is changing out there that no longer binds you to this place," I offered up. "But you need something done to complete it." I looked at this old crone intently. Who is C.S.L.? I pondered to myself; the wand has to be related to this spirit. Glad I didn't speak that out loud. "Like my old master, his soul had moved on. You're just an echo powered by something."

The spirit said nothing.

"I was given a wand. My guess is that wasn't a mistake. You wanted it to be found—me to find it."

I looked over at Kiera still holding the door. "I can't use a wand, it's useless to me. So, who do you want me to give it to?"

"Is that a question or a statement?" asked the spirit smiling at me.

I swallowed. "A statement."

The spirit's mouth widened into a smile. "Go on."

She was looking younger now. No longer a crone, but still old.

"So, what is holding your echo here?" I asked myself. "It has to be something much greater than you."

The spirit nodded at me. "Of course. As you know a spirit must be bound to something much greater than them." As she talked, she looked even younger. A woman in her prime, vastly powerful. Sure of herself, with a wand at her side. The same one Jumper gave to me.

"Petra," said Kiera nervously. I could hear her turn the knob just a little more.

I was close. "We're, technically, in the Bookstore," I said to myself, and suddenly I got it. "There is a book in this room that holds you in place." Suddenly I knew the right question. "You want me to have the book," I said. "But If I pick up the wrong one ..."

"You are almost correct, Petra Abara. My father was an interesting person. A new Merlin is emerging soon. I can feel it. It is time for my father's book to be passed down so I can rest."

My eyes felt like they had gone as wide as saucers. But it was Kiera who shouted out first, "Holy shit! You're Merlin's daughter!"

I looked around me. "Okay, but which book, I wonder?" At the same time, Kiera blurted out, "Who is the new Merlin? What is his name?"

The spirit cocked her head at Kiera. "I never said the new Merlin was a man, now did I?" She smiled at me and bowed. "I would like the wand given to the right hand of the new Merlin. However, for you to leave this place, Petra Abara, you must choose the correct book." Then she faded out.

I heard echoing laughter. "Choose wisely."

CHAPTER 37

Hunters Bond is a complicated spell designed to link an animal to you. If done properly you can see through their eyes, tap their power, as they can yours. Obvious examples, bonding a wolf would provide more stamina, a snake the ability to sense heat, etc. Some considerations: the animal in question needs to be willing and the more intelligent the animal the deeper the bond. It is recommended you thoroughly read all variables before attempting this spell. The original creator of the spell assumed you would want the bond for life, well, the animal's life.

–From the Great Forest Clan master spell list

Both Kiera and I said at the same time, "Well, shit." Then we looked at each and laughed. She was still holding onto the doorknob. After she looked at the glowing outline of the door, then back to me, she said, "Maybe if ..."

I cut in, "The door won't work for me. This is her reality, and she writes the rules."

Kiera bit her lip. I knew what she was thinking. She could leave, now.

"It's okay if you go," I said. I didn't want her to, but I wasn't going to try to stop her. If I didn't make it out, at least James would know what happened to me.

She let out a frustrated growl then kicked the door. After shaking her head as if to clear it, she said softly, "James told me the story of your old master and the spirit he met. My brother didn't run, and neither will I."

"Kiera," I pleaded. "This is different. Before, James and I weren't in the spirit's domain, now we are. Also, this spirit is vastly more powerful."

Ignoring my protestations, she asked, "So what resources do we have?"

I said a few curses under my breath about the stubbornness of certain Vimmer family members. "Fine!"

After turning in place, I said slowly, "My ability to call magic works, or most of it in any case."

"I can cast magic," replied Kiera. She pointedly looked at my amulet. "What doesn't work?"

I shrugged. "Anything that would link to someplace else." At Kiera's questioning look, I added, "Normally, I could reach out to another clan member and mentally talk to them. And, I would also be able to tell you where true north is. Both of those spells don't work here."

"Just curious," she asked. "Could you use it to talk to someone who doesn't wear an amulet?"

I blinked at her. "I don't know," I said slowly. "Never tried. You want me to try with you?"

She nodded. "I'm stuck here holding this doorknob, but if you walk around and we can talk to each other, maybe I could help too."

Just the fact she was staying helped me to relax. I could feel a black terror inside me wanting to take hold. Talking to Kiera helped keep it a bay. I grabbed my amulet with one hand and with my other, my fingers touched her arm. <*"Kiera!"*> I mentally shouted. She didn't hear me.

Inspiration struck. "Um, there are more spells in my amulet that I know are there. I just never really pushed to access them. Let me see if I can. Can you give me a minute? I need to go through a focusing ritual in order to try."

Kiera shrugged. "I'm not going anywhere. Go ahead."

I really wanted a candle, but that wasn't on our list of resources. Okay, something that will burn. Using some of the papers lying around seemed like a really bad idea. I didn't know if they were cursed as well. Then looking at the nearest skeleton, I murmured, whatever works. I uttered a short prayer as I tore off a part of its shirt, careful not to touch the open book in its lap. Poor person; he never got past page three. Considering how easily the fabric came apart, it must have been here for a long time. Next, I drew a circle around myself in the dust and sat down in its center. After scrunching up the old cloth and placing it in front of me, I closed my eyes.

Slow, deep breaths. Mentally reaching out with my mind I felt the circle. It held just a trace of energy. I followed the mantra of my ritual that I'd developed over time. As Royce said countless times, whatever works. One team member had to run a good ten miles before he tried certain spells. We all get there in our own way.

On my tenth exhale, I called the little spell that would light a candle. One edge of the cloth ignited and began to smolder. Just following that simple pattern allowed me to "feel" all the spell's structures jumbling around inside my amulet. As before, I could sense the deeper layers but had never pushed to get to them before. I just assumed as I moved up in the clan, they would become available to me.

I imagined spreading my arms apart to push away the hazy screen. It was like pushing against smoke, nothing happened. I could feel Kiera standing close to me, watching me intently. If felt sort of weird having a person so close to me while I did this.

Open damn you, I muttered to myself. Nothing.

Well, fine then. Let's try something completely different.

I imagined a springboard in the part of my mind that connected with my amulet. Then I backed up mentally and ran for all I was worth, hitting my mental springboard and somersaulting into the black veil. Well, what do you know? The veil is really thin at the top.

Kiera's eyes went wide. <*"I can hear you,"*> she said. <*"Can you hear me?"*>

<*"Yes,"*> I replied. Wow, the new spell worked. Even so, I was using it in a way it was probably not intended for. Story of my life— make it up as I go along. Royce never told me there was a spell which could mentally link up with animals. I just inserted Kiera's image instead of an actual animal, touched her, and I could feel the connection. Apparently, this spell came with extra benefits. Kiera could see through my eyes, and if I concentrated, I through hers.

<*"Well, let's get started,"*> I said and began walking down the corridor. <*"Any ideas?"*>

<*"I doubt it will be a book on the top of a pile,"*> Kiera thought back. <*"Probably part of the puzzle is figuring out a way of moving the cursed books without becoming book-factuated."*>

I blinked. <*"Huh. Book what?"*>

<*"That's what I'm calling the curse, book-factuated. If you have a better name for it, go ahead."*>

I rolled my eyes. <*"Nope."*> I tried her suggestion and borrowed a thigh bone to carefully slide the top book off. The book underneath looked similar and had the same C.S.L. on the bottom.

While looking down at the book, I heard Kiera say <*"The Structure of Light."*>

I snorted. <*"Definitely not light reading. I doubt it's our book. Not sure what 'Merlin's spell book' would look like, but I bet when we see it, we'll know."*>

Kiera responded back, <*"Probably. He designed the Pentwale rune, so I imagine the book would be locked with at least one of them."*>

<*"Sorry,"*> I asked. <*"Pentwale what?"*>

<"I learned about them from my Master. They're considered unbreakable. If you try to break one and it get it wrong some really nasty stuff can happen, including summoning a demon.">

<"Joy. Next pile then?"> I moved to the first turn and repeated the process on a short pile of books.

<"Apocryphal Applied: The Hammer of Light,>"" read Kiera. <"I remember the name Apocryphal from somewhere, it's old.">

<"Kind of odd that there would be two books referencing light."> I said.

<"Petra,"> Kiera said slowly. <"You might be on to something. Do the same on the next pile of books. Let's see if light is repeated.">

Sure enough it was. <"De Sensu: Light of Empedocles,"> read Kiera through my eyes. Then she blurted out, <"Petra, there is no way we could read that title. If I'm right, it's written in ancient Greek from Earth.">

<"Sorry. My knowledge of history pretty much involves what is trying to kill me this week. How old are we talking about?">

<"More than two thousand years ago.">

<"What a minute,"> I blurted out. <"Merlin supposedly was born some nine hundred years ago, give or take. How did this book end up here?">

Kiera laughed. <"To use your phrase, 'I don't know, and I don't know.' But this is the third book on light. That has to be a clue.">

I stopped at the fourth; At first, I thought the pattern was broken. The title simply said Lux. But Kiera said it was a really old way of talking about light.

<"Okay, I agree,"> I said. <"Finding Merlin's book has something to do with light. Got any ideas?">

<"Not yet. Do a circuit. See if anything comes to you.">

I did. I could feel that Kiera was fascinated with looking through my eyes. Stepping around a skeleton, I glanced down at the book. By the clothes, she was a woman. She never got past page three either. Hang on. I could feel Kiera pick up on my excitement. <"What?"> she asked.

<*"Hang on. I want to check on the next skeleton's book."*> Sure enough it was open to page three. I ran to the next one, three. By now Kiera was figuring it out.

<*"So, three. Three what?"*> she asked.

<*"What comes in threes?"*> I asked.

Kiera started rattling off ideas. <*"Father, Son, and the Holy Ghost. It's the first prime number, length, width, and height ... Then there's—"*>

<*"Wait,"*> I said slowly. <*"That last one."*>

<*"Length, width, and height."*> Kiera repeated, but I was already running back to her.

"We're in the Spirit of C.S.L.'s domain. She can make it look however she wants it to be."

Kiera had switched hands holding the doorknob and was shaking out her other hand. "Okay, you know more about spirits than I do," she replied. "What are you getting at?"

"Back in the sunroom at your house. We were talking about the three types of magic, remember?"

Kiera nodded. "Yes. Casting magic, calling magic ..." Her eyes went wide. "And, calling shadows," she whispered. "The three types of magic."

I looked down the hall. "Number three. I bet Merlin's book is hidden in a shadow."

Okay, that had been a trap. Kiera mentally cried at me as I just laid there on the stone floor, looking at the ceiling. <*"Petra, are you okay!"*>

It had been around the second turn that I found a shadow which was just odd. The angle seemed just a tad off compared to the rest of them. Reaching into the darkness unlocked something. I thought at the time gotcha, instead a large centipede creature emerged. I was food, and it was hungry. After I killed it, the creature dissolved into smoke. But I had a cut on my arm and my left knee throbbed. Considering I had to keep jumping out of its way as I tried to beat it to death with my makeshift bone mace, Kiera probably saw a confusing mess of noise and light. My gymnastics training saved me. Without it, I would probably be dead. Another skeleton in this room of books.

<"*Define 'Okay.'*"> I said, breathing hard and holding up my hands to look at them. Ten fingers still there—yay! I call that a win. God, I was so tired. Day ending in "Y." Just need a nap here.

I could feel Kiera almost whimper in relief. <"*Petra, you have to get up,*"> she said urgently. <"*Did the centipede bite you or claw you?*">

<"*I think claw,*"> I said slowly. <"*Why?*"> Just need five minutes of sleep. I could feel my body begin to relax, that felt good.

<"*Petra, GET UP,*"> she screamed at me. <"*I bet it was poisonous. It probably slows your heart down. If you don't move, you'll die.*">

I did feel a rather nice sensation of sleepiness coming on me. If would feel so good just to take a nap. Instead, I rolled over and pushed up. Sitting up, I could feel some disorientation in my head.

<"*Stand up, Petra,*"> came Kiera's voice.

<"*Fine,*"> I growled back, and slowly stood up. Then I took a wobbly step and caught myself from falling by leaning against the wall. <"*Okay, I'm up. Walking now.*"> One step, two. Fall down on my knees.

<"*Petra,*"> urged Kiera. <"*Get up. If you go to sleep, James will miss you.*">

That made my heart pump faster. I felt a little better. I pushed against the wall to stand up again. Kiera kept on talking to me as I walked back to her. I put her on my list of friends.

Sitting down opposite her I asked, "How's your hand?" She had shifted back to holding the doorknob with her left hand.

"Starting to spasm. I don't know how long I can keep this up."

As I leaned my head back against the wall she asked, "What was that move where you twisted. I got very disoriented looking through your eyes."

"Oh, um. A backwards double somersault. I use it in my routines."

"You're planning on competing," Kiera said.

"I hope so. I'm trying out for the silver league, right now I'm just an alternate. Lady Elizabeth thinks I have a shot at getting on the team."

We were silent for a few moments, then I broached a topic that I had been wondering about. "James implied you had two, maybe three offers. Do you know what you're going to do?"

Kiera nodded. "Three. Now that I have my Journeyman badge, Mom wants me to pick one. She really wants grandchildren soon."

"What do you want? I guess, I mean to say, do you like them and their families?" Kiera wouldn't just be marrying a man; she would also be marrying into his family. The elder held a great deal of power over all the other family members. If Kiera disagreed with the family elder, Avalon law was not on her side.

She made a small circle in the dust with her foot. Without looking up, she said, "After Aspen's coming-out ball, Father is going to invite each suitor and their family over for dinner. One family a week." She shrugged. "My parents will probably push me toward one, but they will also listen to me if I have strong feelings one way or the other."

She hadn't said the words. "Do you want to get married?" I asked softly.

Kiera looked up at me. "Yes, and have children. But I don't want to be just a breeding machine to pass along my magic for some other family. I would like to continue my education and eventually become a Master." She shrugged. "It's hard to have both. Mother couldn't do it." She tilted her head and asked, "What have you said to James about your future?"

"That I don't want to stop pushing forward," I replied. "Regarding children, maybe? Still freaks me out a little."

"How does being in the Great Forest Clan change all that? I heard that once you take the full oaths, it's pretty much your life."

Like Kiera, I made a small circle with my finger in the dust on the floor. "It's like signing a codicil. I'm bound to the clan. But some of us get married and start a family." I looked up at Kiera who was staring at me. "You're just still part of the clan." I had enough dust around my finger that I picked it up and tossed it away from me. It immediately spread out and began drifting to the ground. Some of it landed near a stack of books where the light from the outline of the doorway was making a long shadow.

Making a shadow.

"Kiera," I said slowly, standing up. "What if we need a particular kind of light? Light that can only appear with the spirit's permission. Like from the door." I was looking at the shadow about eight feet away from where Kiera stood.

Kiera's eyes went wide, and she held her breath. Exhaling, she said, "Maybe."

I slowly reached into the shadow and felt a click.

I heard a sigh that seemed to come from everywhere. Then the passageway and all its books began to dissolve around me. Suddenly, I was standing back in the Lady Vimmer's sunroom, with a large book clutched in my hands. Its binding wasn't leather, but something much thicker. It felt warm to the touch. Across the front were hundreds of interconnected lines in gold, making some pattern. At the center of this maze was an etched chalice, also in gold. A part of my mind was fascinated by them, but apprehension was gripping me. Where was Kiera?

Just when I was about to scream out her name, a door of light appeared right next to me, and Kiera stepped through. Then the door vanished. Kiera fell onto her knees and began crying while shaking out her hands. I fell to my knees as well and hugged her. We made it out alive!

Chapter 38

It wants to be found.
–Gandolf, Lord of the Rings.

While we hugged, I could feel my amulet begin to relink to other amulets around Avalon. Almost no time had passed. We were gone less than ten seconds.

"What are you two doing?" asked James. I looked around, noticing that he had opened the doors to the sunroom. He was looking down at us in surprise.

I lunged to my feet, handed Kiera the book, ran to him and pulled his head down so my lips could meet his. James was here! He never smelled so good.

James seemed a bit surprised at my sudden aggressive affection but put his arms around me and kissed me back. I'm not sure how long our kiss lasted, but I could hear Kiera beginning to laugh at me, in my mind. Oh yeah, that spell. I wonder how you turn it off.

I broke the kiss with James and came up for air. "I have never missed you so much. Do I have a story!"

James looked like he was about to respond when I noticed the person standing near him. For just a second, I thought it might Lord Vimmer Sr., but then my eyes narrowed. "Why are you here?" I demanded of Sorcerer Petotum. Taking a step backward, I unconsciously began to call energy to me in a way I had never felt before. Maybe it was because I was so pissed at the man! Then rune groups from my amulet appeared before me, floating in the air. That had never happened before, either. Normally I had to go through my ritual and focus in on my amulet to feel them. This time they were all around me, waiting for me to choose one of them. I didn't think James or Sorcerer Petotum noticed my floating runes. Surprisingly though, through my eyes, Kiera could.

<*"Um, Petra,"*> she mentally said just to me. I could pick up on her nervousness at me confronting Sorcerer Petotum. <*"I don't want to die now that we're back."*> Out of the corner of my eye I could tell she was eyeing Sorcerer Petotum and seemed to be waiting for him to explode in anger. Sorcerer Petotum was on the Wizard's Council. You didn't get there by being a lightweight. Even so, I was beginning to put a few of the pieces together. He set me up. I could have died!

James looked confused at my sudden anger. I could understand that. I went from ready to rip his clothes off, to wanting to attack the most powerful sorcerer in Avalon City.

James reached out to touch my arm. "Petra, he's here to help Aspen. Why are you angry?"

I blinked. "What?" But I held my gathering power in check. The runic symbols from my amulet still floated in front of me. I just needed to reach out to one of them mentally to add the connection, so the power would flow. *Try me, Sorcerer. I almost died. You set me up.*

Sorcerer Petotum nodded at me. "Yes, I did."

He answered my unspoken question, like he could hear my thoughts. How powerful was this man? There was no anger or guilt in his words. "But as Lord Vimmer just said, I am here to possibly help his sister. Would you mind if we sat down?"

James let go of my arm to take my hand. "Petra, what's going on? Why are you angry?" He looked over at Kiera for help, then noticed the book in her arms. "Ah, isn't that ..."

"A full Pentwale rune," finished Sorcerer Petotum. And, nodded at James to step farther into the room. "I think this should be a private conversation." His last statement brokered no argument. He was being polite, but I got a sense he wasn't going to allow me to cast any spells here.

I checked the energy gathering about me and yelled out, "You set me up!"

Sorcerer Petotum ignored my shout and followed James into the room. The doors closed behind him by themselves. A part of my brain recognized he was able to bypass the Vimmer house wards effortlessly. This wasn't lost on James or Kiera, either. I could feel Kiera's apprehension edge up a notch.

<"*Petra, please.*"> she mentally said to me. <"*I'm really angry, too. But you have to control yourself.*"> If Sorcerer Petotum could hear Kiera and I talk to each other, he gave no indication of it. After the doors closed, he pulled out a wand. His wand was a bit longer than normal and had gold and silver etchings down the sides of it. He waved it in the air and through my link with Kiera, I could feel a magical bubble form around us. "That should do it," he said, then took a seat in the tallest chair in the room. He sighed and indicated I should sit. "Ms. Abara, you are alive. Celebrate that."

James immediately sat down, as did Kiera. James grabbed my hand and, at his urging, I took a seat as well. "You have some explaining to do," I said to him as evenly as I could. Just the thought that James might be out of my life forever gave me strength to confront this man.

"Ms. Abara, Lady Vimmer," said Sorcerer Petotum. "I think it might be helpful if you tell Lord Vimmer your story."

Kiera began telling the story. It took me a few seconds to get myself under control enough to add anything. However, having James hold my hand helped. Within a minute I was able to join in on the story. Sorcerer Petotum appeared fascinated and smiled at us while James gripped my hand tighter. Toward the end of the story, all four of us were staring down at the book on the floor.

"So that's Merlin's spell book," said James in a whisper. His eyes were huge.

Sorcerer Petotum laughed. "One of them, at least. I received a rather unique visitor three months ago. I suspect it was the same spirit you two encountered."

"We could have died," I said through gritted teeth.

James gripped my hand tighter, probably in an effort not to challenge this man who could probably crush us with a thought. However, James stood up. "I know I would have died," he said flatly. "But if you knowingly put Petra in a place where she could die without allowing her the option of first briefing her, I will challenge you to a duel."

Sorcerer Petotum tilted his head. "I will keep that in mind, young man." After a small smile, he nodded at us and apparently made some decision. "Your points are fair, Lord Vimmer. You and Ms. Abara have both worn the cape of office, however briefly. It would therefore be prudent to allow the two of you in some of our Realm security discussions. I will make sure copies are sent over." He tilted his head at Kiera. "And I am including you in this offer, young lady." He tapped his wand and said softly, "I don't know where this is all going, not really. Everything so far has been best guesses. However, Avalon needs more people like the three of you. We cannot survive without changing." Suddenly his expression shifted, and I could feel power swirling around him. Eeep.

He turned to face James fully. "Regarding a formal challenge, Lord Vimmer. If you cross that line, I cannot refuse. I have no desire to see you, or your family come to harm. But I have a habit of winning such challenges."

Now he smiled, and the brief power swirling around him was gone. "Please sit back down. We are all alive, and I would have given long odds against that several days ago."

James reluctantly took his seat. Okay, I don't care if his father says no, I am ripping his clothes off later today.

Kiera let out her breath. "So, a new Merlin *is* coming. And the spirit implied a lady."

Sorcerer Petotum tilted his hand back and forth. "I think a new Merlin is coming. It not being a man could mean several things, including just meaning it isn't human. But then, Merlin was said not to be entirely human, either. But you have to understand, the signs are vague. I suspect one of several possibilities could occur. But, yes." He glanced at Kiera. "It's somehow tied to bad tidings on Earth, so likely human. Quite possibly female. Depending upon which Oracle you talk to, their best guesses range from six months to eighteen months from now."

James leaned forward. "War? Famine?"

"An event of some kind, certainly. A reasonably reliable Oracle I know had her gazing crystal shatter when I asked her to focus in on the event." He shrugged. "So, I anticipate it will be extreme." He reached over to tap the book. "The fact that you have this now, suggests that the time frame is probably closer to six months. But almost everything we have is guesswork, at best."

Kiera said slowly while looking at Sorcerer Petotum, "The strongest sorceress I've heard of, in recent times, is your old Master. If I'm not mistaken, Lady Victoria Agave. Is she still alive?"

"She is currently running the Calvit School of Magic and Combat. But you are making an assumption which I think is wrong."

Kiera tilted her head. "That the new Merlin is a woman?"

Sorcerer Petotum grinned. "No, that part is most likely correct." He steepled his fingers together. "From the stories, our Merlin came to us as a seasoned adult. No one really knows how old he was." He shook his head. "Subtle hints make me believe this Merlin will be younger than you, Lady Kiera. Perhaps, a young lady who just recently came into her magic."

My mouth was hanging open. "Sir, the spirit wanted me to give her wand to the right hand of the new Merlin. Between you and she, you're making it almost sound like this Merlin will be looking for guides as she grows up."

"If I'm reading the implications right, she might be. The spirit suggested that one of those guides will be a unique person so balanced they could handle standing next to our emerging Merlin and provide guidance without getting lost." Sorcerer Petotum gave me a direct look. "Suggestions? You're holding the book and the wand."

James squeezed my hand harder. Kiera looked at me intently. Sorcerer Petotum just waited, smiling at me.

A unique person so balanced, I thought to myself, and my eyes went wide. "You mean Lady Elizabeth Navartis."

"That would be my first guess as well," he replied. "But not the only possibility. However, you are friends with all the likely candidates."

I think I started hyperventilating. I wasn't sure what to say.

Kiera, wide-eyed, asked, "Sir, who do you think is going to be the new Merlin's left hand?" She gulped and looked at me. "The one the Merlin calls when she's annoyed."

Sorcerer Petotum looked at all three of us in turn. "I have no idea. The two Oracles I trust the most have been getting unusual images. I hesitate to say anything, simply because they are so odd."

"What do *we* do?" asked James.

"That, Lord Vimmer, is an excellent question," replied Sorcerer Petotum. "My recommendation? For now, nothing."

As my mouth opened in surprise, his face became stern. "Ms. Abara, I recommend not telling any of your friends about the spirit's request until you are certain that you should. Having seen my fair share of possible prophecies, they can destroy a person just by knowing about them." He shrugged. "Oftentimes, it begins to shape their lives in very bad ways." He spread his hands wide. "Like them, live your life. Love who you choose and try to make a difference." Then, suddenly standing up, Sorcerer Petotum said with a grin, "Let us go check in with Miss Aspen Vimmer. Perhaps Master Healer Medicus and Healer Hochim have some good news for us."

Just before he opened the double doors, I blurted out, "Sir, about the book."

"Ms. Abara," he said, smiling down at me. "I already have more than enough on my shoulders. It's yours to keep safe."

Then he opened the double doors and walked out. As we followed him, Kiera handed me the book and whispered to me, "How do you shut down your spell?"

"Um," I whispered. "I don't know."

I wasn't certain, but I thought I caught the edge of a smile from Sorcerer Petotum.

Book two, *Healer's Journey* is forthcoming.

If you liked this book, please write a review. As authors, we always appreciate your feedback.

About the Author

By day David Hochhalter is an optical engineer who has designed some of the longest terrestrial systems in the world. Since he was given the 2:00am middle of the night idea brain instead of the 9:00am brain, he decided to try writing instead of reading technical manuals. Besides, imagining stories is more fun than reading about amplifiers. His published books are **Wandmaking 101**, **Wandmaking 201**, and the **Avalon Awakening Series,** starting with *Healer's Awakening*. Currently he is working on another series in the same universe.

Made in the USA
Middletown, DE
15 November 2023

42806123R00168